A
CURSE
R*of*OSES

A CURSE of ROSES

diana pinguicha

Entangled Publishing, LLC
10940 S Parker Road
Suite 327
Parker, CO 80134
rights@entangledpublishing.com

Entangled Teen is an imprint of Entangled Publishing, LLC.

Visit our website at www.entangledpublishing.com.

Edited by Lydia Sharp and Jen Bouvier
Cover design by Bree Archer
Cover images by
arxichtu4ki/GettyImages,
PeopleImages/GettyImages,
CoffeeAndMilk/GettyImages,
South_agency/GettyImages
Interior design by Toni Kerr

HC ISBN 978-1-68281-509-0
Ebook ISBN 978-1-68281-510-6

Manufactured in the United States of America

First Edition December 2020

10 9 8 7 6 5 4 3 2 1

entangled teen
an imprint of Entangled Publishing LLC

to those who have been erased

AUTHOR'S NOTE

I grew up listening to Yzabel's story.

We call her Rainha Santa Isabel—which you can translate to Saint Queen Isabel. She was canonized in May of 1625 by Pope Urban VIII. My hometown, Estremoz, has a statue in her honor, the Castle's Pousada has her name, and so does the high school I went to. A lot of Estremoz still spins around her—and of all the people my hometown could've been known for, I'm glad it's Isabel we ended up with. I do believe she was a truly good person who wanted nothing but to help others. Dinis, as well, was a surprisingly forward king for the time, and together, they were perhaps the best rulers we had. He took away power from the Church and the Nobility and gave it to the people. He was our first literate king and composed poems and songs. He also expanded the Leiria Pine Forest, which later allowed us to build ships and sail the seas.

Isabel herself was one of the most politically savvy queens we had. She fostered diplomatic deals, stopped a war between her brother, King of Aragon, and her son-in-law Fernando, King of Castela. When her son tried to kill one of Dinis's bastard sons, Afonso Sanches, she parked a mule between their armies and made them talk it out to avoid civil war.

That being said, I took a lot of liberties. For one, Moura wasn't a Portuguese town in 1288. It was given to Dinis later, when he tried to wage war against Castela—a war that never materialized because Castela offered lands in return for peace. And while it's true that Erzsébet of Hungary was Isabel of Aragon's great-aunt from her mother's side and they have the same kind of miracle attributed to them, Erzsébet didn't die at eighteen as stated in this book, but she did die young, at the age of 24.

Isabel's age is correct, but Dinis's isn't. He was, in fact, ten years older than her. Their marriage was arranged when she was ten, and it was officiated two years later. Isabel and Dinis would not, however, have children until she was nineteen.

Fatyan's story is also different. She wasn't in love with another Moura named Salúquia—Salúquia *was* the Moura who threw herself from Al-Manijah's tower when the Portuguese took it. I wanted to keep the story but use Salúquia's name in passing so as to give a nod to the original.

In the Miracle of Roses, Isabel didn't turn roses to bread, and there was no Enchanted Moura. But she did sneak out of the castle to feed the poor, and upon being caught by her betrothed, the bread she carried turned to roses. A miracle, supposedly from God, to show King Dinis that his wife's charity was blessed and shouldn't be interfered with. But that didn't make for an entire book, and as such, I set out to rewrite the legend.

We like to romanticize our kings and queens as being madly in love with each other, and while some probably were, most…were not. Isabel had incredible political value, and her marriage to Dinis was one of convenience, an accord signed when she was just ten years old. They did grow to respect each other, and he did include her in making new laws. Theirs was a marriage of friendship; just not a marriage of romantic love.

Unlike many queens before and after her, Isabel only

had two children with Dinis, and had no more when the second was a boy. It's also speculated that she knew of Dinis's infidelities, and instead of detracting him, she was *glad* she was not the center of his attention. Many, many women were glad when their betrotheds paid no attention to them. Sex spelled the possibility of children, and pregnancy and childbirth were as dangerous as a battlefield.

Her lack of children doesn't mean Isabel was gay. But she might have been, as so many women were, and had to hide it because of the way society was. How many still do. I know I did.

The reason why I have such a tense relationship with my hometown of Estremoz is because of how hard I was bullied there for simply being different. Sure, some guys are fine, but I find women much more attractive. And it took me years to overcome the fact that I wasn't broken just because I liked girls, too, maybe even more so than boys. That was the legacy Estremoz left me, one of being halfway into the closet, of self-doubt, and self-hate. It's where I was called "a man" because I liked video games and was good at sports, where people use the term "lesbian" as an insult. (And I will always be grateful for my parents who, when I came home crying about it, always said, "So what if you're gay?")

There's nothing wrong with being a girl who looks manly and enjoys "manly" things, and there's nothing wrong with being a lesbian. There's also nothing wrong with not being interested in boys, or girls, or anyone. I know that now. I wish I'd known it then. I wish someone had dared tell me a story where one of our most beloved queens liked women, too, that queer people have always existed through the centuries despite most of history erasing them. But that story didn't exist for me then, so I wrote it.

Mom, Dad—I know you'll read this. Yes, I like girls, too, and I know that I could come home with a girlfriend and you wouldn't turn me away. But the hateful hometown where you raised me did.

And if you're like I once was, hiding yourself because of society, I sincerely hope Yzabel's story helped you in some way. Writing it certainly helped me.

Kingdom of Portugal
and the Algarves

1288

Part I

Curses

CHAPTER ONE

Festering Secrets

With heavy eyes and weary bones, Yzabel walked past the castle walls and into the narrow streets of Terra da Moura. At her order, her Além-Tejo mastiff, Lucas, took off, checking the cobblestones ahead for any little threat.

"This is ill-advised," Vasco said to her right, his vigilant hand on the pommel of his sheathed sword. "Going to the lower side of town with just myself and your lady's maid. We should at least bring a full squad for your protection."

"Senhor Davide was brave enough to reach out to Brites about the missing supplies." Yzabel cringed as she spoke, leg muscles shuddering against the never-ending chafe of the cilice. With a deep breath, she used that pain to center herself and put one foot in front of the other. "I don't want to scare him away with twelve armed soldiers."

"Why would he fear them unless he wasn't telling the truth?"

"Oh, give her a rest, will you?" On Yzabel's left, Brites adjusted her grip on the wooden box, tins and jars of herbal remedies rattling with the motion. "I know Davide. He wouldn't have come to me unless the situation was truly dire. Plus, you're built like the Man in the Iron Hat. Your scowl alone is enough to detract anyone from attacking the princess."

Yzabel snorted the giggle that sneaked past her lips while Vasco's mouth and nose puckered with a grunt. He turned a narrowed gaze to Brites, asking, "Remind me again, how is it that the lady's maid to an Aragonian princess seems to know everyone between Sicillia and Lishbuna?"

Brites rolled her eyes and scoffed. "If you listened to me when I talk, you'd have heard that I spent some time in this town."

"Yes, when you were a nun. How a convent ever accepted you is beyond me—"

Yzabel gave a pointed sigh, hoping they'd take the cue, but Brites and Vasco seemed to enjoy reenacting the same argument in thousands of different ways. They'd been with her since she'd turned twelve, and after five years, she'd long realized that for some reason trading insults was how they showed friendship.

Both their voices faded to the back of her attention, and Yzabel readjusted her cowl, hiking the collar of her fur mantle to protect her nose from the crisp bite of autumn's air. She blinked away the stars burning across her vision as her eyes darted around the town. Close to the castle, the houses were painted with whitewash, the streets neat—here and there, she could spy children running and playing while their grandmothers sowed nearby, ears alert even if their eyes weren't. With the sun a couple of hours away from setting, most people would still be at work in the fields, but that wouldn't explain the almost-emptiness of the plaza, or why there wasn't a single person lingering around the tavern.

No place was so tapestry-perfect, and as sheltered as

Yzabel had been, she knew better than to take appearances at their face value. No place was absent of poverty, and Terra da Moura should be no exception.

All the more reason why she had to speak to Senhor Davide. When he'd approached Brites after mass, the local prelates had looked from afar, scoffing and dismissing him as a drunk.

"Ah, the town's drunk has come to pester the princess's lady's maid," Baron de Seabra had said then, a slick smirk twisting his mouth. "Don't believe a word he says, Your Highness. I'm sure he's heard the tales of your good nature and is looking to exploit them."

At the time, Yzabel had nodded and assured him she wouldn't believe unfounded gossip. Yet, as she sat next to the king, her future husband, surrounded by nobles of good flesh wrapped in fine leather and expensive silks, the bright glint of gold and jewels peeking between luxurious furs, and rings shining like shackles on their fingers...she saw the baron's words for what they truly were. Brushstrokes made of insults, meant to paint over the image of the man who dared to come to the Carmo Church and to a service reserved only for the nobility, meant to manipulate feelings, to incite prejudice, to foster disgust.

He'd wanted her to see the image of a mean drunk, a selfish man who put his vices before anything else.

Yzabel had seen nothing but a downtrodden man driven to despair by the same beast roaring inside her, with its manic talons clawing at her bowels, her womb, her stomach. It climbed to her head, stabbed shiny stars into her vision and agony into her temples.

Hunger.

The kind of hunger that festered not because of choice, but because of a lack of it. This man couldn't eat because he had nothing to eat; Yzabel couldn't eat because she was cursed. They weren't the same, and yet, they were.

Just as she was absently crossing from the cobbled roads and into the beaten dirt of the low part of town, the afternoon sun stabbed at Yzabel's eyes and pierced straight through her skull. With a wince, she swayed in her steps, and just when she thought her knees would give away, a heavy hand caught her arm.

"That's it," Vasco said while he helped her regain her balance. "We're coming back after you eat. Shouldn't have let you leave in the first place—"

"I'll eat later...when I have to. I'm still fasting, remember?" They both knew she wasn't fasting, not of her own choice. It was the convenient excuse she gave everyone when she sat at meals without touching her food, out of fear she'd turn her meal into a bouquet. That it made everyone think her extra pious was an added benefit she gladly reaped, even if it sat as well in her stomach as the flowers did.

It had been the same with her great-aunt Erzsébet of Ungarie. She, too, had possessed a touch that turned food into flowers, and died young for it. With her marriage to a foreign king, and his qualms against charity, Yzabel's life was unfolding in the very same way as her aunt's had; with a similar curse and engaged to a man of the same kind. At this rate, she too would die soon after her upcoming eighteenth birthday in Januarius. All without even being able to perform a miracle as Erzsébet had; Yzabel could barely eat, let alone hand out food from her own hand. Holding back the curse long enough to pass it as a divine act? Impossible.

Lucas's barking return to Yzabel's side brought her back to the present. A group of five children, all young but not fresh-faced, ran toward them in bare feet.

"The princess came to see us!" one of them said, with a grin that immediately faded when Vasco stepped in front of her.

"It's all right," Yzabel said, attempting to skirt around him.

"I hate to add wood to Vasco's fire, but…" Brites tossed a look to the houses ahead. Squat, little more than four walls of brick held together with lime mortar, dwellings rested in clusters along the dirt road. Their backyards were shared, with a handful of chickens clucking in the communal pen.

The red cloths, however, were what dug claws into her heart. Draped over the windows and doors, the colorful fabric flapped gently in the breeze—a sign the red plague festered inside those walls.

Still, she couldn't ignore these children, with their hollow cheeks and patched-up clothes. Had she been back home in Aragon, no one could've stopped her from raiding her trunks and the kitchens to help them. Here, she had a betrothed to answer to, and he'd made it clear she was *not* to give charity in the form of dinheiros or food. He'd said that she had butter for a heart and needed to harden it if they were to marry, for what good would a princess be if she bankrupted the kingdom with her short-sighted charity?

Under her mantle, her fist tightened. Chin high, she skirted Vasco and kept a hand on top of Lucas's head to still him. "Tell you what," she said to the children, "if you take me to Senhor Davide's home, I'll give you the bread and cheese Vasco is hiding."

"That's reserved for *you*," he protested.

"You're right. It's reserved for me to do as I see fit,"

she chimed back with the full, haughty stubbornness expected of royalty. Lower, so the children couldn't hear, she whispered, "This is what you get for trying to bring me back to the castle to eat when you have a satchel of food hiding under that mail."

The pursed line of Vasco's lips disappeared under his mustache, but when he let out a long sigh and turned back to the children, she knew she'd won. "You heard the princess. Lead the way, but don't touch us."

"We don't have the plague!" spat a little girl. "We've been sleeping at Nana's and bathing in the springs every day so we wouldn't catch it." She was as stick thin as the other, dull and limp black hair stark against the bright fury in her dark eyes.

"Doesn't matter. I'm not risking the princess's health."

There was a collective pout, but the children soon recovered, leading them along the beaten earth that served as a road. Yzabel hiked up her mantle and skirts to keep the worst of the dirt off the fine embroidery, pushing through another wave of nausea and exhaustion that clung to her more heavily than the furs on her shoulders.

Vasco offered his arm—silently this time—and she gladly took it, letting him support her for the rest of the way.

"Careful with what you say to Davide," Brites muttered. "I think the king's having someone follow us again."

It wouldn't have been the first time Denis had sent someone to spy on Yzabel to ascertain whether she was out spending her dinheiros. When she'd arrived on Portuguese soil with her coffers almost empty, the king had taken it upon himself to save her from bankruptcy without even bothering to ask if she wanted to be saved from it. What good was money when it sat untouched in a trunk and not in the pockets of those who needed it most?

Vasco nodded. "Noticed that, too. Whatever you do, Yzabel, try not to speak too loudly. As far as they know, we're only delivering medicine. Let's keep it that way."

They came to a halt, and the girl pointed at one of the houses before them with red cloths over its window. "Tio Davide lives in that one. But *we* are not allowed too close because you know…" The girl threw Vasco a grimace of pure, sassy revenge. "We don't have the plague and don't want to catch it."

Brites laughed, loud and heartily. From one of her apron pockets, she produced a bundle, and from within that, several small slices of cheese. "For that alone, you'll get extra."

"What, now you're carrying food, too?" Yzabel gasped, her voice sounding small amid the shrieking children, who pounced on Brites's offering. Though Yzabel had known about Vasco's constant stash, Brites's was news, and the kind that felt like a personal betrayal.

Looking at those tiny nibbles was enough for the magic to awaken, to burn under her skin and demand she touch it. She closed her fist tighter, nails digging deep in her palm, drowning her curse with pain.

Pouch in hand, the children scampered off, and as soon as they were out of earshot, Brites turned to Yzabel. "I promised your mother I'd help you with your magic, remember? Since I've failed, she made me promise something else." Her hands fell on Yzabel's shoulders. "I'm to keep you alive. For as long as I'm able."

"You place too much worth on me. The world won't end if I die. Or if I don't marry Denis."

"True. We could find another princess," Vasco said. "And we'd be all the poorer for it."

"Why? You know about"—she lowered her voice—"the

curse. To be honest, Vasco, I don't even understand why you still wanted me to be your princess after you found out. Why you stuck around tutoring me for five years while I wither and waste—"

"Because no one else would do *this*," Vasco cut her off, tone strong and steady. "As many headaches as you give me, Yzabel, no other possible contender would tread in the mud, walk in a neighborhood infected with the red fever, to hear out a man who's known to be a drunkard just because he told your lady's maid the harvests they worked all spring and summer on have suddenly vanished." He paused to raise her jaw with his forefinger and make her look into his brown eyes. "No one else cares. Not as much as you do. Denis needs someone like you. *We* need someone like you."

Why did he act like her common decency was an otherworldly trait, and not the bare minimum?

Vasco hugged her, and his strong palm held the back of her head for a long minute before kissing the top of it and backing away. "Now, let's do what we came here to do."

Yzabel nodded while Brites drifted closer to the window to call Senhor Davide. Moments later, the door creaked open and a man emerged. Brown skin marred with scars and dotted with old age stretched thin over his bony frame; wrinkles deep, eyes sagging, slumped shoulders drowning in the sheep's wool capote. He shambled forward, the tanned hide of his shoes so worn there was no inch that hadn't been mended. Pants, vest, and shirt of threadbare cotton, the black faded to brown from too much use.

"Your Highness," the man said, voice wispy in an almost-toothless mouth, rough like the song of broken sugarcanes whistling in the wind. He knelt a few paces from Yzabel, the oil in his hair gleaming in the sunlight.

"You came. Brites said you would, but I…"

"Of course I came, Senhor Davide. And please, rise." She made a motion to help him, but Vasco kept her back, his furrowed brow reminding her not to chance a touch. The red plague was so contagious the clothes themselves could carry the virus.

The old man's knees trembled as he obeyed, and it was only when he had to brace himself on his thigh that she noticed his left arm ended in a stump just above the wrist. "Sorry I can't invite you into my home." He gestured to the red fabric hanging over the door to his eerily quiet home behind him. "The youngest are all down with the plague. Sores just started opening on some of them. Already giving them Saint John's Wort, but you know how this is."

His sigh said everything he didn't—that no matter what they did, some of the children would die. Without enough food to go around, they'd die faster.

"We've brought some lavender oil and other salves to help. Brites…"

Her maid set the box down on the ground. "They're separated by pouches. Can you hand them around the neighborhood, Davide? We brought enough for everyone."

"I will—but lavender oil, Your Highness? Are you certain?"

She gave him a soft smile. "Why else would I bring it?"

Davide bowed his head. "Thank you. Truly. We used up all of ours in the previous bout of the plague, and nothing else works quite like it."

"I only wish I could do more," she lamented. Her dizzy head cast a spell on her, and she would've swayed again had she not been holding on to Vasco. Once it settled, she pushed past the slowness encumbering every muscle and bone in her body. "Do you want to tell me about what you brought to Brites's attention? Your prelates didn't take kindly to your appearance in the Carmo Church. What makes you believe they've been lying about the harvests?"

Thick eyebrows rose. "Because we worked all spring and summer from sunrise to sunset. Carts and carts of wheat, of carrots, peas, kale, turnips, grapes. Yet when the time came to pay us, it was as if we'd brought in close to nothing. We kept cleaning the fields, getting ready for the pomegranates and the quince, and when we asked for our rightful payment, the steward said the mice had gotten in the stores, and he had nothing to give us save for a handful of dinheiros. We had little choice but to hunt for wild animals, and the baron and bishop forbade that, too." He raised his left arm to brandish the stub like a weapon. "This was my reward when Captain Mendes caught one of our polecats returning with a rabbit. Took my hand, and the animals, too."

Yzabel's hand rose to cover her gaping mouth. When Denis had told her to meet him in Terra da Moura instead of Trancoso—where their wedding was to happen—he'd mentioned suspicions of misappropriation from the gentry, and that she should head there instead. That way they could get to know each other before marrying while he investigated the issues himself.

Much as she was loath to admit it, the only reason she *could* come talk to Senhor Davide was because Denis allowed it. And because she was to report to him after. Would marriage be more of this, for the rest of her life? Her actions hinging upon the decisions of a man?

Useless thoughts, to be spent another time. For now, she had to know more. "What made you talk to Brites, and in turn, me?"

"Because when word came that you'd be visiting,

Captain Mendes made the rounds to intimidate us into staying silent. Suddenly, they had dinheiros and food to give us—dinheiros many of them took." Davide threw a spiteful look at the closest church, a more modest building than the Carmo where the nobility attended. "Just like the bishop suddenly had room in the hospital to harbor all the homeless so they wouldn't offend you with their presence."

The breath left her lungs in a rush and the blood drained from her face.

The Bishop had *what*?

"Another person, and I'd have believed you were like them," Davide said to Yzabel. "But Brites was with you, and she doesn't stick around people who aren't worth it, royal as they may be."

Brites shrugged, her lips tight to hide the blooming smile. "I'll take the compliment. And I trust the princess will take your story very seriously. Look at her. Like she saw an alma penada."

Some levity returned to Davide's face. "It's good to see you, even if I can't hug you."

"I wasn't expecting you to still be around, to be honest. Pleasant surprise." Brites winked. "What about Gill and Lionor? Your other kids?"

"Grown and married, the two of them. They live right over there. All of my oldest do." He pointed to another house in their cluster, mercifully free of red drapes. "And you wouldn't believe where some of their young ones are off to. Do you remember the Enchanted Moura?"

"With the time we spent trying to find her? Couldn't forget even if I wanted to." She nudged Yzabel with her elbow. "I've told you her story, remember?"

A series of blinks jostled her memory of an afternoon half a year ago, when they'd been preparing to leave

Aragon to come here. As they'd been sorting through Yzabel's delivery of ointments and salves, Brites had told her of an old friend she'd met in Sintra, how they'd traveled together to Estremoz and crossed Terra da Moura on the way; how, on their night at the hostel, one of the sisters had told them the legacy behind the village's name.

Yzabel frowned. "I do. But didn't you say she wasn't around anymore?"

"I thought she wasn't. When I left, everyone had all but given up on it."

"And we had—until one of the boys swore he heard a voice around the dolmen ways off the river. Then other kids did, too."

"Your children want attention. Enchanted Mouras don't exist," Vasco grumbled his way back into the conversation. "If it's fanciful tales you want to waste your time on, then we should cut this short and get back. The king is waiting."

"Don't be rude," Yzabel hissed. "These children have half their families dying of the red plague, and all of them are starving. Let them have their fantasies while they can." Let them have the fantasies she wished for, but her curse had cut short.

Brites shook her head and sighed. "I swear, Vasco, all that height and not an inch of tact in you." A click of her tongue. "You're right about something, though. We should be getting back."

The sun halfway peeked across the horizon, and the church's bells chimed the fifth hour of the evening. After both assuring Senhor Davide she'd tell the king of what he said, and that they'd come back soon to check on the state of the plague, Yzabel thanked the old man and left.

The Moura story spun in her head, round and round like a wheel. Her gaze wandered along the scenery, at the red over the mud bricks and white mortar, a bleeding wound over those homes and families. At those five children now playing blind goat in the grass.

Her stomach tightened painfully, and Yzabel struggled to keep a smile as she waved goodbye to them. They'd been so happy with scraps of cheese and bread, as happy as she was in the rare event she managed a whole bite of her meals without incident. Had the five of them tried to find the Enchanted Moura, too?

Bright dots burst across her vision. Her belly rioted against the void she'd made of it. She paid them no heed, her head too busy concocting a scheme to somehow bring food into these people's bellies and to spare them from the starvation her own flesh knew so well.

From her great-aunt's fate, and the way Yzabel's own life was unfurling, she could expect the same destiny to befall her in less than four months. If she were to die at eighteen, she first had to find a way to make an impact that would improve the lives of the Portuguese—before hers was extinguished.

CHAPTER TWO

A Thorny Meal

By the time they arrived at the castle, Yzabel's legs groaned as if they were hinges in need of oil. She met Denis at the kennels, where he was inspecting a new litter of mastiffs born three weeks ago. Despite the heaviness that weighed upon her, she couldn't help but squeal at the puppies' antics. Vasco took Lucas to be fed with the other hounds, and Brites left to prepare Yzabel's room for the night. Leaving her alone with her betrothed for a meal that was, by far, the most grueling part of her routine.

They walked in slow, measured steps that took all her concentration to keep up with—she had to lean more and more on Denis as they walked to his chambers. The painful grind of her bones dwindled, the ache waning and waning until it was eclipsed by hunger crawling in her belly, and the throbbing of the cilice's teeth on her thigh.

What she wouldn't give to take that horrible thing from her leg, to walk without its bite on her flesh. But it wasn't as if she could confess to the evil in her veins. Pain was the only way she could pay for the depravity she committed every day.

Only through sacrifices can we achieve His forgiveness, Dom Domingos's words tolled in her mind. She held onto them as they walked, wondering what she was doing wrong, wondering why God did not listen, or if He did, why He didn't help her.

The void roared in her stomach, and she couldn't hide the limp in her next step.

"How long has it been since you've eaten?" Denis asked.

Years would've been the honest answer, the truth she kept from all but Brites and Vasco. She hadn't had a proper meal since her first blood, when the curse had manifested.

"I've been fasting all day," she said between heavy breaths. The stairs loomed ahead, shadows dancing along the lines of the granite steps. A long sigh fanned in her ear, and the world swayed again as Denis lifted her. The mantle slipped from her shoulders, while her body, heavy and rusted as iron when she tried to move, was carried without effort.

"I can make it," she protested, but his pace didn't slow. From the corner of her eye, she caught the shadow of a frown darkening his eyes, pressing down on his lips. "Denis, please. Put me down."

"Only to watch you faint? Isn't it enough that I'm forced to watch you starve yourself?"

His irritation shivered on her skin, and Yzabel curled into herself, crown toppling against her knees as she clutched at the acid burning a hole in her stomach. The curse was killing her, and she hated that she had to lie to him, hated that the devotion everyone praised her for was nothing but selfishness.

"You saw fit to give those children food even though I told you not to," Denis continued grumbling, beard pricking the shell of her ear. It baffled her why he insisted on growing the thing. Patchy as it was, he was better off shaving it clean.

"So it was you following us."

"Did you think I'd let my future wife walk outside the castle walls with just her lady's maid, an old guard, and a dog for protection?" he asked back. "And my man wasn't the one you saw. Matias knows better than that."

Yzabel chewed on the inside of her cheek, thinking. "Then who was it?"

"One of Captain Mendes's men. The local guarda was concerned with your safety among the commoners." The crease between his brows deepened as he frowned at her. "And stop trying to change the subject. Tell me why you gave them food when I expressly forbade it."

"I had to," she moaned. "You won't let me do more."

Denis's retort seethed beneath his rib cage, yet he held it as he nodded to the guard stationed next to his chambers. The soldier opened the door, and when he closed it behind them, Denis let her down on a chair by the table before taking the seat across from hers. Shoulders low and lip curled, the united front they presented before the nobles gave way to sharp tension.

The man who'd been supportive before a crowd was not the same sitting before her now, talking to her in a patronizing tone. "Handouts might make things better for a while. And those children might not starve today, or tomorrow, but what of the day after? Do they ask you for more? Do you keep giving until there's no food in the country and we're *all* starving? What happens, then, when they come clamoring at the gates and we have nothing to give? A revolution?"

Yzabel dropped her hands on her lap. "You have your suspicions about what's happening in this town—suspicions Senhor Davide corroborated today. The poor are starving, and to keep food from children when I have it would've been cruel."

"It doesn't matter. I told you not to do something and you did it anyway. Is this how our marriage is to be?"

She forced herself to meet her betrothed's stare. "If we're to fight every time I try to help those who need it, then yes. It's how it's going to be."

"I'm not saying you can't help them." Inhaling deeply, Denis massaged the bridge of his long nose. "I don't have the energy for this today. Just please tell me what that man told you about the harvests."

Glad for the change of subject, Yzabel did just that while Denis uncovered the candlelit feast, revealing roasted pheasant and turnips glazed gold with olive oil and speckled green with herbs, a bowl of migas, fresh bread, cheese, figs, and marmalade.

So much more than the two of them could possibly eat, a sight so lavish and beautiful it lifted the hair on her arms and raised an intense itch, tickling its way down her fingers like an ant colony moving in tandem beneath her skin. The rich scents held hands as they wafted up her nose, watered her mouth, set off a rumble in her belly that drowned the gurgling wine Denis was pouring into their crystal glasses.

Her curse piled up in her fists, begging to be used. An attempt to smother it only served to magnify its uncanny will, leaving her trembling, helpless to watch as Denis filled his plate with a bit of everything, then did the same to hers.

"That's too much—"

"These things take time, Yzabel, and you can't feed everyone who comes asking until we root out the true cause of their problem." The plate clicked against the wooden table as he placed it in front of her. "And if you bear such concern for the commoners and their health, you must do the same for yourself."

But how could she when magic simmered in her fingertips, ready to pounce on the nearest edible thing? She swallowed under Denis's scrutiny, glad that he couldn't see the light in her hand, afraid of what he'd be able to see if she slipped in the slightest.

"I know." She licked the dryness from her lips. "It's just…"

Denis slumped against his chair. "It's just what?"

"That's easy to say when you've never gone hungry," Yzabel muttered. "Easy to say when you have a country at your feet."

He fixed her with a glare, dark brown eyes peeking from under his scowl. "*Eat*."

With jittery fingers, she grasped the silver cross dangling over her flat chest, earning a long roll of the king's eyes. In her thoughts, she said, *God in Heaven, please take this curse away. Let me eat and build my strength so I can be Your dutiful servant and help those who need me the most. If this keeps going, I don't know how much longer I have left. Please let me eat in peace tonight.*

Her thumb brushed over the familiar dips and ridges in the metalwork, waiting for some divine power to sweep in and stomp out the light filling her veins, light that went unseen by Denis, unseen by everyone who didn't carry magic within them.

Please.

The flames in the fireplace did not stir, and no strange breeze whispered in her ear. No divine intervention would come to her aid today, and why should it, anyway? At seventeen, she was engaged to the nineteen-year-old King of Portugal and the Algarves. Yzabel and Denis had a long rule ahead to prepare for, and God clearly had better things to do than help her with a curse.

But that long rule would only happen provided neither of them suffered an untimely death, and Yzabel was on the verge of one. She could not let this evil magic defeat her and cut short the time she needed to fulfill her destiny.

Lips worried and hand to her heart, she murmured one last prayer before swiftly cutting a bit of pheasant. The magic surged, a tentative heat that traveled down her arm toward her left hand. Teeth grinding, she tried to force the curse back down. It battled against her, stabbing needles into her temples, rendering her body weak, as though assailed by a fever. *Please don't turn, don't turn, don't turn…*

Denis sat, impassive, scrutinizing her and the plate. Eyeing him in return, she shoved the meat into her mouth — the first chew sent juices flowing over her tongue, and she almost moaned as the taste of flesh unraveled in her mouth. Fleeting happiness, though. As soon as she chewed again, her tongue became impossibly hot, her teeth closed on a bitter stem, and she struggled to keep a neutral face as she swallowed, rushing to her glass of wine to wash the horrible taste from her mouth.

The alcohol burned her throat, making her wince, but she *had* eaten something. It seemed to satisfy Denis, at least, and he finally shifted his attention to his own plate. "Thank you for going down there to talk to that man. I would've done it myself if the prelates weren't stuck to my side."

His tone had softened, and she thought the rest of the meal would go by with ease. But then he returned to their dreaded rift between bites of meat and vegetables. "Charity is not a permanent or sustainable solution. An intelligent person like yourself should have no trouble grasping that notion."

She understood where he was coming from. And yet, how could he ask her to ignore the suffering of others when it was so much like her own?

"Then let me help where I can," she cried, unable to stop a pair of inconvenient tears from trailing down her cheeks. "Let me do my duty."

Please let me pay for the waste of my curse before it kills me.

"Oh, you want to talk about *duty*?" He came around the table to loom over her side. She kept her eyes on his chest, too familiar with what came next in this old tirade, too cowardly to meet his eyes.

"Your *duty*, Yzabel, is to give me an heir once we're married," he said. "Something you will never be able to do at this rate because you keep starving yourself. What for? To teach me a lesson so I realize how much the commoners suffer?"

Leave it to men to believe themselves the reason for a woman's actions. But why bother correcting him, when telling him the truth would see her cast out? Their marriage contract would be torn if he found she was living with a curse. At best, he'd send her back to Aragon, and her family's country and name would be washed in shame. At worst, he'd try to cure her, and she knew all too well how maledictions such as hers were treated. She'd seen enough trepanations done at the hospitals back home to know they cured nothing.

Better to let him have his misconceptions; at least those she could use to her own advantage. Denis didn't know the curse was why she couldn't eat. It was the effect, not the cause that mattered.

Determination lifted her gaze to his. "If the poorest of us can't eat, then neither shall I."

He groaned. "Yzabel—"

"If we can't open the castle doors to them, then let us take out spoils to the church and let everyone who needs it have a meal on the Lord's good day."

"*No*. All those worries you bear for the Portuguese— you will put them toward your recovery. You will eat and regain your health, and once we're married, we can ensure the continuity of the Portuguese line. I will think about instilling a charity day after that. Now, *eat*."

He didn't move from her side, and he wouldn't, not until she did as he asked. Trapped, Yzabel sniffed and picked up a piece of migas, soft enough she barely needed to chew. Yet, the curse was hungrier than she was, and as soon as the food slid on her tongue, the heat came back to flood her mouth.

Loathing welled in her chest, sent a current of fiery anger down her spine. She attempted to swallow, but the migas had already transformed behind the curtain of her lips. Prickles sliced her tongue and gums, the roof of her mouth. Briefly, she considered spitting, let Denis see the reason she couldn't eat. Bare her greatest shame and let him do what he will—faults aside, he was known to be a fair man. He might even help her.

Or he might kill her.

Yzabel tried to push the flower past her throat, but she choked on the thorns, on her tears, and she couldn't speak, or breathe, or—

"Are you seriously *crying*?" her betrothed asked, the annoyance extending his syllables into a hiss. "I'm asking you to eat, Yzabel, and you act like I've hit you."

But she couldn't answer, couldn't explain why his words and expectations were as effective as a physical blow. Denis's very presence filled her with inadequacy and despair, and she could not stand to be in his company a second longer.

Cheeks full and tongue bleeding, she looked up at Denis with eyes flooded with anger, and finally, *finally*, he backed away from her. She didn't ask or wait for his permission; she left his rooms with lungs close to bursting and a heart in a knot, his shouts for her to return following her as she rushed across the solar to her chambers.

She barely had time to turn the key in the lock before she bent over.

From her parted lips tumbled not migas, but red petals, crushed leaves, and a fibrous, thorny stem lined with blood. Whenever she ate, this was the result. Flowers in her mouth, that she either spat out or forced herself to swallow.

Yzabel knew she had to end the curse, but how was she supposed to put an end to a force she could not control?

CHAPTER THREE

A Curse of Roses

Kneeling on the cold floor, Yzabel stared at the mangled rose.

She picked up the bitten flower, turned it over in her trembling hand. Such a small thing, no bigger than her finger, and yet it had the power to destroy her life and everything she longed to achieve.

With a sharp, hateful motion, she tossed it into the fireplace, watched it burn away into ashes, and wished the curse would follow suit. The evil trickle of magic remained, pooling in her fingertips, shining brighter than the flames.

Growing hungrier.

Growing stronger.

It hadn't been this persistent when it'd first appeared shortly after her twelfth birthday, when she'd woken to agony in her belly and bloody sheets beneath her legs. Back then, the food only turned if her touch lingered for long minutes—she'd still fasted, but it had been by choice.

Days had gone by. Weeks. Months.

Years.

Until a couple of years ago, when the curse went wild and began leaking at the smallest brush. Like her body was a glass, every meal a ravenous drop, and now that it had been filled, she couldn't stop it from overflowing. And these past few days, the sight of food brought not a single drop, but a deluge.

Until now, the curse had always receded when she put a couple of feet between herself and a full plate. With a grimace, Yzabel tried to push it back down, but the angry light wouldn't stop pulsing, tugging at her head, making her look at the window.

On its perch, the bowl of hard bread she kept for the birds taunted her. The strings of magic carried her on entranced feet, lifted her hand, curled her fingers around a piece. She dropped her heavy shoulders, too defeated to look away as the magic gushed out. The sight took her breath away, its beauty as undeniable as it was unsettling. The bread broke apart and turned green to form thorny stems; petals bloomed from inside out, the red spiraling in on itself until a full flower blossomed. The floral smell thickened the air, tickled her nose. In her hand was not bread, but a rose, fresh as though it'd been picked moments ago.

A mesmerizing curse, but one she couldn't even use to the people's benefit. Senhor Davide and those kids had been famished, and here she was, wasting perfectly good food while they had to ration their bread and vegetables and wine into miserable meals.

It took a few long breaths for her to put a name to the bitterness in her throat. Hate and despair and impotence all merged into one heavy lump. The flower in her hand became her biggest enemy. Nothing else evoked such hatred, and nothing else had the power to doom her in the blink of an eye. She traced its petals of scarlet velvet and their inward spiral, marveled at how their beauty belied the danger underneath. Its sweet scent ingrained itself on her nose. A thorn pricked her finger.

Fury swallowed her world, made it so all she heard was her hissing breath, taken through clenched teeth. Her failures and waste were all she could see.

She ripped the perfect rose into imperfect shreds, barely registering the pain of her rendered flesh as the flower fought back. Blood dripped from her hand, staining the embroidery of the Arraiolos rug under her feet.

The next bit of bread, she put in her mouth. Her tongue burned, and when she spat, it wasn't bread that left her lips, but another rose. Filled with bite marks and blood from where it sliced the inside of her mouth. She put the rose in the empty bowl and tried again.

And again.

And again.

Soon, nine roses looked back at her, their mangled appearance a jeer, a wound, a reminder. Waste, waste, waste. So much waste, all because she couldn't control the curse that blighted her touch.

She flung the bowl against the wall, pieces of clay and roses flying everywhere.

"What was that?" Brites emerged from the small door that led to her lady's maid chambers. One look at the scene had her scurrying over, wrapping Yzabel up in strong arms, whispering, "Shhhh. It's all right," while one hand smoothed her brittle curls.

Had it been anyone else, she would've insisted they leave. But she would've been dead if not for Brites, whose teas and herbal mixtures had dulled the curse for a time before the terrible magic built a resistance and rendered them ineffective. Brites spent however long as necessary sieving soups for her, since the curse had a harder time with liquids—not perfect, but enough for her to hang on to the tenuous grip of life.

She rested her head against Brites's chest. "Why can't I stop it? Am I doomed to carry this blasphemy for life? Why would the Lord saddle me with this terrible thing that just takes and takes and—"

Brites kissed the top of Yzabel's head. Her fingers carried on with their steadying motion. "I've told you before—magic is not the villain you make it out to be. People like me have been using it for generations, and people like you have been born—"

"I wasn't born with this," Yzabel interrupted sourly. "And even if there are more people like us, what does it matter? We're all forced to hide it unless we want to be trepanated, so we might as well be the only ones. And even if we could go public, the only other person who was cursed in this way is dead." A shudder trembled in her lips. "That's how I'm going to end up, isn't it? Dead by eighteen because I can't eat anything other than flowers."

Brites's motions stilled as she sighed. "You won't die if you learn how to control it."

As if she hadn't been trying. "What am I doing wrong, then?" She pulled back to look at Brites and found her regarding her with a mixture of affection and despondency. "Gloves don't do anything, and neither does spearing the food with a knife. Should I pray harder? Fast every day? Go back to wearing the cilice around *both* legs? I spent the last five years doing that, and the curse only grew stronger!"

Her head went into a dizzy spin, throbbing with pain and guilt. "I'm always tired, regardless of how much I sleep. I'm afraid to eat in public, and what I *do* manage to eat in private is not enough to keep me healthy. Even with everything you do, I can't…" She sniffed. "My moon's blood hasn't shown in three years. Denis thinks it's because of the fasting, but if this keeps going, I'll either be dead, or he'll find out I'm unable to bear him heirs because of the curse, then he won't marry me, I won't be queen, and all this pain will have been for nothing."

Brites shook her head. "I don't think it's a curse you bear. If you let it feed—"

"Absolutely not."

"We could give it just the bones—"

"I'll not give this curse *anything*." To do so would be to welcome the Devil in, to give in to the horrible relief that followed the curse's insidious, flowery magic.

Sighing, Brites scratched her hawkish nose. "Then I don't know. If you were a Caraju like me, I could've trained you. We can try soaking you in Terra da Moura's medicinal springs as well, but I don't think that'll make a difference, either." She squeezed Yzabel once before letting go, and her half-lidded eyes caught on her left hand still bursting with magic, unsated, unrelenting.

Shreds of the afternoon conversation with Senhor Davide kindled an idea into life. "What about the Enchanted Moura? You said she grants wishes. Could she... Do you think she could put an end to this somehow?"

Brites bit the inside of her cheek. "She might, if you can find her."

Yzabel had nothing to lose by trying.

"Get Vasco," she said. "We have plans to make."

The curse didn't dim during her night of fitful sleep, and Yzabel woke to a burning left hand and a boiling tongue. With the sun still slumbering, she held her fingers aloft, noticed how they trembled. Either from her own frailty or the proximity of the Enchanted Moura's magic, Yzabel could not say.

At her feet, Lucas raised his ears, a question in his whine as he tilted his head at her. She patted him as she sat up, eyes closed to fight the nausea swaying in her throat and the hunger gnawing at her stomach.

She slid out of bed, naked feet stomping on the carpet as she went to wake up Brites in the room next to hers. Brites helped her dress amid yawns, first the white gown she'd need to wear for the Moura, then a commoner's outfit over it. As they went downstairs, Yzabel fiddled with the rough wool of the skirt's high waist, felt the embroidery in a red-and-gold jacket over a loose chintz shirt. The thick woolen socks chafed almost as much as the cilice, and tanned hide shoes, old and worn, were two ovens baking her feet despite the cold.

"I've packed some bread and chorizo for the day and crumbled some of those honey broas Her Highness likes so much." Brites handed a cloth-wrapped bundle to a sour-looking Vasco.

"I still don't like this," he grumbled. "The Moura's story is pure fantasy."

Yzabel made herself meet his stare. "What if it isn't?"

"It's not befitting of a princess—"

"*I* decide what's befitting of me." She didn't mean the accusation in her tone, but it slipped past her like a poisonous snake. "And if there *is* a Moura, and if she can help, what harm would come of listening to what she has to say?"

Some of the tension lifted from Vasco's shoulders and his glower softened to a frown. "Even if the tale is true, and we find this creature, what do you think will happen if someone discovers you've conspired with a Moor?"

"I'll be killed if someone finds out about the curse anyway, so we better make sure we don't get caught."

"It's *dangerous*. I cannot, in my right conscience, allow you to do this."

This discussion was moot. She so loathed playing the princess card, but sometimes it was the only way. Being confident in front of Vasco had always been difficult because it often meant hurting him, and she hated to see sadness in his eyes.

He'd been willing to look past her curse and protected her the best he could, sought help when Yzabel thought she'd be forever lost. He was more of a papá to her than Pedro had ever been. Which was why she must not let his doubts affect her. Yzabel's own were already hard enough to deal with.

"How long do you think I have if we don't solve this problem?"

Vasco made to answer but ended up chewing on his bottom lip.

"Tell. Me. And be honest."

Remorse darkened his eyes, and at last, he confessed, "Not long. I suspect we would've lost you already had we let the medicus bleed you like they wanted."

To this day, it was hard not to laugh every time she remembered Brites chasing the medicus with a broom, yelling obscenities unfit for anyone's ears. Humor was not appropriate at this instance, so she held firm, face and eyes of unwavering stone. "Then we agree—if there ever was a time to resort to desperation, it's long passed us by. I'll respect your choice to not involve yourself in this, but if you think your absence will deter me, you're wrong." She pierced Vasco with a sharp look. "If there's a chance I can rid myself of this magic, I *will* find it. With or without you."

He nodded, the faint beginnings of a smile playing at the corners of his mouth, and turned to her, encased in hesitation, before placing a fatherly kiss atop her head. "I keep forgetting you're not a child anymore."

She hated him for the reluctance yet loved him for everything else.

While Vasco left to get the horses, Brites pulled her aside. "Now tell me what you need to do to find the Moura," she whispered. Her eyes, as dark as the night, assessed her with uncanny fierceness; she wouldn't let them leave until Yzabel recited the rules without flaw.

She raised a finger, recalling the stories of Enchanted Mouras of her childhood, and said, "Dress only in white, for white is the light that keeps away the darkness of the Moura's curse." Another finger unspooled. "Follow her voice when she begins speaking in my head. The birds will sing their warnings, and the earth will shake in fear. These are attempts to deter me. I'm not to listen." A third finger stood. "And no matter what happens, I must never. Look. Back."

"If you look back before you reach her, it'll be as though she'd never been there." Brites fussed with Yzabel's hat. "Once you're within her range, you have *one* chance. Do not waste it."

"I won't."

Vasco left the stables with two horses in tow. Lucas, who had been grouchy the entire night as if he'd sensed her imminent departure, bumped his head against her skirts and whined. It seemed like only yesterday he'd been a puppy, rejected by his mother and left to perish in the cold, until Yzabel saved him. She knelt on the cobblestones to put her arms around Lucas's neck. He stunk of dog and his fur was damp from the morning mists—she held him tight, nonetheless. "I'll come back soon." A peck on his nose. "Be good to Brites."

Yzabel rose to her feet and stepped into Brites's open arms. "Good luck, little princess," she whispered and kissed her cheek. "And remember—"

"Don't look back."

CHAPTER FOUR

The Deepest Wish

Under October's heavy rains, Yzabel spent her time atop the horse shivering as she went over the set of rules to finding the Moura. Impossible not to imagine Brites's voice as she recounted them in her head, and a grimace twisted her lips. She wished her lady's maid had been able to come, but someone needed to stay back and tell everyone the princess had run out of herbs for her medicines and would spend the day resupplying her stock. If Denis became testy, Brites was one of the few people who could keep him from chasing after Yzabel.

As the sun rose, so did the people, shambling down the hill to work in the fields of their lords while their women and children took care of the house and animals. Skinny girls and boys fed chickens, and she spotted some pigs here and there—likely being raised by the entire neighborhood for slaughter come Februarius. Older girls collected herbs from their gardens, and many houses had red cloths hanging by the windows to announce the presence of the red plague.

She made a mental note on the number of houses marked in red so she could make some medicine and arrange for it be delivered. Although she couldn't adequately fight the plague of famine ravaging the country, she could help with the plague of disease.

The roads proved tricky, the mud slippery under the horses' hooves. They kept a slow pace, bundled in extra layers to keep the chill and raindrops away; nevertheless, she succumbed to sneezing, throat raw and skin burning. She'd blown her clogged nose so many times the handkerchief was sandpaper on her nostrils, and although Vasco insisted she give up and return lest her health grow worse, she insisted they push on.

She looked down at her fingers, the glow of magic becoming sharper the farther they trotted along the gurgling riverbank. The Moura *was* still here—of that, she had no doubt. But there was still a chance she wouldn't be able to find her. If that happened, she wouldn't live to toast São Martinho with watered wine and take in the scents of chestnuts roasting, wouldn't live to hear the Christmas chants carrying into the deep night. She wouldn't live to see the country recover from long years of war, wouldn't be alive to fight for the betterment of the commoners' lives. Those duties had been ingrained in her, had become her ultimate goals. They were all she had left, and she refused to let go of that final lifeline.

The clouds parted in the mid-morning, and sunshine dulled the sharp edges of the breezes. Anticipation built like fire in a crackling log, and she was certain she'd burst open from the growing enthusiasm. It filled her lungs, spread through her blood, coated her sight with sparks that seemed to glint everywhere.

They kept a steady pace along the Ardila River, looking for the marker near the shore: a rectangle of old marble. Impossible to miss, it was as tall as a man and twice as large. When they spotted it, Vasco brought the horses to a halt, casting his sight east as he smoothed his mustache.

"According to Brites, the Moura is supposed to be around here."

With a nod, Yzabel dismounted, the cilice's teeth flaring pain down her leg when her feet hit the ground and with every movement she made to peel off her outer layers. She expertly untied the knot of the flowery headscarf, taking it off along with the wide-brimmed hat that held it in place, then kicked off her shoes and freed her legs from the woolen socks. Her skirt and shirt were the last, revealing the ivory dress underneath. She stashed everything into one of the saddlebags, and from another she took her mantle, draping the fine affair of white fur across her shoulders.

The smile on her lips stretched as sunlight kissed her cheeks and her feet touched naked earth, soft and moist against her skin. The weather was blessedly warm, as if summer had reached into autumn's kingdom for one last reprise.

"Wish me luck," she said.

A tight smile, a comforting hand on her head. "Good luck, my princess. May you finally find peace from your curse."

Peace. That's exactly what she was here to find.

With Vasco leading the horses behind her, Yzabel walked on.

The Ardila River was loud and fast, swollen with October's rains. Frogs croaked along its stony margins, and rabbits skipped across the fields of grass. To her right, the olive trees housed chirping birds, the earth overgrown with grass and flowers.

The feeling that surged when she touched food—the curse and its starry warmth—manifested, unbidden. It took root as a funny twist in her belly grew into a pulsing wave of heat that flared the sharpest on her left hand and tongue. Why those two places of her body teemed with magic, Yzabel could not tell.

Ahead, the air shimmered like the surface of a wind-blown pond.

"Magic," she whispered in wide-eyed wonder.

Intrigue kicked her feet into a run, deadened her to the cringing pain in her bones. The strange imagery drew her, its spell calling her as sirens did sailors in the sea.

"Yzabel, slow down!" Vasco shouted somewhere behind her.

Imbued with sudden vigor, she ran faster still, crossing the glistening boundary. The enchantments in place set her skin on fire, sent the blood in her veins into a burning frenzy, and thickened the air in her throat. The overwhelming need to *turn back* and *go away* overflowed her mind, persuaded her limbs—but she held firm and kept moving forward.

And, at last, a voice she didn't know spoke in her ear.

"*—hear me?*"

"Yes!" Yzabel shouted through shallow breaths, the tug pulling her toward the green fields of trees and grass. As though someone had placed an ember in her chest, the longer she dallied, the longer she took to find the Moura, the fiercer it ached. Her body had one purpose, a single need that propelled it forward—find the source of the voice.

"*Please—so long,*" it said. No, she, for this was clearly a woman that spoke to her. "*Please find me.*"

Birds took flight from their perches in the trees, rustling branches and leaves like a whirlwind. Beneath her feet, the ground seemed to yawn and shift, trying to throw her off balance. She picked up her skirts, ran faster, and the tug pulled harder, burned brighter.

"*Come to me, come-comecomecome—*"

She arrived at a small hill with the dark mouth of a

dolmen at the bottom, a tomb from a civilization long past. Heart in her throat and the taste of metal on her tongue, she briefly leaned against the moss-covered stones, but no matter how hard or how deep the gulps of air she took, she couldn't catch her breath.

At her back, the wind frenzied. Birds swooped, screeching and screaming and demanding she turn to look at them. When she didn't, her sight became a blur of beaks and feathers. Claws raked her shoulders, the nape of her neck, tangled and pulled her hair. There was little else she could do besides hold up her arms to protect her face, cringing.

What if this was the Lord's belated signal that she should stop?

She paused, almost turned around—she would have, had Brites's voice not rung in her head, reminding her that part of the larger spell surrounding the Enchanted Moura was that nature itself would do everything to detract possible curse-breakers from their goal.

"Almost!" the Moura said, in a voice that was all anguish tinted with anticipation. *"Don't stop, please-please-please find me."*

With a scream, she spread her arms and slapped some of the birds away before crawling past the dolmen's threshold. Once inside, the birds didn't follow, and although she wasn't sure they were gone for good, she didn't dare risk a look from the corner of her eye.

No looking back, not until she found the Moura.

"I'm here!" she shouted, her voice reverberating around her.

The damp darkness closed in, and Yzabel couldn't see the way, but the voice called again, and the magic pushed her ahead. The inside had enough room for her to stand,

and with an adjustment to her skirts and mantle, she inched forward, one hand on the steadying wall.

Her heart beat loud and fast. Her entire body became impossibly hot and awash in light, splitting the darkness in half. Right at the center, a stone of weather-worn granite, dotted with specks of red and cut in a rectangle that was not much wider than the palm of her hand.

She knelt, skirts pooling around her in a sea of wrinkles and white. In her head, the Moura spoke again, so close she seemed to be right in front of her.

"Please," she said. *"I'm right here."*

With her glowing hand, Yzabel reached, fingers brushing the surface of the stone. A tremor rocked the dolmen's cave, showering her in pebbles. Gasping, she almost dropped her arm, almost turned back when Vasco screamed her name from the mouth of the anta—but before she could react, reality shifted. A river of air swept her up in its arms, and she fell into the stone, the mysterious current dragging her down, down, *down*.

A shock rattled her bones. An excruciating pain settled on her chest, as if someone had cracked her ribs open and rummaged through her insides.

In her heart, there was only one wish, one word.

Peace.

Peace from the curse and its waste.

Peace to grow strong and be the princess she wanted to be.

Peace in this country that had become hers, so no more lives would be lost to pointless wars.

Her descent slowed. Yzabel's feet met the ground with the whisper of skin on stone. She lifted her gaze to look ahead—mists stretched for as far as she could see, leaving her surroundings clouded in mystery.

A few feet ahead, a small whirlwind spun in the fog. At its center shone a single star, a tiny kernel of light growing larger and larger with each maddening spin.

She lifted an arm to shield her eyes from the blinding brightness, but her skin radiated with its own glow, magic meeting magic. Bigger than what happened if she was near Brites when the woman cast her charms. With Brites, it was a murmur of feeling.

With the Moura, it was an assault.

Every inch of her skin thrummed. Her blood hummed in her ears, each pulse vibrating in her teeth, thumping in her temples. She endured it all, the pain a small price to pay even as she fell to her knees, clutching her head.

A final flash. The whirlwind stilled, and her magic calmed, the brightness inside fading.

She blinked, and blinked, and blinked, until at last, she could see again.

Her heart sped up, jumping to her throat the moment her eyes fell on a woman standing some feet away. The stranger looked down at her hands, examined a strand of inky hair, felt her golden face with her fingertips. Her full lips let out a gasp, appearing as astounded as Yzabel felt. Her eyes, a dark shade of green, found Yzabel's. With a smile, and in a voice lovelier than a lute's song, the Moura said, "Ave."

CHAPTER FIVE

A Promise

Yzabel echoed the Moura's Latin greeting, breathless and unguarded. "Ave."

Wariness stilled the Moura's steps, a frown wrinkling her forehead, followed with a hand to her heart. Big, doe-like eyes the shade of green olives, made more striking in a frame of thick, long eyelashes. Flat and bold brows, her nose strong and straight, her cheekbones sharp, and her lips, round and full, brought up the memory of rose petals, lush and pink.

With slow feet, she approached in a billowing cloud of burgundy skirts, blinking as if Yzabel could disappear and reveal herself a dream. Or perhaps it was disappointment that made her so hesitant. The Enchanted Moura's eyes would see nothing but a waifish girl, ashen pale and malnourished, wearing a fine dress of silk and a beautiful mantle of white fur. She'd see dull brown curls framing a square face dominated by a large forehead, sunken, deep-set eyes black as a void, and a long, thick nose—far from the dashing savior the Moura had probably imagined.

"What's your name?" Yzabel asked, shy uncertainty wavering in her voice.

The Moura's breath caught. "So many have come here

before, and you're the first to ask." She moved closer, every step more mesmerizing than the one before, her voice low and resonant, like the song of crystal glasses. "I am Fatyan, once the favored daughter of Abu-Hassan, Alcaide of Al-Manijah. Enchanted to meet you." Her Latin was slightly different from Yzabel's, but not by much, and it was easy to derive the meaning of her words. After a pretty curtsy, she asked, "And yours?"

She curtsied in return. "I am Yzabel of Aragon, future Queen of Portugal and the Algarves, daughter of Pedro the Third of Aragon and Constanza of Hohenstaufen of Sicily."

"The future Queen of Portugal?" Fatyan laughed, a crystalline, melodious sound that echoed across the mist.

"What's so funny?"

"The irony, dear one. The irony is hilarious." She wiped tears from the corner of her eyes. "That the one person who's heard me in over a hundred years happens to be everything Baba despised—Portuguese, a girl, and a princess."

"I'm not Portuguese, though."

"Aragonian—same thing to him, really." Fatyan went back to regarding her with a quizzical expression. Under the scrutiny, she shifted uncomfortably from foot to foot as a blush heated her cheeks.

"I'm…sorry," she said. "I was told you were cursed into eternity when the Portuguese took Terra da Moura. Taking back a city shouldn't come at the cost of a woman's eternal life. It's not worth anyone's, and I truly am sorry we've caused you pain."

Fatyan's frown deepened, and she blinked. "My misery is not unique, dear one. Others had it far worse."

"It still doesn't make it right," Yzabel said without wavering, "and if I can help you finally end it, then I will."

The Moura's eyebrows arched in surprise before she cleared her throat and regained her neutral composure. "No point in apologizing. It's in the past and not done by your hand. I'd wager you were sold to a king, same way I'd have been sold had the Portuguese not taken Al-Manijah. Not to mention…I'm here by my father's hand, not your people's."

"You're not angry?"

"I was, for a while. But when you've been stuck so long in a place such as this, where time is so warped you lose track of it, anger and bitterness become tiring. Eventually, I stopped feeling them. I stopped feeling anything, and all I did was wait, and sleep, and wait, and sleep…" Melancholy tinged her smile. "Then you came, and I was asleep no more." A step closer. "So, dear Yzabel. Tell me why you've come."

Hearing her name in Fatyan's lips heated her cheeks further, and her closeness breathed wonder into her lungs. No stranger had come so near her before, and she almost stepped away—but then her eyes found Fatyan's and the tender curiosity reflected upon them, and the enchantment of it all rooted her in place.

"I need your help," Yzabel said.

"I know. I need yours, too." A slight tilt of her head. "What would you ask of me?"

Yzabel tensed, her fingers matching the white of her dress as she clutched it. "You have to promise not to tell anyone. Even after we leave this place."

Understanding blinked in Fatyan's eyes, and she tilted her head to the side as she asked, "Is it the sahar?"

"Sahar?"

"Magic." She motioned toward Yzabel's left hand that was still glowing as though someone had spread embers under the skin. "It's what woke me up, even though you were far away."

The curse *had* been reacting to Fatyan's. Yzabel's lips fell open. "Can you tell me why it turns all the food I touch into flowers?"

Intrigue drew Fatyan's lips into a pout and her fingers to her chin. "You turn food into flowers?"

"Yes. That's why I came to find you." She looked at Fatyan, and her tongue darted to wet her lips. "I need this curse gone."

Pensive eyes studied her, then Fatyan raised her hand. "I need to feel your sahar better." Fatyan stilled, left her fingers to hover above Yzabel's jaw. "May I?"

An answering nod came without Yzabel's command, and she stepped forward so Fatyan brushed her cheek. The Moura closed her eyes as she fully cupped the side of Yzabel's face, and she wasn't certain what spell had her enthralled so completely, if it was the stone's or the Moura's, but her heart was racing, and an odd feeling forming in her stomach, so much like hunger and yet not.

The magic inside her surged, and heat spread from where their skin touched. Her heart tried to climb up her throat. When she swallowed it back down, the throb rose to her ears, numbing her to anything that wasn't Fatyan.

A crease appeared between the Moura's brows as she opened her eyes, and her hand moved across Yzabel's jaw, down the slope of her neck, mesmerized as they trailed her own gesture. Yzabel looked down when the Moura stopped at her shoulder and gasped at the sight before her.

Under Fatyan's touch, Yzabel's skin came alight, as though she had candles underneath her flesh and Fatyan's fingers were the flame that lit their wick.

"This is no curse," Fatyan said under her breath. She

trailed her hand down the inside of Yzabel's arm, and it was like watching lightning cross her skin. "How long have you had it?"

"Since my first blood, five years ago," Yzabel replied bitterly, but did not pull away. "And it's been growing worse ever since, to a point I can barely eat anymore."

"Gifts such as ours tend to grow wild if they're not accepted and centered." The Moura gave her a perplexed look, brow low over blinking eyes. "You hate it. No wonder it's angry."

"Angry?"

"Your sahar is starved, driven wild by your revulsion." Fatyan took her hand away and then backed up a step. "I cannot take or change it, dear Yzabel, no more than I could rip your heart from your chest and turn it into a lung."

The shock from Fatyan's words struck her in place. She was sentenced to die, to be devoured from within like a mite-infected tree. "You…can't help me?"

All the suffering and despair, the isolation and the sickness… All for nothing.

It was as if a violent storm raged around her, and she but a cracked reed whipped in every direction, soon to be violently uprooted and lost in the wind. Reduced to a footnote in history as the first woman promised to the King of Portugal, a princess who would give no heirs and leave behind no legacies.

All because of the cursed magic she unleashed at every meal, magic that would finally kill her after all these years.

Stars and darkness overtook her sight. The pressure mounted in her lungs, and wind stirred the mist, snaking around her legs, lifting her up, and Yzabel could not breathe, she couldn't—

"I never said that." Fatyan's soft statement anchored

her. "Your sahar isn't that different from mine. Ours is the gift of transformation, but yours flows outward instead of inward. Either way, if you learn how to properly wield it, you can control how it acts."

Yzabel's throat bobbed as she looked away, biting the inside of her cheek. "I've been trying to do that all my life. I've never been able to suppress the magic."

"That's where you went wrong. Those of us born with magic are meant to use it. We're not meant to choke it, but to give it shape and set it free. You can turn food into flowers on your own, but Yzabel…" Fatyan tucked one of Yzabel's curls behind her ear, lifted her chin with an index finger. "You *can* learn to do the reverse and turn flowers into food. Of that, I'm sure."

The gates of her imagination opened, showing her pictures of the Portuguese fields packed with wildflowers ready to be plucked by anyone who wished. She could turn all that into food people could eat, without spending a single dime. "How?"

"The same way I did—practice, patience, and a small ritual." Fatyan smiled, and sunlight seeped through the mist, kissing Yzabel's cheeks with warmth. "On my life and blood, break my curse, dear Yzabel, and I will help you become a master in the arts of sahar." Her hand returned to Yzabel's face, startling her into motionlessness. "I will help you turn flowers into food."

How had she not seen this before? How had she been so blinded by terror that she'd failed to grasp the most obvious of possibilities?

Denis had restricted Yzabel's charity to measly alms that were nowhere near enough to make an impact. And God had known Denis would forbid her from being as charitable as she wanted; He'd known the Portuguese would need her, so was it possible He had equipped her to deal with it?

Eating alone, avoiding public outings, staying hidden out of fear of being persecuted for the magic she carried… That was not her fate. It was a challenge, given so she could truly understand her calling and take matters into her own hands.

The tentative relief overwhelmed her into a stutter. "H-How do I get us out of here?"

"Ah, this is where even more irony comes in," Fatyan said. "Our legends are always made with men in mind. Women are the object of a curse, not their breakers. Yet, in all these years, no man has been strong enough or brave enough to come. You did."

"What do you mean?"

A lopsided smile of mischief. "A kiss, dear Yzabel. The curse is broken with a kiss."

A kiss? Kisses were supposed to be between husband and wife—and she'd barely kissed her own betrothed. The few times she'd subjected herself to the experience had left her so underwhelmed, she hadn't had the courage to try again recently. To do it with someone else in the meantime seemed…dishonest. "Is that the only way?"

"It is," Fatyan said simply.

Thinking about kissing her flustered Yzabel more than thinking of the marriage bed. "I couldn't have been the only woman to find you."

"You weren't, but the others weren't like you. They came with wishes of marriage and riches, and the curse shaped me into whatever their hearts desired—always a man." She bit the corner of her lower lip. "You were the perfect loophole—someone who came to ask for *peace*. I believe that's why I retained my original shape."

She wasn't ready for this; it was one thing to seek the help of the uncanny, but to kiss a woman? Surely the Lord would strike them where they stood. "But the Bible says a woman cannot kiss another woman."

A sudden gust of wind rose to freeze the air, chilly fingers sinking into her ankles to seize bone and muscle. Darkness swept in, coating the mist in shadow, and Fatyan, so warm a moment ago, stood as rigid as a statue.

"I didn't take you for one of their puppets," she said, the low notes of her voice tolling like bells, echoing in the emptiness around them. "I didn't think you'd be so opposed to the idea of a simple kiss shared to help someone *and* yourself."

The wind spun harder, lifting Yzabel's mantle, her skirts, her heels—the balls of her feet were all that tethered her to the ground, as tenuous and as fragile as spider's silk. The refusal to kiss Fatyan was driving her out of the stone, away from the one person who could help her.

She fought the force pushing her up. "I'm not a puppet."

"No?" Fatyan's glare didn't wane.

The air stole one of Yzabel's legs out from under her, left her poised on the tip of a toe.

"I don't believe you."

A whip of air slammed into her stomach, knocking her off balance and the mantle off her shoulders. For a split second, she hovered in the dark, one arm blindly reaching for Fatyan, whose icy facade had broken into a visage of terrible sorrow and despair. Loneliness dripped from her in waves, the solitude of more than a century burrowing in Yzabel's thoughts.

Fatyan had been so alone, for so long. If a kiss was the price to pay for someone's freedom, should a princess not give it willingly, and gladly? And perhaps kissing a woman was the lesser of two evils and would lead to less complicated entanglements. If she had to bring someone new to the castle to teach her magic, it was far easier with another woman—no one would find it amiss if they spent too long together, or if they slept together, even. Should they succeed, Portugal's citizens would be better off.

What was a sacrilegious kiss in the face of all that?

"I'll do it!" As soon as the shout left her lips, her feet met solid ground, and her outstretched hand met Fatyan's shoulder.

The warmth returned, as did the light. The Moura took a small step forward, the space between them a hair's breadth. "First, an exchange of vows." She brushed the hair away from Yzabel's face, a gesture so tender that she fought the sudden urge to lean into it. "I promise to help you learn the sahar and will not leave your side until you are its master."

It took Yzabel a moment to realize it was her turn to speak. "I promise to grant you freedom once I control the magic inside me. Should that prove impossible, I'll free you nonetheless."

Fatyan's eyes widened as though she hadn't expected that last part. Little dimples appeared in the corner of her mouth, and her fingers grasped Yzabel's chin. "And so it shall be."

The breathy words teased her lips in a way she did not understand. She wanted to inhale them, roll them around in her tongue and swallow them whole. Her eyelids closed, casting her into a darkness that heightened every other sense. The tender heat from the hand holding her chin firm, and the one snaking around her waist. The hectic beat of her heart when their chests touched, the aching of her lips in anticipation until, finally, they met Fatyan's.

It was just a soft brush at first, barely there at all. She didn't know what to do, and although she repeatedly told herself to stay still and let it be over with, another instinct— something buried deep inside, a part of herself she'd never met—made her lean forward.

The flavor of cinnamon danced on the tip of her tongue, the scent of almonds on her nostrils, but before she could get a better taste, the heat of magic enveloped them both. Fatyan pulled away, and Yzabel opened her eyes to see her smiling as sunlight soaked the two of them.

The same invisible current that had swept Yzabel into the stone lifted their feet from the ground, and like two stars, they shot upward into the mist. Fatyan clung to her, and Yzabel wrapped her arms around the shaking Moura. Vibrations hummed around them as the stone's realm crumbled, the magic pieces a river flowing into Fatyan, condensing the timeless prison into its inhabitant's flesh.

Fatyan groaned through gritted teeth. Yzabel's ears popped, her eyes blind against the bright light, and then—

Solid ground. Damp air, the scent of earth heavy upon it.

In a small voice, Fatyan asked, "Did we…?"

Yzabel ran a comforting hand across the other girl's back. "Yes."

Slowly, Fatyan opened her eyes to the cave, a slow laugh building low in her throat. She giggled as she kissed Yzabel's alarmed cheek, hugged her tight, and said, "Thank you."

Strange as it was, Fatyan's warmth wasn't an unwelcome feeling. As Yzabel let herself bask in it a second longer, she wondered if it was even possible to grow used to this.

CHAPTER SIX

A Thread of Hope

As soon as Fatyan took her first glimpse of the orange sunset, she launched into a run, leaving Yzabel behind in the dark.

A lick of her tingling lips brought back the cinnamon, and with it, the twisted rumbling of hunger. She gathered her breath and composure, the familiar exhaustion waking up inside her, but as she started to follow the giggling melody outside, her toe met something hard and sent it spinning forward.

Amid the roots and earth, sat a stone. *The stone.* Back aching and knees groaning, she bent to pick it up, inspecting it with a frown. A trace of magic hummed against the flesh of her hand in an ominous warning, the terms of their deal whirling in her head.

Her last shred of hope lay with someone she barely knew, her faith in a single promise that could be broken at any time. Her practical side, asleep inside Fatyan's cursed realm, erupted with berating thoughts about the precariousness of her situation, of what she'd have to do just to keep Fatyan nearby. It hadn't even occurred to her that freeing a Moura from her prison would bring its share of lies and trouble.

A sound from outside scattered her thoughts and guilt. Vasco asking, "Who are you? Where's Yzabel?"

She immediately scampered out of the dolmen, shouting, "Here!" as she forced her sluggish feet to crest the dolmen's entrance. "I'm fine."

"I couldn't find you for most of the afternoon. You went in there, and when the mantle came flying out, when hours passed, I thought…"

Yzabel had thought it odd that the sun had come close to setting in such a short amount of time, and she looked to Fatyan, who read the question without her needing to voice it.

"Time passes differently in the stone," the Moura explained. "Sometimes slower, sometimes faster, and you can never tell which is which. Especially when you're stuck in a cave without sunlight."

Shaking his head, Vasco lowered dazed eyes to Yzabel's cloak draped in his arms like a blanket of snow, then came over to place the heavy warmth back on her shoulders. He grabbed both her arms for a second as if to ascertain she was truly here, then settled his attention back on Fatyan. "Is she…?"

Under the setting sun, her guard and the Moura exchanged a glance that brimmed with mistrust. Fatyan bristled at the way his eyes raked her over from head to toe, her arms coming to a defiant cross over her chest.

Yzabel stepped between them. "Yes. This is Fatyan, the Enchanted Moura. Fatyan, this is Dom Vasco Pires, head of my Guarda."

Vasco's thick-eyebrowed glower intensified. If Fatyan was uncomfortable, however, it didn't show in the flamboyant bow that followed, or her teasing, "Enchanted to meet you."

Vasco didn't move, and the unamused dark of his eyes didn't leave Fatyan. "I assume she managed to rid you of the curse, then?"

A fierce scowl took over Fatyan's face as her hands became fists, ready to demand respect over being ignored. Yzabel needed to smother the suspicions between these two before any conflict could escalate.

"There's been a change of plans. Fatyan will stay with us a while, and you will not speak of her as though she's not present."

The bags he carried fell to the ground with a heavy *thump*. "She didn't end the curse?"

The gall of him to do it right after she told him not to. Yzabel fixed him with a glare, not speaking until Vasco apologetically turned to Fatyan and reframed his question.

"You couldn't take it away?"

"No. It's impossible to take away someone's magic when they're born with it. All I can do is teach her to control it."

Vasco regarded Fatyan with a critical eye. "You are going to pose problems."

Fatyan snorted. "Why, because I'm a Moor?"

"No, that part of you blends in just fine, since most Moors *are* Portuguese nowadays. The problem is that you'll be a beautiful stranger staying with the princess." He turned to Yzabel. "Surely you don't need to be reminded of whom you're engaged to."

Yzabel's sigh was as guilty as her avoidant gaze. As much as she was loath to admit it, Vasco had a point—she couldn't show up with a woman out of nowhere. Especially one who was bound to draw Denis's gaze; one who smelled like almonds and tasted of cinnamon.

The stone dangerously heated up in Yzabel's hand, and she could've sworn Fatyan *flickered*—there, then not, then there, then not.

"What does he mean?" Fatyan's wispy question barely reached Yzabel.

"That my betrothed is a known philanderer and you're... Well." The flashing heat of the stone climbed to her face, and she cleared her awkward throat. "But as far as I know, he doesn't tend to chase unwilling skirts." Her own included. Come to think of it, Denis had rarely spent a night out at the brothel, and much preferred to keep the company of Aldonza, one of Yzabel's future ladies-in-waiting.

"All right." Fatyan relaxed, and Yzabel released her pent-up breath before putting the stone in her pocket.

"Do you have any idea how long it might take for me to master the curse?"

"Hard to tell." The Moura looked up to the sky and the already visible close-to-full moon. "If we can get you to accept your sahar, we can perform the ritual in a couple of days. We need a full moon, plus some herbs and spices. After that, controlling your gift should be easier—but I'll have to remain at your side until our bargain is sealed."

"And it won't be until I can make bread out of roses." Yzabel chewed on her lip. "Might be best if we sneak you in and we stay in my rooms until then."

Face drained of color, Fatyan took a step back, hugging herself as if struck by an onslaught of cold. From her lips tumbled out a plea, "I can't be locked up again. I can't, I can't, I can't—"

The harrowing sorrow heated the stone again, and before it could burn a hole in her dress, Yzabel rushed to envelope Fatyan in a hug. The gesture surprised even herself, as she wasn't prone to touching others, but the instinct to comfort Fatyan had been so strong it overpowered the rest. This poor woman had been locked away for half a century, no wonder this was her reaction.

"It's all right," she whispered, hands circling comfort around Fatyan's trembling back. "We don't have to hide you, but we do need to come up with a story. If we tell the wrong person you're an Enchanted Moura, they'll either try to pry the supposed demons from our skulls or execute us for black magic."

Fatyan nodded against Yzabel's neck. "Thank you. I just... I can't bear the thought of being a prisoner again."

"You won't be," Yzabel said, Fatyan's nerves quieting under her touch. As she racked her mind for ideas, what she'd witnessed this morning came back to haunt her with full force. Overworked men, incredibly thin children, the red cloths over windows.

Denis wouldn't let her give them food, true—but she could give them poultices to help with the red plague. An extra pair of hands to help with the task wouldn't be unthinkable. "If you want to walk around freely and go unmolested, we can say you're a young sister from the Carmo Convent, and that the Abbess asked me to train you in the making of herbal medicines. Does that agree with you?"

"I..." Fatyan stepped back, biting into her lower lip as she considered. "I can do that."

A s a princess, Yzabel never had the need to share a horse with anyone. When she rode, she did so alone, and proximity wasn't a common aspect of her life, much less so when riding.

Now, she had Fatyan's arms around her waist, the

Moura's body pressed against her back. Her breasts were soft, and her arms and hands would sometimes brush against Yzabel's leg. Touches that were casual yet sent a shiver up her spine and cut her breath short. Not even the chafing of the cilice wrapped around her leg was enough to drown the fleeting sensations creeping along her skin.

It bothered Yzabel that she didn't understand those reactions. She wondered if it was because of her magic and Fatyan's pushing and pulling at each other, or if it was something else entirely.

Perhaps she'd know what it meant if she hadn't lived her life in forced isolation. Other than Vasco and Brites, only Denis had hugged her. Her future ladies-in-waiting, with whom Yzabel spent her better afternoons listening to their gossip as they embroidered, had never been this close to her, and she hadn't tried being close to them. Maybe if she had, she would've known what the fluttering in her stomach was, or why her heart thundered in her chest.

Why she couldn't forget how Fatyan's lips had felt against her own, or how her tongue slid across them as if attempting to catch that taste of cinnamon.

Our Lady of Agrela, no one like her in this era, please purge these thoughts from my head. Please purge them, please purge them—on and on she thought, hoping to distract herself from Fatyan's closeness. In vain, it turned out. Fatyan laid her head against Yzabel's back, and her heart jumped so high she almost flew from the saddle.

Her kiss was a business transaction. Like your engagement is. And, like Denis, she's only chosen you because you're the best choice in a sea of none.

They slowed their horses to a canter when the walls of Terra da Moura emerged ahead, the castle tower illuminated in torchlight from below, the details of its crenellations lost in the blur of Yzabel's weak eyes. At the sight of it, Fatyan tightened her arms around Yzabel's waist and turned to frigid stone.

"That tower is where I died. At least, where I tried to," the Moura whispered, snuggling closer.

She found one of Fatyan's cold hands and held it to her chest. "Are you all right?"

The hesitation that followed answered her question. As if realizing as much, Fatyan shook her head and gave Yzabel's hand a squeeze. "I will be. But thank you for asking."

Their hold didn't break at the gates; it did not break as they guided the horses up the small hill and into the village's center.

It was only when they reached the castle and Vasco led them around the back did Yzabel let go of Fatyan's hand. While her guard went ahead to make sure the path was clear, Yzabel dismounted and helped Fatyan down.

The Moura swayed upon touching the ground, leaning against Yzabel when her legs threatened to give. "It's… been a while," she said apologetically, and hugged Vasco's cloak tighter as she looked at the tower. "They call this Terra da Moura now?"

"Yes." Yzabel looked about their surroundings, empty now that night had fallen. Light flickered behind some of the windows of the living quarters—a long, two-story building painted white, as buildings often were in Além-Tejo. "Named after the young Moura who jumped from the old tower when the city was taken." Her gaze fell on Fatyan. "Named after you."

A snort. "Did they really?"

"Yes. As the story goes, the Brothers Rodrigues were so moved by what you did they could never forget the sight, so they started calling this Terra da Moura to honor your memory. I think…" Yzabel narrowed her eyes in thought and wet her lips. "I think they blamed themselves for your death."

"From the way they cut down my people, I can't imagine how that's possible." A sardonic snarl disfigured Fatyan's lips. "Either way, my fate wouldn't have been much better had they not invaded."

The air chilled inside Yzabel's lungs. "What do you mean?"

"What does the legend say about me? About why I jumped?" Fatyan asked back, eyes hooded in bitterness.

She stroked the horses' snouts absently. It had occurred to her that not everything in the story was true, for victors rarely left the history of the defeated intact. The story of a Moor princess who killed herself out of heartache told a lot better than the one about a Moor princess killed by her conquerors. "They didn't…push you, or anything?"

Fatyan let out a low chuckle. "No."

"Then—"

"What does my story say about it?"

Yzabel blinked before answering. "That when you saw the Portuguese wearing Bráfama's clothes, you were so heartbroken by your groom's death, you jumped. And that your spirit, restless without the love it'd been promised, haunted the castle, so they had to move you someplace else."

Fatyan's face was impassive for one tick of the clock; the next, she broke into a dry, short laugh. "Love. Of course they had to say it was love." She shook her head and scoffed. "My spirit didn't linger by choice, dear Yzabel. My father was the one who cursed me—and when given the choice to be captured or be trapped in a stone, I tried to go out on my terms instead. As you can see, it didn't work out exactly as I'd planned." A long sigh rumbled in her throat, and she spun so her back was to the tower with agony plain on her face. Whatever the full truth was, it sat locked behind her lips.

Yzabel couldn't pretend to know what would drive a man to curse his own daughter, or the despair that had driven Fatyan to jump. Prying into it, however, was out of the question. Had Yzabel been in Fatyan's place, she would certainly have been unwilling to talk to a girl she barely knew. Even if said girl had broken her curse.

A short while after the castle's bell chimed with the eighth hour, Vasco appeared around the corner, motioning them to follow him inside, and guided them across doors and hallways, deserted in the early hours of the evening. Before they could begin climbing the last spiral stairwell between them and Brites's rooms, Fatyan came to an abrupt halt, shivering under Vasco's cloak.

"What's wrong?" Yzabel asked, one foot on the first stair.

Fatyan took a hand to her belly, stepped back. "My sahar, it—"

"Dom Vasco!" exclaimed a voice from the top. "I wanted to talk to you about the night shift—might we do it over supper?"

Yzabel reached for Fatyan's ice-cold hand and turned the closest knob. Linen closet, as it turned out. "He can't see you without a habit. Quick."

Vasco's and Matias's voices faded as they hid behind the closed door. The Moura's trembling intensified along with her grimace, and she clutched at Yzabel's arm as if it were a lifeline. "Who's talking to your guard?"

"Matias," Yzabel whispered. Heart pounding in her

chest, she knelt to spy through the keyhole. Brites's son, whom Vasco had taken under his wing and into the Princess's Guarda. "He has the night shift guarding my door."

"There's…something about him. Like I've heard his voice somewhere." Fatyan pursed her lips in the darkness and shook her head. "Never mind. It's probably an overreaction from my sahar, since it senses danger, and there's plenty of it all around us."

The words sat uncomfortably in Yzabel's ears as she waited for Matias's silhouette to pass the closet. Had she not been told, she never would've guessed he was Brites's son. Where her lady's maid was warm and honest, Matias was cold and slippery. And although Brites swore her son knew nothing of either her magic or Yzabel's curse, there were times when she'd catch him scrutinizing her in a way that made her skin crawl. As if he knew of her hidden affliction and was disgusted by it.

Footsteps faded in the servants' corridor. The echo of a lock, of a door slammed shut.

When she was sure Matias wouldn't see them, Yzabel tiptoed out the closet with Fatyan at her side. Up the steep stairs, Vasco awaited with arms crossed and an annoyed curl to his face.

"What did he want?" asked Yzabel.

"Nothing of relevance." He ushered them into Brites's sparse quarters, furnished by a single bed and a lonely table, and then they came to Yzabel's room, still unfamiliar to her in its unnecessary opulence. Flames crackled in the fireplace, candles cast their light from atop the drawer and nightstand, tapestries hung from the walls, and the four-poster bed was made with layers of white blankets and furs. On the small table by the settee, a jar of pansies cheered the room, and a jug of wine waited to be poured into the two glasses beside it.

"Brites is fetching food. She'll be up here shortly," Vasco said, leaning against the door he'd just closed.

Lucas immediately woke from his slumber, stretching his legs before pouncing on Yzabel in a blur of fur. His warm, wet tongue trailed a sticky path across her face, drawing a giggle from her lips. "Lucas... Lucas stop! Down!"

The dog calmed, settling to lean his head against Yzabel's hand. She scratched him behind the ear and looked over her shoulder to find Fatyan plastered to the wall, eyes wide with terror—a reaction she'd seen before in some of her ladies-in-waiting.

"He won't attack you," she reassured.

No effect. "B-but he's. So. Big. Do all princesses keep *bears* for pets?"

A knock diverted their attention to the door. Vasco opened it to let Brites in, who carried a large tray with two bowls of stew, a clay pitcher, half a loaf of dark bread, and honey broas. The scent of chickpea stew watered Yzabel's mouth and brought Fatyan away from the wall.

Brites's eyes widened when she spotted the Moura, the grin spreading her lips a stark contrast to Vasco's apprehension. "I knew you could do it, little princess."

"Brites, meet Fatyan. Fatyan, this is my lady's maid, Dona Brites Sande."

"A friend and I tried to find you some forty years ago," said the older woman as she set the tray on the table. "When we couldn't hear you, we thought someone had already freed you."

"I was asleep and determined to be left alone. But you can only slumber for so long." Fatyan's mesmerized gaze wouldn't leave the food, and it was with wonder that she picked up a slice of bread and bit into it. Poor woman must be starved after so long in that stone.

"And Denis?" asked Yzabel.

"He's livid you were gone all day. Wanted to go find you and bring you back. I…" A tight breath left Brites's nose. "I had to call Aldonza. They've been in his rooms since."

Some of the weight lifted from Yzabel's shoulders, and her eyes slid to Fatyan devouring one of the bowls of chickpea stew with voracious appetite while Vasco watched her like a hawk. The memory of the Moura's naked fear at the mention of Denis noticing her, how the stone had heated as if ready to claim its prisoner, wilted the relief blossoming in her breast. All this time, she had been so blinded by her selfish reprieve from the attention of her future husband, she'd never wondered about Aldonza.

She should ask. If Aldonza were with Denis of her own free will, or if he had been coercing her for years—and she would, soon. Just not tonight.

"Fatyan has to stay with me for a little while, so we're telling Denis she's a novice from the Carmo Convent, sent at my request," Yzabel said, changing the subject. "Can you get her a habit? She can help us make poultices for the families afflicted with the red plague."

Brites regarded the Moura thoughtfully. "My old one should fit."

Fatyan lowered the bowl from her lips, gaze flitting from the food and Yzabel, and she hurriedly put the bowl down. "I'm sorry. I shouldn't have started to eat without you."

Did Fatyan think she'd offended her by not waiting? "You don't have to apologize. You've been in that stone for the last hundred and twenty-one years!" Yzabel gestured to the food. "Go on, eat."

Brites straightened her back and placed her hands on her hips. "I'll get that habit for Fatyan and bring it."

Before Brites could leave, Yzabel swept her in a hug. "Thank you for everything you do for me."

"It's my pleasure, little princess." Brites kissed Yzabel's cheek before speaking to Fatyan. "Should you need anything, please tell me." She turned to the dog. "Lucas! You're staying with me tonight. Your master needs her focus and we both know you don't help with that."

The dog looked to Yzabel, trying to scrounge an ounce of pity. She knelt and kissed him on the nose. "Go with Brites, Lucas. We'll be together again tomorrow."

Lucas obeyed, but not without tugging at her heartstrings. He whined as he followed Brites with his head low, and he looked back with sad eyes for every one of the four steps he took to cross the room. Fatyan visibly relaxed once he was out.

Vasco made to leave in silence along with Brites, but the sourness on his face plucked Yzabel forward. She wrapped her arms around him, rested her forehead against his chest. "You as well, Vasco. I appreciate you greatly."

Something she'd said so many times. Something she knew he needed to hear.

Vasco leaned away a bit, taken aback by her sudden display of affection. It seemed to soften something inside him, and he rested his hand atop her head, his thumb rubbing her scalp. "You are a rare treasure, Yzabel. If this helps you find the peace you need, I'll object no further."

It was all she asked.

Hand on the doorknob, Vasco added, "For what it's worth, I still think you should try the springs. Brites has talked to the sisters in charge of running them, and they've agreed to vacate the springs at your request, so you can use them in privacy."

"But I don't want to keep others from—"

Vasco groaned his exasperation. "You have to learn how to be selfish once in a while. It's *one* day where people can't use the springs—it won't ultimately matter."

No, but it was the principle behind it—that for her to enjoy something meant others being deprived of it—which she refused to accept. "I'll use them along with everyone else, then."

"It's beneath your station—"

"*I* decide what's beneath my station."

"It's a security issue!" Vasco shouted.

She rolled her eyes. "What, you think someone will try to drown me in a room full of people?"

"Yzabel, *listen* to me—"

"No, *you* listen. I will not use the springs if it means closing them to everyone else."

"So this is what Brites meant by you being petulant," Fatyan said from her place at the table, a humorous lilt to her voice. The look she gave Vasco was one of begrudging respect. "Now I know why you're so strict and wary. Someone has to save Yzabel from herself."

"You, too?" She couldn't believe they'd paired up against her. So many people in town were sick and in need of the springs' treatment. It wasn't petulance that she refused to deprive them of it.

Fatyan cleared her throat, her expression sobering. "Those springs *are* blessed, and they do help with a variety of ailments. I can help your sahar settle if we go there together, and Vasco is right that we must be alone. There's no saying how your gift will act when in contact with blessed waters."

Yzabel sighed, recognizing a battle she could not win.

"Fine. But we'll go at night, after they're closed to the public."

If they were right about the springs, it wouldn't hurt to try. Still, a jittery nervousness lingered at the thought of bathing *with* Fatyan. Exactly three people had seen Yzabel without her clothes on: her mother, her former chambermaid, and Brites. She shouldn't feel this uneasy at adding another woman to that number, especially when she would be acting as her lady's maid.

It made no sense for fear to breed in her breast, but that's what this was. Fear at the reaction her magic would have to the water, and fear at what Fatyan would think when she saw what Yzabel looked like under the layers of fabric.

CHAPTER SEVEN

Wasteful Necessity

By the time Yzabel finished washing her hands and pouring herself a glass of wine, Fatyan had already set aside her empty bowl, a contented smile curving her full lips. "That was good harira—and these!" She bit into a broa, moaning as the sweetness unspooled in her mouth. "Oh, I missed ghoribas!"

It was impossible not to smile at Fatyan's sheer joy, or at how she used Algarvian terms for the cozido and broas. Yzabel's chirpy laugh broke through the Moura's ravenous appetite. After finishing the cake, she downed a sip of wine and asked, "Why aren't *you* eating?"

Embarrassment heated Yzabel's cheeks and she lowered her eyes. "I don't want to waste food when you're hungry."

Footsteps padded on the carpet as Fatyan drifted to her side. A finger slid under Yzabel's chin to gently lift her head, and shock jolted through her. "You'll have to waste some of it regardless. I need to see your magic at work if I'm to help you master it."

"I—I know." A whisper said with eyes that refused to leave the floor. "I should tell you, the curse makes it, um… challenging to eat, to say the least. It's not an elegant effort."

"And my gurgling the harira was?" Fatyan tugged her along, gently pushed her to sit on the chair while she leaned on the side of the table.

Recognizing defeat, Yzabel placed a napkin on her lap, then pointed at Fatyan with the wooden spoon. Although her face was serious, her voice chimed with humor. "You've been warned."

With fast, short motions, she stabbed at the stew with the spoon, breaking the carrots and chickpeas into smaller pieces so she could swallow them without chewing or choking. "The curse travels through the spoon if I linger too long," she explained as she kept on murdering the legumes.

As if unable to sit by and watch, Fatyan held out a hand. "Let me do that for you?"

"Oh." She dropped the spoon and nodded toward the bowl. "Thank you. That'd be very helpful."

Fatyan set to grinding the stew as best she could without a sieve—it wasn't perfect, but it was better than Yzabel's rushed stabbing, and soon enough, she asked her to stop.

"That's good enough." She took the bowl from Fatyan and put it to her lips, tilting her head back so the stew fell directly into her mouth.

From the corner of her eye, she caught Fatyan maneuvering herself to better watch what unfolded before her. Glimpses of heat flashed inside Yzabel's mouth, down her throat, fading when they landed in her belly, and her left hand hummed with glowing energy.

Halfway into the bowl, Yzabel choked and coughed a few times before spitting up a chewed-up daisy with only a handful of petals still attached.

"Extraordinary," Fatyan muttered.

"An extraordinary bother, more like," Yzabel countered. "Brites made a tea that used to dull it, but it no longer works.

She serves most of my meals pre-mushed and pre-cuts the cheese and bread so I can eat with minimal chewing—I guess with all the commotion she forgot to do it today." She crushed the daisy in her hand. "Either way, such options aren't available when you're hosting dinners. It's even more unthinkable that touching food forces me to waste precious sustenance in times like these."

"And when it showed…who told you it was a curse?"

"My mamá. She said that some crafty noblewoman had cursed me, jealous I was to be Queen of Portugal and the Algarves. The very same curse my Great Aunt Erzsébet suffered from over fifty years ago, and one that ultimately killed her at a young age, shortly after she performed a miracle." Yzabel refilled both their wineglasses and cradled hers to her chest. "The curse grew worse with time, and up until now, I thought I would die the same way my aunt did. Seems…silly, now that you've made me see I'm meant to master it. Not just to keep Denis from finding out, but to feed the people without breaking his rules about where and how I spend my dinheiros."

Fatyan cocked her head and raised an eyebrow. "And you think your betrothed will kill you if he found out you bear sahar? If your aunt had the same gift, and hers was seen as a miracle…"

"Aunt Erzsébet's husband was a man of God. When he caught her sneaking out to feed bread to the poor and she turned bread to roses in front of him, he took it as an act of the Lord, meant to humble him into allowing his wife to continue her charitable exploits." Yzabel's mouth tightened. "Denis is many things, but devout isn't one of them. His reaction will not be that."

"Does he treat you wrong?" Fatyan asked, darkness consuming her eyes.

Yzabel's movements slowed, then became flustered. "No! Lord, no. He's just very, how do I put this… Strict? A miser who can't see how privileged he is? And I don't think he'd forgive another betrayal from me. He's still upset I went behind his back with my charity and almost spent my dowry before we were even married."

Fatyan tapped her jawline as she thought on that last sentence. "But to kill you… Do you truly think he'd do that?"

"He would. If not for the betrayal, then out of pride." She looked down at her hands, picked on her cuticles. "Kings don't let princesses drag an engagement for years, and a princess who hides terrible secrets can't risk the ire of the men who hold her fate in their hands."

Fatyan pointed at the three robust slices of bread neither of them had touched and said, "Show me more of your magic, then."

Yzabel instinctively made to argue, but she had to do this. Her slender, small fingers reached for the bread—the magical glow emanated from her hand, rushing forth as if it hungered for the sustenance before it. It enveloped the food in a white light that broke apart to become a thick stem, elongated and thinned to green leaves, swirled into nested petals of deep red.

It was beautiful.

It was a waste.

But if Fatyan could teach her how to control it, this waste would open the way for miracles.

Wordlessly, the Moura plucked the rose from her hand and examined it with enraptured attention. Yzabel tried to contain her anxious jittering while Fatyan looked at the rose with fascination. Closing her eyes, the Moura smelled the crown of petals, then trailed her fingers across the stem, carefully testing the prickles against the flesh of her thumb.

"No wonder you thought it a curse; no wonder the sahar turned into the image of one, too," Fatyan mused. "I think I understand what's going on. It shouldn't be too hard to do what you need to do."

Hope fluttered in Yzabel's chest. "Truly?"

"Yes. But just in case..." Fatyan held out a hand, palm up. "Turn another while you touch me. My sahar should react and give me a better idea."

Something still wasn't clear to her, though. "Shouldn't you have lost your magic now that you're out of the stone?" she asked as she placed her hand on Fatyan's.

"I will never lose my sahar. It's been with me since I was born." She traced her thumb over Yzabel's knuckle, the simple touch erupting in complex emotions she couldn't place. Fatyan brought her face closer. "Magic like ours can never be killed. Only mastered. Now. Tell me what you feel when you turn food into flowers."

Yzabel pursed her lips and closed her eyes, trying to recall the sensation that came when she let her curse roam free. "There's a tingling, like I have ants crawling on my skin. Warmth, too. And it's always worse in my tongue and my left hand."

"I noticed. But we'll leave your tongue out of this for now," Fatyan quipped with a smile and a wink.

The too-fresh memory of their kiss fluttered in Yzabel's mind, and heat flooded her cheeks at the *for now*. She did not know what to do with it, and so she cleared the awkwardness in her throat and asked, "Where do I begin?"

A hum began in the back of Fatyan's throat, the low, gentle sound a caress in Yzabel's ears. "Try to replicate the feeling you get when you touch food."

She tried. She recalled the heat, the numbness, tried to

force those into her hand, to push the magic roaming inside her into doing what *she* wanted instead of what *it* wanted.

Nothing.

"Hmmm… Let's try another way." Fatyan picked up another piece of bread. "I want you to touch this, and as you do, focus, *really* focus, on the changes happening inside you."

Hand hovering a hairsbreadth away from the slice, Yzabel closed her eyes to better concentrate on the curse's magic. As if it was a ball in her veins, the energy traveled from her chest, down her arm, collecting at the cusp of her fingertips.

Though she wasn't touching the bread quite yet, the magic reached out to it, hungry and eager, eating through the dark dough like bright mold.

"Tell it to stop," Fatyan urged.

Yzabel bit into her lip, sweat beading on her forehead as she tried to bring the curse to a halt. Willing it to obey, she pictured a leash choking the magic and forcing it back up her arm. It whiplashed into her, making her yelp as it sliced at her stomach and burned the roof of her mouth like a trapped wild creature tearing a cage apart.

Her fingers jerked. The magic spread. Hoping to save the bread from becoming a rose, she closed her hand and pulled it to her chest before the light had completely enveloped it. Fruitless effort, for once the curse took hold, there was no turning back. The contaminated bread broke from the untouched segment, and between one blink and the next, a second rose, smaller, but as red-petalled and fresh as the previous one, fell soundlessly to the floor.

How was she supposed to stop something that had a will of its own?

Impotence and anger blurred Yzabel's sight with tears.

Her head swam, her throat ached, her breath refused to slow down, and her body became so hot. She had to get her clothes off, cool down. Her shaking fingers tried to pull at the strings around her neck, desperate to rid her from the burden of the cloak, and—

A tug on her arm, and awareness returned. Fatyan held her hand still, and Yzabel looked to find an expression of painful uncertainty on the Moura's face.

Shame covered her in a blanket of panic and self-derision, and she looked away to let the dim candlelight mask her wet cheeks. Fatyan was going to realize just how weak and useless Yzabel truly was; she would tell her she'd been wrong, and she'd be stuck with this cursed touch forever.

Something soft touched her jaw to catch a stray tear. "Why are you crying?"

"Frustration," she said, unable to stop the ridiculous flow of tears. "Silly, isn't it?"

"It's not, and it happens to the best of us," Fatyan whispered, one hand cradling Yzabel's cheek with gentle patience while the other traced the inside of her palm.

Her heaving chest expanded, close to bursting, as if all the magic inside her roiled like the Tenebrous Sea during winter storms, as if she were made of brittle glass and was about to shatter.

"The only reason you can't do this is yourself. Or rather, your perception." Fatyan thumbed away the tears on Yzabel's face with delicate motions, her eyelids low with concern. "You can't treat the sahar as your enemy and hope it'll obey."

The motion of Fatyan's fingers reassured her somewhat, and Yzabel managed to resume breathing evenly. "Then how?"

"Accept it for what it is—a part of yourself, like your nose"—she tapped Yzabel's nose with a finger—"your ear"—she traced the shell, eliciting a small shiver—"your hand." She brought their joined hands between them. "You don't try to cut your nose off when you have a cold, do you? Or your ear, when you can't hear well enough? Or your fingers, when they drop something?"

Fatyan was so warm, her words so gentle. Yzabel looked at their joined hands—how nicely they fit together, Fatyan's long brown fingers threaded with Yzabel's small white ones. "I don't know. Maybe I should've cut off my hand. And my tongue."

"Then you would've been one-handed and tongue-less, and the food would still turn," the Moura jokingly retorted before becoming serious again. "You refer to your magic as a curse. And because you've shunned it all your life, it's become a starved animal, hungrier and hungrier every day. Until you see it as the gift that it is, it will remain unruly and feed itself every chance it gets."

"Surely that can't be all."

"It's not. But it's important." Fatyan released her to sit back on the corner of the desk, crossing her arms over her chest, concentrating as if trying to assemble a torn letter back together. "Have you tried to just...keep turning food until the magic's dried out?"

"No. To do so would waste too much, and I—"

"You've been starving the sahar," Fatyan interrupted. "Like you, it needs nourishment, and all that denial and hatred you bear has been slowly turning it hostile. You have some serious neglect to make up for."

The shame from before returned at full force. Marriage, intimacy, public outings, asserting herself, the curse... Could she truly do nothing right? Was she doomed to fail in her endeavors until her frail health caught up to her?

Fatyan edged closer. Her knees pressed against the side of Yzabel's thigh, and she quietly waited for Yzabel to do *something*. She didn't know what, and when she reluctantly lifted her gaze to the Moura's—her eyes so beautiful, the lashes thick and long, the irises so green—she couldn't tear herself away.

"Don't look so down, Yzabel," she said. "Everyone goes through this; gifts like ours are often wild, especially when we fight them."

"You also went through this?" she asked with a rough, broken voice.

"I don't know anyone who hasn't." A bittersweet smile lifted a corner of her lips, and a faraway look settled on her eyes. "The morning my gift manifested, I woke with sheets stained with blood, aching bones, and in a face and body that weren't my own. Instead of turning food into flowers, I kept turning myself into someone else. It took me months, but eventually, I accepted it. Still, the sahar is a temperamental beast, and before anyone can use it effectively, it needs to be centered and leashed.

"So, on the next full moon, our Benzedor took me to a circle of herbs and cinnamon. A snake was laid at my feet, the scare triggering my gift into action and the ritual into beginning. After that, my gift was easier to control, and after many, many nights of practice, I could change anything about myself in the blink of an eye." Pain creased her face, trembled in her voice. "But now my sahar isn't working as it should."

"Why?"

A sad shrug. "I don't know. I've never come this far with anyone else, so this is all uncharted territory for me. The sahar is here"—she pointed to her chest—"but it will remain inaccessible until my curse is fully broken, which won't happen until our bargain is met, which won't happen until you accept the blessing into your heart."

It wasn't just about herself anymore. Mastering the magic meant reducing the waste of her meals, meant stopping Denis's nagging about her health *and* meant giving Fatyan her freedom. "What happens if I don't? Can we still do the ritual?"

"We can, but it will be dangerous." A grave pause and a dark look. "The sahar can turn on you. You might die."

A lump hardened in the back of Yzabel's throat. "How do I begin accepting it?"

"Every time you find yourself wanting it gone, think the opposite. Think that you *want* the magic, that it is part of you and always will be. When you're afraid that you're going to waste food, remind yourself that it's a necessity—the sahar needs to eat as you do. Remember that the sooner you embrace it, the sooner you will be able to control it." She winked. "After all, didn't the Holy Spirit come down on the Apostles to give them gifts of power? Why can't it be doing the same for *you*?"

"I…" Yzabel meant to say she didn't believe it'd be enough, but she bit her tongue before any sound could leave her lips. What did she know of curses—no, of *magic*? And Fatyan was right; the Holy Spirit was God's helper, and all this could've been His doing to set her on the right path. "I will try."

Nodding, Fatyan rose to her feet, taking a moment to stretch her legs. "What happens to me once we're done? You said I could go anywhere I want, but…this world is not the same one I knew."

Yzabel pondered on it. "There are many other Moors who swore vassalage to Portugal and live freely in places such as Sintra. I can arrange for you to go there. They're still your people and—"

"My people are all dead," Fatyan said, low and harsh. "I have no one to return to."

Yzabel's mouth slammed shut so fast her teeth clicked together with painful force. How careless of her to assume Fatyan would want to live among Mouros when she'd been separated from her culture for over a hundred years. "You're right. I-I apologize," she quickly stammered. "But do think on where you want to go after our promises are fulfilled—I will do everything I can to make it happen."

Fatyan blinked as if in surprise. "That's…beyond generous. Are you sure?"

"Yes. So…think on it, all right?" A long yawn forced its way past her lips, and she covered her mouth with a hand.

"We can talk more about this tomorrow," Fatyan said. "Right now, you need to sleep." She stared at the bed. Which Yzabel now realized was *singular*.

Her heart raced like the wings of a hummingbird; her stomach fluttered like a rainbow of butterflies. She squashed both, telling herself there was no sense in getting so worked up over sharing a mattress with another woman.

She must've been immobile for too long, for Fatyan added, "I can sleep on the floor."

Perhaps that would be for the best, if Yzabel's intrinsic need to please would let her. Which it didn't. "No! Don't be silly. The bed's big enough for the two of us."

The thought of undressing brought the curious jitters back, but if Fatyan were to act as her lady's maid in the future she'd have to see her naked. Yzabel went to the commode and handed one of the larger nightdresses to Fatyan—her stone slumbered inside Yzabel's pocket still. A surreptitious movement later, and it was in the drawer, a memento of the incredible things she'd seen, and a reminder of the challenges still to come.

She blew out the candles, the firelight enough illumination for her to make it to the bed, where she made a point to not stare at Fatyan while they prepared to retire.

The sheets were cold, their breaths and the dying flames the only sounds in the night. Though exhaustion weighed on her eyelids, Yzabel couldn't find her slumber. Despite her earlier discomfort toward the Moura's proximity, something was still unsaid, and she wouldn't rest until she voiced it.

"Fatyan?"

"Yes?"

"I'm…" Cowardice stuck to her tongue; she forced it out through sheer will. "I'm glad I found you."

A breath. Two. Under the covers, Yzabel squirmed, certain she'd said something wrong.

"I'm glad you found me, too," came Fatyan's whispered reply.

A smile on her lips, Yzabel curled herself tighter. With Fatyan, she had answers, and for the first time in years, she had hope as well. Because if Fatyan was right, and Yzabel succeeded in controlling her magic, the specks of color scattered in the fields around them—the white of the estevas, the purple and yellow of the pansies—could be used to feed a village. Many villages, for a long time. Flowers bloomed everywhere in Portugal, even in the Além-Tejo's dry plateaus that stretched to the horizon.

She would control this magic. She had to.

CHAPTER EIGHT

Small Lies

In the morning, Brites came with Yzabel's usual breakfast, plus an extra chair for the room. Yzabel donned her robes, insides screaming for the warm milk and honey in the mug.

Lucas's nails scratched stone, and Fatyan gave a little shriek as the mastiff jumped out from behind Brites.

"It's just my dog. Remember?" Yzabel skirted Fatyan to meet Lucas, kneeling to hug him and bury her face in his stinking fur that smelled better to her than the cursed roses. "Oh, my baby, I've missed you, but that's no way to act. You've given poor Fatyan a fright!"

Fright didn't seem to cover it, with Fatyan's wide eyes and shallow, wild breath as she gave Lucas a wide berth on her way to the table. Only when the furniture stood between them did she dare to speak. "That is not a dog. That's a wolf-bear-thing."

"Hah!" Brites said with a lopsided grin. "I noticed you looked at him like he was about to eat you. It's why I took him last night."

Lucas headbutted Yzabel's fingers, then leaned against her with eyes closed as she stood to look at Brites. "Did he behave?"

"If by that you mean 'stayed the entire night by my door, waiting for me to open it,' then yes. He behaved. And hurry with that milk." Brites pointed at the steaming mug. "Denis has been asking for you since he woke, and he's expecting you in the Steward's Office."

Fatyan clicked her tongue when Yzabel picked up the mug and gave the honey a good stir. "Are you telling me *that's* all you eat every morning?"

"Why, yes." Unfazed, Yzabel took a large gulp, the richness of the honey sweet on her tongue, the warmth of the milk velvet on her throat. "The curse doesn't work on liquids, and it's enough to keep hunger at bay without breaking my fasting."

Eyes closed, Fatyan pressed her thumbs on her temples. "Yzabel," she grumbled. "What did we talk about last night?"

The next chug fell on her stomach like a rock. Beneath her skin, the magic roiled, spreading to her fingertips, desperate for sustenance and raging upon finding none. "I can't…" She flailed on what to say, on how to properly express herself. "This is more than fine to start the day with."

"It's not. And you called it a curse again."

"See? Petulance," Brites interrupted with a groaning sigh. "Starving is what our princess thinks she deserves."

A shock straightened Yzabel's spine. She took a step back, defensive, shrill. "What else was I supposed to think when I kept choking on flowers?"

"You do have a difficult blessing. I'll give you that." Fatyan's voice softened along with her mien. "But all great acts come with sacrifice, and in your case, you need to sacrifice food."

Yzabel gnashed her teeth behind pursed lips. The mug had gone cold, as had the milk, but she forced herself to drink it anyway, not looking up as Fatyan came to stand in front of her, not listening to her steps, ever so close—

"Your selflessness won't help anyone if you're dead, and you *will* die if you take the ritual in your current state," the Moura said, a dark portent shivering in her tone. Sharp, but not uncaring, she went on, gentle hands covering Yzabel's on the mug. "We have a bargain, Yzabel, and I need you to eat if I'm to fulfill my part. Can you do that for me?"

She made to ask for another way; the worry on Fatyan's face stopped her.

Your selflessness won't help anyone if you're dead.

"Only stale bread and bones," she conceded. Lucas threw her a pitiful whine, big yellow eyes pleading. "I know. I'm sorry—but you have plenty of bones as it is, and we could use the narcissus. And the roses."

That last sentence she added belatedly and with a hint of spite. A waste it might be, but while not as precious as food, rosewater and narcissus paste would help with the red plague.

Fatyan's fingers, still on Yzabel's, stiffened before she dropped them, and she bit her lip as she looked at the door with a one-eyed squint. Not two seconds later, a knock followed.

"Your Highness, the king's requesting your presence," Matias said from the other side, cracking open the door so she could better hear him. Ever concerned with Denis's wishes, which was remarkable considering he'd been in the king's presence for about two weeks while he'd known Yzabel for five whole years.

"He is *insistent* today," Yzabel hissed, stalking to the commode as she shouted, "Tell him I'll be there soon."

"His Majesty told me to escort you," was the reply.

Brites slid the door a look from the corner of her eye.

"*Now* he learns how to take orders." A sigh escaped the corner of her lips, and she shook her head. "Come, Fatyan. Let's get you into the habit, and I'll show you around."

The Moura followed, but before she could disappear into the lady's maid's chambers, she looked over her shoulder. A wink, and a smile, and the words, "I'll see you at lunch."

Yzabel found herself answering with a smiling nod, though once she was alone, consternation sunk a grimace in her expression. Lunch, where Yzabel was supposed to use the curse, and as necessary as Fatyan claimed it to be, Yzabel had trouble accepting the forceful waste.

She quickly changed into her day clothes, the modest silk kirtle too large on her frail frame, hips so thin she had trouble fixing the golden sash to keep the brown surcoat in place. The whisper of fabric pulled at the cilice nipping at her thigh. Foot propped on the chair, she gently hiked up the skirts and unfastened it with care, wetted the edge of a towel on the basin and dabbed at the punctured flesh, cleaning it of blood. Then, teeth on her tongue, she wound the spiked garter back where it belonged, where it could constantly remind her of her sins and make a dent in her perpetual penance. If she was going to be wasting food, she needed it now more than ever.

As she washed her face and hands on the basin, the cold water bit into her brittle fingers, its icy needles pierced her joints as she pinned her curls back before pulling the cowl over her head. In the mirror, an apparition of eyes ringed with shadows, sallow cheeks, purpled lips, gray skin, unbearable to behold.

Before the bed, she knelt, tilting her chin to the cross above the headboard as she prayed a quick Pai Nosso and an Ave Maria, thanking them for bringing her Fatyan, and to please help her tame the curse—no, the *blessing*—bestowed upon her.

Matias interrupted her again, incessantly rapping on the door frame until she emerged from her room. He stood at attention, blinking eyes fixed on her. "I apologize, Your Highness, but the king—"

"Yes, yes." She waved him away and threw her mantle over her shoulders. "Let's go."

Nausea roiled in her belly, and bile swayed on her tongue as she crossed corridors and hallways with Matias at her heels, and she had to brace herself on the wall for a second to keep the milk down. Hung tapestries surrounded her, embroidered images of hunting scenes, kings past, Jesus Christ, Santos and Santas whose woolen eyes followed her as she passed, their weight that of cotton compared to the iron of Matias's gaze.

"Mother said you've brought someone from the convent to help her." His voice reverberated along the passage, raising the hairs on the back of her neck. "That you let the sister stay in your rooms."

Brow strained, Yzabel asked, "What about it?"

"It's a security risk, Your Majesty. With the local prelates so angry, how can you be sure this woman isn't here at their bidding?" His breath hissed with a sharp intake. "I don't know what it is exactly, but something about her isn't right."

Inhaling deeply, she paused at the office door. She couldn't tell Matias what Fatyan truly was, but neither could she dismiss him easily. As with Brites, suspicion ran thick in Matias's blood, and he wouldn't let go of an idea until proven wrong. "I appreciate your concern, but I assure you, Fatyan has nothing to do with the local gentry. And neither does she wish me harm."

"But my princess—"

"Vasco interrogated her before she came and found nothing amiss." Not quite a lie. "He would never let her come with me if he thought her dangerous."

"I'll…" He looked down at her with black eyes under a thick, straight brow, so much like Brites's it was impossible for Yzabel not to soften. "I'll talk to Dom Vasco, then."

"If you must," she said, dismissing him with a nod before turning the doorknob and slipping inside. Her betrothed sat behind the desk in the steward's office, polished mahogany shining among countless leaves of parchment. Shelves stacked with books and folders lined one of the walls, and a large chest and cabinet sat on one corner. By the fireplace, chamberlain, treasurer, and chancellor inspected files from three armchairs of red velvet, and next to them, a small table sat with a pitcher of wine and three glasses. Thankfully, no food lay about to tempt her magic, or her already-groaning stomach.

"Good morning," she greeted from the doorway.

"Your Majesty." The three men bowed their heads, barely acknowledging her as she strode through the cramped room toward Denis.

He looked up through red-rimmed eyes, his lip curling with unhappiness. "Sometimes I wish it wasn't common knowledge that I know how to read," he muttered under his breath. "It was much easier to find corruption when the prelates thought they didn't need to hide it."

"So, no luck?"

"None." At a flick of his hand, the book he'd been examining slammed shut. "You were gone all day yesterday—and what's this I hear about you taking in a nun from the convent?"

Rumors did travel faster than the wind, it seemed. "I have brought in a sister, yes." Afraid he'd see the lie on her face, she busied herself with stacking the assorted papers into a neat pile. "I visited the Carmo Convent and talked to the Abbess about the red plague devastating the poorest quarters of Terra da Moura. She agreed to send a novitiate to help and learn from us. Brites could also see if the sister is a good fit to replace her when the time comes for her to retire."

Denis's hooded eyes blinked. "Huh."

"Huh, what?"

"I always thought Brites would serve you until her dying breath," he said with a shrug. "You *are* extremely attached to the woman."

The hairs on her arms bristled, and she looked at him with a furrowed brow. "You speak like it's a bad thing."

"Must you always answer with seven stones in your hand? It's not like it's a lie."

"Must you speak so critically of how I choose to treat my servants?" she barked back. "Brites is like family to me. I fail to see the issue."

"*Jesus*, Yzabel. There is no problem. Your staff is your responsibility, and so long as this nun is as competent as the woman she'll be replacing, I couldn't care less." Denis rubbed the sleep from his eyes, pinched the bridge of his nose. "Now can you help us go through these?"

The sudden change caught her off guard. "Of-of course."

"You can take that pile over there." He gestured to a stack on the far side of the desk. "I'll bring you more later. With lunch, so I can be certain you eat."

Meals with Denis were never easy, and if she had to accept the cur—the *blessing*—he could not be in the vicinity. An excuse, she had to come up with an excuse, fast, before her breath got out of control, before she couldn't open her panicked lips and move her dry tongue. "I told you I'd keep fast until the matters in Terra da Moura are resolved."

A fearsome growl burbled in Denis's throat. "Yzabel—"

"Truly, your devotion is astounding, my princess!" Dom Domingos interrupted, black choir dress whispering on the floor as he came to lay a thin hand on her shoulder, the purple cassock and amaranth trimming the only specks of color in his attire. "We should all be as pure of flesh as you are."

"You ask me to let my future wife wither before my very eyes?" Denis scolded. "She looks half-dead already!"

"As so many of your citizens do," the Chancellor-Mor gently argued, the weight of his fingers straining Yzabel's neck. "The princess's devotion is but another reason for us to solve the nation's problems as quickly as we're able. The Lord shall keep her safe in the meantime."

Yzabel smiled at him, weak and trembling, but the relief that usually followed Dom Domingos's defense of her practices didn't visit her this time around. The praise he bestowed upon her piety blinded him to what Denis saw so clearly. What used to make her feel better brought an onslaught of queasiness, for Dom Domingos would rather see her starving and virtuous rather than well-fed and healthy. And she had no doubt that if he knew of her magic, he'd tie her to a chair and drill at her skull until he pried the demon out of her head.

Denis leaned back against his chair. "Fine. But you will have dinner with me."

She acquiesced with a bow of her head and collected the pile of parchment and folders. "I'll have Brites fetch some more of these for me later."

"And do introduce me to this girl before we leave this town," Denis called after her as she was about to depart.

"I want to know who you will be spending time with."

A jolt in her chest, a seedling of fear taking root. Part of her truly hoped that Fatyan would never have to share a room with Denis and his inevitable lecherous glares—and if the ritual succeeded tomorrow night, the curse would be reversed more quickly, and there was a good chance Fatyan would be gone before the king got any ideas. One thing was to know Denis kept mistresses everywhere they went, or that one of his favored dalliances sat across from Yzabel when she joined her ladies-in-waiting. Another would be for him to take Fatyan as well.

Yzabel didn't know why panic drummed in her heart at the thought. Only that it did.

CHAPTER NINE
Transformation

Yzabel spent the rest of the morning poring over her portion of Terra da Moura's accounts, fingers buried in her hair as she tried to decipher the steward's terrible penmanship—which she suspected to be purposeful. It didn't help that he also seemed to enjoy littering the borders of every page with dreadful, lascivious poetry that would put Denis's to shame. Propriety demanded she not pay them any attention, but curiosity pulled a heavier weight, and she kept on reading regardless of how many shocked gasps and uncomfortable blushes it took. God would forgive this transgression done in the name of thoroughness.

The scent of garlic and pennyroyal fished her from the sea of parchment, while the shadows of blurry letters swam in her eyes and a migraine stabbed at her head. Fatyan, now clad in the black habit and white veil and wimple of a novice, cleared the table, making room for Brites to set the tray down in front of Yzabel.

Two soft-boiled eggs floated in the bright green assorda, still steaming on its brown bowl, a plate with two fat fillets of fish, a bread bowl cut into small pieces, and dark golden broas by a jug of red wine. The brightness of magic swelled in her breast, dripped down her arm, jerked at her fingers to touch, touch, *touch*—

Pressure against her forearm, the rough scrape of crust. She jumped in her seat, twisting away, but to her squeaking dismay, the bread followed, and the light under her hands shot directly into it. Joyous magic encroached upon crust and crumb, stole her breath away as it stretched to a stem. Leaves and prickles bursting along the stalk—

Belatedly, she shrieked, "That's enough bread for six assordas, *Fatyan, what are you doing*?"

The Moura held up a finger, furrowed eyes set on the changing lump of magic. At its peak, the curled blooming of a rose as big as Yzabel's head. Nose against the blossom, Fatyan inhaled and said, "Transforming three arráteis of week-old bread into three arráteis of roses." With a playful tilt of her hand, the edge of the flower tapped Yzabel's nose and filled her nostrils with its scent. "*Transformation*. Not waste."

"You tricked me," Yzabel muttered, but it was futile to hold on to the sourness of the small betrayal. A lightness washed on her limbs, brought stillness to her shivering hands.

"You agreed to bread and bones. Plus"—she handed the rose to Brites, who shredded it into one of the boiling pots around the fireplace—"we're going to need more roses. And narcissus. So…" A pivot on her heels made a grandiose gesture as she revealed the second tray sitting on the bed in all its menacing fullness of dry bread and bones picked clean. Fatyan brought it over, placed it next to the food and held out her hand.

Her eyes flitted between the Moura and the tray, uncertainty weighing on her arm.

"Don't lose sight of what you'll be able to do when you

master your sahar," Fatyan urged. "Trust me, Yzabel."

It could be the knowledge that Fatyan was bound by a promise she couldn't break; it could be the sincerity in her pleading gaze, the tenderness in the susurrus of her voice; but Yzabel's hand was already in Fatyan's, taking in its warmth as it guided her fingers down. Smooth bone gave way to a yellow corona nesting in a delicate cup of white petals, bread became more roses. The panic of so many years stirred in her chest, and she tried to take her hand away, stitch it to her palpitating heart.

Fatyan held it tighter. In Yzabel's ear, she said, "Eat."

Tongue in a knot, she turned to her meal, gingerly reaching for the soups. The magic stayed busy with Fatyan, and she swiftly dumped some bits of bread into the assorda's broth. Next came the fish, and as soon as her nails scraped the soft flesh, the blessing suddenly changed direction, hungry for something tastier than bread and bones.

Yzabel barely had time to drop the fillet into the bowl before the curse claimed it. To her left, the bright red and yellow of roses and narcissuses of all sizes brought bile to the back of her tongue, each one a tear in her composure that left her determination fraying and tattered. Sweat piled along her hairline, stewed in her cheeks, the heat unbearable. "How… How much *does* it need? How much do we have to waste before it's happy?"

"What does fish become?" Fatyan asked back.

"L-Lavender."

"Which we can also use," Brites reminded, hands full with the mortar and pestle, where she ground the narcissus flowers into a paste. "Not just for the red plague."

"It's not an equitable exchange," Yzabel protested.

"Not *now*. But it will be." Fatyan's free hand glided on

the line of Yzabel's shoulders, coming to a shuddering rest at the nape of her neck. "You need to heal your relationship with the blessing. Waste some food now so you can produce hundreds later. Now turn that fish and tell yourself it's all right to do so."

Yzabel swallowed the sickness in her throat, forced herself to grab the second fillet. The magic poured out of her, and with eyes slammed shut, she thought, *You can have this, you can have this, you can have this* —

The soft fragrance and buds of lavender caressed her fingertips. Heavy lids lifted, tired fingers grasped the flower, larger than its wild counterparts she gathered during Iunius and Iulius. A drop of its oil kept nightmares and anxieties at bay; enough of it over a wound would keep the flesh from festering.

Yzabel had been so fixated on not eating she'd been too obstinate to look around. Too stubborn to listen to what Brites had been telling her all along.

Fatyan's grasp traveled to her shoulder, pinpricks of light following in a shiver, then Yzabel's gaze. She tilted her chin, found the Moura smiling down at her, more brightly than the magic, more brightly than the stars in the darkest of nights.

"I understand now," she said. Then to Brites, "I'm sorry. I should've listened to you when you told me to turn as much food as I could."

"At least you're listening now." Brites clicked her tongue as she scooped the narcissus paste into a glass jar. "Better late than never, I suppose."

Yzabel returned to her meal, and although the nervousness remained, she no longer feared the waste, because she had never been cursed to waste.

She'd been blessed to transform.

Hands clasped around the cross at her chest. *Holy Spirit, take what I've given you as appeasement. I'm sorry I doubted. But I see. I see.*

Yzabel took a spoon of broth, bread, and egg, and although the magic played on her fingertips, it didn't try to steal the food from her mouth. She chewed, swallowed, took spoonful after spoonful, even managing a few bits and pieces of boga before the familiar heat danced in her tongue.

Her first reaction was to scream at the first bite of lavender, throw a child's temper tantrum at the unfairness of it all. All she wanted was to *eat* something without this happening.

But right now, lavender was as precious as that nugget of meat. Yzabel swallowed the growl as it bubbled in her throat, unlocked her jaw, and set the flower aside. The spoon grew heavier each time she took it to her lips, and black tendrils snaked around her sight. Sheer effort kept her going, and she managed half of the assorda and most of the remaining fish before nausea ripped through her stomach, too used to fasting and starving to receive anything else.

Hand on her bloated belly—laughable, how so little could feel like so much—Yzabel leaned back on her chair. "I can't anymore."

"Unsurprising, given how little you've been eating for years." Shaking her head, Brites took the tray away and set it on the floor, where Lucas was happy to be of service. "And that's all you'll have until supper. Hear me, boy?"

A wagging tail and the sound of slurping were the only answer the mastiff deigned to give them. It was only fair he got what remained of the assorda, seeing that all those delicious bones had become narcissuses.

Fatyan sighed with a pitiful look at the leftovers. "Not to rain on your festivities, sweet Yzabel, but you have a long way to go still. Hopefully the springs will help it along. At least enough for you to take the ritual and come out alive."

"I pray that they do." Yzabel covered a yawn with a tired hand, sleep dangling on her eyelids. "Why do I feel like I've been awake for days? It's only midday."

"The sahar demands a healthy body filled with stamina. Neither of which you have."

Even though Fatyan had meant no offense and had been merely stating a fact, even though Yzabel *knew* she wasn't healthy, the declaration stung, filled her with the numbing poison of unworthiness.

Rather than let the petty misery sink her further, she honed it to determination and returned to the lurid poems and blotted numbers, re-calculating every sum. Of the many battles she waged daily, this was one she could win. She wrestled the successive yawns, the hefty eyelids, the fuzzy sight, the selfish desire to give in to sloth and rest her head on the table. Since when did hard wood appear so plush?

Sitting by the fireplace, Brites gave assertive instructions on how to make lavender oil. "The buds we use as they are, but the leaves, we have to dry—both to use them, and to keep suspicion off Yzabel, since lavender is not in season. Lucky for us, I know just the trick."

Scissors snipped flowers, and the thrum of magic shivered in Yzabel's ears, the familiar words of one of Brites's spells whispering in the air. The warmth of steam, the small crackles of wilting flowers, a delightful gasp.

Fatyan's laughter chiming behind her. Truly a beautiful sound and one Yzabel found herself clinging to as she tried to make sense of the letters in front of her.

Once Brites dried the lavender, she and Fatyan began storing it in jars for safekeeping. By the time they finished with the herbs, so had Yzabel with her papers, and as she'd told Denis, she sent Brites back for more. When her maid returned, it was with a sour expression, as well as Dom Domingos on her trail.

Fatyan, who'd come to sit beside Yzabel, straightened her shoulders, green eyes fixed on the Chancellor as his brown ones did the same on her.

"Look who I found." Brites grunted as she came to lay the new papers on Yzabel's desk, her tone implying that she had tried to keep him from coming.

Unease flitted in Yzabel's belly; no one had reason to doubt that Fatyan was a nun, but Dom Domingos was a man of the cloth. If anyone could tell the difference between a sister and someone who dressed like one, it would be him.

She rose from her seat and put on her brightest smile, trying to appear unconcerned. "Dom Domingos. I didn't expect to see you again so soon. Did you find anything in the documents?"

"Not yet, Your Highness," he said as he approached, giving Brites a wide berth as he passed. Dom Domingos disapproved her choice for a lady's maid, something Yzabel had never quite paid heed to, as all the reasons he gave for such distaste were the reasons she kept Brites in her employ. "This must be whom the Abbess sent to help you." He turned to Fatyan. "What is your name, child?"

Yzabel tried not to look too panicked even as the goose bumps pricked her arms.

Fatyan stood to give him a full bow. "Fatyan, my lord."

"Fatyan," Dom Domingos repeated as if to test it, then looked at Brites from the corner of his eye. "Is there a reason as to why you'd bring a novice and not a sister?"

"I didn't want to deprive the Carmo Convent of one of their members," Brites answered without blinking. "And with me being so close to retiring, I thought it prudent to train someone who's as devoted to the Lord as our princess."

"And out of all the novices, you couldn't find one that was less..." He stopped, attention briefly going to the ceiling as he searched for a word to settle on. "*Vivacious*."

Vasco had had much the same reaction when Yzabel had emerged from the stone with the Moura. She supposed it was natural, since it wasn't every day someone as beautiful as Fatyan graced their eyes, but as understandable as it was, she didn't care for how they spoke of it, as if the Moura was to be doubted because she looked the way she did.

"I'm a nun," Fatyan said, brows crunched. "What does it matter what I look like?"

Dom Domingos lowered his attention to Fatyan's hands, folded in front of her. "There is no ring on your finger. You've yet to take your vows and could change your mind at any time." He halted, a dramatic pause he often employed in his sermons. "From what I've been told, you've got plenty of suitors already."

"The only man I'm comfortable around is our Lord Jesus Christ." Fatyan spoke without wavering, a tight smile gracing her lips. "That will not change."

Dom Domingos returned Fatyan's affected smile. "Not even for a noble?"

Yzabel rotated her shoulders to mask the full-body squirm that came. This was what this was all about, concern that Fatyan would end up using her wiles to make men act like fools.

If Fatyan felt any unease at the Chancellor's words, it didn't show in her polite, "I assure you your concerns are woefully misplaced."

The answer didn't satisfy Dom Domingos, who'd taken on the look of a ferret keen on finding rabbits in a hole. The knot in Yzabel's belly tightened as she thought of ways to end this conversation before he realized Fatyan was no novice and only here temporarily. "Dom Domingos, surely you don't need to question Fatyan's choices."

He held out his hands in a gesture of mild surrender. "I apologize. It is not this novice's intent that I doubt." A brief glance to Brites, not bothering to hide it was *her* he had a bone to pick with, something he'd made no secret of after they'd arrived from Aragon.

"It's been a few days since your last confessional, Your Highness."

Days ago, Yzabel would've accepted the invitation without blinking. At the moment, however, she had more important things to take care of.

"I told him that if you wanted to confess, you'd have gone to him," Brites said tersely.

"And I told you that I'd let the princess answer for herself," Dom Domingos said, equally curt. "Not everyone follows your wayward ways, *Brites Sande.*"

The hissing with which he said Brites's name dripped with poison, allowing Yzabel to see his reasoning all too well. He believed Brites would lead her astray, and although she wanted to tell him the reasons why Brites wouldn't, she could not. To do so would be to admit to having magic, something Dom Domingos would not be lenient on. Not to mention that Yzabel's most recent sins were not something she could confess to him, thus rendering the point of such a session moot.

"My apologies, Chancellor, but I fear I must decline. We have much work left to do here, and little time." Keeping

her tone gentle, she gestured to the new pile of documents
Brites had brought. Still, she had to placate him somehow,
lest his animosity for Brites fester further. "The Lord will
understand, I think, if I delay confession in the name of
seeing the matters in Terra da Moura solved as quickly as
possible."

"Of course. I understand." He ambled to her side, black
robes swishing, and placed his bony fingers on Yzabel's
shoulder. "Regardless, should your soul grow weary,
remember that I am at your service."

"Thank you, Chancellor." *Remarkable,* Yzabel thought,
that such a feeble hand could weigh so much. Yzabel took it
in hers and knelt to kiss his amethyst ring as was expected
of her.

"The offer stands for you, too, Sister Fatyan," Dom
Domingos said, extending his hand Fatyan's way. "If you're
to stay with Her Highness, my door is always open."

The Moura kissed the ring the same way Yzabel had
done. "Thank you, Your Grace."

Dom Domingos turned to leave without acknowledging
Brites, and Yzabel resisted the urge to make him. Beyond
impolite, it was rude, but her lady's maid shook her head,
signaling her to let him leave.

With Dom Domingos gone, Yzabel breathed deeply,
but the tension did not wither. Fatyan grimaced at the
Chancellor's back; Brites had her lips thinned into a line,
arms crossed over her chest. Dom Domingos lingered
at the door and said something to Vasco too low for her
to hear. Although the Chancellor was someone she was
supposed to trust, she found herself reluctant. He disliked
Brites, and always sought to undermine her at every turn.

Whatever words Dom Domingos had imparted to
Vasco, Yzabel truly hoped he did not listen.

CHAPTER TEN

Springs

Yzabel woke to a stiff neck, a dry mouth, and a jaw crusted in drool.

Limbs and muscles groaned as she stretched and wiped at her face with her sleeve. The last wisps of the setting sun's light clung to the edges of fabric and furniture, lining them with a faint orange glow. By the fireplace, Lucas snored, while Brites and Fatyan traded hushed questions on whether to wake her.

"You shouldn't have let me sleep all afternoon," Yzabel complained, a latent yawn robbing her tone of any accusation.

"You needed it. But it's good you're awake now." Fatyan brought Yzabel's mantle and draped it onto her shoulders. "They're waiting for us at the springs."

Right—they were going to the springs nearby, with their sacred waters that mended wounds, seen and unseen. "We have to be back before supper, though. Denis is expecting me."

"We have time," Fatyan assured.

Vasco awaited them in the solar, and Yzabel greeted him with a kiss to the cheek before the three of them headed out. Fatyan spent the walk between the castle and the springs pointing out the differences between the Terra da Moura it was now and the Al-Manijah it'd been before. The fountain was exactly where she remembered, except it was now decorated with carved marble as white as snow; the plaza had been remade with new pavement, the cobbled roads between houses narrow.

The light of fires burned behind closed windows, the sounds of families scattering across the air. Infants crying through mothers' lullabies, children playing with their siblings, parents demanding silence. A group of drunkards meandered out of the closing tavern, the owner screaming at them from the doorway about how tomorrow was another working day.

Meanwhile, the gentry's conviviality lasted into the late hours of the night, with food and drink flowing freely all evening. It seemed unfair that they could enjoy such luxury when the people who worked for them could barely unwind before curfew struck.

Halfway down the sidewalk, Yzabel paused to wipe the beads of sweat along her hairline with the back of her hand, exhaustion narrowing her sight and spinning in her head. A touch on her elbow steadied her, and she found Fatyan looking at her with concern. The Moura's arm slipped to twine around hers, a silent offer for support that she took with a smile, leaning against Fatyan for the rest of the way.

"These also haven't changed much," Fatyan mused, eyes trailing along the entrance of archways and the ground paved with cobblestones. The Roman Empire had had its faults, but they certainly knew how to build lasting facilities.

Past the central arch, Vasco veered left into a vestibule operated by an old nun. He gave her a handful of billion coins. "Thank you for allowing the princess to use the baths this late."

"My pleasure, Dom Vasco." The woman looked beyond him, skirting the counter to come kneel before Yzabel. "It's such an honor to receive you, Your Highness. I see the rumors of your devotion weren't exaggerated!" the nun exclaimed with appreciation as she kissed Yzabel's surprised hands. "You must fast often to achieve such a pure form. Truly worthy of being called Holy Princess."

She hid her wince with a weak smile. "It's the Lord's will that I starve," she said, scratching her leg through the skirts, drawing a little bit of pain to compensate for not telling the truth. "This is my new lady's maid, Fatyan. She'll be accompanying me inside."

With an enthusiastic nod and more compliments, the nun gave them two towels and a bar of soap, then ushered them into the dressing room.

Fatyan was quick to kick her shoes under the wooden bench. "You have no idea how much I missed these springs," she said, giving Yzabel a glimpse of smooth leg as she unfurled the socks.

She hurried to draw her eyes away, concentration curling her features as she folded each sock, before setting both on the shelf above their heads. Unbidden thoughts of Fatyan's states of nakedness heated her cheeks like embers, and even though she ached to peek, she didn't dare. It was improper, indecent, unbecoming—

"And it will help you ease up for a little bit," Fatyan added softly, shoving her discarded clothes next to Yzabel's neatly folded socks. "Relaxation is what you need right now. It'll help with the sahar, too."

"I-I know, but…"

Hands wrenching the band wrapped around her waist, Yzabel looked at her feet, at the ceiling, at the door— anywhere but Fatyan.

"Dear Yzabel, are you embarrassed?" Fatyan asked.

That was part of it, but not all. Next to her, Yzabel couldn't help but feel inadequate, and not just because of Fatyan's beauty. "I'm not used to bathing in company," she grudgingly admitted, looking up long enough to see an impish smile that was enough to give her stomach a twist.

Fatyan tied the towel under her arms. "So? You don't have anything I haven't seen before."

"That's…not it." Her hand went to her leg, over the cilice, jaw moving along with the grind of her teeth. It was pointless to drag this further, and after a long moment, she stilled. Exhaled. Stood a little taller. "But you're right. It's not befitting of me to be so cowardly."

The cloak came off, as did the sash, the sleeveless overgown, the kirtle.

But when Yzabel shed her chemise, a gasp sounded behind her, and breathless fingers trailed over the lines on her back, some red and recent, others old and faded, leaving her shivering under their path.

"Who did this to you?" Fatyan asked, her voice hard. She skimmed her fingers farther down, where the cilice's teeth dug into her thigh, every one of its previous bites a circle of tracks around both legs. Droplets of blood welled where it punctured red skin, a hideous contraption worn for no reason other than to suffer. "Who makes you wear this?"

Each welt the road to a painful memory, each bruise a settlement populated with inadequacy. She couldn't bear to meet Fatyan's gaze when she said, "I do."

With an ethereal touch, Fatyan traced the thin, angry lines crisscrossing Yzabel's salient ribs. "When I see these, I picture you squirming with hunger while whipping yourself." A dry swallow ate whatever it was she was going to say next.

Screaming quietude hung between them as Yzabel

tried not to dwell on the wretchedness of her physique, defaced by wounds and thinned by hunger. Tried not to dwell on how inappropriate she felt next to Fatyan, who was everything a princess should be—fearless, beautiful, and of full flesh.

She kept her eyes down and her body still while Fatyan trailed a finger along the cilice. "Why do you hurt yourself?" she asked, cautiously, the sound barely registering.

Something complicated in her core woke under the touch; flustered, Yzabel was quick to reply, hoping speech would take away the riotous sensation. "I told you. I tried many things to take the curse—the gift—away. Mortifying my flesh was but one of them."

The Moura opened the device on Yzabel's leg, and a hiss fled Yzabel's lips along with a stab of pain as Fatyan peeled the device off, blood welling in every little puncture.

"You must never do this to yourself again. No matter what is being preached, no god wants to see their subjects suffer. Especially when they've blessed said subject with a great gift."

"You don't think suffering brings you closer to the Lord?" Yzabel asked—the notion seemed foreign to her.

"No. And it doesn't. God only cares if you're good, which you are." She fluffed Yzabel's hair, sending shivers up her spine. "Never believe the interpretations of men. They distort the original meaning to suit themselves."

"But the Bible is sacred, and—"

"I was raised on the Bible, too, Yzabel. It's just something else written by men as well. Like history. Like my own story."

"That doesn't mean it's wrong about this," she countered.

"And you don't question parts of it? If I were to believe everything unconditionally, then I'd believe the lie you tell about my people and how we invaded Al-Andalus, or the lie about my loving Bráfama. We never invaded, and I never did."

The revelation almost knocked Yzabel off-balance as she tucked her clothes in the shelf. Not because of the part about the Moors; she'd known as much from her teachers back in Aragon, and it was supported by the Moors left in Portugal and the Algarves as well.

But the rest… "Why do they say you loved him, then? In your legend."

"The men who disseminated my story must've been romantics at heart," Fatyan said as they walked out of the dressing room and into the bath antechamber paved with a shallow pool of cold water. She paused for long enough that Yzabel wondered if she'd offended her again. But just as she was about to ask, Fatyan continued. "I guess they wanted their women to be like I am in that tale. So already in love with a man our parents choose for us, we'd rather die than to live without him."

"That's…" Stunned speechless, Yzabel took a hand to her chest, where her heart beat fiercely against her rib cage.

As if sensing her disquiet, Fatyan stopped at the threshold between the antechamber and the springs. Steam swam in the air beyond the door, wisps reaching around her, almost like ghostly fingers trying to pull the Moura in. "It is what it is. Any story is bound to change if enough time passes, and even more so when said change comes from the mouths of the powerful. And the men who wrote the religious texts we guide our lives by might've distorted the words to benefit their own desires."

It should bother her that Fatyan spoke of heresy, but the crux of her statement rang true. So many stories were changed with the passage of time.

"Have you noticed how you've been fixated on creeds that tear you down?" Fatyan went on with breathless determination, each question widening her eyes more and more. "Noticed how they tell you to starve and suffer, when God's own son wanted us to love each other? How they tell you every kindness you do is never enough, even though one small act of goodness enriches the soul and the world better than unnecessary pain?"

Outright denial stormed to the tip of her tongue, but the memory of Dom Domingos's voice and the cold phantom of his touch on her shoulder welded her lips shut. His encouragement that she keep fasting even though she was so close to death, his advice that she should strengthen her flesh by wounding it even though she barely had any. She'd become skin and bones and scars, and for what?

Acid swept her mouth. "Why would anyone who could do good resort to defiling the Lord's words?" It was inconceivable to her that someone would bastardize something sacred. Yet she'd seen it happen, greedy vicars hoarding gold instead of using it to help the citizens, noblemen and women mistreating and overworking their charges rather than protecting them. "We're supposed to help each other, not—"

"Not everyone has a heart like yours." Fatyan sighed sadly. "Their words were enough to convince you that you'd been cursed, when in fact, your sahar is quite the opposite."

Conflict waged within Yzabel, her upbringing warring with Fatyan's provoking statements. She shouldn't believe a woman she barely knew over the sacred book she'd been baptized on. But on the other hand, Yzabel *had* believed the magic to be a curse all her life solely because the Bible told her so, and there had been nothing in the other religions that explained it, either.

And once she mastered the magic, her blessing would let her do wonders instead of horrors.

"I understand your point," she acquiesced with a tight smile. "It might take me some time to fully absorb everything you said, however. It's…hard to question what you've always taken as mostly fact."

"I only ask that you consider nothing is as it seems. Now…" Fatyan looked toward the springs. "Shall we?"

Together, they walked across the torchlit bathing chamber. A rectangular pool of marble took up most of the heated room, and the steam escaped through the narrow windows along the top of the white walls.

Yzabel followed Fatyan down the stairs and to the springs, where the Moura dropped her towel without ceremony. She went ahead into the bath, waves of black hair trailing behind her. In a fluid motion, she threw herself backward, letting the water cover her entirely before she rose again, the crystals dripping along her curves.

Yzabel swallowed. No matter how often she pulled it away, her gaze insisted on straying to Fatyan and her round breasts. How differently would they feel from her own, which were small and barely there? Would they be soft like a pillow, or hard like muscle?

Questions she told herself to be driven by mere curiosity brought on by their differences—how Fatyan's breasts were fuller and bigger than hers, the nipples brown instead of pink, or how she seemed to have more hair on her belly, or how her hips were broader, her buttocks generous. That she was jealous of the Moura and that was why her eyes kept darting to her—because she wanted to look more like Fatyan and less like herself.

You're staring. Stop staring! Lord Almighty, what is wrong with you, Yzabel?

Scared of her own thoughts, Yzabel let the towel fall and all but stumbled into the water, with the hot steam making the steps hard to gauge, and all the wild ideas playing distractedly in her head.

To her mortification, she ended up landing right in Fatyan's arms, who enveloped her with their steady softness.

"Careful," the Moura said. "We can't have you break your head open."

"S-sorry." Yzabel quickly stepped away from their tangle of slick limbs, thankful that the hot air masked her blushing embarrassment. Realizing she was clutching the soap tight as if her life depended on it, she set it on the edge of the baths. "I slipped."

Yzabel sank into the warm water, and it *did* feel nice. She dunked her head, lingering under the surface before rising for breath. Keeping herself emerged to her neck — which wasn't hard, as the springs were deep enough that she could do so if she was on her knees — she waded over to Fatyan, who leaned against the corner with a contented smile on her face.

"Feels good, doesn't it?" asked the Moura.

Yzabel sat with her back to the wall, head leaning on the warm stone. "It does." Closing her eyes, she soaked in the springs, let the warm waters ease away the weariness. Yet the restlessness in her limbs refused to settle, and the thoughts running through her head found their way back after she tried to lay them to rest. The magic inside her twirled in every direction, tugging at her fingers and toes, spreading numbness on her tongue.

Under the water, Yzabel fisted her hands, fighting for control. The effort lined her face with a grimace, had her eyebrows trembling and her muscles spasming.

A drop landed on her cheek, startling her out of her

trance. She opened her eyes to see Fatyan playfully kicking the water next to her face. "I have an idea," she said with an impish smirk.

Yzabel closed her eyes so as not to fall into the temptation to steal another glance at Fatyan's breasts—which she was keenly aware was an odd, worrying fixation, but...

They floated.

Larger breasts were capable of *floating*. She hadn't expected them to be so buoyant.

Overly aware of her own small assets, she resisted the urge to cover them. No one else was there, and it seemed like an exercise in vanity to be so self-aware. Clearing her throat, she made herself hold Fatyan's gaze. "An idea?"

"Yza," Fatyan called, so close Yzabel had no problem seeing the smaller details, such as the water tying some of Fatyan's thick lashes together, or that the green of her eyes was specked with brown, or the freckles dusting the top of her nose and cheeks. "You need to accept the sahar into you—and for that you need to lower your guard. To relax and let the magic in these waters do what they do best."

"You think I'm not trying?"

"I know you are. But you need help." She drew a circle on the surface of the water. "Turn around."

"What for?"

"Trust me."

The argument was persuasive. Oddly, she *did* trust Fatyan, in a strange, instinctual way.

But it was the wink that did her in.

Yzabel did as Fatyan asked, almost jumping out of her skin when her curly curtains of hair parted in half, and the Moura gently swept it over to her front, leaving her back exposed.

"Back in my day, sahar-bearers went to springs such as these to center their powers. It makes the ritual easier when magic and body are in synchrony." With deft touches, Fatyan found the stiffness on Yzabel's shoulders, and although it hurt at first, there was a certain release that came with the painful kneading. Her eyes closed of their own volition, and she let her head droop forward.

Wariness had stalked every waking moment of Yzabel's life. It had been mandatory she be careful, never too trusting. Then Fatyan had come into her life, scraping away at the rock of her defenses with each deft touch, and with her questions, she chipped at the foundation of Yzabel's beliefs. She often reminded herself to be wary, that this was nothing but a transaction to benefit them both, yet she couldn't bring herself to harbor it for long. It ate at her that she couldn't figure out why. Nor could she understand why she felt *safe* with Fatyan, as though she could tell her anything without fear of breaking confidence.

Was this all a facade, or did Fatyan care?

Why would she lie?

Why would she not?

"Relax, Yza. Let the sahar come to you."

Even her ears seemed to grow numb, eating pieces off her name as it left Fatyan's lips. In that warmth and safety, it was as if her soul had become untethered. Her bones lightened, the bath and Fatyan's ministrations slowly peeling away the layers of exhaustion. The anxiety that plagued her every moment fell away, melting under Fatyan's touch, which moved from her neck, to her shoulder blades, her spine, then back up again.

She looked down, saw the magic settle on her chest, a sunlit snake coiling tighter and tighter around her heart. With every beat, the wisps of light traveled farther into her veins, blood and blessing flowing in perfect harmony. Steady, the gift progressed to her throat, and the air tasted cleaner, fresh even though she was in a room full of steam. Then it moved to her eardrums, and her hearing sharpened to hear the birds calling to each other outside.

In that moment, encased in wonder, Yzabel could see her destiny sprawled before her, what could be if she simply let the magic exist instead of fighting it at every turn. She could see herself, one with this wonderful force, feeding a nation with nothing but willpower and wildflowers. Everything she wanted to be, there for the taking—and she tried to take it, to catch it and bind it to her heart—yet years of neglect were not so easily undone, and the blessing scattered along with her breath.

The gift wasn't in tune with her yet, but it was closer than this morning. Not an enemy, but a skittish stranger willing to approach. Not much progress, but progress nonetheless.

Yzabel wasn't aware Fatyan had stopped until she leaned forward to speak in her ear. "Feel better?"

She was in such a delirium that for once, she wasn't bothered by the other girl's nearness, or by their nakedness when she turned around to pull Fatyan into a fierce hug. "You were right," Yzabel said. "You were right. It's a gift. It was always a gift."

And with that gift, she would change the country.

CHAPTER ELEVEN

Secrets

Their bath finished, Yzabel and Fatyan returned to the changing room with towels wrapped around them, a new lightness in her steps. Since the curse—the *blessing*—had shown, it was as if a shadow had been following her trail. An invisible weight shackled to her, one she'd believed to be dragging her down.

Yet, if Fatyan was right, it had never been a burden. A weight, yes, but that of responsibility, a cross she was meant to carry for the good of the world. One she'd willingly bear.

Yzabel's giddy humming filled the changing room with song while they dressed; however, by the time they reached Vasco—who'd also taken the opportunity to bathe—the blessing, so calm moments ago, roiled back to life in her famished stomach.

On the small of her back, the Moura's firm hand steered her along the empty streets. "Don't give in to the vicious cycle of blame and doubt. Remember what you felt at the springs and keep it close. As long as you do, the ritual to center the sahar will succeed."

Nonetheless, the ritual and the magic weren't Yzabel's only sources of worry, and with a frown upon her brow, she asked, "What do I do in front of Denis, though?"

"We'll give the sahar a meal before you go. A sumptuous one, so it's not tempted while you're with him."

"If you're so certain it's a blessing, perhaps you should tell him," Vasco said. "End this web of lies you've been spinning."

Yzabel looked over her shoulder to see his glower and threw him a matching glare. "You were the one who suggested I hide the gift in the first place," she reminded. "And you know I cannot tell him—at least not until I've mastered it and shown him it can give instead of take."

"And what happens when Dom Domingos eventually talks to the Abbess of Carmo Convent about this sister you've taken in?"

She snorted. "That would be a first. In all the years we've been engaged, neither he nor Denis bothered with my affairs with the nuns. Not unless dinheiros were involved."

"But men talk amongst themselves, and women overhear. Then, they gossip. Dom Domingos is already suspicious." His eyes narrowed. "The longer Fatyan stays, the more rumors will breed, and sooner or later, her origins will be called into question."

Must he always be so dour? She turned her eyes to the cobbled road ahead, a defensive arm wrapped around Fatyan's. "Then I shall endeavor to work harder, so Fatyan is free before that happens. Can you please go on ahead and tell Brites to bring extra food to my rooms?"

Unhappy to be dismissed so inconsequentially, Vasco pelted her with a look of "this isn't over." He veered off to the servants' passage, closing the door with a violent bang that rattled the wooden frame.

"And women are the dramatic ones." She rolled her eyes.

Fatyan's, however, were shrouded in pensiveness as she tucked a stray lock of hair back into the white wimple.

"Vasco's concerns do have some merit. Men *do* talk. And I…" Consternation weighed on her half-lidded eyes, and grim teeth chewed on a worried lip. "Brites had to smack a young page across the head this morning when he asked to marry me."

Under the swaying torchlight of the castle's archway, Yzabel noted that the straight, loose cut of the black dress didn't diminish the promise of her curves, and that the veil didn't take away from her lovely face — if anything, the modesty shone light on Fatyan's beauty, made her green eyes seem bigger and her lashes thicker, her nose more regal, her lips more luscious.

"You *could* marry someone. If you wanted," Yzabel found herself muttering while a cold breeze shivered on her spine, and a queasy knot tightened in her belly.

"And lose the freedom I've craved all these years?" A little *harrumph* and she waved her hand over her chin, tilted in haughty dismissal. "When you fully control the sahar, I'll make myself uglier and tell all of them I burned my face. No one will bother me then."

"You shouldn't have to. It's not your fault men think they're entitled to every woman they fancy," Yzabel spat.

They came to the stairs and their daunting steps. Trembling hand cold on the freezing wall, Yzabel put one foot in front of the other, letting Fatyan support her when she needed. Her legs ached, her lungs burned, her tongue dried, and every time she swallowed, a metallic taste lingered on the back of her throat, but she could see the top. A few more shaky steps, taken with heaving gulps of air, and the corridor stretched before them in its dim, candlelit glory.

Clutching her midsection with one hand and Fatyan with the other, Yzabel stumbled forward. Farther ahead, a silhouette caught between the solar and the main passage, one hand on the door's knob, the other smoothing her disheveled hair.

Her feet faltered, frozen in the prospect of exchanging pleasantries while pretending not to notice Aldonza's frazzled state. Since discovering the affair between her lady-in-waiting and her betrothed, awkwardness had pervaded her demeanor whenever she looked or talked Aldonza's way, leading to some very unprincessly avoidance on Yzabel's part. But she'd already seen her, a similar plight unraveling in her expression.

In the corner of Yzabel's eye, Fatyan raised an inquisitive eyebrow.

"M-my princess!" the lady-in-waiting piped, smoothing the wrinkled skirts of her green overgown, the bright yellow sash snug around her wide hips. "We've missed you for so many afternoons, and you appeared so ill at court the other day, I...I came to check on you."

A bold-faced lie told through swollen lips, but Yzabel couldn't summon the courage to call it out. To tell Aldonza she knew, to ask her if she was happy being Denis's lover. Was she as glad for the other mistresses as Yzabel was for her, or did it eat at her as it had eaten at Yzabel's mamá? Would she hate her for asking?

"How kind of you to worry," she said, a practiced statement through a plastered smile. "I'm feeling a bit better, but it'll be some time before I can join my ladies-in-waiting in the sewing room."

Aldonza twined her hands behind her back, the curve of her pouty lips as strained as Yzabel's. "We've heard that Terra da Moura's finances are in quite the disarray, yes. I imagine you've been helping the king with them? He's always so complimentary of your intellect." Her eyes slid to Fatyan's blank face. "And this must be the sister I've been hearing about. Fatiana?"

"Fatyan," the Moura corrected, unflinching. "Who might you be?"

"Aldonza Rodrigues da Telha." A swift curtsy. "And I'll be going. Please do join us sometime, Princess. Have a good evening."

Yzabel nodded. "You as well."

The lady-in-waiting disappeared down the stairs, an absent hand rubbing her belly—were Yzabel's eyes deceiving her, or had it grown bigger and rounder since she'd last seen Aldonza?

"Does she know you know? About her affair with your betrothed?" Fatyan asked.

"I don't think so. Same with Denis. And I know I should at least ask Aldonza if she's happy, but…" Shaking her head, Yzabel meandered into the solar. "One day. After I've mastered the blessing."

Curiosity tilted Fatyan's head. "That woman is a risk to your position, and you're concerned about *her* happiness?"

"She's no risk to my position," Yzabel scoffed. "And why wouldn't I be concerned? It's one thing to be engaged to an adulterer; another to be engaged to a rapist."

Fatyan's lips parted. Closed. A crease dug between her eyebrows, but whatever she was going to say evaporated when Yzabel opened the door to her rooms, hitting the two of them with the ungodliest of scents.

"Did something die in here while we were gone?" Fatyan asked, ripping the wimple and veil from her head and holding them in front of her nose.

Brites stepped away from the window with a grimace toward the offending meat at the desk. "Bedum. Vasco said you needed something to turn, and that was about to be used for compost. The only thing that drunkard of a butcher butchered today was good lamb. Not even the dogs will touch it."

No wonder—the stench alone was enough to make her gag. The blessing had never taken to decomposing items, but although its taste had been spoiled, the meat itself was fresh, if unpalatable to a person's tongue. She rushed over to the desk, magic already swelling on her fingertips. The bits and pieces of cooked lamb were still warm and soft to the touch, and the blessing took them eagerly, leaping from her skin in a surge of liberation.

Putrid stink gave way to a flowery fragrance as hyacinth vines sprouted in the place of a shank, ribs, head. In fire's glow, golden light exploded into a rainbow of green leaves, purple stalks and bean pods, bulbs of white, blue, pink, and violet.

Hyacinth vines, like the ones her teachers used to grow in her home in Aragon, like the ones that had bloomed everywhere in her mother's Sicilian home.

Fatyan scrutinized the light beating under Yzabel's chest, and without an uttered word, she picked up the bowl by the window and unceremoniously shoved aside the greenery to make room for the bread.

Yzabel didn't need to be asked to pick up a piece. Bread on her fingers, she waited for the familiar surge of heat to travel from her heart to her shoulder, down her arm, a slow march that halted at the edge of her fingertips. It was eager, playful, and this time, slowing when she thought it to a halt.

A rose the length of her finger bloomed in her hand; when she tried with a second piece, it was very much the same. The breath of wonder filled her nostrils, and she said, "It's answering. Not fully, but…" A third bit of bread, and with focused will, the light stopped at the wrist, unmoving while she held the air in her lungs.

"See?" Fatyan said in Yzabel's ear. "Accept it as part of you, and it will begin to answer like any other."

She managed to keep her composure through a thundering heart, spinning around to look at the Moura. An urge overtook her when she met those green eyes, and she gently brushed Fatyan's hair behind her ear to pin it with the small rose. "Thank you."

"Why are you always thanking everyone?" Fatyan asked, genuine puzzlement in her low voice. The red of the rose brought out the earthy tones of her skin, making her somehow even more stunning.

"It costs nothing to say, and there's no value in appreciation if it's not freely given."

A little frown marred Fatyan's forehead. "Had someone else said that, I'd have taken them for an insidious manipulator. But you…" The lines deepened. "You do it for no reason other than to be *nice*."

"And believe me, that's our princess's greatest fault," Brites said. She pulled a small chest out from under the bed and brought it over to the vanity then collected the hyacinth vines. "I'll get started on these while you dine with Denis. Might as well have a few more bottles of salve for when I go into town tomorrow." After chucking the hyacinths into her quarters, Brites turned, hands on her hips. "Now let's get you changed before Matias comes knocking like he did this morning."

Fatyan's lips twisted, sour at the mention of Brites's son. Neither of them knew why Fatyan's sahar flared when Matias's name was floated or when he was in close range, only that it did, and it sickened the Moura every time.

"I can change by myself," Yzabel offered.

Brites shook her head. "Not when you've just bathed

and have a rat's nest for hair. You know how Denis is."

She blew a curl away from her face and crossed her arms. Her betrothed didn't insist on a lot of things, and although he didn't mind her disheveled appearance during the day, he required she be presentable when they dined together.

"I can attend to her," Fatyan offered. "I'll help you with the hyacinths once we're done."

"You don't have to," Yzabel protested, abruptly alarmed by the thought of the Moura helping her, of her hands revisiting her naked flesh with incidental brushes. "You're not a servant—"

"I don't mind."

"Thank you." Brites smiled at Fatyan. "Do you remember what to do?"

"I do."

Yzabel groaned and rolled her eyes, waiting for Brites to leave the room before she turned to Fatyan. Her bearing softened, as did her voice. "It's just… I don't want you to think I see you like that."

"You worry too much," Fatyan said as she stepped in front of the princess. "Now, let's get you out of those clothes again."

At once, it seemed like all the meager heat in the room was on Yzabel's face. The fresh memories of the springs flitted behind her blinking eyelids. "Y-yes. B-but r-really, you don't h-have to—"

"But I want to, dear Yza," Fatyan said with a small smile that belied the gravity in her voice. Then, pointing to the bread, she added, "You still have to turn all of that into roses. Finish feeding your gift so today's work won't go to waste."

Begrudgingly, Yzabel began to turn more bread into

roses, huffing as she went through them.

"Yza…"

That again. Those first few times, Yzabel had thought Fatyan had just given up halfway through her name, but then she used it again, and again.

"Why do you keep calling me that?" she asked, curious.

"It's faster to say than Yzabel?" A mischievous smile turned her lips upward. "And it's also a cute way to shorten your name? No one else uses it, so that makes it something that's just between the two of us. Do you need more?"

Yzabel's smile was a thief sneaking up on her. Her heart, too, beat a little faster, seemingly pumping more blood to her already hot face. "You have more?"

"Oh, yes. I like how it sounds when I say Yza, and how easily it rolls off the tongue. Yza. Yza. Yza. Yza." A wink. "Should I go on?"

By then, Yzabel's cheeks had grown so hot, she must be scarlet. Hoping to reduce the terrible awkwardness, she touched one piece of bread, let it unravel into a rose. Thorns dug into her skin, and she cast it aside.

She so absolutely, irrevocably *hated* roses.

"Yzabel?"

"Mm?"

"You're frowning. Does my calling you Yza offend you so?"

Yzabel relaxed her expression instantly; she hadn't realized how hard she'd been scowling until then. "I'm sorry. I'm just…frustrated. The sight of roses alone infuriates me. To see them is to see my failures on display, and my hope dies as they wither. But—" She paused to lick her lips. The blood rushed back to her face as she made herself look at Fatyan's eyes, at those thick lashes. "I don't mind that you call me Yza. In fact"—she smiled—"I rather like it."

Although, it was one thing to like it, another to have Fatyan call her Yza in a room full of people. "Please don't refer to me that way in front of anyone else, though. It doesn't offend me, but others might take offense on my behalf, as unwanted as that is. Vasco especially."

Fatyan inclined her head forward. "I'm aware. Would you find it strange if I said I'm glad for it?"

Well, that was the opposite of what she expected. "Glad?"

"Yes." She brushed one of Yzabel's curls away from her eyes, and she failed to suppress the shiver that ran up her spine. "That way it's another secret we get to keep between us."

Yzabel's grin widened her lips further. She decided to follow her impulses just this once, and kissed Fatyan's cheek as a good friend would. "Thank you."

"There you go again," she said with amusement. "What am I being thanked for now?"

"Keeping my secrets." She bit into her lip as she tried to understand the odd tightness in her breast. "I have to come up with a nickname for you now. It's only fair."

"Baptize me, then," Fatyan offered with a quirky sigh and roll of the eyes.

"All right." She tapped Fatyan's nose. "Faty."

"Faty?"

"Y-you don't like it?"

"I do." She placed her hand on Yzabel's shoulders. "Yza and Faty, the rebellious princess and the Enchanted Moura."

"There's a nice ring to that."

"There is. Now…" Fatyan turned her around. "Let's get you changed."

She complied even though the thought of Fatyan unlacing and unbuttoning her garments flustered her beyond comprehension. She remembered the springs, the way Fatyan had touched her, the wake of heat following her fingers.

It's because you're unused to strangers touching you. Of mostly everyone *touching you*, she repeated in her head until she convinced herself that it was the truth.

One tug at the silk, and the sash dropped with a tickling whisper. Yzabel threw the surcoat and kirtle over her head while Fatyan fetched clean ones, leaving her shivering in her chemise and socks.

The scent of almonds spread in her nostrils as Fatyan guided a fresh, creamy kirtle down Yzabel's body, then the heavy surcoat of blue linen trimmed with fur. She tried not to shiver as Fatyan tied the sash into place, each motion twisting her heart in queer ways.

It wasn't like this when Brites helped her dress.

Why wasn't it like this when Brites helped her dress?

She swallowed her titillated breath while Fatyan fetched the comb and oils from the chest. Yzabel told her which ones to use and where, then turned bread into roses while Fatyan tried to tame her hair.

She applied lavender-scented oil to Yzabel's brittle curls. Gently, she combed away the knots and mats, careful not to pull too hard, grimacing when hair fell away regardless of her care. Inadequacy sprouted on Yzabel's tongue. "Brites was being generous when she called my head a rat's nest," she muttered as a piece of bread changed into a rose. "I wish I had hair as thick and straight as yours."

Fatyan's face scrunched with something akin to disappointment.

Yzabel bit at the bitterness in her mouth, looking down at the roses in her lap. "Does it upset you that I wish I looked more like you?"

"You don't want to be more like me," she answered, equally softly.

"Why not?" Their eyes met in the mirror. "You're beautiful. I'm—"

"Better than beautiful." Fatyan grasped Yzabel's chin, tilted her head so she could look her in the eye. "Sure, your eyes might be sunken, and your hair may be weak and your skin sallow, but those will improve as you eat better. What truly makes you shine, though, what makes you more precious than anyone else, is your heart." Her other hand found the left side of Yzabel's chest, over her heart thrumming wildly beneath her fingers. "It's the most beautiful of any I've seen."

A small, bitter chuckle, and Yzabel bowed her avoidant eyes. "You barely know me."

"True. But against all your teachings, you came to look for me. You were willing to make a bargain with me, an enchanted creature of the people you've called enemies for centuries; you're painfully worried about the less fortunate; when it came to food, you were worried about *me* starving. Not just that, but when you came into the stone, I saw your heart, and it was *good*." A wink. "Why do you think I allowed you to get me out of that stone?"

A tiny giggle. "I thought you were just desperate."

"Oh, I was plenty desperate. I still would've turned you down if there had been ugliness in your heart." She wet her lips. "It might not look like it, but I was raised in privilege. I assume you, being a princess, were as well. People like us are often entitled and have a way of forgetting the sorrows of those below our status. Having a powerful sahar running through your veins has taught you hunger, weakness, and determination. You had the courage to hunt a legend, and the flexibility to adjust your approach when I said removing the blessing was impossible."

Yzabel's jaw closed for a long moment. "You're saying it was all to teach me a lesson? A *lesson*. Even though all my life I've devoted myself to the Lord and His word."

"So many people do that, and they have flaws in their compassion nonetheless. Like the Portuguese Knights, who cut down anyone who opposed their Reconquista. Like my baba, willing to curse his daughter into an eternal existence."

Back in the Stone, Faty had mentioned she'd stopped feeling anger at what had been done to her, and when she'd first spoken of her father, it had been with sadness. Now, fury began to seep through, sharpening her voice, and Yzabel couldn't blame her for it. It had been a cruel thing that had been done to Faty, crueler still that it had been done by a hand that was supposed to protect her.

Then again, had Yzabel's papá not done the same to her? He'd decided whom she'd marry and spend her life with. The only difference between Faty's baba and Yzabel's was that one had used magic, and the other had signed a paper.

The last of Yzabel's braids finished, Fatyan reached for the gold crespinette on the vanity. Nothing but the whisper of hair and jewels between them as she twirled the braids around Yzabel's ears, then set the bejeweled cap atop them to secure them in place.

Fatyan rounded the chair to kneel in front of Yzabel, joining their hands atop the many roses on her lap. "You've been forged in despair, Yza, and tempered in hardship. It's made you considerate in ways many wouldn't be. That is why we were given a power that could not just feed a nation but temper it, too. Because you, of all people, will use it for good."

"You sound like Brites," Yzabel said.

"Well, Brites is wise."

"You barely know her, too."

"I don't need to see her heart to know she cares deeply about you, and that it hurts her to see you suffer. Same with Vasco." She lifted Yzabel's face with a finger under her chin. "Same with me."

Yzabel's eyes widened, and that heat crept up to her cheeks once more. "What if I don't deserve it? What if I end up disappointing everyone?"

"So long as you keep being who you are, I don't think you will. So." She stood and searched the tins until she found the one with red beeswax. "How's your sahar?"

She searched for the presence of magic inside her, the power answering with fingers of warmth tight around her chest. "I think I'll be able to manage in front of Denis."

"Hmm. Keep still." Faty dipped her finger in the cosmetic, then slid it along Yzabel's mouth, a slow trail of rouge and sparks following in its wake, parting her lips with a gasp.

She couldn't look at Fatyan now, not with her cheeks so hot they didn't need painting. She focused on the magic in her hand instead, at the light shining under her skin before meeting the bread between her fingers, turning it into another rose. "It's so beautiful to watch."

"It is."

"I guess I'm lucky most people can't see the magic." A test she'd done with Vasco and Brites before, revealing that those without blessings couldn't see the light of others' gifts.

"We had to have some way to defend ourselves," Faty said. "Otherwise, many of us would've been dead before adulthood."

"I've always hated the peace that came after. The relief.

How could I feel such a thing when my touch brought nothing but beautiful waste?" Yzabel shook her head, and the Moura's fingers caught on the back of her neck, grazing the golden net and jewels of the crespinette. "I see, now, how I was misguided. I was always meant to own this."

"You were." Soft touch of lips touched Yzabel's forehead, spreading comfort and chaos all at once. "Because once you do, you will be able to better the lives of thousands."

"You're so sure that I will, but… Do we even know how to reverse the magic?"

"Trust me. Once you go through the ritual, it will be like instinct. Practiced instinct, but still…"

A knock on the door. "Your Majesty?" Matias called roughly from the other side. "The king is asking what's taking you so long."

Behind her, Fatyan quivered, then tensed, green eyes fixed in Matias's direction. Yzabel wondered why a gift to sense danger flared at Matias's nearness, but that was a question Faty herself had no answer to. It pained Yzabel to know she could do nothing to ease how Faty felt around Matias other than to take him as far away as possible.

"I'll be there in a moment." She stood, looking at herself in the mirror; there was no helping the thick bridge of her big nose, but with the rouge giving life to her lips and the crespinette hiding most of her big forehead, she had to admit she looked *presentable*.

She turned to Fatyan one last time, flashing a smile. "I know I'm always saying this, but… Thank you. For everything you've been doing."

Fatyan smiled back.

It was small, but it brought a rush of victory to Yzabel's heart.

...

Silent prayers filled her head as she marched across the solar to Denis's room, where her betrothed already waited at the table, shoulder-length hair neatly combed back behind both ears. "Evening, Yzabel," he said as she took a seat across from him.

Without the magic running rampant, dinner with Denis became less charged. It brought her great relief that they could finally have a nice meal together, without fear hanging over her and flowers blossoming in her mouth. Her stomach couldn't hold much yet, but she made it through enough spoons of lamb and peas that he looked at her with amazement wide in his eyes.

"I think this is the first time I didn't need to remind you to eat," he mused out loud.

"I *am* trying to be better about it," she said, choosing not to elaborate any further. Denis probably figured it wouldn't gain him anything to press her, either, and soon the subject of their conversation moved on to the lewd notes the steward had scribbled all over the margins of his documents.

"And they're so…*bad*. Even I can write better poetry than that." In the span of a few seconds, Denis went from giggling at the poems, to covering a yawn, to sipping on his wine; the red on his eyes and the dark circles around them marked his bad sleeping habits—Yzabel doubted he'd caught a wink between Aldonza and the steward's books. "Dom Domingos made me swear I would start ignoring them because I kept laughing."

Yzabel nibbled at her cheese tartlet, the sweet crumbs so bright on her tongue even her belly wanted to make room for more. "It might make a good parlor game if you want to get everyone drunk."

"What, take a sip every time it doesn't rhyme?"

An excited chuckle. "And every time he misspells, and every time he counts the times he'll—"

Her lips stopped working as an idea struck thunder in her head. Slowly, her eyes drifted to Denis's and found him frowning.

"What?" he said.

"It's *code*." Yzabel left the dinner table for the desk, returning with one of the many leaves of parchment Denis had brought to his rooms. "See, here, for instance. 'À caputa disse/mete quinze ameixas no culis/e vai pagar ao Benzedor…'" At Denis's boisterous laughter, Yzabel crossed her arms over her chest. "Could you stop? You may be a young king, but you're still a king. Not a blushing squire."

"I never imagined your lips capable of speaking such words! I wish I could be there when you inevitably confess this to Domingos." His chuckle died before her exasperated scowl, and he made room on the table for the sheet of parchment. "Fine, fine. Tell me about the plums."

"The plums aren't plums, but something else. And the Benzedor…" She looked through more papers before bringing them over to Denis. "Look. When the poems aren't referring to the writer, they invoke someone else. The Benzedor. The Olhapim. The Rosemunho, offered something to appease them, and there's always a quantity of something—breasts, fruit, erm…*parts*."

"They're code for what was taken from the stores, and to whom it was delivered," Denis finished for her, brown eyes wide with wonder. "Yzabel, if this is right…"

"We have the players, and we have the game." Not

enough, if they were to remove them from power. "But it won't be anything without hard proof. They have to be hiding their profits somewhere."

Denis traced the small notes on the margins. "The inquisitors we sent beforehand haven't found anything. It's possible they've already traded everything for a profit." He looked at her from the corner of his eye. "Just as it's possible this is just bad poetry."

"But Denis…it was working. You said it yourself, it was terrible to the point you stopped paying attention to it." She twined her fingers behind her back, standing tall next to him. "A secret stash of *something* exists. All we have to do is look hard enough and I'm sure we'll find it."

"I'm glad to see you so determined." He rose to place a heavy hand on her shoulder, his thin lips curled in a smile. "And to see you finally eat. The country needs you at full strength."

With their similar heights, all she had to do was look ahead to see the genuine affection in his expression. Yzabel searched for a flutter in her chest, a pleasant tightness in her stomach, for the overwhelming need to kiss him.

All she felt was a sputtering pleasantness touching happiness and pride to her heart, the same kind she'd felt when her brother would compliment her on French well spoken. That strange enthrallment that enraptured her where Fatyan was concerned was nowhere to be found with her betrothed.

Yzabel leaned forward, brushing her lips to his on a whim, hoping to ignite the spark she'd felt with Fatyan. Denis, shocked into stony stillness at first, had just begun leaning into her when she pulled away and stepped back, thoroughly confused and underwhelmed.

"I'll try to be the princess the country needs, too," she

said, struggling not to scratch at her upper lip, where she could still feel the specter of his mustache. "I'll see you tomorrow. Do try to get some sleep."

Her feet hurried back to her rooms, her body attempting to flee the terrible thoughts that nipped at her heels.

CHAPTER TWELVE

Danger in the Night

Controlling her wayward imagination proved more of a challenge than it ought to, and as Fatyan undid the buttons on the back of Yzabel's dress, she made herself think of serious matters. Such as where the prelates could be hiding the profit of their misdeeds.

"When you lived here, did you have any secret passages or rooms?" Yzabel asked as she put on her nightshirt. "Some place to hide valuable treasure, perhaps?"

"You mean aside from my stone?" Fatyan joked as she folded the evening gown. "There were some, but from what I've seen, the Portuguese built over them."

"I need you to take me there." The crespinette's mesh and jewels caught on her hair, causing Yzabel to hiss as she tried to pull it off her head. Fatyan took it from her, carefully prying it loose.

"After the ritual, all right?"

Faty seemed so confident they'd succeed, but Yzabel failed to summon the same. She'd accepted the blessing, true, but what if it wasn't enough? What if she died tomorrow, never fulfilling the contractual obligations her papá had set for her? Not just her marriage — Yzabel's death would exact its toll on two bargains. Faty would return to the stone if this ritual failed. Her future hinged on it, too.

Yzabel pushed the negativity away, and said, "All right."

They lay down in bed, and even though they weren't touching, Yzabel's stomach knotted with bittersweet agony. Quietude fell over her as the mattress dipped behind her, her throat tightening as Fatyan's warmth reached her cold skin.

"Are you worried?"

Yzabel licked her suddenly dry lips. "Yes."

Not quite true.

Not quite false.

"Yza, look at me."

Begrudgingly, she turned to her other side and came face-to-face with Fatyan, their noses almost touching. Yzabel's heart thumped in her throat, and the air froze in her nose when Fatyan traced her prominent cheekbone with the back of her hand, leaving her torn between shrinking away or giving in.

Her eyes slid shut as Faty palmed the side of her face. She feared if she kept them open, she'd keep looking at her lips. Everything that should've been present for Denis was here, with someone she barely knew but who'd already become a friend.

"Everything will go well." Fatyan's whispered words drowned out the crackling fire, the howling wind. "We'll both be free soon."

Not trusting herself to speak, Yzabel nodded. Faty began to shimmy back, retreating to her half of the bed. Her absence left room for a draft to slip into the sheets, the cold chattering Yzabel's teeth, sending her hand forward to hold onto Fatyan's.

When Yzabel turned around, Faty followed, draping one arm over Yzabel's waist and closing the space between them. It was cold. Fatyan was warm against her back. She told herself that was just it, that the quickening low in her belly was from settling into comfort.

This was friendship. Kinship between two people with magical gifts. Two souls reaching through time to meet in a mutual beneficial arrangement.

Nothing else.

The following night, Brites brought everything Fatyan had asked for the ritual, naming every item as she placed it on the table.

"Chalk, dry basil, laurel, and calendula." She fished a tiny pouch from her pocket. "The cinnamon was harder to get, but I managed."

Fatyan turned to the window and the raindrops hitting the glass. "We've a problem, though. The ritual has to be conducted under the light of the full moon—if it's to reach Yzabel, there can be no clouds or rain."

"Let me worry about that," Brites reassured. "Calling or driving away rain is my specialty."

Yzabel had no doubt the woman could handle it. Fatyan had explained how Brites's gift differed from theirs. Carajus like Brites were taught their gifts, not born with them, and required no ritual to increase their control. So long as they were connected to the earth, all they needed were the right words to bend its forces to their will. When the moon closed on its highest point, Vasco and Brites escorted Yzabel and Fatyan to the empty garden next to the eastern wall.

"I slipped valerian into the guards' stew," Brites whispered as she unlocked the last door standing between them and the open sky of the garden. "With that and the storm, no one should bother us."

Nevertheless, worry gnawed at her. So many things could go wrong. Sleeping herbs didn't work on everyone the same way, and a guard or servant could walk in on them. More than that, Denis could be coming to Yzabel's rooms, a first brought on by her sad attempt to kiss him. Ill-begotten as that choice had been, she had initiated it, and there was no telling when she'd reap the consequences.

"And Denis?" Yzabel asked.

"Sleeping. I told Matias you wanted to know if more women were coming to visit your betrothed in the middle of the night. He needed no more convincing to stay behind and watch Denis's door." Brites looked beyond the threshold, where the relentless melody of rain hitting stone and trees filled the air, before turning to Fatyan. "You'll have to be fast. I won't be able to hold back the rain for long."

Beyond them, cobblestones made a path between two large patches of earth, where stalks of parsley and sage, thyme, and mint swayed in the wind, and the tree branches, heavy with lemons, persimmons, apples, and olives, rattled their shadowy arms and leafy fingers.

At Fatyan's nod, Brites rushed ahead, coming to a halt in the middle of the garden. A brief hint of steel as she drew a small knife from her apron and held it to the palm of her hand. One sharp motion and blood sprung forth, mingling with the rain.

Yzabel stiffened, made to run to her maid, but Fatyan held her back with a hand on her shoulder. A slow hum filled Yzabel's ears and every hair on her body prickled as Brites's sahar swelled along with her voice.

"Vento, vem!
Vento vem!
Arrasta p'ra fora as nuvens!
Leva a chuva também!

E das brumas pesso eu um véu,
Das gotas de água espelhos,
P'ra nos guardar de ouvidos,
E de olhos alheios!"

Brites chanted the same eight sentences over and over, each time louder, each time more commanding.

The clouds above swirled. Thunder cracked, a bolt of pure energy piercing the sky to hit Brites's raised hand. Yzabel screamed, her screech echoing through the air as the lightning flashed blinding white. Many times she'd seen Brites's magic, but never to this effect. Was this supposed to happen? Was she going to find her lady's maid lifeless on the ground once the brightness cleared from her eyes?

Fatyan hissed, burying her head in the back of Yzabel's head, holding her in place.

Brites's voice rose higher still, stronger than ever, repeating the rhyme one last time. She was unharmed, and the sky now clear above her. Ears ringing, Yzabel breathed again, not realizing she'd stopped.

"I'll be damned," Vasco breathed, drawing the sign of the cross.

Yzabel glared at him. "Do you also bless yourself whenever I turn bread into roses?"

"Your magic doesn't let you take a bolt of lightning and walk away unharmed!"

Fatyan pursed her lips, but whatever she was picturing must have been too comical to resist, and she let out a snort.

But Yzabel didn't find the situation amusing. "It's

magic nonetheless. For all you know, it *does* let me survive lightning."

Vasco opened his mouth, only to close it immediately after and look away. At least he had the decency to look guilty. His wide eyes went back to Brites, but his voice didn't shed its fearful coat. "I never knew she could do this."

"What are you doing standing there?" Brites asked. "*Hurry!*"

Fatyan rushed into the night, tying a long ribbon around the stick of chalk. "Step on it," she told Brites as she slipped the fabric underneath the maid's foot. Keeping it stretched, she drew a perfect circle. "Paint it white. I'll get the rest ready."

While the Moura lined the circle with cinnamon and spread herbs over it, Vasco laid a heavy hand on Yzabel's arm. "Please. I beg you to reconsider—there has to be a way that doesn't invoke yet more sorcery."

"There's no more sorcery to this than there is to my touch." Yzabel shook off his grip, only for him to tighten it.

"*Your* sorcery is holy—but this?" Vasco bit his lower lip, eyes flashing with feverish conviction. "Look at what they're doing, Yzabel. Their chants, and herbs, and powders. They're opening a doorway to the Devil himself!"

Jaw set and eyes narrowed, Yzabel yanked her arm free. "They're not."

"How can you be sure?"

She couldn't explain, and even if she could, Vasco wouldn't understand. She could tell him Brites's and Fatyan's magic was as divine as nature itself, that there was no darkness to Brites's chants or Fatyan's knowledge, that if this was indeed devilry, she would feel wrongness oozing in the air and not the magical wonder of a storm gone silent.

"I just am," she said, already moving before Vasco tried to stop her again.

Fatyan pointed to the circle, instructed her to step inside and kneel. She flipped the bag open, surrounding Yzabel with bits of bread and remnants of dried herbs. "After I light the circle, you need to use your gift on the bread." She held Yzabel's gaze as she produced a flint from her pocket and took the knife from Brites. "Ready?"

Yzabel breathed in. Out. She had no choice but to be ready. This was the only way.

"Ready."

The flame sputtered a few times before catching, spreading across the dry herbs to fill her nose with the scent of basil, laurel, and cinnamon. A scream soared up her throat as the fire rose around her, and in her head, the voice of doubt rung in protest.

"Turn the bread!" Fatyan urged from outside the circle.

An anxious wound festered in her breast, but she did as she was told. Roses bloomed under her fingers, the tendrils of magic spreading hot across her body, her skin thrumming as it glowed, hotter and hotter. Akin to how it'd behaved in the springs, only with the intensity of ten midday suns at the height of summer.

Her chest readied to burst, and when Yzabel tried to take one hand to see if it had cracked open, she found herself unable to move. Her ears captured no sound other than her blood, pumping wildly through her veins; a force brought her to stand, tilted her chin up toward the hypnotizing full moon, and then…

Her toes scraped the floor as she floated upward. Pain raged, tearing at her gut, ravaging the breath out of her lungs. The magic within her roared, a beast unleashed, clawing at her eyes, making her *see*. A feral wail ripped past her lips—it was hot, so hot, her tongue an ember, her throat full of smoke, her heart—

"Stop this at once!" Vasco shouted. Yzabel made to move, but the ritual held her afloat, immobile as her skirts and hair whipped all around her. Rushed, anxious footsteps, and louder, he demanded, "Stop this before it kills her!"

Yzabel clenched her teeth, tried to turn again, but she was trapped, drowning under the moonlight and the magic, asphyxiating her—

A smack sounded in the darkness, and Brites screaming, "Vasco, let her go!"

"Domingos is right—you've been corrupting Yzabel, and I've encouraged it for too long. This charade ends now." Vasco's voice filled the night, the strength of his anger and threats a violent blow. How could he do this? What could Dom Domingos have possibly said that would turn him against them so quickly?

"I've told you he's not to be trusted!" Brites shouted back. "We've known each other for years, and you believe him over—"

"You will stop this witchcraft, or I swear to God I will tell Denis everything!"

"We can't," Fatyan said, weak and strained as if struggling for breath. "The only way for Yzabel to come down is for the ritual to run its course."

"So let her go!" Brites demanded. "Vasco, let that girl go and put the knife down!"

Knife?

Distant thunder roared, but it was Vasco's hiss that cut through to deafen her. "Her business with our princess is done."

A shriek, shrill and terrified. The faint rustle of grass, a choked cough, and all sound was lost to the ring of magic in her ears, an acute buzz that scratched at skull and teeth.

Fingers closed on Yzabel's ankle, tried to yank her down as brilliant moonlight shocked her arms open, their bright fingers swaying in the sharp wind. Each one was an extension of herself, and when she closed her arms—she could move now—the light curled inward, folding and folding until it reached her chest.

The magic of her gift, once a shell isolating her from the world, crumbled into specks of dust as she welcomed it into herself. It was only then, as she finally allowed the magic to fully coexist with her, that she realized that the anger and hatred gnawing at her had been born of incompleteness. No longer did she feel like a foreigner in her own skin, sharing a body with another entity. She'd come to terms with the gift the same way she'd come to terms with her curly hair, her big forehead, her small hands.

The blessing became her, and she became *more*. The muscle she'd been training to control the magic now flexed as easily as any other. Light and warmth sung underneath her flesh, a river at her beck and call. Hearing returned to her as she floated back down, as did her breath—her legs buckled her as soon as her feet touched down, and she fell forward, gasping. In the corner of her eye was a lump of flesh lying on the ground, the stench of singed hair and charred meat making her gag.

"Yza...bel..." he groaned.

"Vasco!" She hastily crawled toward him, gathering his head on her lap. Charred black puckered his skin and deformed his lips. The hand on her leg, trying to bring her down when she'd been exploding with energy... It had been him.

She did this to him.

"Oh Lord, Vasco..." She leaned closer, her tears falling

to mingle with the ashes of his skin. "Why did you try to stop me?"

"The Moura…lied. Brites, too." He closed his eyes and inhaled deeply. His neck stiffened, and from his lips sprouted flowers, stems growing and petals swirling. Though he was gagging, he had enough strength to touch her cheek with a burned hand and say, "Don't let them replace you."

He choked on a breath.

It was his last.

CHAPTER THIRTEEN

Beautiful Death

The rain returned, washing away the ashes of the magic circle as Yzabel cradled Vasco's head in her lap. Tears fell on his forehead, not on skin but on rough bark, not on hair but stalks of barley. Branches of flowers grew out of his mouth, and more ripped his stomach open in a swirl of roses and daisies, pansies and gardenias, dandelions and daffodils—flowers of all kinds, some of which she'd never seen before, bearing colors she couldn't name, rising in an intertwined rainbow of petals and leaves.

Yzabel didn't know death could be so beautiful, or that betrayal could cut so deep.

Paranoia swirled, a disease twisting the acid in her stomach, nausea up her nose. "What did he mean, don't let them replace you?" A hesitant question, each syllable breaking out in a bitter sob. Was that what Fatyan had been trying to do in the springs, feeling Yzabel's body in lazy, casual touches to replicate every line and lacking curve? Looking up, she found Brites helping the Moura up, a complicit look passing between them, a pool of light at their feet washing away in the pelting rain. Louder, Yzabel asked, "Is that your true goal? To replace me as princess when you regain your freedom and power?"

Eyes wide and eyebrows raised, Fatyan tried to speak, but all that left her mouth was a wheezing croak. Hand on her throat, she desperately shook her head and turned to Brites.

"Vasco cut her too deep. She won't be able to speak for a little while."

Agony twisted its dagger in her gut, and her hands froze on Vasco's shifting form, the delicate touch of vines and flowers razors on her icy skin. Shocked eyes landed on Fatyan exposing the white line bisecting her neck, spiderwebs of flesh knitting it together. The knife forgotten on the cobblestones finished the story Yzabel had missed while suspended in air and moonlight, unable to move or speak or hear.

"We didn't lie, little princess. But we did keep some secrets from you." Brites came closer, voice and footsteps nearly drowned in the storm. Despondent loss glistened in her crestfallen eyes. "I wish he'd talked to me before he decided to turn on us."

Yzabel wiped the rain from her eyes, a moot gesture, considering how strongly it pelted them. "What did you keep from—"

A burst of energy turned her question into a yelp, and she crawled backward as roots broke out from Vasco's body of wood and flowers, digging between the cobblestones. The plants parted, rearranging themselves as the bark of Vasco's skin curled upward to become a sapling, and she fell back as the trunk swelled and branches stretched up into the night.

"Fatyan's life is tied to yours. The only thing that can kill her is *your* death, and the only reason I know this is because a long time ago, I freed an Enchanted Moura of my own. Regardless…" Brites gave the growing tree a look that simmered with anger and sadness, sniffing at the water running down her cheeks. "We have more pressing matters to take care of."

Yzabel's mind raced to grind the conflicting emotions tearing her in different directions, and words piled on her tongue, hurtful questions and selfish demands knotting together into an angry rant. What else did they know, what else had they kept from her, the *other* Enchanted Moura Brites had freed—but the expression on her face snuffed all those thoughts out, and all Yzabel could mewl was, "You can't."

"We have to. No one will be able to explain a tree sprouting in the middle of the night. They'll start looking, and they will find us. Find *you*." Brites retrieved her knife again, fixed her gaze on Yzabel as she said, "I won't let that happen. Fatyan, take her back to her rooms. Use the servants' passage just in case and avoid the kitchens."

"No," she said, rising to her trembling feet, crossing her sodden arms over her chest. "I won't move until you tell me what you've been hiding."

"You might be my liege, Yzabel, but you're not entitled to every one of my secrets. Especially when they aren't mine to tell." The harshness of her sentences slapped Yzabel harder than the freezing rain, rocked her worse than the thunder roaring above their heads. "If you want the truth, you'll leave. Now."

The skies began to lighten, sunrise fast approaching in the horizon. Pressure formed around Yzabel's hand as Faty's fingers wrapped around hers, tugging her along. She resisted, planted her heels on the cobblestones until Fatyan wheeled around to grab her face.

"I would never…" Fatyan's wispy voice cracked and broke, and she coughed until it cleared. "I would *never* try to replace you. Even if I wanted to, I couldn't. No one can." She brushed rain and tears away from Yzabel's cheek. "You're irreplaceable."

The newfound heat made her realize how cold it was, how her wet clothes clung to her skin in a freezing veil. And Faty's eyes, so wide and earnest, her lips tucked into a despairing pout—how could she not believe her?

Yzabel turned to Brites, her maid's accusations of entitlement pushing to the front of her thoughts. It was the blatant remorse on her expression that stopped her from voicing them. Daylight seeped further in, shining on them the threat of discovery.

"You're telling us to go, but what about you?" Yzabel asked. "Someone might see you. Or the fire. And what about the ashes?"

"I'll take care of everything. Now *go*."

That last command uttered, Brites held the blade to her palm, then pivoted to the adult cork oak and its crown of flowers in the middle of the garden. A sharp movement, then blood mingling with rain on bark and leaves. Sniffing, she ran her arm across her face, and a long breath trembled in her nostrils as she placed her hand on the trunk.

"Da chuva nasce óleo,
Do meu sangue fogo nasce,
Pr'a queima até à cinza
Esta árvore de desastre."

The wind howled, a beast come alive. Brites's blood caught fire, a sputtering flame, then a pyre, consuming the tree that had once been Vasco.

Numbness spread on her senses, and she let Faty guide them through the servants' corridors. The silent halls haunted her, the swishing of her wet skirts on the stone floor bouncing off empty walls, but she heard nothing but the beat of her own heart, heavy and fast, thumping in her ears, flooding her with a bedlam of emotion.

Vasco had died in her arms after trying to interrupt the ritual.

After trying to kill Faty.

After screaming that Dom Domingos had been right about Yzabel being corrupted.

Knowing Vasco had gone to the Chancellor-Mor behind their backs brought more questions than it answered. Did Dom Domingos know about the magic, or did he simply mean Brites was corrupting Yzabel by insisting she eat and take care of herself, therefore foregoing the hunger and pain that purified the body?

But above all—Vasco was dead. Never again would he kiss her forehead goodnight, never again would his steady presence be at her back. The closest thing she had to a father, gone in a flash of light and a cornucopia of vegetation.

In her rooms, the embers smoldered in the fireplace, the promise of warmth hypnotizing her to follow. While Fatyan threw kindling in to bring the flames back to life, Yzabel shed her sodden dress and donned her robes and nightgown. The events of the night hit her straight on, and she didn't fight the weakness that made her legs give and her knees hit the rug.

Sorrow emptied her heart and filled her eyes, and once she started crying, there was no stopping it. Loss gnawed at her chest, bobbed in her throat. Yzabel hiccupped, startled as an arm covered her shoulders, brought her around into an embrace. She buried her face in Fatyan's neck, let her hold her through the tears, comfort her through the sobs.

"Oh, Yza…" Fatyan said, perching her cheek on the top of her head. "Someone who has kindness hanging on her every move shouldn't have to pay so much to have miracles at her fingertips. I wish things had gone differently. I wish Vasco hadn't suddenly judged what we were doing as terrible."

Her fingers closed around the neckline of Fatyan's shirt. "He could've retired to a vast fortune and a coveted title, but he chose to stay by my side to protect me. Since our first meeting, that's all he's ever done."

"I tried to stop him."

"I know." She sighed against Fatyan's neck, traced the vanishing line made by Vasco's knife. "I can't believe he tried to kill you. Or that you didn't die." She pulled away. "Or that you didn't tell me you couldn't."

Guilt flashed in Fatyan's elusive gaze. "You were dealing with so much, I...I didn't think it wise to add to the pressure. But yes—the life of an Enchanted Moura is tied to whoever breaks their curse. Even after I'm free, even if we're apart. I'll die when you die."

It was in her own interest to keep Yzabel healthy and alive, yet Fatyan had no way of being certain how long Yzabel's life would be, or if she'd recover from her mal-nourishment. "And you risked making a bargain with *me*?"

A shrug. "I'd rather have a short life through someone who's good, than a long one through someone who's not."

The strings pinching Yzabel's features snapped, and the doubt Vasco had cast on Fatyan evaporated. Belatedly, she realized her hand was still on Faty's neck, thumb brushing her throat. "I'm sorry. I'm so sorry."

She'd lost Vasco. She'd almost lost Faty. And Brites... Oh God, Brites had stayed behind, holding on to secrets while she burned away the remnants of tonight.

"Even now, you take time to be kind," Fatyan mused in a whisper full of curious wonder.

"That's something Vasco taught me. Kindness isn't

something you are. It's something you choose to be, every single moment of every single day." She almost smiled, remembering his face that day, the seriousness in his voice. "When we met, he made me promise to choose kindness always. Our own secret deal—I'd be kind, and he wouldn't tell Denis about the magic." A small sniff, a long yawn. "He might not have believed it in the end, but I still do."

"Still, you don't have to apologize for something he did."

"But I do—he was in my service, had my trust. Misguided as it was, it was in my name he tried to kill you." Yzabel shook her head, wiped her face with the back of her arm. "He mentioned Dom Domingos. Do you think he told him who you really are?"

"I don't think so. But it's possible Vasco heard one of the less flattering versions of my tale and thought it the real one. Namely the one where I lure people into my domain, and then kill them so I can assume their identity." She scoffed. "The reason why I refused to leave for so long was because I wanted someone who didn't want me to be anyone but myself."

Sleep tugged at Yzabel's eyelids, questions at her mind. And Brites—why wasn't she back yet? Was she meandering in the corridors trying to buy herself time? Would she run so she'd never have to give Yzabel answers on the *other* Enchanted Moura? Why hadn't she told her before? What had she meant by secrets that weren't her own to share?

Had Vasco known them?

Yzabel had yet to reverse her gift, and after she did, she would have to find a way to distribute any food she made from flowers. All of this—finding Faty, the training, the ritual— had been done with those goals in mind. But how was she supposed to accomplish them when grief tore a chasm in her breast and so many different questions vied for her attention?

CHAPTER FOURTEEN

Deceit

The merciful oblivion of slumber didn't last long. It seemed as if Yzabel had just closed her eyes and drifted off when she woke up to Fatyan shaking her, Yzabel's name an urgent whisper on her lips.

Fighting the sunlight, she opened her eyes to the day, hissing as the brightness stabbed at her head. Small, compared to the grief that overwhelmed her, that dug its claws into her heart and tore it to shreds.

Vasco, dead. Brites, still not here. And the tree…

Muffled voices sneaked under the door as she fished a handkerchief from the nightstand and blew her clogged nose. Speech rough in her sore throat, she asked, "What's going on?"

"Matias raised the alarm when Vasco wasn't here to be relieved of his watch," Fatyan answered in a rushed whisper. "And that man you mentioned before, Senhor Davide? His house—"

Before Fatyan could elaborate, the knob rattled on the door and someone banged on the wood. "Yzabel!" Denis's voice called from the other side. "Yzabel, open this door!"

His demand nailed her to the mattress, brought a shiver up her spine and panic to her breath, frozen as the key on their side trembled and fell. The lock turned, ominously slow, and the door swung open to let the distressed king inside.

Denis made it to the bed with hurried steps. When he saw Yzabel, odd relief sighed on his lips. "You're…you're here. And well."

Yzabel barely had time to turn before Lucas jumped onto the bed, nuzzling her neck and licking her cheeks, and she gratefully leaned into him. Nervousness tickled her fingers and nose, and she made a show of blowing her sneezing nose while she gathered her thoughts. "Aside from this cold, yes, I'm well. Why wouldn't I be?"

Her betrothed's face hardened to stone, brown eyes flicking between her and Faty. "Where's Brites?"

She wished she knew. "Not sure—although it's odd she's not here yet." Yzabel hacked into the kerchief and took a hand to her spinning, thrumming head.

"I can go look for her," Fatyan offered, rising from the bed.

"Don't bother," Denis said, encroaching on the Moura's space. "You're the nun."

"Novice." Fatyan stepped back. Denis followed, driving her back until her knees hit the mattress.

"Brites was training you, wasn't she? To take care of Yzabel?" His nostrils flared, his teeth clenched. "Did she teach you anything else? Anything *uncanny*?"

Yzabel's heart skipped a beat. "Denis, what are you—"

"Quiet!" he screamed at her, rage roaring red in his cheeks. "I know what you've been hiding—keeping a Carajua as your lady's maid. Inviting pagan witchery into this house and country. And this one…" He grabbed Fatyan's arm, pulled her toward him. "Dom Domingos talked to the Abbess this morning and she knew nothing about sending a novice to help you."

The air hitched on her sore throat, and Yzabel wished she knew exactly what Denis was thinking, wished she could come up with quick lies that rang true. But she didn't need to lie, only to omit.

"Let go of her. She's done nothing wrong," Yzabel said. "But you're right in that she's not a novice. We made up that story, so she'd be unbothered by your men. Not that it worked." A spark of outrage flared in her chest, and she allowed it to spread, to seep into her words. "You really should discipline *them*. Inflicting their leery gazes and rowdy words on a nun."

Denis's fingers twitched, his glare never leaving Faty. "Then who are you? Is Dom Domingos's story true?"

Impassive, Fatyan lifted her defiant chin. "That depends. What *is* he saying?"

"Do not play coy with me." He seized the Moura's jaw so violently Yzabel couldn't stand by any longer. She bolted from her nest of pillows and blankets, but Denis's grip was too tight, she too weak. Lucas, too, sensed her anguish, but when he looked at the source of it, he tilted his head and looked between them with a confused whine. Thank God for small mercies, thank God for giving her a dog smart enough to know he should never bare his teeth at the king.

Yzabel tried again to pry his hand from Fatyan's face, but it was like trying to change the pose of a statue carved in marble. "Denis, stop this."

He paid her no heed, shoving her aside and talking over her. "Is what Matias told me the truth? Are you or are you not the Moura named Salúquia?"

Yzabel blinked away the surprise. Matias had told Denis that Fatyan was an Enchanted Moura, so it was only logical he was the one who'd told him about Brites and the Caraju.

Fatyan's mouth parted, then thinned into an angry line. "I'm not Salúquia. I have *never* been Salúquia."

Was that pain, jittery in her determined statements? Why did Denis think the Enchanted Moura was named Salúquia? Had they changed Faty's name in one of the stories? Was that why she'd been surprised when Yzabel asked her name? And why *have never been Salúquia*?

Questions for later, questions that didn't matter when Denis was manhandling Yzabel's friend right before her eyes. "I can't believe you'd fall for such a ridiculous tale," she said instead. "Or why Matias would conjure such a thing. Especially the part about his own mother being a witch."

"I do," a fourth voice chimed in from the threshold between the quarters of princess and maid. Brites, haggard and haunted, the wrinkles on her face deeper than they'd been the day before—as if she'd aged ten years overnight. Gentleness blinked in her dark eyes. "I might be his mother, but that boy's hated me for years. Looks like he finally got over his fear of being a Carajua's son."

Denis's hand went slack, and he pivoted to Brites. "Then you admit to practicing paganism when you serve the future Queen of Portugal? Have you any idea what it'd do to her if this gets out? What do you think the Pope will do if word reaches him that my wife has been associating with a Carajua?"

"Then make sure it doesn't," Brites said. "And don't blame the princess for this. She didn't know."

Yzabel made to protest, but a slight shake from Brites's head closed her open mouth. She was spinning falsehoods to protect her, willing to take on the punishment for Yzabel's faults.

"And what were you doing in town at night? Matias says he saw you return covered in soot and ash." Heavy feet stomped on the floor to loom over the maid. "Coming from the direction of Senhor Davide's house shortly after it burned down."

"That's because I sent her," Yzabel interceded, lurching to stand between them, the lie already spilling from her lips. "She was to distribute the medicines we made, and Vasco went with her for security."

Denis regarded her with cold assessment. "Why didn't you tell me you sent them into town? You know I have no problem with you giving the people your herbal remedies."

Something else, she had to give him something else that would be plausible for her to hide. "Because I also told them to give food."

He sent a withering glare her way, fury barely contained in the grind of his jaw, before shifting it toward Brites. "And the fire?"

"We came just as someone set it. Vasco went after them, while I used the Caraju to summon rain. I managed to delay the fire just enough so Senhor Davide and his family could escape before the house crumbled." Brites's breath shuddered, the too-fresh loss shadowing her eyes. "But if Vasco hasn't returned, then...then I fear whoever tried to kill Senhor Davide ended up killing Vasco."

"You think Vasco's...dead?" Denis's mouth and arms fell, aghast in a limp moment of surprise.

But Yzabel couldn't take her gaze away from Brites, couldn't stop herself from reading the many ramifications her statements implied. Like a tapestry unfolding stitch by stitch, the story unraveled in her imagination. Vasco had already been dead, and there had been no fire in town after she and Faty had left Brites with the tree. After burning

Vasco, Brites had done the same to Senhor Davide's home while constructing the narrative of an attack.

All to draw the attention away from Yzabel.

"I *know* he's dead," Brites said. "There's no other reason why he wouldn't be here."

Yzabel cast her gaze down, not bothering to mask the horror she felt slipping across her features. Agony wrenched a hiccup from her throat and sent tears to her eyes. So much destruction in such a short time, and although the decisions hadn't been made by Yzabel herself, they might as well have. It was in her name that Vasco had tried to stop the ritual, in her name that Brites left a brave man and a family homeless.

Dazed and blinking, Denis asked, "Why did you not report this immediately?"

"Because I've been looking for Vasco since!" Brites cried. "When I couldn't find him, I came back, thinking— *hoping*—he'd be here to greet me."

The king massaged his temples, then pressed his thumbs against closed eyes. With a sigh and a slight shake of his head, he straightened his shoulders and said, "The fact is, you remain a Carajua. You used your incantations last night, in plain sight. What if someone saw you?"

Cold grasped Yzabel's chest, and she forgot the terrible possibilities around Brites's acts, forgot there were secrets she had kept, forgot everything but the need to keep someone so dear safe. "Denis, don't—"

"Brites Sande, for the practice of Caraju, your services are now terminated. You will stay in the dungeons while we conduct the investigation on Vasco's disappearance, and you never, *never* talk to Yzabel again. And the only reason I allow you to keep your head is because of your son's proven loyalty to the Portuguese Crown."

"That foolish boy," Brites muttered under her breath.

Yzabel echoed the insult in her mind; she'd always known Matias was devoted to Denis, but she hadn't known his loyalties to her betrothed superseded the bonds of family.

"That 'stupid boy' is the reason you still draw breath, and if you try to contact Yzabel in any way, not even Matias's loyalty will stay my hand." His tone lowered to a chilling threat. "And if anyone asks why you've been dismissed and are stewing in a cell, you'll say you were caught stealing."

Brites kept her dauntless chin up, her demeanor steady. "Is that all?"

"Yes."

Yzabel tried to get to Brites, but her betrothed kept her still with a vicious grip on her arm. "No," she said. "Denis, you can't."

"It's all right, little princess." Brites's reassuring smile became a harsh grimace as she shifted her gaze to the king. "Everything I did, I would do again because it was done to help the greatest treasure this country has. And if you hurt her, *my king*, you will wish you'd never been born."

"Are you threatening me?" he hissed.

"Yes." Brites turned to Yzabel, voice soft once again. "Goodbye, little princess. Stay strong. Make us proud."

Denis keeping her still, Yzabel could do nothing but watch her leave. Loss on top of loss, each one different, each one as final, each one leaving her with more questions than answers.

Yzabel's jittery fingers grabbed onto her skirts, and she looked down, containing herself; interfering would only make it worse. Hatred welled inside her over her powerlessness in this situation, of how even though she'd dedicated her life to this marriage and this country, she could not save the people she cared about if the king wanted them gone.

To think they'd been laughing the night before, joking about offensive poetry.

Brites was at the door when Yzabel managed to wrench herself free, dashing across the carpet to envelop her in a hug. Brites's strong arms snaked around her, brought her closer still, and in her ear, the words, "We'll find a way out."

Reprieve gurgled in Yzabel's sobs, her tears rained on Brites's shirt. The warmth of a kiss blossomed on her forehead, in a squeeze on her shoulder, then nowhere, leaving her adrift in a sea of sorrow and grief.

She spun around, anger grumbling in her throat, in her footsteps, in the accusing finger she pointed at her betrothed. "You had no right," she said.

"We're not done yet," he countered. With Brites gone, his focus went to Fatyan. "If this one isn't a novice, then who is she?"

A sharp intake of breath snorted on her clogged nose. While she coughed, Fatyan produced another kerchief from the nightstand, offered it to Yzabel as she spoke, even and without pause.

"Her Highness found me when she was out picking herbs." Fatyan took a moment to wet her lips, and when Denis didn't remark on anything, she resumed her fiction. "I'd been traveling with my father—he was a metalworker commissioned to do a job in the Algarves. We were on our way down there when bandits attacked us on the road, and Father…" A long, closed-eyed sigh. "Father distracted them so I could escape. I'd been running aimlessly for a day and a night when the princess found me, and when I told her of my plight, she was kind enough to offer me a place to stay."

Denis pinched the bridge of his nose, shoulders sagging, mouth frowning. "Why wouldn't you tell me, Yzabel?"

"Would you have let her stay if I'd told you?"

A pregnant pause. "No." He sat on the edge of the bed, the mattress sinking along with his weight.

"Then please, don't be angry." She took his hand, hoping the contact would ease his grudge even as she glimpsed Fatyan's nose wrinkling with abject distaste. "She had no one to turn to. I couldn't abandon her."

"I'm not upset you took in another stray; I'm mad you kept it from me!" The anger returned, not alone—there was hurt in there as well, genuine pain over broken trust. "I'm your betrothed, Yzabel. I care about your well-being, and all this time, I've been nothing but patient with you. Patience you reward with lies." He tore his hand away from hers. "The one reason I don't have your head lopped off is because I *know* you're incapable of a single bad thought— but I am done letting you do as you please." He stood, brought his heavy hands to Yzabel's shoulders. "You are not to leave this room until we find who killed Vasco. For your own safety."

She swallowed the impotence knotting in her throat. "You can't keep me here."

"I can, and I will. The Prelates of Terra da Moura are the only people who could be responsible for Vasco's disappearance. And I don't trust anyone in this village until we find out who exactly did it, so, yes. You *will* be staying here until then, and I'll be coming here to check on you for every meal, starting with lunch today."

Protests bubbled on her tongue, burst on the barrier of her clenched teeth. She couldn't confess that Vasco had died trying to stop a magical ritual, couldn't tell him that Dom Domingos had poisoned her guard's mind to doubt her, and her blessing, beating quietly against her ribs.

When she said nothing, Denis whipped his head around to look at Faty. "And you're to stay with Yzabel, meet her every need, and never leave her side unless I'm present. Keep watch over her while I cannot, and should she do anything against her well-being, you are to report to me immediately. Am I clear?"

Fatyan raised her head, touched the bruising skin of her jaw. "Like water."

The door slammed shut. Without his smothering presence, the thin veneer of strength slipped from her body, and the torrent of agony snapped the strings holding her up. Yzabel crumbled, folded into Lucas's awaiting support.

Her pain, her despair at being locked up, her grief over Vasco and Brites; it was small compared to Faty's, who knew no one else in this present world, and had been grieving alone inside a stone for over a century. Faty, who wanted nothing but to be free and was now trapped in these chambers along with her. She was the one who was supposed to be crumpled and weeping, Yzabel the one to comfort her. Instead, it was the other way around, Faty wrapped around her, stroking her hair, holding her close. In her arms, Yzabel tried to put her broken heart back together, tried to cover the void left by Vasco's death and Brites's incarceration. It was like trying to reconstruct a shattered crystal glass, and no matter what she did, a part of it always ended up missing.

"I think," a sob croaked in her throat, "I think Brites burned down the house knowing Denis would suspect the local prelates. So he'd think they're the ones who killed Vasco. I…" She sniffed miserably. "I can't let them take the blame for something that's my fault."

"It was doubt that spelled his end. Not you." Fatyan

tucked a stray curl behind Yzabel's ear. "And if someone needs to be held accountable, let it be someone who's already guilty of great wrongdoings."

Yzabel closed her eyes, hating the relief that came with knowing she was safe from suspicion. Hating that she was glad they could use Vasco's untimely death to condemn a guilty party of the wrong crime. Hating that it was no different than using her inability to eat to strong-arm Denis into letting her give more to charity.

"And we still haven't checked your gift. Vasco interfered before the ritual finished, so I'm not sure…" Faty furrowed her brow and held Yzabel at an arm's length as she studied the light beating on her chest.

"No, it worked." The blessing lay where it belonged, next to Yzabel's heart—and now that she understood it, it understood her as well. A flex of the right muscle, and the magic traveled to her shoulder, down her arm, to her hand, then back up again. An obstacle so insurmountable days ago now effortless to overcome.

"I should get us something to eat and practice with. The sahar might be answering now, but you still need to make food out of flowers. You still need to learn to reverse this."

Cold kissed her back as Fatyan sat on her heels and made to stand, but Yzabel clutched at the other girl's skirts, clinging to her presence, to her warmth.

"Yza…"

"Please don't leave," she pleaded, eyes cast upward. The dark of loneliness peeked in the shadows of the room, stitched her lips with the trembling thread of sorrow. Vasco and Brites had kept her moored in the storms of the world, and now that they were both gone, Faty was all Yzabel had left to keep her from asphyxiating on her own secrets.

Softness surrounded her hands, pried stiff fingers from

fabric, and Yzabel thought Fatyan would drop them, tell her to cease being pathetic, to get herself together and look to the future instead of dwelling on miseries of the past.

But she did neither of those things. She sank back to Yzabel's side and held her tighter still.

CHAPTER FIFTEEN

Burning Ash

It was lunchtime when her door opened again. Yzabel had thought Denis was exaggerating when he said he'd be there for every meal.

She should've known better than to doubt his word.

"Your food is here," Denis announced, tone as serious and as unamused as it'd been earlier. "Brought some for your beastly pet as well. You're welcome."

She was supposed to be grateful he was feeding her dog? Denis's patronizing ways awakened a dark desire, something cold and ruthless and terrifying. She kissed Lucas's snout and rolled out from under him as the guilt gave way to something else.

Denis was the reason she was trapped in a room, the reason Brites was no longer at her side. True, it was Matias who'd sold his own mother out, but it was Denis who'd dismissed Brites. Denis who wanted to keep her under lock and key. It was beneath her to seek vengeance. But she could have justice. And what bigger justice than to be healthy and feed Denis's own nation with nothing but flowers?

The king made himself at home in her rooms, claiming one of the two seats at the table. Yzabel sat opposite him, and Fatyan came to her side, as maids often did when present for their masters' meals. The Moura kept a hand to her stomach and an eye on the door, features sour. Although she could not see him, Yzabel had no doubt that Matias stood on the other side.

Near the food, Yzabel's gift simmered below the surface, but the ritual had worked, and when Yzabel told it to bide its time, it listened. She ate without a glance at her betrothed or a word in his direction, made her bites slow and her chewing slower.

"How's the assorda?" he asked.

"Salty." Yzabel drank water from the glass. "Brites's was much better."

"Brites chose the consequences the moment she used her Caraju in public."

"No. You chose them." Before an angry retort could leave his mouth, she asked, "Is Fatyan also a prisoner here, or just me?"

He tossed Fatyan a pointed look, and without the morning's fury veiling his perception, annoyance became attraction as he *saw* her for the first time. Jaw locked, Yzabel found one of Fatyan's hands where it lay on the back of her chair, a protective instinct, bringing lines in Denis's brow to a twitch. "Now it bothers you when I look at other women?"

"With her, yes," Yzabel stated, unable to answer for the possessiveness from her tone. "Fatyan isn't one of your girls."

Denis snorted. "You think you could keep me from her if I wanted her? Either of you?" The chair groaned as he rose, the table creaked when he braced himself on it, leaning over.

Yzabel matched his stance.

He scoffed. "You're lucky I don't want any woman who doesn't want me back."

Her fingers curled. "You want praise for basic decency?"

"No." Denis sat back down, legs crossed and hands steepled as he regarded Faty. "But I am trying to figure out why exactly she'd want to serve you."

Fatyan's tone was stiff. "Why wouldn't I?"

"Why would you? Someone who looks the way you do would have no trouble finding a husband. Perhaps even one above your station." He rolled his eyes and shook his head. "Hell, half the bachelors in my court have asked *me* about you."

Worry curved Yzabel's lips into a grimace. Next to her, Fatyan's stillness was that of death, her voice the low growl of doubtlessness. "Then you can tell them I'm not interested in marriage."

"Then you have no ambition to use your proximity to Yzabel to climb the social ranks?" Denis asked, unconvinced eyelids narrowing with mistrust. "You'd choose a life of servitude over running your own household?"

"No, I choose a life of serving the woman who's to be the Queen of Portugal and the Algarves over a life of serving a husband," Faty spat. "You want to know my ambition? It's to be free to make my own choices."

Yzabel didn't care for Denis's line of questioning, or for his silent scrutiny of the Moura. "What's the point of this?"

"The prelates swear innocence on last night's incident, and all of them have witnesses to vouch for their whereabouts. My men have searched the rubble, inquired the neighbors, Senhor Davide and his family, and found no evidence tying the Prelates to the fire." He gnashed his teeth, one hand coiling into a fist. "As with the town's resources, I *know* they're responsible, but have no way of proving it. We have the records of what the prelates have stolen, but we've turned this town upside down and haven't been able to find the hard proof we need. Even when we do, there's a good chance many of my vassals will stand with Terra da Moura's gentry. They're too used to their own power, too used to getting away with much the same."

The nobles and the clergy were the reason why most of the Portuguese starved, and when Denis had shared his inquisitors' reports regarding Terra da Moura being on the brink of collapse, they'd seen it as a sign it was time to intervene and change a few laws. With proof of mismanagement, Denis could take the lands away and redistribute them as he saw fit—the rest of the gentry might feel threatened and try to depose him to maintain their lavish lifestyles.

The moments stretched into a long pause, broken with a question from Faty. "And what does that have to do with me?"

"The Baron of Terra da Moura has predilections. All of which you meet. If you were to ingratiate yourself to him, he might just make the right mistake trying to impress you. You might become privy to secrets, invited to shuffle through his belongings."

Yzabel's heart thumped, and a shiver shuddered in her spine. "You can't mean to whore her—"

"It's not your choice," Denis said with no inflection to his tone. "It's hers. A favor for me, to prove she's trustworthy; blackmail if she's not."

Fatyan's grip on Yzabel's hand tightened painfully. "I'll spy for you if you give both of us free reign of the town."

Yzabel readied herself for Denis's outburst, for his screams and threats, but he remained neutral and unfazed. "I'll give you the castle only. Provided Yzabel is here in time for her meals and Matias escorts you."

"No," Yzabel said.

"I'll think about it," Fatyan said at the same time.

Twisting around in her chair, Yzabel craned her neck to look at the Moura. "You don't have to put yourself through that for my sake."

"That's what you say now. Give it time." Denis let his words hang suspended in the air as he made his way out. "Matias will stay outside, so make sure you behave."

"I want someone else," Yzabel said. Not just because Matias had turned on Brites; Fatyan got physically ill with his nearness, and she wanted to spare her that.

Denis pierced her with his stare. "You will get no one else. Fatyan is permitted to leave to fetch anything you need, but if she lingers longer than half a chime"—he shifted his gaze to the Moura—"I will assume you're conspiring with someone and throw you in the dungeons. I'll be back when it's time for dinner."

"Wait!" Pushing through the lump in her throat, Yzabel asked, "What about Vasco's funeral? We might not have a body, but—"

"We'll keep looking until we find him." His hand lingered on the door, and his next words came out with some hesitant difficulty. "If we don't, we'll hold a service in his memory once our investigation concludes."

She didn't know she'd been tense about it until then, but there was relief to know Vasco would have some form of funeral, even without a body to bury. Denis didn't deserve a drop of gratefulness, not when he was the reason Brites rotted in a dungeon, but the seed bloomed nonetheless. She hated him for tugging at her strings in such a manner.

In a mournful susurrus, Denis added, "He was my friend long before he was yours. I mourn his death, too."

It wasn't a lie. She hated him for that, too.

Once he was gone, Fatyan sank against the chair across from Yzabel. "And you said he was good."

"I betrayed his trust. He's right to be angry." Her tongue embittered at the defense that came so naturally to her. Denis didn't deserve her excuses, either.

Shaking her head, Yzabel picked up one of the many pieces of bread on the tray. So easy to keep it from becoming a rose, and what should've filled her with joy brought yet another pang to her chest. Another one of her shortcomings Vasco would never see overcome.

She hated he wasn't here to see her in control. She…

"Just because Vasco's not here doesn't mean he isn't watching," Fatyan said softly.

"I know." Yzabel blew her nose on her napkin and lifted a queijada toward the ceiling. "To you, Vasco. May the Lord forever keep you in His arms."

The sweet richness of the small cake spread cinnamon and sugar on her mouth; oddly, there was comfort to be taken in that—a superficial sort that lasted only seconds, but as fleeting as it was, she cherished it. It was better than the emptiness rumbling in her heart, at least, and she reached for a second tart while finishing the first, stuffing her face so she wouldn't have to feel her ravenous sorrow.

"Slow down before you choke!" Faty admonished, but the laughter in her tone stole any credence her warning might've had.

Yzabel took gulps of wine to wash down the tartlets. "The food makes it better, and for the first time since forever, I can eat without worrying. Let me have this." She reached for a third queijada, moaning as the sweetness broke apart in her mouth.

"Still, it's good practice to chew," Faty pointed out.

"I am chewing!"

She was most definitely not, but her blushing denial drew laughter to Fatyan's lips. "Yes, like a rabbit munching on grass."

"Rabbits are adorable, so…" She shrugged, but the haughtiness she'd invoked slipped with a tap on her nose.

Faty's radiant smile blinded her, and the wistfulness of her voice filled Yzabel's ears with its softness. "That, they are."

The cinnamon of the queijadas sitting on her tongue brought back the memory of their kiss, the hint of spices, the shortness of breath. Cheeks flushed, Yzabel realized she'd forgotten to swallow, so she did it then, hid herself behind the glass of wine as she drained it in small gulps. Denis hadn't been so cruel as to bring food for just himself and Yzabel, at least, and she motioned to the table, berating herself for her inconsideration. "Don't let me eat all of this."

She nibbled on the almond tosquiados, the crispy shell melting on her tongue until Fatyan finished eating as well. A few slices of bread and cheese remained; Fatyan pushed them her way. "Go on. Turn them into flowers, then try to turn them back."

With her right hand in Fatyan's, Yzabel picked up bread with the left.

"Flowers won't trigger the sahar as food does," Fatyan said. "You'll have to do it yourself."

Eyes closed, Yzabel pictured the light traveling to her fingertips.

"Well done." Fatyan's fingers brushed against Yzabel's. "Now, as you direct the magic, grab the image you have of bread turning to roses, and picture it backward."

Yzabel directed the threads of magic toward her hand, to the rose, imagined it glowing and transforming into bread. A hopeful gasp parted her lips when the magic jumped to the rose, encompassing it in its bright light.

"Please," she whispered, pouring more of the gift into the flower. It shone brighter, so bright she couldn't bear to look directly at it anymore, brighter than the fire, brighter than—

It *burned*.

With a loud yelp, Yzabel dropped the glowing rose. Absent her touch, the light turned to flame, the rose scattering into ashes. The pain in her hand small against the anger building in her chest, her limbs—

"You lost your patience and used too much." Faty gently turned Yzabel's hand, inspected the searing line along the length of her palm. Warm breath coated it with tingling as Faty blew on it, and the entirety of Yzabel's being shuddered when the Moura placed a kiss upon it.

"Better?" Faty asked.

She couldn't feel any pain anymore, agitated as she was. "Y-yes."

The fact that Yzabel couldn't forget Fatyan's kiss, that it had left an imprint in Yzabel's head, that her thoughts always strayed back to that moment before realizing they were already there, beneath her eyelids, the ghost of it on her lips.

Putting her trembling heart out of mind, Yzabel turned all her concentration on turning bread to roses, and roses to bread.

CHAPTER SIXTEEN

Hidden Stories

Three days into her entrapment, Yzabel couldn't stand the smell of flowers anymore. Aside from the meals shared with Denis, every waking moment was spent trying to turn roses into bread, then screaming and growling when she failed to do so. The floral scent smothered chambers that seemed to grow smaller with every failed attempt, the walls tighter, the ceiling lower. She went to the window, but the outside air was stale when filtered through that tiny square. No space for her to breathe, and she couldn't—

"Let me out!" Yzabel shouted, rapping at the door. "Matias, I know you're there! I need fresh air."

Her fists bruised on the unyielding wood, that accursed barrier standing between her and the outside. The lock turned, and a hard shove against the door threw her backward; balance lost, she fell on her bottom, and before she could get up, Matias was there, looming over her with a dissatisfied grimace.

"Your Highness, it's not safe for you to be out."

"I don't care," she replied as she got to her feet. Matias could intimidate her, but she knew his threats were moot—he wouldn't lay a hand on her. "I'm going out for a walk."

Faster than she could blink, Matias grabbed Fatyan

by the hair, shoving her on the carpet at Yzabel's feet and holding her down with a knee to the small of her back. Steel slid against leather; the cold bite of the knife pressed against Faty's cheekbone. "The king said I could hurt her if you did not comply, Your Highness."

"He would not!" Doubt quickened her breath and shook her head. "No, he wouldn't."

"He would." A hand tried to push into Fatyan's mouth to hold her still. She sunk her teeth into it, and Matias screamed, banged her head against the floor—Fatyan's eyelids shivered, dazed before slamming shut, a movement echoed by her teeth. She bit again, seemingly keen on taking a finger if it was the last thing she did.

"Fine, I don't need to get out." When Matias made to slam Fatyan's head again, Yzabel threw her hands between the Moura and the floor, screaming, "Stop this. Right. *Now*!"

The outburst stunned Matias into stillness and Fatyan into releasing his hand. He let go, but not before sinking his knee farther into her spine one last time. "Sahiqa scum."

"Don't use words you don't know, you ass-face hiding in plain sight," she spat back, crawling to her knees. "I can't believe you came out of Brites."

Yzabel stood between them, holding a hand to Matias's chest when he tried to make for Faty again. As evenly as she could, she asked, "Have you talked to your mother? How is she?"

Matias's sourness remained on the downturn of his lips. "She's my mother in name only. I've no reason to listen to her vile spewing."

"Why not?"

"She's not the woman you think her to be. It's not just using the Caraju; she has a sickness she hides, a dangerous thing that perverts everyone around her." He slid a harsh look at Faty. Both his and her fingers trembled with antagonism, as if they were under the influence of opposing forces. "The same sickness this one has."

"Don't be ridiculous," Yzabel said, dismissive. Fatyan couldn't even die, so by logic, she couldn't be sick.

"You may not believe me, Your Highness, but I speak the truth. They carry the sihaq, both of them." His heavy brow lowered, Adam's apple bobbing up and down with a rumbling growl.

Sihaq? Yzabel racked her mind for a definition, but among all her knowledge of medicine, she couldn't remember coming across such a malady.

Faty, on the other hand, furrowed her brow, a glint of *something* shaking in her eyes. "Where would you have heard of that?"

A humorless chuckle. "You're not the first Enchanted Moura I've met." He turned to Yzabel. "I know the king doesn't believe it, but I know what she is. My mother and her *friend* have been trying to free every Enchanted Moura out there for years now. And they sometimes mentioned one who was trapped in Terra da Moura since—"

"Enough!" Yzabel commanded as a shudder traveled up her spine, the stab of betrayal slicing her heart anew. Brites had kept so many things from her, things she wouldn't be able to ask while she was trapped in her room and Brites in the dungeons. Matias wouldn't rattle her until she heard the answers from Brites herself. "You can return to your post."

He gave her a nod, but before he left, he stopped on the door's threshold to look over his shoulder, dark eyes meeting Yzabel's. "Ask her, Your Highness. Ask her about the disease, and what it makes her do."

She waited for the door to close and the lock to turn. Though they'd hidden the flowers in the drawers of the lady's maid chamber, their scent drenched the room still, sickening and sweet, but she made herself calm down, inhale deeply. "What does he mean by disease? What is this..." The unfamiliar word rolled awkwardly off her tongue, "Sihaq?"

"It's a...term from my time. Used to refer to women who find men unappealing." Faty crossed her uneasy arms over her chest, blew the air out of her puffed cheeks. "But it's as much of an illness as disliking olives."

Yzabel blinked her confusion. "So it's a matter of taste? Why would he claim it a disease? And the name he called you..."

"Sahiqa. It's...what you call someone who carries the sihaq. As for why he'd claim it a disease..." Faty shook her head with a snort. "Men take personal offense when a woman identifies as a sahiqa. They're so used to being the center of attention that when a woman doesn't see it the same way, it's because they must be sick."

Yzabel's head spun, and it took her a few breaths to gather all the threads together. She'd never found any man desirable. Even her betrothed, who had so many hearts fluttering, failed to affect her own, and she'd always assumed the starvation and bodily penances had numbed her to desire. And men *did* like to make everything about themselves. God knew Denis had made her reluctance to eat all about himself as well.

Matias claimed Brites had the same condition—if that were true, then why had she never told her? Why had she never told Yzabel of the possibility that she might be affected by this sihaq as well? Did she think her too weak to bear the knowledge she'd never want her betrothed in that way, so she'd chosen to keep her in ignorance?

A hesitant frown tugged at her brow as she asked, "Do

you think I carry it, too?"

Faty regarded her intently for a long moment, eyelids falling and rising in the slowest of blinks, arms unfolding to drop at her side. Yzabel's heart drummed in her ears; her breath dried in her mouth. The howling wind fell to a murmur in the background, the dive of raindrops mute on the glass window. The quietude stretched, drowning her in anticipation as Faty came closer.

Closer.

Gliding toward her with soundless footsteps, hair as black as the habit she still wore like an inky mantle around her shoulders. She had one of those looks again, where teeth ever-so-slightly trapped a corner of her lower lip, the slightest of lines marring her brow, an intent squint holding her eyes ajar.

In the end, Faty gave her three words only.

"I don't know."

CHAPTER SEVENTEEN

Paranoia

The days started to blend together in an interminable haze of failure and frustration.

She woke up next to Faty, and they changed out of their nightclothes. Denis came in the morning, and while Yzabel ate, Faty would leave to store more wood by the fireplace, empty the chamber pot. Refill the room's jug of water. Every time, she'd return with wearier eyes and leave with unease scrunching her shoulders. The men kept bothering her, and although Faty brushed it away, the discomfort was evident in her grimaces. After some insistence on Yzabel's part, Fatyan began to take Lucas with her, initial fear offset by how effective a deterrent the dog was.

Four or so outings later, and Faty no longer referred to Lucas as a wolf-bear-thing. From time to time, Yzabel would catch the Moura petting Lucas with a distracted hand while she scowled at the mirror as she tried to access her own powers. To see her precious dog and her precious friend finally accepting each other filled Yzabel's heart with so much warmth she almost forgot her current predicament.

Almost.

Once he'd deemed Yzabel had eaten enough, Denis would leave. Fatyan would break fast then, and Yzabel would take whatever was left, turn it into flowers, and try to change it back to whatever food it'd been. But she was still too overcome with grief and anger, and the sheer despair of it all burned every flower to a crisp.

The scene would repeat itself at lunch, then at dinner. By the end of the first week, Yzabel had attuned herself to Denis's comings and goings. Thrice a day he came to her, each visit more miserable and strained than the last. Yzabel could've cut him down had she been able to take the tension and fashion it as a weapon; she seriously considered sticking him with the letter opener, at least.

Every time, he told her, "If you want out, you know what must be done."

Every time, she replied with, "I refuse to let you coerce me into borrowing Fatyan so she can spy for you."

And once Denis left, Fatyan would always say, "I can do it, Yza."

"You don't have to do anything for me. You shouldn't even have to stay anymore." Her voice wavered, and bewilderment pinched her brow as she looked out the window. "I'm in control of the gift. You're not bound to me anymore."

"But I am." Fatyan's approach shimmered through Yzabel like summer sunshine casting away cold shadows, wrapping warmth around her waist, laying the weight of her head on the back of her neck. "Our bargain won't be met until you turn roses into bread and prove mastery of the sahar."

Another reminder of her failures. Bitterness rose to her tongue, disappointment sunk her stomach. She kept expecting Fatyan to say something different, to hear her say she was staying with her because she *wanted* to, not because she had to.

On Second-Fair, while the kettle warmed in the fireplace and Faty had left to grab broas from the kitchens, a gentle rapping nudged Yzabel from her place at the table. She swiftly hid the roses under the bed, swept the bits of bread into a bowl and set it by the window before asking, "Who is it?"

"Dom Domingos, Your Highness. May I come in?"

The hairs on the nape of her neck stood with palpitating nerves and hesitation. The Chancellor-Mor hadn't seen her since before Vasco's death, and not for lack of trying. Several times now Yzabel had heard them talking in the solar, Denis telling Dom Domingos she was resting and not to be disturbed. The several days of continued insistence to convince Denis she was not at risk of falling prey to the Chancellor's preaching had paid off at last.

Dom Domingos had soiled Vasco's thoughts against Brites and Faty, sowed doubt that had killed as efficiently as a dagger to the neck. Wariness straight on her shoulders, Yzabel sat on the three-legged bench before the fireplace, moved the kettle around just for the sake of it and said, "You'll have to ask Matias to unlock the door."

The familiar tumbling noise of key on lock, and Dom Domingos crossed into her chambers, short white hair catching the light in contrast to his black robes as he looked around the space with a calculating eye. Satisfied to see them alone, he shambled toward her, hand on his back as he lowered himself onto the bench next to hers.

"I've yet to offer you my condolences for Dom Vasco," he began. "Such sudden loss must weigh heavily upon you."

She narrowed her eyes. "It brings me much grief, yes."

A small smile tugged at the Chancellor's thin lips. "He was a great man. I still remember when he recommended you for queen as if it were yesterday. How he stayed with you for five years until you were prepared to come."

"Yes, I…" The memory chipped at her cold resolve, softened her demeanor and tone. "I owe him much and shall miss him even more."

For championing her. For protecting her. For letting her bring Brites.

"And just as I'd convinced him to finally denounce his friendship with that unholy woman, too." He shook his head and let out a breath. "I realize your affection for her blinds you, my princess, but Brites Sande is a dangerous woman, with a head full of dangerous ideas."

What little gentleness she'd gathered slipped through Yzabel's fisted hands, and very slowly, she turned to face the old man. "And what dangerous ideas might that be?"

Flustered, Dom Domingos shifted on his seat. "Surely you've heard of her disease. Of her pact with the Dark Lord that allows her to command nature. Brites's very presence threatened your place at our Lord's side, and it's a shame it took Dom Vasco's passing for His Majesty to do something about her influence."

If she told him of her own magic, would he accuse her of bargaining with the Devil as well? Keeping the sneer from her features, she asked, "Is that why you wanted to see me? To stomp on Brites's good name?"

"Good name? With the things Dom Vasco and her own son have confessed to me, her name is anything but!" Dom Domingos reached for her hand. She let his bony fingers wrap around hers, parchment-thin skin smooth and slippery. "Your Highness, the sickness and the paganism are only the beginning. Brites's most nefarious plan is yet to unfold."

Yzabel loathed the curiosity that made her ask, "What plan?"

"The…" He leaned in, drawing a sign of the cross

over himself before whispering, "The Enchanted Moura she brought you." She tried to yank her hand, but Dom Domingos's grip, surprisingly tight for a man his age, held her prisoner. "Dom Vasco told me everything before he passed, and Matias corroborated. The king might not believe it, but that girl you have serving you now... she's an Enchanted Moura that Brites has been seeking for years, going so far as to rope in a nun from the São Francisco Convent in Estremoz to help her. As the stories go, to free such a creature requires a bargain, and..." He inhaled sharply as if to prepare himself to speak of hideous things. "I'm afraid she offered *your throne* in return for the Enchanted Moura's power."

Yzabel's mask cracked at the audacity of it all, and she could no longer help the flippant laughter from bubbling in her lips. She couldn't even be angry at Vasco's memory for telling the Chancellor about Fatyan and using Brites as a shield, not after hearing the wild tale he'd spun. A bargain existed, yes, but it was between Yzabel and Faty, and it was without the involvement of the Portuguese throne.

"My princess, this is serious!" Dom Domingos chided, pulling at her hand. "Dom Vasco and I shared the same suspicions and talked about it at great length. This Fatyan is trying to rob you of your place. And someone who looks the way she does would have no trouble convincing the king to annul your betrothal and take her as his sole mistress. If he stays unmarried, it leaves the way free for her children to inherit the throne."

Newfound strength hardened her limbs, and she reclaimed her hand with anger grimacing on her face, hissing, "Fatyan's not interested in that." She'd told Yzabel many times that she valued her freedom too much. That she found men as unappealing as rock. She'd told Dom

Domingos as much when he'd interrogated her about it.

"That's what she tells you—but I've seen her conversing with the king, all batting eyelashes and pretty smiles. And while our king may have many virtues, he has one great weakness. He's young still, prone to the temptations of the flesh, and that one, well…"

He let his words hang in the air, and somewhere deep down inside her, doubt began taking root. Faty had been talking to Denis? When? And had she been truly smiling, or had Dom Domingos misread the situation? Why did wondering twist at her heart and steal her breath?

Willing calm into her body, Yzabel crossed her legs and asked, "And that's different from every other mistress how?"

A question asked softly, yet it had Dom Domingos reel back as if slapped. "It's not. But in this one, you at least have a choice. Your betrothed's soul is at risk as it is, and there are only so many dalliances the Lord can forgive him. Even before you're officially married." A touch on her knee brought a creepy shiver to her leg. "I beg you to take pity on the king. Dismiss that woman and the temptation she brings."

Without an utterance, Yzabel didn't move her eyes from the hand he'd placed upon her knee. He tucked it away with embarrassed apologies, but she was done with him, done listening to his horrible ideas meant to trip her into feeling guilty. Ideas that made the fate of the king's eternal soul all about her when it was only about Denis and Denis alone.

At least now she knew exactly how he'd poisoned Vasco's mind—tall lies and baseless conjecture, born out of the notion that every beautiful woman *had* to be an ambitious temptress who longed to birth kings. After all, what other heights could they possibly aspire to?

"My betrothed is his own man, Dom Domingos, and I do not appreciate you referring to him as an animal that can't think for or control himself," she said. "Neither do I appreciate this malice toward Fatyan, and if you continue spewing it, then I shall invite you to leave."

He opened and closed his mouth before clearing his throat and rising with a nod. He hesitated, swaying on his feet like a branch in the breeze. "One more thing, if I may?"

She looked at him from the corner of her eye. "If you must."

"His Majesty informed me you're no longer fasting." Before she could interrupt and tell him to get out of her sight, he hastily added, "Which I understand, since you will need to give him an heir after you're married. For that, your body needs sustenance. As such, you need to purify your flesh in other ways if you're to remain in the Lord's good graces."

Although he didn't say it out loud, his meaning was clear, and the judgment in his voice throbbed on the scars along her back and around her thigh. Yzabel hadn't worn the cilice since the springs, hadn't brought out the cat o' nine tails for almost as long. Whenever she'd felt the need to, she'd remember Faty's hands chasing the length of welts, asking, *Notice how they tell you to starve and suffer, when God's own son wanted us to love one another? How they tell you every kindness you do is never enough, even though one small act of goodness enriches the soul and the world better than unnecessary pain?*

Dom Domingos accused Brites and Faty of wanting to replace her, when in truth, it was he who wanted someone else on the throne. The conditioning of years finally lifted from her eyes, and Yzabel saw his intentions as clear as daylight; saw how he only liked her because she'd taken everything he'd said about the Lord's teachings without question. Teachings that had left her feeble and pliable, for he sought not death of the body, but of the mind, chipping at her willpower all these years so she'd become a husk of her former self. A wooden doll filled with *his* ideals, and not her own.

And still, the pull to put the cilice back on lingered. The need to use the whip and let the pain overwhelm everything else simmered under her thoughts. There was sound logic behind Faty's words, yes, but... What if she was wrong? What if God *did* want her to suffer for the lies she'd pervaded between herself and Denis?

Yzabel didn't give him the satisfaction to see how much he'd affected her. "I'll think on it," she said without granting him a look. "Have a good evening, Dom Domingos."

Alone, she hugged herself, rocking back and forth on the little bench, the fire's warmth lost to her numb skin. Her head dropped to her lap, and Yzabel didn't know how long she sat that way, curled on herself as terrible feelings hosted a ball in her head.

Faty talking to Denis, waltzing with, *You need to cleanse yourself*, draped in a gown of *You need the pain*.

She found herself moving, kneeling before the commode and sliding open the bottom drawer. Under nightgowns and socks, the stone, pulsing with faint energy. Farther back, against the corner, supple against her fingers, the cat o' nine tails. Her hand closed around the handle, leather strips whispering as she dragged it out —

"Are you looking for something?" Faty asked.

Lucas bounced across the room to come lay his snout under Yzabel's arm, and she dropped the whip to hug her dog instead, burying her face in his neck to hide her blushing guilt. "No, I..." She slammed the drawer shut. "It's nothing."

Two clicks on the table as Faty set the plate of cakes and bowl of bread down. "Then why are you scowling?"

"Dom Domingos came by while you were gone. He..." She wanted to ask her if it was true, if Faty had been talking to Denis behind her back, but the question couldn't make its way past her dry throat or her swollen tongue. To give it voice was to admit she didn't trust Faty, that she didn't believe her when she'd said she wasn't interested in sitting on the throne.

It would be to call her only friend a liar. Her friend, who beheld her with apprehension slanted on her brow and lips. Worry Yzabel refused to question. "He asked me how long it's been since I've mortified my flesh."

Warmth enveloped her back, arms closed around her waist. Faty rested her chin on her shoulder, hugged her tight, tight, *tight*, and whispered, "Don't let his words affect you."

It should be easy to cast Dom Domingos from her mind. Should be easy to remember all the things Fatyan had done for her. Too many to count, especially in this past week, when everything Yzabel did involved Faty in some way. Talking, braiding hair, eating, or simply *being*. While they sieved and crushed herbs for salves, stories flowed between them, two rivers of memories merging into a sea of shared experiences. When she'd begun to yield to despair and sob out of nowhere, when she'd wanted to do nothing but scream, Fatyan had always come, always held her until the raging fits passed, always let Yzabel sink into her and breathe the scent of almonds from her skin.

Faty wouldn't have done those things if she didn't care.

"Come on. I brought more bread for you to practice."

Faty's nose nudged the curve of Yzabel's neck, climbed to her jaw, and she was suspended in that motion, imprisoned in the kiss placed upon her cheek. Every syllable brushed against her skin with a hot whisper; something so small shouldn't leave her short of breath and speedy of pulse, but it did, and she was.

Neither of them moved as the chords of fado winked in Yzabel's ears, wondering if they'd always been meant to meet. That God had made her starve to leave her without options and kept Faty trapped through more than a century so she could guide her into the path she must take. Terrible atrocities and excruciating pain, done in the name of a greater good.

Or was it a symptom of constant proximity? Of friendship? Of something else? When they were like this — which was often over the past three weeks — she found herself remembering their one kiss, done in the name of breaking a curse; found herself remembering how she hadn't *needed* to return it but had done it regardless; then found herself picturing it happening again. Would she still taste cinnamon, and would her mouth still feel as soft as velvet?

It'd be so easy to find out. All she had to do was turn around, to hold Faty's face, lean forward —

Yzabel laced her imagination with wine and set it on fire. This wasn't the time to wade in the miasma of misguided feelings warring in her breast, and it was with bleak resolve that she shed Faty's arms and marched to the table. She took a piece of bread, held it between her fingers. "I'm all that's keeping you here," she muttered, willing the gift into the flower.

"You are." Fingertips trailed fire along Yzabel's left arm to wrap around her hand, winding her so tight she released neither breath nor grip on magic. "But not for the reasons you think."

When she said things like that, with unnecessary touches that always lingered too long, Yzabel was sure Fatyan knew the effect she had on her and did it all on purpose. And therein lay the problem, for if seduction was Faty's plan, then Denis would've been the better target.

Cold shock speared her breast. Yzabel had never opposed his affairs—why would this one be different?

Why *was* it different?

Unable to keep those thoughts from spreading, Yzabel's hold on the gift loosened, letting the magic unspool in tendrils of light. The stem and petals widened and thinned into paper-like pieces that crumbled between her fingers, not to ash but—

"Flour," Fatyan said, catching the white dust in the palm of her hand. Yzabel leaned closer, squinting as she touched the little mound.

Not the slice she'd started with, but it was something.

"You're almost there," encouraged the Moura. "Keep trying."

Yzabel did.

But she still couldn't stop thinking of Fatyan and Denis entwined as man and woman. Neither could she stop the ugly jealousy from festering, or the pain from flaring every time she imagined them.

It wasn't there when she pictured Denis and Aldonza. Why was it there with Faty? Was it because Yzabel thought her a friend? Because Faty was here to help *her*, not Denis?

And why was she so afraid to learn the answers to all these questions?

CHAPTER EIGHTEEN

Persistent Doubt

Morning came again. Afternoon. Evening. Yzabel asked about the prelates, and the king told her they'd found no more evidence yet. A funeral would be held for Vasco and no, she could not attend the service. Not unless Fatyan did a favor for him.

"I can't believe you'd use his funeral for such a self-serving purpose," Yzabel said, fisting the fabric of her skirts. "Have you not a drop of kindness in your heart?"

"I've kindness aplenty—but not for a lying fiancée who'd keep secrets from me. And speaking of *fiancée*..." He looked her over. "You're looking better. At least this whole ordeal hasn't been for nothing."

Lips pursed, Yzabel looked down at her lap. Denis had spoken true—she did look better, and much healthier. In the almost three weeks since the ritual, the blessing worked *for* her rather than *despite* her, and she was recovering her weight twice as fast as a regular person would. Her smiling dimple was deeper on her rounder cheeks, her hair stronger, skin pinker, eyes brighter.

It shouldn't be long until her moon's blood returned, and she had no more excuses to give her betrothed regarding the making of legitimate heirs when the time arrived.

Alone with Faty once more, Yzabel returned to her training with anxious concentration. Sitting on the bed, the bread on her lap turning to roses at a touch. The mounds of flour were getting bigger but using the gift so much and so often was as tiring as running from here to Ulisbuna, driving exhaustion to yawn on her lips, and the weight of iron to her lids.

"It hurts you to be unable to attend Vasco's funeral, does it not?" Fatyan sat beside her at the foot of the bed. "If I go tonight, you will be able to leave these rooms tomorrow. We can—"

"You heard what Denis said about using the baron's preferences. I won't let you denigrate yourself so I can attend Vasco's funeral. He wouldn't want you to, either." She rubbed the sleep from her face. "None of this would be happening if I'd been a dutiful princess, anyway."

"You *are* a dutiful princess," Fatyan amended. "Few in your station would care as much about the commoners as much as you do."

"It's not enough."

Under the silence of the crackling fire, white particles piled on her lap like snowflakes, and so did the frustrations in her head. One by one, they trickled into her thoughts, spilling from her tongue, out her lips. "I can't turn these roses." A rose came undone. "I can't feed the Portuguese." One more. "I can't give this country a prince." Another. "I'm the reason you're not free."

The next rose she grabbed so tight, thorns punctured her flesh—she savored the pain, willed God to take it as payment for her faults. Bitter anguish burned her eyes, soured her throat. "I'm holding your life back."

"I wouldn't have a life if it weren't for you." Fatyan brought Yzabel's hand to her lips, startling her into releasing it.

The strange tightness returned to coil between her legs, and she knew she should take her hand away but couldn't bring herself to do it. Fatyan's touch carried such an exquisite ache it was impossible not to lose herself in its lingering briefness. Her back arched, her chest swelled, awake with a feeling she had no name for—it was painful, sweet, too much, and not enough.

"I could say the same," Yzabel said. "You're as indebted to me as I am to you."

"Then stop saying you're holding me back." Fatyan turned Yzabel's hand palm up, fingertips trailing shivers over the fresh cuts.

Recalling how Fatyan had planted a kiss on the affected area last time Yzabel burned herself with her magic had her light of head and panicked of heart. She hurriedly swept her hand away to grab another rose, clearing her throat as she tried to appear nonchalantly focused. Warm light seeped from her fingers, catching just a bit of the stem at first, then spreading gold into the entire flower.

When she felt she'd poured just enough, Yzabel blinked the sweat away from her eyes, and insides hummed like the plucked string of a lute, vibrating softly as she imagined the flower becoming wheat, flour, bread. She kept her hold firm when the light turned radiant. The rose widened, thinned, and when Yzabel cut off the flow of magic, it splintered into a hundred pieces, soft on the palm of her hand.

Breadcrumbs.

In a trance, Yzabel repeated the process, making another rose, getting more crumb.

The image chained her in miraculous wonder and breathless relief, and it was with wide eyes that she turned to look at Faty, expecting to find her radiant. Yet a furrow marred her brow with something between guilt and concern as she looked over the fragments that were bread, yet not.

Yzabel's smile vacillated. "Faty?"

Green eyes looked at her from under thick lashes. "Hmm?"

Yzabel's mouth dried, the beat of her heart heavy as if it were made of steel instead of flesh. "Is your curse gone?"

A shake of her head. "No. The stone's still tugging at me because *crumb* isn't exactly *bread*. But…" Faty put her hands to her face, pensive lines burrowing deeper on her forehead.

"But what?"

It started with imperceptible shifts — wider nostrils, smaller mouth, a sharper brow — then the stark ones. One moment, it was Faty she was staring at; the next, a stranger with a head of flaxen hair and a gaze of murky brown.

Breath trapped, Yzabel reached for Faty, tracing the rounder cheekbones, the bow of thin lips. Had she not witnessed the transformation, she wouldn't have been able to tell who lay under the pale skin.

"My blessing returned," Fatyan whispered against Yzabel's fingertips — even her voice was different, higher in pitch, less melodic in tone. "Baba used to call me his little chameleon because I could blend into any surroundings. That was before he hated me enough that he had his Benzedor curse me." A lingering sigh filled the air between them. "Sometimes, Matias reminds me of him."

Faty had never told her what it was that had turned her father's opinion on her, and Yzabel had no heart to ask. Whenever the Moura came close to speaking of it, her lips would twist, and her eyes would mist — pain, she had assumed. She wouldn't waste this chance to find out more, and so she gently asked, "Of your father?"

"No. Of Benzedor Yusef. My sahar teacher." Faty squinted at nowhere in particular. "It's strange, because our Benzedores wore veils that left only their eyes visible, and I never really saw his face. But Matias looks at me the same way Yusef did. Talks in the same way, too. It's just a similarity, but it's enough to trigger all those bad memories, and those bad memories trigger the sahar." A shudder racked her shoulders, and she shrugged it off with a sigh and a shake of her head. "Yusef's long dead, and so is Baba. Neither can force me to do anything I don't want to."

The way she said it, with bitterness dripping from her lips, made Yzabel wonder if Faty had used her powers to do something so terrible she dared not voice it. The nefarious obsessions in her brain drove her to take a step back, suspicion building ugly clouds over her head. She dumped the crumbs that had accumulated in her skirts onto the dinner tray Fatyan had yet to take back to the kitchens.

"Did they make you become other people?"

Fatyan met her eyes as she gave a hesitant, slow nod. "Remember when Denis asked if I was the Moura named Salúquia?"

She did, but with so much happening, it had slipped her mind to ask. Now that Faty brought it back up again, however, the pieces fit. "The marriage to Bráfama. It wasn't *you* who was supposed to marry him."

The saddest glint shone in Fatyan's eyes. "Sal was my best friend. And when she died with a marriage contract to fulfill, Baba thought to use me to ensure it went through. We needed Bráfama's forces to defend Al-Manijah, and if I had to be someone else for that to happen, Baba saw no problem with it."

Yzabel swallowed the lump in her throat. So much

sorrow wrapped around Faty, and though Yzabel wanted to cut the Moura free, her thoughts seemed to be stuck on the fact Faty had been made to take another's shape in order to go through an arranged marriage.

Was this what Vasco had been worried about? The doubt that had driven him to turn against Brites, and ended up taking his life instead?

With a deep breath, she asked, "Could you become me?"

"I could." Fatyan's face and skin changed to Yzabel's, and it was like looking at a mirror image that had a will of its own. It crossed the space between them, leaned forward to whisper in her ear, "I could become Denis, even."

When she stepped back, she *was* Denis, with his deep-set eyes and severe brow, his wide shoulders and sparse beard, assailing Yzabel with so many conflicting emotions she couldn't make sense of her own thoughts.

She picked up a lock of wavy hair, the exact same shade of reddish brown as her betrothed's. Faty's gift could be used for so many purposes, and if she wanted to, she could replace anyone she wished. A princess. A king.

"But I don't want to become him. Or you." A stubby hand brushed Yzabel's cheek in a way Denis's never had. "And I would never use my gift to harm you, Yza."

She believed it. She doubted it. And hearing the nickname Fatyan had given her in Denis's voice, through his lips, was a dichotomy she couldn't wrap her head around, and neither could she understand the feelings tugging at her stomach. It was Denis, but it was also Fatyan. One was the person she was supposed to love, who she was supposed to want. The other…

Would her lips taste the same? Would her touch awaken light in Yzabel's breast, or simply leave her lukewarm? Under the linen nightdress, was there a new appendage between the legs, and why did the possibility make her shudder as if hit with unpleasant cold?

Why did it feel like death would take her if she didn't find out?

It hit her that this was the very first time she *wanted* to kiss her betrothed, and the reason was because she knew it was Fatyan under a mask. She didn't know what it meant, and neither would she find out, because Fatyan had no reason to stay, and if she wanted to leave, Yzabel would have to let her go.

Tears returned to her eyes, raining torment on a moment that should've been of joy.

The hair between Yzabel's fingers flattened and elongated, darkening to the black of night, and Faty became herself again. It was her arms that hugged Yzabel close, her voice that asked, "Yza, what's wrong?"

"I-I'm s-s-sorry." Yzabel couldn't help but think that their embraces would soon come to an end. "I'm so thankful, and yet..." She pulled away to look at Fatyan's face, the curve of her lips fickle. "You're still not free."

"Neither are you."

Yzabel shook her head. "I never was. My privilege is my cage, and one I cannot break. Or want to. I must shoulder my burdens, Faty. But you..." She wiped her eyes with a shaking finger before looking at Faty again. "You can be free for the both of us."

Hurt flashed across the Moura's face. "Do you want me gone that badly?"

"No! That's not it at all," Yzabel hurried to correct the misconception—but how could she explain that she didn't want her only friend to be as trapped as she was? "I just... I want you to have a choice."

"Then I choose to stay. With you."

No hesitation in her voice, no doubt in those searching eyes. The paranoia stormed back into Yzabel, and there it was again, the vivid image of Denis and Fatyan together, locked in passion, whispering promises of love to each other.

She didn't have the courage to look Faty's way anymore. "Why would you want a life of servitude when you can have true freedom?"

"Why would I want true freedom if taking it means I can't stay here to help you?" Two fingers swept across Yzabel's jaw, persuading the rest of her face to follow. "We both know making bread out of flowers is but one step in your plan to feed the people."

Several times during the week, they'd talked about what Yzabel would do with her blessing once she controlled it, and had come to two realizations. First, no one could know she was secretly feeding people; second, Denis could not notice Yzabel's absence.

As if reading her mind, Fatyan said, "If I'm here to take your place when you're gone, your betrothed will never find out."

And if he came by during that time bearing thoughts of heirs, it'd be Fatyan he'd lie with. Fatyan who'd bear his seed, his touch, his needs—

Unable to keep wondering, she asked, briskly, "Is it because of him?"

Fatyan blinked up at her. "Him who?"

"Denis." She held her hand against the twisted pain in her chest. "I...I am aware that I've asked a lot—too much— of you. If you want to stay because you feel compelled to bed him, I will not hold it against you. I know some women have those needs, even if I don't."

A long pause withered in the air.

"Why is it so hard to believe I want to stay for you?" The susurrus of a question barely heard over the drumming of Yzabel's heart.

She had to get away, put space between them so she could think without her body urging her to lean forward, to wrap herself around Faty and breathe in her scent. Her feet moved, skirting around the Moura. "Why would you?" Yzabel said.

Warmth caught her fingers as she passed by. "There's not an arrátel of malice in your bones, no trace of selfishness in your actions — to a fault, I might add." Yzabel couldn't move between the polarizing desires warring inside her, couldn't help but let Fatyan embrace her from behind, or take Faty's hand away when she placed it over her thundering heart. "I've seen this," she whispered into Yzabel's ear as her other arm tightened around her waist. "And it was filled with light and goodness. Of all the people who found me, you were the only one I *wanted* to leave with, the only one I could see myself staying with. And I will, for as long as you want me."

Words that should've been water to her parched throat were a gag of regret. Fatyan wouldn't be saying them if she saw Yzabel's heart now, with its ugly jealousy and unwarranted suspicions. "I'm not that good."

A long, exasperated sigh heated the curve of her neck. "Learn to take a compliment."

"I know how to take one when it's deserved," Yzabel countered.

"You really don't." Fatyan chuckled before releasing her. "It's endearing, until it becomes annoying."

"And you still want to stay and help me." She hugged herself against the cold of Faty's absence, wishing it would mitigate the void in her every pore as she watched the

Moura open the bed and settle under the covers.

"Your plan to deliver bread won't work unless someone stays behind to cover for you," Fatyan pointed out, patting the mattress next to her, a siren's song that lured Yzabel into the sheets with her and their little dance of spooning for warmth. "What happens once you're married and Denis comes to your rooms at night to find you gone?"

"He spends most nights with his mistresses anyway," Yzabel muttered, closing her eyes to better savor the pleasant shivers Fatyan trailed along her arm. "All I'd have to do is go to him first in the nights he does not."

"Is that something you think you can do?"

She buried her head deeper into the pillow. "It's something I must do. Being with Denis in that way is as much my duty as helping the poor."

"But you don't love him like that."

"Love isn't a steady foundation to build a marriage on anyway." Yzabel swallowed the quiver in her throat. "In a way, I'm glad there's no passion to cloud our relationship. Better for the country that volatile emotions aren't sitting on the throne along with the king and queen. And as much as the prospect of lying under Denis terrifies me, I can endure that if it means bringing stability to our rule."

"That's…" Fatyan sighed. "That's so sad. Someone as kind as you deserves happiness, and it hurts to see you resigned to never having it."

Yzabel shrugged. "It's not anything many women haven't gone through before. Love is a small price to pay for a lasting marriage and just ruling."

"And why must you pay it alone?" The mattress shifted as Fatyan propped herself up on one elbow. "Your betrothed has lovers aplenty. Why can't you?"

The snort was out of her nose before she could help

it. "And risk a bastard? The law isn't as lenient on women as it is on men when it comes to that. Even then, I…" A furrow came upon her brow as she thought back on all her encounters with supposedly handsome men. That every woman she'd come across swooned and sighed over Denis, and all Yzabel could nurture for him was a warm buzz of friendship, which had dwindled to tepid tolerance over the past three weeks.

She turned to lie on her back, her sight full of Fatyan's firelit features. "I've never felt the need to be with any man. I just can't fathom how shoving a rod of meat inside me can be anything but painful."

Fatyan swept the hair away from Yzabel's face, so gently it was as if she ran a brush dipped in starlight. Under the shower of easy sparks, slumber began to tug at her conscience, and she was almost out when Faty said, "It doesn't have to be."

Yzabel snapped her eyes back open, suddenly alert, mind reeling.

CHAPTER NINETEEN

Rift

*I*t *doesn't have to be painful.*

"How would you know?" Yzabel said. "You told me you'd never been with a man."

"I didn't. Didn't have to." The air became heavier, charged with danger and allure, and so did her hand where it rested on Yzabel's hip. "I spent a lot of time alone, and without anything else to do, you're bound to explore. And the one thing I could explore besides my sahar was my body. As much as they want us to believe otherwise, we don't even need a man to have pleasure."

The question of how scratched the back of Yzabel's throat, but only shallow breaths passed her lips. A caress on Yzabel's chest, barely there—Faty's bosom, so close, and she had to grab at the sheets to keep her hands from closing on it, to keep herself from finally knowing the feel of her friend's breasts.

The aching heat built low in her belly, her legs closing on their own to suffocate it as Fatyan leaned in. Yzabel licked the warm breath tingling along her lips. A distant part of her mind told her she was supposed to say something, but she couldn't remember what they'd been talking about— Faty's closeness was all there was, all she could think about.

"Yza?" Fatyan's tender call, spoken right over Yzabel's nose.

"Yes?" her whispered answer.

Faty's free hand moved, trailing languid fire along Yzabel's chest, her collarbone. "Do you want to know?"

Her insides melted, and a strange feeling of wetness built between her thighs, making her squirm with the need for *something*. Fatyan held her at the cusp of expectation, and in her hands, Yzabel felt like a twisted rope, aching for Faty to untie her and set every knot loose.

"You'll teach me?" The question came out breathless. She couldn't tear her gaze from Faty's cherry lips, or her fingers from twirling a lock of Faty's silky hair around them.

A shift. A caress of temptation along Yzabel's jaw. "I could. What else are friends for?"

Faty sank lower, pressing them together. Skin sizzled where their bodies met behind thin chemises, and she realized she'd arched her back to press them closer still.

"This feels different." It was something else, but what was *something else* when the two parties were women? What was the tug between them, if not that?

Fatyan palmed one of Yzabel's cheeks and gave the opposite one a kiss. "What does it feel like, then?"

Sweet pressure flickered in her chest, her lungs, devouring every other one of Yzabel's thoughts until she lived solely to pursue its name. "I don't know."

The shadow of Fatyan's lips dipped to find the shell of Yzabel's ear, drawing a delicious whimper. "I do."

A moment flooded in unspoken promises and secret knowledge, and like with water, Yzabel drowned in it, and she would die if she did not breathe in an answer. "How?"

"Because I spent more than a century trying to forget it." The tip of Fatyan's sharp nose bumped Yzabel's broad one, and she left her mouth hovering over hers, every syllable a fleeting stroke of soft lips. "And now I remember."

The green in Faty's eyes gave way to dilating black before disappearing between lowering lids and long lashes. Her weight shifted as she planted a kiss on Yzabel's temple. Another on her nose. Her cheekbone. Each fed the agonizing flame sputtering in her gut, bringing it higher, higher—

A tentative brush of lips on lips that lasted forever and then not at all, and yet it stole everything away. Her breath, her words, her sense. Confusion locked her in place, and Fatyan pulled away, blushing, hand to her lips, like she couldn't believe what she'd done.

"I'm sorry. I shouldn't have—"

Yzabel's heart pounded once, twice, heavy with need, and her lips hungered for another taste, another kiss. Every moment she hung in that breathy stillness stretched into a small eternity, and when Yzabel tilted her chin up and captured Faty's mouth in hers, the quietude unraveled along with everything else.

A gasp opened Yzabel's mouth, letting in a sleek, slow caress of a tongue and the taste of cinnamon. Her body came alight, and it was not unlike being able to eat after starving for so long. This was another part of her she'd neglected, a type of affection she'd never feasted upon, and now that she had, she couldn't keep herself from seeking another taste, from devouring every morsel.

Yzabel cradled the back of Faty's head, fingers lost in luscious hair while the rest of her got lost in everything else.

A hand slipped under the hem of her nightshirt, hiking up the fabric as it skimmed the curve of her waist to come to a splay on her ribs, thumb resting right under the small curve of her breast.

Her legs lost their strength and fell open, letting one of Fatyan's slip between them. The tightness at her center pulsed, and every inch of her flesh throbbed for more. A hot, shallow breath left her lips when Faty took hers away.

All so new. So strange. So wonderful.

Fatyan's mouth came back to hers, rough and soft, demanding and giving. Yzabel moaned, needing more of that taste, more of that feeling as she swallowed the chuckle spilling from Faty's lips.

"Oh, Yza…" The stars of kisses on her jaw, behind her ear, goose bumps in their wake. "I waited so long for you."

Yzabel still didn't know what she meant by that, what exactly it was that she had that Faty hadn't seen in anyone else—but she was so close to finding out, so close to unwinding the growing frustration that followed Fatyan's touch like a moth did to a flame.

Faty's hand traveled lower, while she ate the gasp right out of her lips before whispering, "Yza, I love you."

Love.

So that's what it was.

Another sharp flare of pleasure froze Yzabel in a whimper, and the four letters of that word swam behind her closed eyes. Faty swirled her tongue around the peak of a nipple, her finger slid to tease the growing tightness between Yzabel's thighs, lifting the buildup to new heights.

A violent jolt of rapture opened her eyes, roused her from the madness that was this waking dream of carnal pleasures. The sight of Faty's lips on her gave her a shiver of pleasure and a shudder of horror.

Women shouldn't want other women to touch them like this, shouldn't come apart under another woman's touch, shouldn't be curious as to what awaited her at the end of whatever it was that Faty was doing to her.

Panic shallow in her breaths, she sat up, scrambling out from under Faty's warm weight and hating the empty ache that blossomed in her lower parts, the ache that told her to return, to beg for more of that ecstasy, to let herself return to the labyrinth of Fatyan's caresses and get lost in it again.

She recalled the talk her mother had given her before the wedding. How, even if it hurt, it was a woman's duty to lie there and wait for the king to fill her with his seed. An empty receptacle whose only purpose was to be filled with babies.

She'd heard it could be different, too. Overheard the maids and her ladies-in-waiting confess wicked things in hushed tones, caught Aldonza talking about her nights with the Portuguese king. Catching those glimpses of conversation always made Yzabel wonder if there was something *wrong* with her. Why was she so uninterested in sharing a bed with Denis, or any other man? Why did the thought of him hovering over her fill her with such fear instead of wanting, or at least, curiosity? Why had she felt nothing but lukewarm when she'd pressed her lips to his, whereas with Faty it'd been like coming up for air after being underwater too long?

They'd said she'd lust when she grew up, or when she met her future husband, but such emotions had never visited upon her, not even upon meeting the man she'd share her life with. And yet…the women had been right. Yzabel realized now that she *did* lust. Only it wasn't for the person she was supposed to.

She thought God had sent Faty to help her, and He had—but the Devil always lurked in every one of God's boons, and she'd succumbed to the temptation as easily as men did. The rush of heat that invariably blossomed when Fatyan touched her, when she smiled, when she hugged her, when she looked at her—when she was simply *there*, in Yzabel's vicinity. The flips of her stomach, the lightness of her breath, the feeling that her chest was about to burst. She'd thought it friendship, and although *friendship* was part of it, she realized now there was something else in the mix as well.

Something wrong. Something that once known, she would never be able to forget.

"This can't be," she breathed.

"Yza?" a confused call, spoken with concern. Movement shifted the mattress as Faty crawled toward her.

Before she could touch her again, Yzabel rushed to leave the bed, to put as much distance between them as she was able. "This can't be," she exclaimed again, this time through tears and terrible shame. *Love* like this couldn't happen between two women, which meant whatever was happening between her and Fatyan was wrong. Unnatural. A sin.

Fatyan recoiled, her look of hurt and fear scratching at Yzabel's heart. "What's wrong about love?" Faty said.

"You don't love me! You can't. It's against natural law—"

"Then why did you kiss me back?" Faty came to stand before her, and Yzabel turned her eyes away, shut them tightly to keep herself from glimpsing the flesh that had been under her hands moments ago, trying to forget how soft it'd been, how warm, how perfectly it had fit against hers. Her lips could still taste the cinnamon, and the scent of almonds lingered on her nostrils still. "Why didn't you ask me to stop then?"

"I don't know. I…" Yzabel shook her head, curled into herself and against the wall at her back. Her head drowned in opposing thoughts, flashing her images of Denis, of Fatyan, of herself, all the ugliness she'd bottled over the last week spilling its poison into her tongue.

Fatyan seized her uncertainty to reach for her again, to say, "No, listen —"

She dodged the hand coming toward her shoulder, afraid that contact would bring back the lustful chaos from the bed. "Don't touch me!"

Faty stepped back with a grimace. "Yza, please —"

There was no stopping the hideous accusations from falling out. "You're trying to take me away from the Lord's grace, aren't you? Trying to stain my soul with unforgivable sins, using His blessing to turn me to the Devil's ways."

She waited for Fatyan to contest her, to say she'd read things wrong somehow. But when she dared to steal a glance, there was only sorrow and hurt. The urge to apologize, to take away those lines of pain from Faty's face, jumped to the tip of her tongue, and the need to return to Faty's embrace began to build up again.

"I should've known you'd be just like Baba," Fatyan said. "Just like any ignorant fanatic who picks and chooses the parts of the Bible that fit their biases and excuse their crimes." An angry flare of her nostrils. "Do you want to throw me out a window, too?"

That's why she'd never talked about the real reason she'd been cursed — her father had caught her with another girl. And even though Yzabel wanted to deny it, to say she'd never hurt Faty, to go back into her arms and kiss the sadness away, she couldn't free herself from the spell that kept her immobile.

Her silence was the worst of choices, implying an agreement she didn't mean.

Fatyan snorted. "I was a fool to hope I could be free with you."

Words that struck like thunder, final and deadly.

Words she could try to undo, and yet no sound formed in Yzabel's throat, no correction was given voice. In her tearful, shameful silence, a gust of wind kicked around the space between them, and when she lifted her watery sight, it was to find Fatyan at the center of the turmoil, the glow of her skin washing them in a flash of light. As if made of thousands of pebbles, parts of her began to flake off in a landslide, a solid mountain crumbling under the force of broken promises.

Under Yzabel's feet, the floor rumbled and tilted. The bottom drawer of the commode rattled ominously before falling open with a *pop*, and there, nestled amid the nightgowns, the stone radiating the burning energy of magic, demanded Faty's return.

Her vow to give Faty the liberty to be herself had freed the Moura of the stone, and now, her ugly accusations were putting the Moura back. Her voice came unshackled then, as did her limbs. Mouth, desperately crying, "Don't go!" Hands reaching for a face, seeking, finding—

Her fingers slipped right through, eons too late. The arms that had wrapped around Yzabel, the eyes that had *seen* her, the lips that had kissed her, dissolved to specks of light and dust. All was still in loud silence as the cloud that was Faty lingered around her until the breeze stirred again.

In a current of sparkling powder, the mist disappeared into the stone, forever to stay out of Yzabel's reach.

Part II

Miracles

CHAPTER TWENTY

Denial

Yzabel did not understand her wretched heart that bled for Faty, or her traitorous body, where the ghost of Faty's touch remained, haunting her with those terrible sensations of pleasure even after the Moura had gone. As though the ground vanished from under her, Yzabel sunk to the floor with a hand to her rushing heart and tried to make sense of everything that had happened.

The kisses. The touches. The words.

Faty, conceding defeat. Faty, returning to the stone, where Yzabel could never find her. She'd had her one chance and she'd destroyed it in a fit of offensive rage.

Yzabel ran her hands across her face, tangled her fingers in her hair and tugged, as if pulling on her curls would rip away those unholy memories and sensations from her mind. They remained, their sinful roots strong, and she couldn't—

A sobbing scream erupted from her lips. She was made of anguish, filled with sin, her body unwashed with impurity. Yzabel bit into the soft flesh of her hand, hoping the pain would rip Fatyan from her mind, but she was there even as she tasted blood.

The sting of her teeth retreated, and there it was again,

the sweet agony that shouldn't exist, the temptation to surrender. Emotions Yzabel should revile but couldn't bring herself to.

She wrenched herself away as her mind raced, still trying to process, to understand. Why had she liked what Faty had done to her, why had she indulged when she should've instantly put a stop to it? Why was heat returning to her lower parts, along with that odd wetness that had made it so easy for Faty to—

Yzabel didn't know what was worse—that she loved someone who wasn't her betrothed, or that the person she loved was a woman.

"It's wrong, it's wrong, it's wrong." Wailing her litany of regret, Yzabel's feet scrambled across the floor until she reached the commode, searching for the whip.

She'd stopped mortifying her flesh at Fatyan's request, stopped atoning for the sins she couldn't confess. Weakness exploited by this unholy lust, by these untoward cravings. She wanted to blame them all on the magic, that this had happened because she'd invited the Devil's forces into her rooms, let them cradle her to sleep in bed.

But that couldn't be; her magic was God-given, and she finally could use it to the people's benefit. It was everything that had come along with it that had been the problem.

Fatyan, staying with her, lying for her—Yzabel could've put a stop to that. She could've put some distance between them, kept things cordial, ripped the roots of this terrible attraction before they even bloomed. Kept herself from enjoying their time together instead of seeing it for the trap that it was.

It'd be so easy to cast blame on Fatyan, but that would be to deny her own faults and compliance. It'd be to deny that she *had* hungered for Fatyan's kiss, for her touch, for her *love*, that she'd made Yzabel's insides spark with careless lust. But Faty had been alone and trapped for so long. Her declaration must've been nothing but despair, nothing but the need to keep the one attachment she had to the current world. Fatyan did not love Yzabel, not truly; her affection was born of desperation and solitude and kindness she hadn't expected.

Her fingers ran across the hard, cold handle, stretched the supple leather tails.

The harsh truth was that there was no one else to blame for Yzabel's sins.

She held the whip tighter and immediately brought it down over her shoulder, breaking flesh. A line of blood trickled down her back, pain flared and faded.

Not enough.

"Lord, please forgive me," she said. "Please cleanse me. Please," she told herself with another blow, wincing when it connected, then treasuring the blossoming pain, for when there was pain, there was no Fatyan.

But she came back, between blows, between tears, between sobs, between gasps of air and bursts of agony. Vaguely, Yzabel was aware of the noise stopping, the sound of the lash echoing alone in the night. Her blows grew weaker, the pain so intense it blackened the edges of her blurry sight.

The whip fell from her tired hands; every little movement became excruciating, pulling at her raw back. Blood painted the carpet red, and Yzabel let it spread along with the hurt, let it smother her in its cruel embrace. She welcomed the agony, welcomed the cold hard floor beneath the rug as she lay down on it, barely hearing the door open, or Denis's scream—she only noticed he was there when his boot was in front of her eyes.

Her betrothed.

She'd betrayed him, betrayed her promises to him. He'd been patient and kind, and she'd rewarded him with nothing but treachery and deceit.

"Yzabel…Yzabel, what have you done?" Gentle arms gathered her up, carried her to the bed.

"How else will the Lord forgive me for my transgressions?" She looked at him through wet lashes and aching eyes. "I lied to you. I betrayed you."

Surely, he could see her shame, read her sins on the lines of her back, hear the regret in her voice—

He turned around, and she thought he'd leave as his footsteps faded. But after some rummaging, Denis returned with the emergency box and sat next to her. She hissed as he began to peel the shreds of nightgown from her wounds, his fingers so tender, his face so worried.

"I'm sorry."

His apology crushed whatever was left of her heart, brought new tears to simmer behind her eyes.

"All you wanted was to help. I should've listened to you instead of demanding you forsake something that matters." The cold sting of salve mingled with the heat of his hands as he spread it across her wounds. "I've released Brites from the dungeons; she doesn't deserve to lose her life when she's not to blame for Vasco's murder. She'll be following the Court's caravan back to her home in Estremoz—but you must understand, I cannot invite her to be in your employ again."

He was trying to make things better; it made her feel worse. Denis *did* care about her, and her opinions, her happiness. So long as Brites came out unharmed, she couldn't complain—at least she'd still be able to visit her former maid.

Yzabel curled into herself further. God had given her everything, and instead of accepting His gifts, she'd acted the petulant child, made herself believe her life fraught with curses and a betrothed who didn't want her. All those nights she'd been relieved to see him spend with other girls, she should've been trying to make things better with him.

She should've been trying to love him as God had ordained, instead of letting Faty lure her into sin.

"Is this… Has your maid finally told you she did what I asked?"

She had? But how? When? Why?

The conversations Dom Domingos had witnessed between Faty and Denis. The increased absences from the room. It had all been there, and she'd refused to read what was so plainly written.

Yzabel buried her head on the pillow. She couldn't think of Fatyan, for to think of Fatyan would be to remember this night, and all those before.

His hand pressed on the small of her back, thumb brushing the salve's soothing coolness on another open wound. "Is that why you did this? Because you think I made your friend do horrible things?"

"No."

The truth, and yet, Denis didn't buy it. "I *did* want her to befriend the baron, but I never intended her to go through with anything. You assumed I did, and I was so angry I never corrected it."

Her and Fatyan's weeks of isolation could've been over in a day. If she'd just asked Denis what he'd meant, if she hadn't presumed the worst about the man who'd be her husband—

"I'm not sure how she did it, but she had results. She found Vasco's family rings hidden in the baron's belongings and says he keeps Vasco's dagger on his person. She also found where *all* the prelates hide their profits. It was written here…" A rustle of fabric, and a shoddy book appeared next to her head. "The baron had it hidden among his things."

Yzabel read the fuzzy letters out loud, "*Recipes of Além-Tejo*. A cookbook?"

"With terrible poetry written on every page." He closed the jar of salve. "Poetry that matches the one we found in the steward's books—at least, verses related to the Olhapim. The Steward and the Captain had the other two." A brief, concerned pause. "Can you sit up?"

She did, the remnants of the nightshirt sliding down her body, and she embraced the pain that came with the simple movement, staying still as Denis wrapped a linen strip around her torso. His fingers brushed the same places Fatyan's had, but they evoked no spark in her skin or a flutter in her depths.

Even now, when she lay bare and vulnerable before her caring betrothed—a betrothed who hadn't seen her naked until now—she couldn't summon a drop of desire. She told herself it was because the pain drowned out everything else, but there had been pain with the cilice, too, a pain she remembered vividly. Fatyan trailing one finger over it, the tingle of pleasure following its aching path.

"Where was the hiding place?" Yzabel found herself asking in a tiny, tight croak.

"The tower—the one where they said the Moura Salúquia jumped from. There was a hidden trapdoor at the bottom, leading to a stone cellar full of barrels of wine and bags of grain. Pouches of spices, jars of olives, silver, and gold. The theft from the people, it seems, goes back since the Reconquista." His attention flitted around the chamber. "Where *is* your maid?"

Yzabel's guilty gaze fell on the commode's open bottom drawer, on the gray stone humming with unseen power. Faint, the scent of almonds tickled her nose, and she wondered if Faty was still awake or gone back to sleep. If she was screaming inside that rock, or if she lay still and shattered, if she boiled with hatred for Yzabel, or if she trembled with regret.

Whatever she might be doing, Fatyan was gone.

Gone.

Disappeared forever, and the last Yzabel would remember was how she'd rejected her. The look on her face lined with disbelief and colored with hurt. Willing to return to a prison in order to never have to see Yzabel again.

For the best. It was for the best.

"She left my service last night," she managed to say.

Denis's motions stilled, but her present condition answered any other questions he might have. "That doesn't surprise me. Not everyone has the stomach for your sanctimonious spectacles." He neatly tied the strip under her arm, placed a hand on her shoulder. "You can't do this to yourself, Yzabel. This country needs you strong, and not—"

"Bleeding and starving. I know," she completed. "I'll… I'll try to be better." Allowing herself a final sniffle, she tilted her head back to keep yet more tears from reaching her eyes and forced herself to bring reassurance to her false smile. "Thank you for freeing Brites."

When Denis left the bed, he held out a hand. She took it.

. . .

Vasco's funeral took place in the Carmo Church, the entire court clad in black and sitting in silence while Father Paulo spoke his sermon.

The Church, once Yzabel's favorite sanctuary, now sent an anxious jitter to her legs and fingers. The somber air fell heavy in her lungs, and although she tried to catch Dom Domingos's words, they arrived as nothing but distant echoes. She was afraid to behold Christ upon the cross and see him look away, afraid to look at the Virgin Mary to see her cry blood, afraid of the statues of Saints and the paintings of the scripture. Thus, she focused on what she could, the closed empty casket, arrangements of purple wild saffron, hortensias of pink and blue, and pansies of yellow, black, and red, laid around and over the wooden bed.

Vasco had died because she'd hidden things from her fiancé. Another tragedy of her own doing, one she could never voice to anyone other than the people who'd witnessed it.

Blood began to ooze down her back, and she sunk against Denis, hiding her face in the crook of his arm as they followed the casket across the narrow streets until it was laid to rest on a cemetery of marble graves and mausoleums.

On their way back to the castle, a shiver tittered on Yzabel's spine, lifted the hairs on her arms and the back of her neck. The scent of almonds tickled her nose, the magic inside her rising to its call, halting her feet, spinning them around. A wave of ink-black hair, the flash of a hand the color of dark copper in the corner of her eye.

Wishful thinking. Trickery of the mind. Faty couldn't be among the throng behind them—she was back in Yzabel's rooms, inside the stone tucked away in the commode. All alone, as she'd been for over a century. Her thoughts spun and spun, back to Faty in the mist, waiting, and Yzabel had to press on the cilice so the stab of pain would drown them out.

Fatyan was pain.

Pain was Fatyan.

Perhaps once she went through enough of it, her head would associate the Moura with torture and not desire.

CHAPTER TWENTY-ONE

Placebo

Next to Denis on his throne, Yzabel sat in black furs and a black dress. Though she didn't wear the queen's crown yet, he'd insisted she be there as if she did, and though her face was hollow and dark circles surrounded her sunken eyes, her expression was unwavering, her spine straight. Inside her, the magic was a swirling storm of white, raging in tandem with her wild emotions. At her feet, Lucas lay with his ears perked, alert to the nervous atmosphere; behind them, the Guarda Real stood to attention, Matias among their number.

The torches on the walls and the fireplace to the left had been lit, the cackling of flames lost to the howling winds outside. Yzabel kept her hand in Denis's, giving an image of silent unity as the gentry filed in, first in trickles, then in pours. When the room was packed to the brim with nerves and rumors, Denis stood and cleared his throat.

"Ladies and gentlemen of the Court, I bid you good evening," he began. "It's no secret I've brought us here to conduct investigations on this village's governance. Today, our efforts finally came to fruition."

Denis motioned to her. "It was Princess Yzabel who first noticed something amiss in Steward Mendonza's accounts. Messages that once decoded, detailed just how much of each harvest had been pocketed by the people I've trusted with these lands." His scowling eyes roamed the crowd from one side to another. "My father and some kings before me ruled the nobility with a light hand and let the clergy enrich at the cost of the country. But I am not that sort of king, and I will not tolerate unjust behavior."

A hubbub rose from the gentry, whispers growing louder until Denis screamed, "Silence! Ramalho"—he turned to the Grand Prior—"arrest Baron de Seabra, Steward Mendonza, Bishop Carvalho, and Captain Mendes."

Denis's guards moved to pluck the men from the crowd, throwing the throne room into chaos. Matias tackled the steward as he tried to escape through the back; the captain drew his sword, screamed for his men to aid him—none did, and he was knocked down with the pommel of a sword to the back of his head; the Bishop was under the Grand Prior's grasp, and the baron…

"You Aragonese cow!" He dashed toward her, a knife glinting in his hand. Yzabel froze, and the baron took two steps before her mastiff jumped him, sharp teeth sinking into his arm, cutting flesh to ribbons. Lucas yanked until the knife clattered harmlessly on the floor. The man toppled soon after, leaving his wife and daughter screaming from the stands and blood flowing across the stone floor.

The four men were brought to their knees before Denis, all silent save for the baron, who cried and whimpered as he clutched at his arm—Yzabel doubted it could be saved, even if her betrothed didn't sentence the four of them to death.

Denis's footsteps echoed above the whispers. He picked up the knife de Seabra had used and slowly made his way back to the line of men, hand closing around the baron's scalp. A strong tug pulled de Seabra up, exposed his throat. "Where did you get this dagger?"

"It's mine, Your Majesty."

"Is it? Then why do I recognize the engraving?" With a flip of the wrist, he held the blade in front of the baron's eyes. "I sent this dagger to Vasco as a gift for negotiating my marriage contract. My marriage to the woman you just insulted. Crassly, I might add. Yzabel."

She shifted on her seat, straightened her spine. "Yes, my king?"

"This man tried to do you a grave injury. His possession of the dagger proves he is responsible for Vasco's death." He slipped the knife under the baron's throat before meeting her eyes. "His fate is yours to decide."

Her gaze flitted to the other man, whose paling skin shone with sweat. He held his mangled arm to his chest, the black sleeve of his surcoat ripped open to reveal the gnarly wound, and his eyes fluttered in a struggle for consciousness. Matias stood behind him, and although his expression was serious, Yzabel could swear she saw a mysterious glint in his eye that she did not know how to interpret. Only that it unnerved her.

Lucas pressed his snout against her leg, and she scratched the top of his head, behind the ears. De Seabra *had* tried to come for her, and if it hadn't been for the dog, he would've hurt someone. He had a soul blackened with ill-intent, diseased with egoism; he had abused his power for his own gain, kicked the downtrodden further into starvation and disease. At her word, his evil would be cut at the root, never to plague the world again.

But no matter how hard she tried, she couldn't summon the words of death. Jesus had forgiven those who'd put him on the cross, had urged his followers to love and forgive, for no sinner was without redemption. And although the baron might be guilty of the crimes concerning this town, he was not guilty of killing Vasco. Denis used Vasco's dagger as proof, but Yzabel knew better, even if she didn't understand *how* the baron had come to possess it. Had Fatyan done that, too, when she'd been helping Denis behind Yzabel's back?

"Let him live," she said. "Strip them of title and rank and make them live among the people they stole from. Let them choose between seeking redemption or damnation."

A buzz of surprise traveled the room. Yzabel looked to no one but her betrothed, and the slight frown he gave her a silent question of "are you sure?" At her nod, he released the baron, who'd since passed out and hit the floor with a heavy thump.

"Dom Domingos, take note of this decree," Denis said as he made his way back to the throne. "I, Dom Denis by the grace of God King of Portugal and the Algarves, revoke all rights to explore land from the prelates in Terra da Moura. From this moment on, such rights will be given to the people working them."

The rest of the prelates from Terra da Moura raised objections from their places among the crowd. Denis muzzled them with an effective, commanding shout. "You might not have perpetrated this deceit, but you are complicit in your silence. I do not for one second believe that you were not aware."

The scribbling of a quill on parchment. "Is that all, Your Majesty?" Dom Domingos asked from his scribe stand at their right.

"Yes. I suggest everyone at Court to consider how they run their lands, lest the same happen to you. The Royal Treasurer will stay behind to assure the new distribution is done evenly, as well as guiding the citizens in their efforts." He rose from his seat, and Yzabel took his extended hand. "Court is dismissed."

"I can't believe you did that," she said after they'd left the commotion behind.

"I can't believe you asked me to let them live," he grumbled back.

"Cruelty leads us nowhere. They're going to have a hard life as it is." She looked down at Lucas, trotting beside her. "Imagine the baron working in the fields without an arm."

"I didn't think this dog had that in him; should've known better than to doubt an Além-Tejo mastiff." Denis snapped his fingers, and Lucas veered to receive a pat. "Maybe we should get you another. They can guard you and our children together."

A flush heated her cheeks at the mention of children, and what had to happen for them to be made. Memories of Faty flooded her thoughts, dried her tongue, had shame pushing her on one side, and regret pulling her on the other.

Shame because she *had* wanted every bit of it, and more.

Regret because she would never see Faty again, would never be able to apologize for saying those mean things, would never be able to tell her that even though it was wrong, she loved her, too.

"Why are you so afraid of it?" Denis asked, misreading her silence.

"It's not that," she hurried to say. "My blood still hasn't returned. I need to gain more weight before we…try."

"We'll see how you're faring once we're married."

Yzabel made herself smile in their exchanged glance.

"If not then, after. I'll trust you to tell me when you're ready, then."

She let him place a careful arm around her shoulders and said, "Thank you."

For too long, she'd been letting her betrothed down — her betrothed who was ultimately patient and fair, who'd waited five years for her to profess herself ready to join him, who made no unexpected demands and gave her many freedoms in return.

He could've kept her from making medicines, could've kept her from the smaller charities she devoted herself to, could've controlled her dowry lands, could've forced himself on her, could've had her persecuted for witchery. Kindnesses she'd repaid by being willful and dutifully righteous. Kindness she'd repaid by falling in love with someone else and not him.

But she could still make things right.

She could still make herself love Denis.

The next morning, their departure from Terra da Moura was as somber as the overcast horizon. Under heavy rain, their pace was twice as slow, and the chilly wind made every moment grueling. But it was the solitude that made it truly miserable.

The first day she spent in the clutches of moroseness, humor as bleak as the black of her mourning clothes. During dinner, she made herself pay attention to Denis and his plans to build a university.

"In Ulisbuna, maybe," he said between bites of stuffed quail. "A place where people can learn Art, Law, Medicine, and their rights."

"Most of the population won't be able to afford that,

though. Or want to." Yzabel played around with the julienned kale on her plate. "They need their children to work the fields, not sitting in school."

"No, but it's a start for those who *can*. We're losing young people to other nations because we do not have a university of our own. Most end up staying where they complete their studies." He took a sip of wine. "We have them finish their education here and keep their brilliant minds here as well. I'm the first Portuguese king who knows how to read. That…isn't right. We're supposed to trust our advisers and our stewards, but how can we know they're doing their job unless we verify it ourselves? Same with the people, and for us to move forward, our citizens need to move forward as well."

Another good thing, one that would help the entire country. "You're right. Not everyone will be able to afford it, but it should be an option."

"You could take charge of the project."

Yzabel's knife clattered on the plate.

He trusted her again. He wanted her opinions, her expertise. Again. She should be elated, not hurt, not fighting the twisted pain in her heart.

"If that's not something you want to do…"

"No, I do." She pushed herself to smile. "But why me?"

"You were tutored by the same scholars as your brother Jaume, were you not?" Denis wiped his fingers on a slice of bread before eating it. "Men of all faiths were invited into your home for their expertise—you were raised in the breast of theology and culture, and you won't hold someone's beliefs against them if their hearts are in the right place. I can think of no better person."

Her face heated at the compliment, and she looked at her betrothed from under her eyelashes, hoping to find desire in the wake of her flush. To feel that odd flutter in her stomach, or the urge to seek his touch.

There was nothing beyond the warmth of friendship.

Yzabel cleared the pain in her throat. "The prelates might oppose out of sheer stubbornness."

"We're lucky that you're more stubborn than they'll ever be, then," Denis said. "If there's anyone who can convince them of its benefit, it's you. Which brings us to our dilemma: The prelates have too big a hold on the country. Their first concern isn't Portugal, but the Holy Church. That needs to change. The people can't control their future when they give most of it to the prelates."

He was testing her devotion to God now, poking the arrows of her moral compass. And while she *did* believe in the Holy Church and its goodness, she wasn't the naïve little girl he'd promised to marry. She realized not every prelate was good. She'd *seen* it, with her own eyes.

"I may be devout, but I'm not blind. Or stupid. The Church is already responsible for our spirits; they shouldn't have to be responsible for our bodies as well. It's on *us* to make it right. Now that you left the farmers in charge of their own lands, they can sell more, profit more, and stop needing charity. More money for them, more taxes for you." She lifted her chin, looking him square in the eye. "The Church can keep on gathering its funds the way it always has, by relying on the good will of the people."

A smiling tug played in the corner of his lips. "The Pope might take offense, you know."

"The Pope is Saint Pedro's successor. He will understand." She took a bite of turnip, washed it down with a sip of wine. "And people are *good*, Denis. They will give as much as they can if they know it'll help someone else. Should you do this across the country, and rescind your limits on donations, the Church will have no reason to object."

He blinked. "You've really changed."

Yzabel looked away. "I had to."

It was God's will she change, God's will she accept her gift of the Holy Spirit and use it for the people. God's will that led her to Fatyan. And where there was God's light, there was the Devil's shadow as well. She should've held strong against the darkness instead of letting the lust fester like a wound.

That wound bled still, along with the ones on her back, along with the punctures of the cilice's teeth.

"You're finally seeing the big picture, Yzabel. This change...it's for the better." From across the table, his hand folded over hers. "I'm glad we're discussing how to run the country again."

She turned her fingers under his. "So am I."

But at night, when she was alone with Lucas in her cold tent and couldn't turn roses into bread, she wished again for Fatyan to be with her, wished she'd open the flap and climb inside. She'd sit behind Yzabel and whisper exactly what was wrong, that she should remain calm and keep practicing. Before the hopelessness and regret flooded her again, Yzabel sent magic spinning into a rose, a quick succession of images flashing in her attentive eyes—stalks of wheat, grinding flour, a splash of water, a dash of salt, a bit of yeast, a ball of dough sitting on a tray over embers, bloating, browning.

The rose compacted, widened, swelled, and instead of a prickled stem, there was the rough shell of the bread. A loaf smaller than the palm of her hand.

Food she'd made from a flower.

Her lungs expanded with overwhelming relief when it

did, her breaths growing bigger when the next rose became bread, too. Lucas licked her face, and she smiled as he gobbled up the loaves in single bites.

The lightness in her being didn't last long, for even though Lucas was company, he was still a dog. He lacked the capacity to comprehend the miracle that had just transpired, and as much as she talked to him about it, he would never answer. He wasn't Vasco, or Brites, or Faty.

Faty, who would've been now free if Yzabel hadn't lost control of herself.

A blanket drawn over her thoughts, she crawled to the trunk where she'd placed the stone for the journey. The rock was warm on her hand, alive with magic, and she held it in front of her between index and thumb.

"Faty," she whispered, unsure she could be heard, certain she'd choke if she didn't try. "Faty, our bargain's done. You can come out."

She waited for Faty to answer inside her head as she had the day they'd found each other. Waited for the stone to erupt, for the ground to shake, the birds to stir. But she'd had her chance, and now that it'd been wasted, all the stone held for her was silence.

As soon as she lay down to sleep, her tired eyes drifted to where Fatyan used to sit beside her, and Yzabel would find herself wishing she could place her head on Faty's lap. Faty would run her hands over Yzabel's curls, wrap them around her fingers like rings; when Yzabel could barely keep her eyes open, they'd lie, curled against each other—

She pulled at the wounds in her back until she could feel them bleed again, falling asleep to the sound of her sobs and the taste of her tears. The morning would come with Denis's gentle rebinding of her wounds, getting better despite her tugging on them at night.

That was how much God wanted her to recover. The gift of the Holy Spirit wasn't just helping her regain her flesh but healing the lash's marks as well.

The Lord loved her still. Even though she'd let herself crave another woman's touch, He cared for her, mending her body so she could fulfill her purpose to bring true peace to this country.

She thought on it, desperately. How to tip the scales of balance without eliciting a revolt that could bring civil war upon them, how to make everyone's lives better in ways that would hurt no one. But how could she hope to bring peace to a country when there was no peace in her heart?

The days passed. Her relationship with Denis improved, returning to the cooperating friendship it'd been during their long correspondence. Whenever there was a settlement, he'd let her give alms to the poor so long as she kept them small, merely enough to keep starvation at bay for a week. He wasn't aware that she ended up giving more, and although she knew she shouldn't lie to Denis about anything any longer, Yzabel couldn't bring herself to tell him of her magical gift.

A gift she controlled because of Fatyan.

With the mastery achieved, Yzabel now had to find a way on how to use it to its fullest potential, and she had to do it by herself. As they rode, she thought on ways she could bring food to the people. The easiest way would be to involve the servants, but after what happened to Brites, Yzabel couldn't risk it. This meant she'd have to distribute the bread herself, but with her job as future queen consort, she had little spare time available to her. Short of duplicating herself, Yzabel had no idea how she was supposed to do it.

When the caravan stopped for lunch, Yzabel plucked as many estevas as she could and placed them in her apron's pocket.

"Your Highness, why those?" Lady Aldonza asked. "They're a weed!"

Yzabel shrugged, keeping things short and courteous. "Estevas are powerful medicine. I like to keep our cabinets stocked."

Truth was, she hated picking estevas. Their resin left her fingers sticky, her skin stiff, but they were *everywhere*, and could be used to disinfect wounds, or to soothe flea bites. She'd keep some of these to make some salve, but most had another purpose.

Surely, she could turn estevas into bread as easily as she did roses. As such, whenever they stopped, and she walked the streets with her ladies-in-waiting or her betrothed, she'd slip the poor a coin, then linger back a moment longer to shove her hand into her apron and sneak in a loaf of bread as well. It was tricky, with Matias now the head of her Guarda and lingering at her back, but she learned to work the dead angles in his sight and how to use her dog's massive frame to hide her surreptitious movements.

Everyone, Matias and Denis included, thought the thanks that came after was for the money. She didn't bother to correct them. It was keeping things from her betrothed, yes. But sinning was forgivable if done in the name of good.

Unnatural love between women wasn't a good cause, even if love itself was the noblest of causes.

Was that why loneliness clung to her like an illness? Because she still wasn't being too honest with her betrothed? Or was it because she truly *did* love Faty, and to be without her was to starve her sick heart?

The araba was full of women, Estremoz several days

away from the horizon, and still she succumbed to the bitterness of saudade. The melancholy wouldn't lift, the pain in her chest wouldn't fade, and even if she wanted to run back to Fatyan and apologize, she couldn't.

Fatyan was gone.

The stone now lay dangling between her breasts, wrapped in ribbons of silk tied to a fine silver chain, beating with the same rhythm as Yzabel's heart. So close. So far. Every night, she fell asleep with the stone clutched in her hand, whispering things like *Sorry. I love you. We can never be together. I want you by my side.*

Every time, the stone responded with taunting silence, its magical glow shuddering as if to say, *You've had your chance.*

"I must say, you've been looking better with each passing day," Lady Aldonza's statement plucked her from dark daydreams. "The king must be relieved."

"It's good to see a man thusly concerned with his future wife. That he insisted to see to your every meal before you're even married, oh!" Countess Mariana fluttered her rich eyelashes with a sigh. "It's not just his verses that are romantic, but his gestures as well."

Yzabel swallowed the lump of memories that surfaced. "I'm lucky to be marrying him."

"Has he visited you at night?" asked Aldonza in a too-innocent chirp.

Their marriage had all but been formalized, with their long engagement and Yzabel's subsequent delivery to the Portuguese lands, so it wasn't too odd a question or implication. Still, prickling unease curled her toes, the discomfort lowering Yzabel's gaze to where her hands rested in her lap. "No. There would be no point, considering my health."

She was still healing. All she could do for now was eat, get better, and wait for her womb to be fertile again. There would be no point in her bedding Denis until then, anyway; an unwillingness that had nothing to do with the fact she *still* thought about Fatyan, and everything to do with the lack of moon's blood.

God must've been listening to her thoughts, because the following morning, when she went to the chamber pot, drops of red colored her bodily fluids pink.

CHAPTER TWENTY-TWO

Despair

Breaking open the little box of necessities filled her with unexpected relief. The cotton rags with strings would finally be put to use, as would the small necklaces she filled with lavender and sage to hide the smell. All of which she'd made with Brites while expecting the flow to come back.

She tied the string around her hips to keep the rag in place; it was uncomfortable to walk with the cotton between her legs, but it was either that or let the blood run freely. With the pendant of flowers behind her clothes, no one even noticed she'd reached her time of the month.

The cramps were the worst, periodic stabs to her womb that made her grimace and groan. She longed for mint tea to ease the pain, but to deny herself a woman's aches was to go against God's wishes. He'd sent her this pain as a sign that she could now love her betrothed the way she was supposed to. Perhaps if she let him do what men did, she'd stop thinking of Fatyan's hands on her skin, of her lips upon her own.

But God was as cruel as He was merciful, and the tide didn't last long—three days later, it was gone. The next, the familiar donjon of Estremoz rose from atop the hill. The sun hung halfway down, and around the road, men and older boys tended to the fields, cleaning the earth from weeds and other maladies.

"*Esh-tre-mous*," Marquise Júlia said from across the araba. "Quaint name."

"As the story goes, it's because a group of settlers found a tremosso tree somewhere around here," Aldonza explained as the araba rolled over the portcullis and into the city walls. "They returned to harvest it every year, and the place where the tremossos grew eventually became Estremoz."

Yzabel tuned out, taking in the familiar small houses painted in quicklime to reflect the oppressive summer heat, with blue or yellow lines trimming their bases, doors, and windows to keep the flies and mosquitoes away; the cobblestone-paved roads, and the sidewalks in the traditional Portuguese style, with white and black stones. The village's women and young children tended to their own small gardens—some were lucky enough to have a chicken or two, maybe a neighborhood pig they were fattening up for slaughter come Februarius. A loathsome custom come at the end of winter, with the pig's cries finding her regardless of how hard she covered her ears or how far away she stood.

Pigs were such smart, sweet animals, and eating their meat invariably made her sick. The Bible forbade it, too, yet another rule ignored in the name of survival to no cataclysm. No part of the pig went to waste, either. Every bit of flesh, every drop of blood, every sinew and organ and nerve turned to another purpose. She couldn't fault the Portuguese for it, not when pigs fed so many; that she could go without eating it was her privilege, and not something the commoners could avoid.

It was a sin God allowed because it saved lives; and yet, why did she keep comparing it to her agonizing feelings for Fatyan? Was it because her absence made a different part of Yzabel starve, and she feared the saudade would kill her with its melancholy as starvation nearly had?

This had to be a test from God, as the blessing had been. Yzabel had almost failed the first; she couldn't fail the second.

As she examined the town on their way up to the castle, Yzabel committed the streets to the map in her mind, making note of where the guard postings were stationed and more places she should avoid. The open terrain of the plaza between the city center and the poor quarter would be her biggest obstacle; she'd have to swipe a copy of the city's blueprints from the Steward's Office later, to see if there was a way around it.

Her rooms in Estremoz's castle were as opulent as they'd been in Terra da Moura, save for the pile of letters waiting for her in the desk. Yzabel took her time going over the weekly reports from her many castles and villages, riches she'd gained when her papá signed her hand away to the King of Portugal and the Algarves. Come summer, she'd have to visit them all, make sure everything was as stated. If Terra da Moura had taught her anything, it was that the absence of a just hand gave way to greedy deceit.

Yzabel turned back to her letters, making note of the advancements in her own lands. Her shelters in Porto Mós and Óbidos should be open, giving aid and shelter to old or sick prostitutes who couldn't find work, as well as to women who'd been ostracized from society. She wanted to build another in Odivelas, too; it was, reportedly, Denis's favorite place for philandering, and God knew those poor women needed shelter once the men began finding them unappealing. She wanted to know if the hospital she'd ordered to be repaired in Alenquer had been done properly.

So many liked to call those women names, to spit on them and cast them out, for they were unrepentant sinners who deserved no charity.

To Yzabel, they were simply people down on their luck who deserved to be granted basic needs. Jesus had risen to Maria Madalena's defense, and for women, so would Yzabel.

She kept her mind and body occupied. After she broke fast at dawn, she tossed the leftover crumbs to the birds at her window, small blackcaps and warblers, as well as large crows. They stayed on the sill after the meal, and she took to singing to and with them during the busy mornings spent running her own estate, boosting her spirit through the often-tiresome business. The afternoons she spent with her ladies-in-waiting and evenings in prayer and poring over the city map. Matias followed her around everywhere she went, and Faty's Stone pulsed against her breast when he came too near as if to remind Yzabel not to trust him. Her relationship with Matias was cordial at best, strained at worst, yet regardless of how often she complained to Denis that she did not want him in charge of her safety, the king would not budge.

Every night, there would be great feasts awaiting them in the dining hall, boar braised in clay pots, kale and chorizo shredded into thick caldo verde, sweet rala bread, endless cheeses and limitless wine. But while the Court gorged on every bite, the people were still starved.

Yzabel saw them when she and her ladies-in-waiting walked through town when the weather allowed. Children so thin it was a wonder the strong wind didn't take them and send them flying across the sky. Still, they laughed as they played games before the sun fully disappeared and they had to go to bed. From some houses came the cries of babies and infants, of tired wives and husbands. When they were outside as the workers returned to their homes with empty cork tarros dangling from their arms, Yzabel couldn't ignore their slumped shoulders and half-closed eyes.

They needed her help still.

But Estremoz wasn't a passing village on the way. They were to remain here for the next four months or so, and she knew if she gave people bread in the open, her actions would eventually reach Denis. He'd ask where she got it, and that was a question she couldn't answer.

Still, she had to help.

First, however, came another duty. One she had to prove she could do.

Yzabel called for the servants to prepare a bath, then placed the stone's necklace on the small table by the tub, arranging soaps and oils around it as she waited.

By the firelight, she soaked in foam, rubbing away the dirt on her skin, the impurity between her legs. The hot water reminded her of the springs, of Fatyan's fingers kneading her back, her shoulders, relieving one tension to awaken another. Yzabel hadn't understood it then, but she did now, when the ghost of touches past brought a tightness to her core, tears to her eyes, and a beautiful ache to her chest.

She missed her. So much.

How had Faty woven herself into Yzabel's soul so fast? Why couldn't she untangle the threads between them, how did absence make the longing greater? Was it because there had been no parting words between them, no closure as to *what* those kisses had truly meant? Or because the last Yzabel had seen of Faty was the pain of rejection on her face?

I love you, Yza.

The glow of magic swirled in the palm of her hand, and she wished the Holy Spirit had given her the power to reverse the hourglass of time.

At least she could've told Fatyan she loved her back.

And even then, what good could've come of that? Adultery was adultery regardless of gender, and to tarnish the marriage bed was sin.

Denis tarnished it all the time; he *sinned* all the time without reprisal from God. Should his seed never take in Yzabel's womb, his adultery would provide him with an heir, the country with a king. His sins had a purpose; Yzabel's didn't.

Gooseflesh prickled her skin as she dried herself by the fire. Her white mantle draped over her shoulders, Yzabel bade Lucas goodnight and walked the candlelit hall to her betrothed's room. The nightgown's silk was as heavy as iron, the nerves thick in her throat, in her quickened breath.

She'd been only ten when her marriage was arranged, and as such, her parents had insisted she stay with them until she was the age of consent. But then her papá had died, and she'd been able to buy two and half years with her family before her brother shipped her off to fulfill the seven-year-old contract.

Before she'd left Aragon, her mamá had pulled her aside, and said, "Give him a son as quickly as you can. Even if you have to get started before your wedding is officialized." Rancor had lined Mamá's face, and Yzabel understood that this was the same advice she had once been given. Women could be intelligent, they could be kind, but more importantly, they had to be fertile.

Denis had never tried to touch her, and she'd convinced herself that it was good; that Denis's lack of interest in her would keep her out of the marriage bed—and, consequently, from the birthing bed's likely possibility of death.

If she hadn't ignored her duties, if she had faced her fear of copulation, then maybe her affections would've already been taken when Fatyan had come into her life.

In her chest, her heart hardened, her resolve stiffened. The marriage bed might be painful, but how could she complain, when every other woman had to go through it? She'd never gone cold, or in need of clothes, and while she'd experienced hunger, it had never been due to a lack of food at her table. Compared to the commoners, she had it easy.

But the pain wasn't what she feared. If it were, her arm wouldn't be heavy as she raised it, her mind wouldn't be racing.

What she truly feared was that she could no longer deny that her body craved women instead of men, and that she couldn't effectively pretend otherwise. But she had to do this before she went out to deliver bread. Questions would undoubtedly arise once loaves showed at people's homes, and spending the night with Denis would be a foolproof alibi should those questions turn her way.

Breath in. Breath out. Yzabel knocked on her betrothed's door.

"Come in."

She crossed the threshold, that invisible barrier between them as tall as the Pyrenees. "Am I interrupting?"

Denis looked over his shoulder. He sat at the desk, a candle shining light on the papers spread across the surface. "Yzabel. What are you doing here?"

Surprise widened his eyes, stretched his face. Yzabel walked up to him, the map on his desk drawing her attention. Denis moved over to let her see it.

"You're planning to increase the pine tree forest in Leiria?"

"Yes. The way I see it, it's pointless to pursue conflict with Castela. We've been playing tug-of-war with them for so long, and now that relations are stable, I wouldn't strain them unless I had no choice. But"—he pointed to the blue part of the map, the ocean beyond Portugal's western shores—"there may be a way for Portugal to grow that does not involve the Iberian Peninsula. But I don't know yet. We have bigger concerns, such as our own stability. I might leave the plans for a future king. Our son, perhaps."

Swallowing her indecision, she undid the knot of her mantle, brought the nightshirt over her head. There she stood, naked and shivering, waiting, unable to meet his eyes until—

A hand on her chin, lifting her face up. "We're not married yet. You don't have to do this now."

"I know," she said without wavering. "But we'll be married soon enough."

Denis's gaze burrowed deeply into hers for a long moment before he asked, "Are you sure?"

Yzabel made herself hold his attention, to appreciate the firelight dancing on the harsh angles of his face. "Yes."

Denis kissed her then, his beard scratching her skin, his hands heavy on her hips. Yzabel fought the urge to squirm, reminded herself to open her mouth to his seeking tongue. Things that had come so natural in that brief time with Fatyan were forced with Denis, but Yzabel had to endure it. This was the cost of her privilege, the cost to be able to change people's lives. He tasted of wine and something acid, bitter to her palate—she told herself it could be worse, that at least she liked and trusted Denis despite all his flaws.

That he could've been less patient, more forceful, but he'd respected her instead.

Then he touched her chest, and she couldn't help it—she cringed.

That hadn't happened when Faty had done it; then Yzabel had leaned into it, wanting more, needing more—

Denis stopped, looked at her with a frown. "Yzabel, if you don't want this—"

She tried to shake Faty from her head. "No. This needs to happen. It has to."

He sighed, but he took her to the bed with exploring hands. His weight dipped the mattress, his thin beard scratched at her face, and she decided it best to just close her eyes and let him take the lead. But as his mouth moved to her neck, down her body, it was Fatyan's lips she imagined. It was Fatyan's hand between her legs. It was Fatyan beneath her eyelids, touching her, kissing her. All of it felt so irrevocably wrong, made even more obvious by the fact she had to keep thinking of Faty to get through it.

Yzabel couldn't hold the tears back any longer, wiping them as they escaped, hoping her betrothed wouldn't see them, that he'd ignore them, that he'd just do whatever and get this over with. On Denis's brow, a frown began to form, and it was with consternation on his mouth that he said, "This isn't happening."

He rolled off her, leaving her looking at the canopy of the bed in a state of dazed shame. Something really was wrong with her. Wrong with her body that, even after being under the betrothed God had given her, ached for someone else's touch. Wrong with her heart, who decided to pledge itself to another woman, to pine for a love that could never be.

"I'm sorry," Yzabel said, pulling the sheets up to cover

herself and dry her tearstained features. "Something... Something's wrong with me, and I can't—"

Wordlessly, Denis picked up her nightgown and mantle where she'd forgotten them on the floor and handed both to her. As she haphazardly put them on, he sat beside her, seriousness in his worried gaze, the crackling of the flames the single sound passing between them.

"We don't have to do this if you don't want to," he said, breaking the silence at last.

"That's not what you said a month ago." Yzabel's hands fisted the sheets, knuckles white and trembling. "And you were right. For the throne to be secure, for this country to be secure, I will need to give you an heir."

"That had more to do about your state of sheer malnourishment than with children. Nothing else seemed to bring you to your senses." He sighed. "You're healthy now. That's what matters. Well..." His tone stayed calm, if a bit embarrassed. "I've got bastards aplenty."

"Bastard children can't inherit the throne, Denis."

"They can if I legitimize them."

Her pride should've been wounded at such statements, and yet Yzabel couldn't find anything within herself but relief for the way out he presented her with. Still, it was unfair of her to take it, unfair for her to ask so much, unfair of her to put this burden on another woman. "You and I both know that won't go over well with the gentry."

"If you want me to force myself on you, I can. But neither of us will enjoy it, and I know that if I do it, you'll end up resenting me until you die."

He spoke with such softness and understanding her tears turned to hot frustration, her chest withered with worthlessness. "I don't deserve such kindness. Or patience."

"Ai, Yzabel," he said her name in a breathless cuss,

complete with a palm to his forehead. "I'll be here whenever you want to try, but I will *never* force you. Not to mention the main reason I'm marrying you is because it'll bring much-needed stability. Anything happens to you and I have to contend with your brothers threatening war."

A statement that should've reminded her of her value served to humble her instead. It was chance that she'd been born into her family, chance that she had enjoyed great privilege and would enjoy it still simply because her brothers were kings of Aragon and Majorca.

"More than that," his voice softened, and the warmth of his hand spread over her left hand. "I wouldn't be able to find another wife who'd make as good a queen as you."

That was what thoroughly undid her, and Yzabel almost blurted the whole truth out. Denis deserved to know that she would never desire him, he deserved to know her heart belonged inside a stone, but humiliation stuck to her tongue and stitched her lips shut. She couldn't stand to stay under the understanding in his brown eyes or the comfort of his words when she still had truths she couldn't share.

Yzabel turned her hand so it was palm to palm against Denis's and squeezed. "Thank you," she said, wiping her tears as she bolted from the bed. "I'll leave now. I'm sorry I've made you waste your time."

She was halfway across the room when Denis called after her, "You can stay, you know."

It touched her that he offered, and her stilling feet pivoted her to look at him. But she still had work to do tonight, something she was desperate to throw herself into. "No, it's all right. You have work to do. I don't want to keep you."

"You make my work better. I would discuss some more things with you."

"Oh." Yzabel didn't deserve his confidence, not when she was still hiding truths from him. But she couldn't turn it away, not when he offered it like an olive branch. "All right then."

That night, they debated as equals, without volatile passions to muddle their thoughts or decrees.

CHAPTER TWENTY-THREE

Discoveries

Both Yzabel and Denis could barely keep their eyes open when they bade each other goodnight. With barely a sound, she padded back to her rooms, where she changed into a dress of long skirts and stuffed it with the flowers she'd picked in the afternoon. Fatyan's stone was back around her neck with its cozy weight, the magical lull throbbing against her heart.

Although relations between Portugal and Castela were tense, these were mostly peaceful times, and the patrols were scarce in the streets. If she remained vigilant, she could avoid them, as well as any detection. Steeling herself with a deep breath, Yzabel climbed over her bedroom window, Lucas jumping after her. Together, they slid across the grass of the small hill and hit the paved roads with nothing but moonlight illuminating her path.

Under the drizzling rain, Yzabel clutched her cloak, sent Lucas ahead, waiting in a dark corner as her dog checked the streets for late-night wanderers. He'd return if the way was clear, bid her to follow him to another street if it wasn't. After clearing the more affluent area, she began to stop at every door. As swiftly as she could, she picked estevas from her skirts—she'd been practicing with them for days now—and turned them to bread as easily as she did the roses. In fact, she could turn *any* flower to bread now, and although it miffed her, she couldn't figure out why pork would become estevas, but estevas wouldn't become pork, she took her victories where she could. If bread was all she could make out of blossoms, then she'd make as much as humanly possible.

She turned the esteva into a loaf and wrapped a linen strip around it. Her original idea had been to leave the bread by the door, but with the ever-changing winds, she wasn't confident the rain wouldn't ruin it, even with the added shelter of the beirais. Fortunately, the people stored their wood outside, under small sheds next to their homes, so she left the bread there, certain it'd be safe from the willful weather and found whole in the morning. Under the arches of each church, she left a dozen loaves, and more in the hospice.

Then, there was the matter of the windows and doors clad in red. They needed food more than anyone else, yet Yzabel couldn't risk getting too close to them even if the odds of catching the disease were low when not directly exposed to a contaminated person's skin. She had come too far, had too many things left to do, to leave a potentially fatal illness to chance.

Dogs, on the other hand, were immune, and she'd trained Lucas well enough to deliver a package. Yzabel took shelter under whichever tree was closest to the red houses and called Lucas to her side. On her knees, she wrapped a second string of linen around the bread and held it in front of her dog's snout. "Take this and put it under that shed."

Tail wagging, Lucas bolted off. Without her sentinel, Yzabel leaned against the bark, tension tight in her shoulders as she carefully listened for the sound of voices or footsteps between raindrops and whistling branches. Were she to be caught, at best, she wouldn't be recognized, and would have to contend with the guards' interrogation; at worst, she'd be brought back to Denis and face *his* interrogation. Neither was an outcome she could afford. A regular girl could not have a possible justification for such late an outing, much less a princess.

Unease built in her bones as she repeated the process for the other plagued houses—six of them in total. On the fifth, Yzabel thought she saw the mist darken and shift, and on the very last one, while she hid next to an empty pigpen, the sound of boots squelching in the mud chilled her ears.

She'd been seen, and now she was being followed.

A peek wasn't needed to know someone was skirting the pigpen and coming her way. Keeping herself low, Yzabel took one step to the right for every one she heard to her left. Heart in her throat, she made herself breathe slowly, through her nose. From the corner of her eye, she spotted her dog, returning from his task. All Yzabel had to do was nod toward the man, and at once, Lucas jumped.

Caught unawares, the man fell backward into the pigpen with a shocked scream and Yzabel launched into a run. She found herself veering right, down the road— halting briefly when she spotted a light on, then crawling under the window to avoid detection, hitting her chin on the pavement when her hands slipped on wet cobblestones. She dashed to the closed doors of São Francisco's Church, past the plaza, turned left to the last road parallel to the wall.

Crows swooped down, cawing loudly. Yzabel recognized them as the flock she'd been feeding, momentarily stunned until she recalled that crows weren't only highly intelligent, they were loyal. She'd treated them well, and now they tugged at her sleeve, telling her to move on, their urgency evident. She began to gather herself, shifting her grip on her skirts. The sound of boots hitting stone echoed in the street. A step. Another. Lucas howled to the mist at her left—a warning that someone came from that direction.

The crows circled around, swept past her. Yzabel didn't wait—she ran, turning the corner, then another. Somewhere in the vicinity, the flutter of many wings. A man's voice shouted in the next street over. She didn't stay to find out who it belonged to.

Yzabel didn't stop running until she was safely back in her chambers. Wet to the bone, she tossed her cloak aside, then closed the window after Lucas had joined her inside.

She'd done it.

The thrill beat fast in her chest, and her throat was sore from running in the rain, but she'd given so much bread away, without spending a dime. Come morning, almost everyone in town would have a loaf at their door, and many more waiting for any who asked their parishes.

Yzabel laughed, effervescent with joy, with the incomparable feeling that was fulfilling one's divine purpose.

And she had no one to share it with.

Her tears changed from jubilant to bitter. Vasco should've been here to see this. Brites, too. And so should Fatyan.

It wasn't fair that it was her absence that stung the sharpest.

...

Yzabel managed to stay awake during the early morning, busying herself with writing letters to prospective teachers for the University. She wrote to her brother Jaume in Majorca, her tutors in Aragon, to the Bishop of Ulisbuna, then began drawing plans for classes and budgets for construction until the bell rang for midday mass. For an hour, she listened to Padre António's sermon, a rosary between her intertwined hands.

After the choir boys finished singing a joyful hymn, she joined Denis and the court in the Great Hall for lunch, then followed the ladies-in-waiting to their afternoon embroidery session.

A good princess spent time with her peers, and Yzabel had avoided these women for far too long. But as it turned out, focusing on cross-stitch and gossip after a sleepless night and a full lunch proved to be more challenging than Yzabel had thought. Her head began to sink, her eyes to close, and a yawn was leaving her mouth before she could attempt to contain it.

"Long night, Your Highness?" Violeta giggled. "Have you finally met the king's mighty sword?"

She still couldn't understand why any woman would voluntarily submit herself to it. Or how she could enjoy it to perdition. Faty had brought her more ecstasy with a single kiss than Denis had with his everything.

"You know he's been waiting for the chance," Aldonza muttered, so low Yzabel barely heard. "He's set on his pure-blooded heirs."

Her tired eyes drifted to Denis's mistress, who stabbed her needle on the aida cloth with furious intent. Noted the other woman's generous forms, straight brown hair that gleamed gold in the light, a dainty nose, pouty lips thinned into a line. Noticed the full roundness of her belly, thick with a child to come. Another bastard for Denis, who might take the throne if Yzabel never delivered.

Yzabel should be angry at the two of them for fornicating under her roof. Should demand Aldonza stop now, tell her to seek Denis no more. But what right did she have? When she looked at Aldonza, it was obvious why Denis would want the court lady. Aldonza wasn't as beautiful as Fatyan—no one was, really—but she was still beautiful, and Yzabel hated how effortless it was to recognize it.

She'd never been attracted to men. All her life, she'd looked at beautiful women and think the heat in her face came from admiration. She'd have spent her entire life thinking that way if Faty hadn't come along.

The regret ate at her, a pulsing pain in her rib cage that never went away. If only she'd reacted with patience and kindness instead of anger and fear.

It was clear now that she would never love Denis in the way a wife should love her betrothed. But Aldonza might. Yzabel had never delved into her betrothed's affairs, but perhaps it was best she did.

Did Denis love Aldonza, or was she yet another pastime, nothing but a warm body willing to do anything for her king? And, as important, did Aldonza love Denis, or were there underlying motives in her affections? Did Aldonza think about her sins when she was with him, and she loved him so much she didn't care? Or did she let him have her way with her because he was her king, and to deny him could bring catastrophe upon her?

"Is he worth it?"

Aldonza's shoulders stiffened into a straight line. "Pardon?"

"Denis." Yzabel slowly raised her head. "Is he worth

the sin it brings upon your soul?"

The room took a collective breath. Aldonza took her hands to her heart. A hint of fear widened those big, light brown eyes framed in long dark lashes and worry rounded her parting lips. "M-My princess, I don't know what you mean."

Any other time, Yzabel would've looked away and let the matter rest. But she was done ignoring what happened around her.

"Answer me, Aldonza."

"I..." She looked to the other ladies around them, all of which conspicuously looked only at their own cross-stitch. Finally, she gave up with a sigh. "Since when have you known?"

"Since I arrived in Portugal."

Someone coughed—Yzabel thought it was Violeta. "Told you she wasn't stupid."

"Why did you not say anything?" There was genuine confusion in Aldonza's small voice, softening Yzabel's own.

"My silence doesn't make it less of a sin on your part," she said. "So, I ask again, is he worth the stain on your soul?"

A peep trembled from Aldonza's mouth, tears shimmering in her eyes. "I'm...I'm so sorry," she whimpered. "He said you didn't care, that you encouraged him to seek others, I..."

For two ugly heartbeats, Yzabel considered letting the other woman keep on apologizing, let her feel the shame her own sins had brought on her.

Kindness is a choice, she remembered hearing, remembered saying. *And you must choose it every time.*

"I'm not asking because I'm jealous." Yzabel knelt before Aldonza, took away both hands covering the other woman's face and held it in hers. "I'm asking because I want to know if you love him. Do you? Or do you allow him simply because he's your king, and you have no choice?"

"No, I…" A sob racked with shame. "I know it's a sin to be with someone who's promised to another, but—"

"But you love him," Yzabel completed.

"I do. Forgive me, but I do." Her head hung low, her breath shook. "It happened, and once it was there, I…I was too weak to deny it."

It *happened.* Yzabel's feelings for Fatyan had just happened, too. One moment they'd been mist, something intangible, the next a flame that couldn't be put out, not even with a torrent of denial and the pain of the lash. She hadn't asked for it, hadn't willed it into existence.

But even if it *was* indeed love, they could never be. The Lord forbade any carnal pleasure that wasn't suffered in the name of procreation, and two women couldn't make a child.

"Aldonza." Yzabel cradled the woman's wet cheek, gently turning it to face her. "I'm not the one who needs to forgive you. It's you who must forgive yourself, you who must bear the cross of tainting a betrothal, and in the future, a marriage. If that's something you can live with, then you'll face no hostility from me."

At least, Yzabel didn't say, *your desires aren't unnatural.*

Aldonza shook her head. "I don't deserve such kindness. I…" She inhaled deeply. "I harbored ill wishes toward you. I wished your womb would sour and for your moon's blood to never come. I wished—"

"Hush. It's all right." Yzabel embraced her—a clumsy effort, with Aldonza sitting, but she managed. "Thank you for loving him in all the ways I can't."

Aldonza's love for Denis was improper.

But Yzabel's love for Fatyan was worse than that. It was unholy.

She had to keep reminding herself of that. Eventually, it'd become true.

"You really are a saint," Aldonza said when they parted.

"I'm truly not." Yzabel sighed, wishing people would stop calling her that. No saint would've yielded to debauchery. Sinking to her knees, she placed a hand on Aldonza's stomach. "What are you going to call it?"

A beautiful smile sent her way. "Afonso if it's a boy. Maria Afonso if it's a girl."

Yzabel snorted, much to the room's shock. "I swear he's set on naming all his children the same thing."

"He really is." Aldonza laughed.

Yzabel went back to her seat feeling lighter than before. After tea was served with honey broas and almond gadanhas, she excused herself for a nap. Matias shadowed her yawning steps, always close ever since Denis had seen fit to give him Vasco's position. Nights were the only time she was free of his constant scrutiny.

Hard to believe he'd come out of Brites.

"Have you talked to your mother?" she asked. "Did she arrive well? Where is she staying?"

He stopped, standing with his feet planted wide, his hands behind his back. "The king had me escort her to our family house, where we lived before she came to work for you." His thick brows pinched together. "We didn't speak a word. I'm done with her ilk."

"What ilk is that, caring mothers who don't tolerate tantrums?"

"People who've made pacts with the Devil." His frown deepened. "You've seen what she can do, the charms she weaves. That is not a holy power."

"Any gift is holy if used for holy purposes."

Matias took a step forward, looming to intimidate. She had to crane her neck to look at him. "Brites is not the kind mother you think she is."

"Or maybe you're a difficult son."

A shake of his head. "You'll see, my princess. When I catch her, you'll see."

Disturbed, Yzabel pivoted away and headed back to her chambers. It was Matias who'd been following her last night, Matias that the crows had steered her away from, and like a dog with a bone, he wouldn't give up until he caught her. And Brites…

She had to warn Brites soon.

CHAPTER TWENTY-FOUR

Mistake

Yzabel crashed into her bed, eager to catch a couple of hours of rest before supper. It should've been easy, given the exhaustion that sickened her to the stomach. Yet, regardless of how hard she tried to empty her mind, how desperate she was for slumber, when she closed her eyes, there was Fatyan. She would always be there, in the space between breaths, in the silence between words, in the darkness of every blink—and the more Yzabel tried to forget her, the sharper the memories became.

When sleep did come, it was with dreams of Faty. Of her hands, of her kisses, of their bodies pressed together. Then she turned into Denis, leaving Yzabel cold. He leaned down, told her to relax, then asked, "…dinner and supper?"

Yzabel's eyelids fluttered. "Hmm?"

"I asked why you skipped dinner and supper," Denis's very real voice said.

"I overslept," she moaned from the bed. "Can you please ask one of the maids to bring me something?"

"In a moment."

The click of the latch speared her chest, blew the laziness from her eyes. She sat up, gut twisting, "Denis?"

He looked at her with condemnation in his eyes. "Did

you hear about the bread?"

She gave him a most innocent blink, as confused as she could make it. "What bread?"

"The bread that showed up this morning. In the churches. The hospice. The *poorest* houses."

"I don't care for the accusation in your tone," she snapped back, immediately regretting her outburst. Part of her had been expecting this; it was the reason she'd spent the night with Denis before going out in the first place.

"It sounds like something you'd do," he pointed out. "Like something you've done."

"You told me to never use the crown's money without asking for your consent first. Have I asked you for more dinheiros than usual?"

His voice turned grumpy. "You have not."

"Was I not with you last night?"

"You were."

"Then how could I have time to give away all that bread?" She meant to sound as curt and as annoyed as she did. Theatrics went a long way into selling her half lies. She hadn't been using the Crown's money, hadn't been using anything other than wildflowers and the Holy Spirit.

Denis's lips trembled and his gaze narrowed—but he didn't press further. "Matias says it's his mother. That he saw her do it."

Yzabel resisted the urge to roll her eyes. "He would say anything to earn your favor. He's thrown his mother to the wolves before, remember?"

"He acted in the right."

She bit her lip, not wanting to fall back into this argument and lose the current one. "My point is, he is obsessed with his mother and her…practices. It makes him believe things that aren't true."

"Someone *did* put that bread where it was," Denis stated. "It might've been a one-time incident, but I have a feeling it's not."

Yzabel kept her expression blank. "Why are you saying that as if it's a threat?"

"I was stating a fact." He opened the door again, looking over his shoulder one last time. "I'll tell someone to bring you dinner. Rest."

While she waited, Yzabel washed her face, tied her hair back. Tonight, she'd have to pick flowers as she went — there were plenty in the wild terrain between the poorest houses. Brites lived near that area as well, in a small brick house with a roof of red tiles. She'd spoken often of living there before Yzabel's mamá sent for her, after which Brites had packed her bags and moved to the other side of the peninsula with her son. The house had been abandoned, waiting for Brites to retire, or for Matias to start a family.

Dinner came as migas with braised pork, of which she ate the former and gave Lucas the latter.

When the church bells tolled midnight, Yzabel stole into the night.

The first street went by in a quick dash, and she stuck her back to the wall as she peeked around the corner. Farther down, the torches of the ducal palace cast a hazy halo on the mist, the guards underneath undoubtedly ready to react at the smallest noise.

Giving them a wide berth, Yzabel veered right, to the plaza where the fair took place every Saturday. Past the dark tavern, already closed and empty, then the Church of São Francisco, kneeling behind the bushes around the building when heavy steps sounded nearby. Lucas tensed, ready to jump, and she placed a quieting hand on his head, knelt to hug him close.

The patrol passed, and she was on the move again, sticking to dark streets on the way down. Moonlight illuminated her footsteps, and quietude dominated the air save for an occasionally barking dog, or the faraway voices of guards chatting.

Her path narrowed with the streets, slowing her pace to a crawl. Hiding spots became harder to find, and Yzabel found herself curling in the shadows, sure her heaving breath and pounding heart would give her away to the passing guards. But the heavy rain smothered the sound of her steps, the dark night shielded her from view, and she managed to avoid any detection.

Finally, she hit the untamed fields close to the wall and began to pick as many wildflowers as she could—mostly estevas, but some pansies as well—then set out to deliver them. The lack of sleep must be affecting the gift, making it harder to turn the flowers; her sight began to blur and twist, and she leaned against the wall, taking deep breaths to steady herself. She pressed on, even as the nausea sent her stomach roiling and coated her tongue with the bitterness of bile.

Tumbling feet drove her shoulder against the wall. Clutching her dress, Yzabel closed her eyes for one moment, steeling her mind and body to keep on pushing through. The light drizzle stuck her hair to her face, and Yzabel kept to empty streets, hanging back in dark corners when voices traveled near her, hearing them talk about the witch they looked for.

"It's supposed to be Matias's mother—the one who used to attend the princess?"

"Poor boy. Having to turn on your own flesh and blood..."

Yzabel stopped hearing them over the sound of her

gnashing teeth. The crows returned, she noted with relief, sweeping the skies over her as she emerged from her hiding spot by the fountain. She wished Brites still worked for her, so she'd keep her former maid safe from mean gossip and ill wishes. She wished Fatyan was there, too, for no reason other than she wanted to curl up against the Moura again, to fall asleep and wake to her warmth, to hear her encouraging words that left no room for doubt.

Warning Brites was but one reason Yzabel had to see her. She placed a hand on her chest, over the hard lump of the stone—through layers of cloth, it heated beneath her fingers as if saying, *Ask her about me.*

The weight of Yzabel's desires slowed her feet, made her second-guess her every choice. Her confusion spread to poor Lucas, who whined questioningly as he regarded her from down an empty street before pounding across the cobblestones and disappearing into the mist.

She followed him toward the poorer district, where the houses were smaller, some clustered together, others far apart, each home with its own sound. One was racked with the coughing of many people; another had a crying baby and desperate mother trying to console him; another had the hushed whisper of children, and their father shouting for quiet. And all of them had empty sacks under their sheds, hoping for another visit from the person who'd given them bread the night prior. So much poverty clogged Yzabel's throat and dragged down her heart. And this was just Estremoz. How many more, in other cities? In other countries? She was trying to do good, but…it wasn't enough. It would never be enough.

And these people… They left her gifts, too, small things such as woven baskets, embroidery, small soaps, bundles of herbs. The gifts they could spare, to pay back a single act of kindness. Yzabel smiled as she held an embroidered towel to her chest. Leaving it behind felt like spitting on generosity, but she must. They had need of these precious things. She did not.

Would they be gifting her if they knew it was their princess leaving them bread, and that she was not as holy or as saintly as everyone believed?

Yzabel reached into her skirts for a pansy, transformed it into bread, and placed it in the waiting sack. Her lungs seemed to want to scramble out of her chest, as no amount of air she gulped could sate them. Wet skirts whipped at her legs with lashes of burning cold, and her head swelled and spun with dizziness.

As she made her way to the houses dressed in red, Yzabel prayed her symptoms were of exhaustion, perhaps a bad cold, and not the plague. Back against a tree, she used the time it took for her dog to drop off the first parcel to turn another loaf. The magic heated her a bit as it worked through the flower, stilling her trembling fingers while still-warm bread formed in her palm. She quickly wrapped it in the linen strips she kept in her skirts, ran to another tree that was closer to the next house.

A couple more left. Then she could go to Brites, whose house was farther up and closer to the outer city walls.

"There's bread over here!" a man's voice cut through the mounting wind. "Find whoever's leaving it!"

Carefully, she looked over her shoulder and around the trunk. The hazy lights of torches moved in the fog not too far off, and Yzabel's entire body froze as she ransacked her head for what to do. If she went to Brites's house or hightailed back to the castle, someone might see her, and the ensuing commotion would wake the slumbering citizens. For now, her only choice was to hide, and the best place to do so was among the red-curtained houses.

From the branches above her, the cry of a crow sounded a warning. Lucas returned to her side, and Yzabel didn't wait any longer. She wrapped the spare linen strips around the lower half of her face and took off toward the nearest pigpen she could hide in, hitting the dirt road between a cluster of homes as more voices emerged behind her. Her hold on her skirts slipped, her remaining flowers falling, fabric catching around her hurried feet, and down she tumbled into the mud. She made to quickly stand, ignoring her aching limbs and pounding head.

"Lucas, draw them away," she commanded, throat scratching with every desperate lungful. Her dog left as she hopped over the short wall and crawled into the empty shelter.

At least she thought it would be empty—but a foul smell burned through her clogged nostrils, and she had to bite her tongue not to scream when she noticed where it all came from. Below her, blood-stained, pus-streaked rags littered the floor. The families must be dumping them here to be burned.

The surest way of contracting the red plague was to be in direct contact with the sores that burst from the skin, and she was sitting in a sea of contagion.

Still, the light of torches crept closer. Shivering and wet, Yzabel held her knees to her chest, made herself small against the shadows and waited for a rampage of boots to pass her. Brites would know what to do about the red plague, about Faty, about everything, and so she ironed her focus to one thing—go to her former maid.

Lucas howled, and the footsteps drifted away. Carefully, Yzabel slipped out, making toward Brites's home farther up the quarter. It was removed from the rest, surrounded by trees laden with persimmons, oranges, pomegranates, lemons. The chicken coop and pigpen beside it were empty but showed signs of having been cleaned recently.

Dim light seeped from the cracks under the door. Yzabel checked behind her to make sure no one had followed her, and when the night came up empty, she knocked. "Brites?"

Nothing.

Yzabel pressed her ear to the wet wood—there seemed to be fumbling, and angry whispers. A knot of dread tightened in her stomach, became a stone at the back of her throat. "Brites?" she tried again.

The door swung open, throwing her back and out of balance—Yzabel fell flat on her bottom, a sharp pain spiking in her lower back. She winced, crawling back to her feet, freezing in her spot when she took in the sight before her. Matias, leather boots specked with mud, creaking on the wooden floor, squelching on the wet earth.

"I knew it was you," he growled. "Just as I knew you'd come if I mentioned my mother."

Panic welled in her throat, and she scrambled to her feet. "Where is she?" Yzabel asked, her voice strong despite her nerves. She bit her lip, considering her next action. With no weapons to defend herself, could she run fast enough to lose him in the streets, then hightail back to the castle?

"She went to the convent as soon as we arrived." He took another step toward her. She took one back. "But don't worry—I'll see to it that she gets her due. She won't lure in anyone else with false concern or rot them from the inside with her notions about magic and the Lord."

"That's ridiculous."

"Is it? Then why are you out here, alone at night and making false miracles?" Righteousness trembled in his brow, in his lips. "I know you freed Fatyan. What deal did you make with her so you could use the sahar?"

Yzabel's hand went to the lump underneath her clothes, Fatyan's stone hot against her skin. Matias had known about Brites's magic, that much was true, but her former maid had sworn he had no idea about Yzabel's. Had Brites played her, or had Matias played them both?

"I don't know what you're talking about," she said, choosing to feign ignorance.

"I might not have paraded my knowledge, but that doesn't mean I'm not in possession of it." He threw her a patronizing smirk. "You've been using the sahar to put bread in people's houses. You've used it before, on the way here, when you thought I wasn't looking, to slip loaves into people's hands."

Yzabel's hands clenched. There was no more denying that he saw her magic, which meant he commanded it, too. Despite the many things Brites had hidden, Yzabel trusted her still. She trusted her more than she ever would Matias, and if there was a reason Brites never mentioned he had magic, Yzabel had to believe it had been done to protect her.

Yzabel didn't wait any longer. She dashed around the house, somehow keeping her balance in the underbrush, slippery from the night's mist and torrent, and whistled for Lucas. But Matias threw himself at her, knocking her forward. The side of Yzabel's head hit a rock, and she saw black, then stars. She struggled against him, but he had her pinned under his weight, and all she could muster was a flailing of her legs.

He leaned closer, knees adjusting to lock her arms in place. "How will the king react once he learns you're the one feeding his people the Devil's bread?"

"It's not the Devil's!" she hissed, careful not to scream and draw more attention. "All I'm doing is giving them food."

"I doubt that. Just like I doubt the king will want anything to do with you once he learns of yet another betrayal from you." He spun around, shifted his weight so he sat on her upper back and shoved her hands together. Rough rope circled her wrists, scraped her flesh raw. "You ask me, I'm doing this country a favor by burning you along with the house she raised me in."

The will to survive drove her to kick and flail, but she might as well try to move a mountain by blowing air. She forced herself into stillness—she had to get out of this herself, through her own means. That meant buying time until Lucas found her, so she asked, "Why?"

"So Brites will be blamed for it. Do you think it will be hard to convince Dom Domingos that a ray of light came down from the sky to set Brites's home on fire? That it's all the Lord, telling us to smite the woman who once lived here and dared take refuge at the convent?" His voice was at her ear, hot with delusion. "Do you think it will be hard to convince Denis you slipped out of your rooms to come meet her, disobeying him yet again, and divine punishment struck you?"

Birds flew above her, but no sign of Lucas. Was he lost—or worse, had one of the guards hurt him? As the magic within Yzabel rose, so did her frantic heartbeat, yet she blocked out all the ominous thoughts, swallowed all her fear, and whistled a sharp, desperate note.

A sharp yank, and she was standing, a hand smacking her across the face. "Don't you dare call attention to us, Aragonese witch," he hissed, and tore the linen wrapped around her head to shove it in her mouth. Rain fell, freezing droplets hitting her face as he leaned to whisper against her ear. "You will join the Dark Lord in Hell and take Fatyan with you."

Horror spiked in her chest, in her throat, in her skin. Yzabel's magic swelled and burned, jumping to Matias's hands where they closed around her arm, dragging her. Thunder ripped through the clouds, its cracking blaring, its light incandescent—Yzabel yelped, and when she opened her eyes again, white fire consumed her bindings, then engulfed Matias before burrowing into his flesh, leaving behind charred skin and lines of black ash.

"What—" He choked on his words as a large shadow tore through the air. Lucas collided with Matias, throwing him off Yzabel, gleaming teeth aiming straight for an exposed throat—

"Lucas, don't!"

Too late. Lucas sunk his jaws onto Matias's neck, ripping flesh with a ferocious shake of the head. Matias twitched. Stopped moving.

But no blood spurted out where Lucas had wounded him. Like with Vasco, flowers spiraled from his body, rising to the sky in a canopy of petals and leaves.

Her head screamed at her to run, and yet Yzabel could not keep the scent of scorched meat and hair from bursting through her nose like acid, nor tear her gaze from the body and the flowers rising in the night. The weight of what had happened dropped on her, at first a pebble, then a crushing boulder.

Matias was dead. Brites's son was dead. He'd been dead before Lucas tried to rip his throat out.

Her breaths came fast and shallow, tears blurring her sight. She'd taken a life to save her own, a sin bigger than any other she'd committed. Now she wouldn't be a harmless saint who fed the people. She would be a murderer who poisoned the world.

Tears mingled with rain as she sank to the ground, whispering, "I'm so sorry. Lord forgive me, I'm sorry."

This was it, the irrevocable sign that she was to stop. For how could God absolve her of this? How could *Brites*?

First, Yzabel had taken the woman's oldest friend, and now, she'd taken her son. Yzabel's sodden garments froze her bones and skin as she looked up at the clouds. Maybe it was best she remain here, let everyone find her with flowers on her hands and judge her for her crime.

Tears mingled with rain as she sank to the ground, whispering, "I'm so sorry. Lord forgive me, I'm so—"

Beside her, Lucas growled, his entire body rumbling with menace. Yzabel lifted her gaze to the flowers that had been growing rampant moments ago, now shuddering to a halt before beginning to retreat. The black, sooty lines etched along Matias's flesh cracked like an egg's shell. Underneath, new skin emerged, pale and glistening. The wound in his throat closed, the evidence of Lucas's teeth no more than a bad memory.

Shock slackened her jaw and stole the litany from her tongue. Head shaking and hand to her mouth, Yzabel crawled backward, unable to tear her eyes away. Matias was healing, like Faty had the night Vasco had tried to kill her, only for Yzabel to accidentally kill him in return. And as the bells tolling the fourth hour reverberated in the air, so did what Brites had said that day.

A long time ago, I freed an Enchanted Moura of my own.

CHAPTER TWENTY-FIVE

Trust

Who is Matias? Who is Matias? Who is Matias?

Yzabel ran to the one place she could get an answer—the convent. Her lungs and heart seemed to want out of her body, but she pressed on, only coming to a halt when the São Francisco Church was in front of her. Beyond, all the streets leading up to the castle were alight; while Yzabel had been waylaid by Matias, the night patrols must've called for reinforcements from the barracks, and when they'd failed to find her in the poorest quarter, they'd resorted to blocking every street.

However, the sentries posted in front of the church hadn't moved. Yzabel sunk to the floor, using the two tall steps to the church's marble porch to hide her as she crawled, with Lucas low behind her, then prayed the guards wouldn't look her way while she slithered along the cobblestones between church and convent.

She allowed herself a deep breath when she hit the bushes, and then used their path and the heavy rain to mask her slow creeping toward the convent's archway. Once safely in its shadows, she turned the knob as softly as she could. There was always a sister inside the foyer, and it didn't take long for the shuffle of footsteps to reach Yzabel's ears.

On the other side, metal slid against metal, the latch lifting. The door creaked, and standing there, framed in candlelight and holding out her hand, was none other than Brites.

"I've been waiting for you, little princess," she said.

The sight of her, safe and in a nun's outfit, crashed through the thin dam Yzabel had erected to contain her emotions on her way here. Sobs and tears burst out of her as she stepped into the convent, and she wanted to wrap her arms around Brites but couldn't.

Yzabel shook her head rapidly, and somehow managed to unlock her voice to say, "Red plague."

Brites's demeanor instantly changed to alarm. "We have to burn your clothes." She closed the convent's door and gestured at Yzabel to follow. "What happened?"

"Matias. He-he was going to kill me and have you take the blame—" Words withered on her lips, the terror too fresh on her mind. "I panicked. All I thought about was getting away, and the magic..." She inhaled through her nose, but her breaths lumped in her throat, a knot growing bigger the harder she tried to take in air, to stop the panic from building. But her mind was taken with the consequences of tonight, of how Matias had seen her, how she'd killed him, how he'd healed.

When they came to the large cloister, she made herself look into Brites's dark eyes. "Why didn't you tell me he was an Enchanted Mouro?"

Consternation deepened the wrinkles on her former maid's features. For a long moment, there was only the sound of the storm outside, rain pelting against the shaking shrubs and trees of the garden. When Brites finally spoke, her voice was old, tired. "I was going to tell you once you fully broke Fatyan's curse. Then that whole thing with Vasco happened, so I decided to wait until we came here and things calmed down." She weaved her arm with Yzabel's, and gently ushered her past the bars separating the vestibule from the convent proper. "Out of those clothes first." Brites opened the door to the warming room, where a fire cackled in its hearth. While Yzabel shed her sodden garments, Brites filled a bowl with wine and rags, then went to the fireplace to get the pincers. "Wash yourself by the fire. I'll burn these outside."

Lucas was already lying against the stone beneath the hearth, and Yzabel joined him. The rag was cold and rough, and the wine smelled strong, but the motions served to quell the shaking of her hands and mind.

She was calmer when Brites returned with a bundle of clothes and blankets in her arms. "Do you remember the stories I told you about a Moura named Zaida?"

"The one who was cursed for helping a Portuguese soldier during the Siege of Sintra?" Yzabel frowned.

"Zaida was the Enchanted Moura I freed," she said, adding more twigs to the fire while Yzabel dressed in the old habit. "And for a while, we traveled together looking for others like her. During that time, we found the man you know as Matias in Terra da Moura. He'd gone half mad, consumed with paranoia and delusion—and when he and Zaida saw each other, they also recognized each other, and he attacked her immediately. I managed to kill him, but he rose back up while we were still recovering from the shock." Brites shook her head as if to shake off the unpleasant memories. "I killed him again. And again. When he kept on healing, we tied him up. Zaida asked him how he could still be alive since he'd cursed her to her own stone over a hundred years ago."

Fully clothed, Yzabel sat back down. "And then?"

"He told us he had found a way to use the curse of the stone to make himself immortal." Brites unfolded the blanket and wrapped it around Yzabel's shaking frame. "Not in so polite a manner, mind you. He was laughing the entire time, reveling in his own brilliance, and got so obnoxious about it we decided to put his spell to the test." She knelt and used the tongs to break the embers off a burning log, sparks jumping, crackling, fading. Brites looked at it as she spoke, eyes half lidded against the sharp heat and brightness. "It's gruesome work, killing a man. It became even more so when he healed from everything we tried. Limbs grew back. Organs regenerated. Finally, I decided to just go for the head—literally. I cut it off from his neck and set it on fire."

She was still stabbing at the log. Yzabel leaned against her former maid's side, while Lucas moved his head to the woman's lap and looked up in the way only dogs could. The tongs clicked against the stone floor, discarded, and with a deep breath, Brites began to pet Lucas and resumed the tale.

"When we found him, Matias had the appearance of a man who'd seen fifty or so springs. With his head destroyed, his old body fell away like a husk. His ribs cracked open, and between the blood and guts, was a weeping newborn."

Yzabel's chest throbbed. "And when he turned into a baby, you decided to raise him?"

"It's…strange, to see a man so reviled become something so apparently innocent." Brites slid her an askew glance. "I was stupidly arrogant and stubborn, so I decided I could undo a century and a half of prejudice and spite. We had someone with the gift of memory put a veil on his mind so previous notions wouldn't cloud his judgment, named him Matias so he wouldn't inadvertently remember himself. I taught him to be kind and understanding, to listen instead of judge, and hoped that would stick even if he somehow got his memories back. But sometimes no matter how hard you try to raise your children right, they come out wrong. It hurts to admit I failed with him, but if I had to fail with one of you, let it be the son I chose for myself and not the daughter my heart chose for me."

Yzabel had no way to answer that, unworthy of such love and understanding. "I'm still responsible for this. Matias tried to use me to get revenge on you, and I fell into his trap like a little duckling. I don't deserve your help, or your—"

"I decide what you do or don't deserve from me," Brites cut her off, the authority drying the arguments on Yzabel's lips. "But first, we have to take care of Matias, and for that, we need Fatyan."

"Fatyan?" Yzabel asked with a blink. "Why?"

"She's the reason he's been alive so long. He was the one to curse her to that stone and bound himself to her hatred for him in the process. The more she despises him, the stronger he grows, but if she can look at him and profess forgiveness…"

Her eyes widened as she read the lines of unspoken secrets etched upon Brites's expression and tied them to the clues she'd already had. Fatyan's reaction to Matias hadn't been mere coincidence, and he wasn't just someone who reminded her of the Benzedor who'd cursed her. He was the man himself. "That's why you drove me to find her. You needed her out of the stone so she could put an end to Matias. You needed to break her curse so she would forgive him."

"No, what I said back then was true. Until Davide mentioned the children had been hearing her again, I thought she was long gone, or freed by someone else. I was at a loss at what to do with you and your refusal to eat, so I thought I might as well let you try finding her. If she could make a man essentially immortal, then she'd certainly know how to approach your magic." Brites looked back to the fire. "Still, had you not gone looking for her, I would've done it myself. If Fatyan dies without forgiving him, then he will go on living forever."

Yzabel shuddered at the thought of having someone like him walking around the earth for eternity, and her hand unwittingly went to the stone hidden beneath her clothes.

In the end, finding Fatyan had been for nothing; the Moura was back to where the Benzedor had put her. Telling him the truth about Faty's whereabouts might keep him from targeting Yzabel's life, since it would prove that she and the Moura were *not* bound together, as the original curse hadn't been broken. But that would give him something else to hold over her, the same way he had a hold on the Enchanted Mouras whose lives he'd forever altered.

Lost, she looked at Brites, at the worry softening her gaze; she wanted to tell her so badly, ask for her advice, bask in her understanding — if there was anyone she could talk to without fear of judgment, it was this woman, who had been more than a mother to her these past five years.

The words were there, on the tip of her tongue, ready to fall from her lips as soon as she opened them. Tears of shame and unworthiness spilled down her cheeks, and she couldn't muster the will to bare her greatest indignity, her hideous betrayal. Loss and loneliness rushed at her again, and she slipped the necklace over her head, held the stone in the palm of her hand, and let the gesture speak for her silence.

"Oh, little princess." Brites's arm came around her, pulling her close. "These should be happier days filled with miracles, not bleak ones drowning in tears."

They would've been, had her flesh not been so weak. The teeth of the cilice woke up then, and she scratched their itch for attention, the reaction sending a domino of pain cascading across her thigh. "I deserve this," she said, more to convince herself than Brites.

"Yzabel, I love you like a daughter, but sometimes talking to you is like talking to a wall." She gently rapped her knuckles on the princess's temples. "This should think for itself. It should know right and wrong aren't as black and white as a book paints them to be."

"Not when it comes to this," Yzabel whispered. "I did something terrible and hurt Faty in the process. That's why she's back there. Why I will never see her again, and why we can't do anything about Matias."

Brites took the stone, scrutinized it with a heavy squint. The magic inside flashed and wavered before settling back to its steady thrumming. "That might not be necessarily true."

Hope dared to flare in her heart, and yet, she doubted. "You don't know what happened. I…" Yzabel's forehead touched Brites's shoulder. "She doesn't want to be with me."

"Now *that* is definitely not true. That girl loves you," Brites said. "And Fatyan isn't the sort of person who'll give up on someone she cares about."

Yzabel held the blanket close around herself, wanting to disappear into it, to never confront her inappropriate feelings or admit them out loud. It was pointless to hide in front of Brites, however; her former maid knew her too well and didn't need words to understand her heart.

She pried one of Yzabel's hands from the blanket and held it tightly. "Look at me."

Yzabel couldn't. She was too ashamed, too broken, too—

"I know it's confusing, but you're not the first, and certainly won't be the last."

In an instant, her round eyes met Brites's understanding ones. "Did she tell you?"

"She didn't have to." She squeezed Yzabel's hand. "It was in the way you looked at her; the way you were with her, and the way she was with you. It was bound to happen, sooner or later. My one regret is that I wasn't there to smack sense into you when you started whipping yourself raw."

"How did you hear about that?" Yzabel asked, balking at the memory.

"Dom Domingos came to gloat, claiming my efforts to turn you away from the Lord's good graces had been in vain." Brites sighed. "I thought you knew better by then."

"What was I supposed to do?" Yzabel's voice reduced to a weak whimper. "It was the only way I had to pay for that sin."

"Your unwavering piety was always your biggest fault," Brites pointed out, strong but not harsh. "Remember when Lucas was a pup, and would hump everything—including other male dogs? Black swans and pigeons frequently nest with members of the same gender. And if we're talking about adultery, that, too, is forbidden in the Bible. Do you see your betrothed being punished for it?"

Yzabel shrunk further into herself. "No. But I shouldn't do something just because Denis does it as well. And neither am I an animal who isn't aware of the consequences of her actions."

"In an ideal world, we'd all marry for love and infidelities wouldn't occur. And while some *do* get to marry for love, it's not the same for many of us." She fussed with Yzabel's hair. "Answer me this, did you choose to want Fatyan?"

She hadn't. It had happened the same way a sunrise happened. She'd been slumbering in the darkness of ignorance, and then, out of nowhere, the brightness had come, shedding light on everything, putting names in what had been nameless.

"No."

"Had you a choice, would you have let your father promise you to Denis?"

The question stunned her for a moment. "No. I would've joined a place like this. Dedicated my life to helping others through the Lord." Yzabel bit into her lip. "Alas, I was too valuable for that. I was always to be married off, and when the King of Portugal and the Algarves asked for my hand… Papá couldn't say no."

"A convent is where you should've been. Where do you think women who love other women end up if not in marriages of convenience?"

"You mean to tell me they…the nuns…" It seemed impossible to think as much. No women were purer than those who dedicated their lives to the Lord, and—

Yzabel inhaled, halted her mind's racing. Weren't they pure women still? Did those unnatural desires make them less so because they felt them?

"Some of them, yes. It was the only way they could be themselves behind closed doors, and it works. Almost everyone is oblivious to a woman's true affections if they aren't directed toward men." She gently lifted Yzabel's chin. "You're going to marry for a political alliance. So long as that alliance stays in place, so long as you give Denis what's expected of you, *no one* will even notice you have a preference for women. If anything, it makes it easier for you to follow your heart and be happy in ways your betrothed can't make you."

Happiness. She'd been so full of that when she'd been with Faty, until she remembered how wrong their affair was.

When she didn't speak, Brites continued, "You didn't have a choice in whom your father promised you to, but Yzabel... You have a choice now. You can keep on hating yourself for the things you feel, keep hurting yourself to try to make it go away, throw yourself into your duties until you're too exhausted to think about anything else. It will work, for a while. Then it won't, and by the time you realize you've made a mistake, it'll be too late to correct it because you will have driven away everyone you love." No doubt lurked in Brites's steady tone, or her dark eyes. "And you won't be able to visit me, either, because I won't want to see you."

Dread weakened her voice, weakened her question to a pathetic sob of, "You'd do that?"

"You'd ask me to watch you slowly kill yourself again? I've been through that once. It was enough." Brites huffed. "And if you can't accept Fatyan or yourself, then you can't accept me, either."

A knot wrapped her stomach as puzzlement blinked in her eyes. "What?"

"Like I said, you're not the first. I called myself a widow to hide who I am. I raised an adopted son to hide who I am." Grief trembled in Brites's voice. "And the reason why I accepted your mother's proposal to come to Aragon to help you was because I knew you'd lead me back here, to the person I love."

Yzabel's heart was a thousand pieces slowly breaking apart, for even though she could hate herself and her wants, she couldn't summon the same righteousness for Brites. "Is it Zaida? You *did* talk about her a lot. And she was *your* Enchanted Moura."

"Her, indeed." Brites smiled. "We traveled together for twelve years, but when all that happened with Matias, she refused to stay with me while I brought him up as my own. We settled in this city, and she went to the convent, seeking their protection while I stayed in the house where you met Matias tonight. But I'm old now, Matias is no longer the boy I raised, and I'd rather spend every day I have left with her in this gilded cage rather than alone and in freedom."

That had been what Faty has said, too, in different words, right before their fight.

"I…" Humbling tears fell from trembling eyes. "I didn't know."

"I never wanted you to. You were so set on the Book, on doing everything by it…"

She'd driven the closest thing she had to a mother to secrecy. Although she wished to deny she'd have done it, Yzabel knew it'd be a lie. Had Brites admitted to it before, she would've acted the same way she had with Faty, making her no better than the hypocrites who claimed to want to help but never did anything about it. She was no better than men who waged wars over interpretations of faith, no better than the prelates who stole from the people.

"I'm so sorry," she sobbed. "I had no right to force you to keep that part of yourself locked away and out of sight."

"And I accept your apology because I know you mean it. But Yzabel, dear." Brites smoothed the side of Yzabel's face. "That acceptance has to be for everyone. Including Fatyan. Including yourself."

"But how can I do that?" Desperation lifted Yzabel's voice. "I'm already promised to Denis, and when I marry him,

I'll have to take vows before the Lord. I can't betray them."

And she *had* to marry him. Not just because their union would keep Castela from waging war on either Portugal or Aragon; if she stood to have a chance at changing the world for the better, she had to be Queen of Portugal and the Algarves rather than a princess at the whims of others.

"Ai, Lord give me patience. No one expects you to be a true saint. And no one's saying you have to *act* on anything," Brites sighed and rolled her eyes before placing a hand over Yzabel's heart. "The Lord is here, Yzabel, not in the Bible, not in any book. He loves you as He made you, and He made you as you are—and that is the truth. So long as you share love and not hate, the Lord will *never* abandon you. He knows the world wasn't always the way it is now, and it won't remain like this forever. But we live when we live, and if Rome wasn't built in a day, you can't topple centuries-old misconceptions in a day, either. So don't try. What you do is, you find happiness where you can, and you make sure no one finds out where it comes from."

"But what if people suspect?"

"They don't. Not the men, anyway. They see us as breeding cows and don't really understand that we can want, too. Especially if what we want is what we can't have. That's…too much of a man thing, and in their self-absorbed brains, women aren't capable of the things a man is."

"Not even women?"

"They might, but…" Brites shrugged. "Like you, their brains have been washed into thinking they can't feel that way. That it's impossible. Use their misconceptions to your advantage."

It seemed so easy, so…doable. "How can you be sure?"

Brites scoffed. "Princesses and queens keep the company of other women all the time. So long as you lock the door and keep your deviations behind it, no one will ever know or suspect what goes on between the two of you. Not to mention those behaviors are easier to hide among women. Women can hold each other's hands in public. They can kiss each other on the cheek in public. They can embrace in public. In that, it's easier being a woman with so-called unnatural needs than a man in the same situation. It's unfair, true, and we should all be free to show our love—because that's what it is. Love."

"And Love is the ultimate commandment," Yzabel finished. Once, she would've been shocked to an allusion to such immorality; now, she felt only frustration at the injustice, and shame for doubting God.

"It is." Brites brushed Yzabel's hair from her face. "And the Lord knew you'd never be able to love your betrothed in that way—but He still wanted you to experience it, and all the wonders that come with being with someone who's right for you." A daring, knowing wink. "There's no risk of contracting a bastard in an affair between women."

That much was true. It was almost funny that Yzabel deemed her feelings for Faty unnatural because no child could come of their union, and it'd taken Brites's words for her to turn it around and see it as a blessing.

Just as with her magic, what Yzabel had believed a curse was a gift from God in disguise.

"You called me daughter of your heart." She hugged Brites, kissed her cheek, added, "Thank you for being my heart's mother in return. Thank you for everything."

The sweet pressure of a peck on her cheek. "How much do you trust Fatyan?"

"With my life."

With her secrets.

With her heart.

"Good. That's what it'll take, if you want to get her out." Stone in hand, Brites trudged back to the cabinet, the drawer's creak cringing in Yzabel's teeth, and plucked a knife from within. "I have to curse you the same way she was. You will become pure magic, the same way she did when Yusef did it to her. That means you won't grow old or ill once the two of you get out." Brites came back with heavy steps. "I also don't know what will happen if two Enchanted beings break each other's curses. There's a chance both of you will die if one does; a chance you'll die independently of each other; and a chance you never will." She leveled a stern look at Yzabel. "Are you sure you want this?"

The argument between her and Faty flickered behind her eyes. The look on Fatyan's face, lined with disbelief and colored with hurt, embittered her tongue with regret and despair. The part about them dying wasn't a theory Yzabel cared to test anyway, and she could deal with it when the time came. She wouldn't need to be afraid of the red plague or any other sickness anymore, either.

As for the aging, she supposed she could always ask Faty for help. If she stayed. But neither of that mattered, not when this was a second chance at making things right; a chance to ask Faty to return her friendship, her patience, her guidance, even though she had no right to any of them. Most of all, she wanted to ask her for forgiveness over the hurtful things she'd said, how she'd reacted.

She had no right to that, either. Because in that moment, she'd chosen cruelty over kindness, sowed seeds of ugliness and reaped their bitter reward. All she could do was hope Faty chose differently. Heart pounding and breath held, she answered, "Yes. I'm sure."

"I'll put the necklace around Lucas and tell him to

go back. If all goes well once you're in, you should be in your rooms by the time you get out. And be very, *very* careful around Matias. He might not say anything to Denis about seeing you, but he will find a way to pressure you into making more mistakes." Brites put the still-humid cloak back on Yzabel's shoulders, then held her at arm's length, a long look passing between them, and a gentle whisper rolled from her smiling lips, "Good luck, little princess."

So quickly Yzabel barely caught it, Brites grabbed her hand and slid the blade across, pressed it against the stone as she chanted,

"Ó pedra encantada,
Que este sangue seja
O pagamento de entrada—"

A loud *crack* thundered in Yzabel's ears, and radiant energy struck her with the speed of lightning. Her body splintering and shrinking; Brites a giant holding a mountain as a tug at her center pulled past the hard, jagged edges and into the stone.

Immaterial, Yzabel floated in the never-ending mist.

Below her, steam puffed around a replica of the springs in Terra da Moura, and *there*, sitting on a granite edge with her legs in the water, black hair a coat around her shoulders...

Fatyan.

Yzabel tried to scream for her, but she had no mouth; she tried to feel for her throat, but she had no hands. As with the flowers and bread, she focused on her magic—that was all she'd become, pure and undiluted magic—imagined her toes, her feet, her legs, her torso, her arms, her head, falling like a star at midnight and crashing straight into Fatyan's waiting arms.

"You're here," she stammered, sinking her face into Faty's hot neck, half expecting her to dissolve and vanish from under her. "You're here."

Warmth bloomed in Yzabel's brow, on her cheeks, of lips and kisses and tears. Faty hugged her as she always had in their brief time together, a span of weeks that felt like years, and perched her chin on Yzabel's head.

Softly, as if afraid, as if dreaming, Faty whispered, "I'm here."

CHAPTER TWENTY-SIX

One Last Trade

Yzabel didn't know how long they stood there, simply basking in each other's touch. Too long. Not enough. Eventually, she scraped up enough courage to look at Faty, who was still wearing the nightgown of that fateful night. "I thought I'd never see you again," she whispered. "I tried to tell myself it was for the best, but…"

"I did, too," Fatyan admitted. "You said some very cruel things."

The harshness stung—but she deserved it. "I'm sorry for how I reacted. I…" She suffocated on all the things she wanted to say, all the apologies she had to make. "I wanted to take it back as soon as I said it. I talked to the stone every day, hoping you could hear me."

"I know. I've been listening." Faty let go of her, a critical glint in her eye. "You should've been smarter about how you give away your bread. What possessed you to do it alone at night?"

"It's the only time Matias isn't around to follow me and report my every movement to Denis." She wetted her dry lips. "Did you know who he was?"

"I suspected it when he mentioned the sihaq. But no, I didn't know, not until he found you tonight. He was older, back when I knew him, and always wore a veil." Faty let go of her, sunk back onto her seat by the spring's edge. "I realize you came here through great trouble because you need my help to deal with him. But it's moot. I can't forgive him."

Shame coated Yzabel's cheeks with red. "That might have been the catalyst, yes." She dragged her feet to Fatyan's side and sat beside her. The water was as warm as she remembered. "But I would've come for you regardless."

Impassive, Faty slid her a look from the corner of her eye. "Are you still afraid of me?"

Yzabel winced, the question stabbing at her as effectively as any knife. "If there's anyone I was afraid of, it was myself. I acted in confusion, and I hurt you."

"You did." Her legs kicked small waves on the water. "But I should've known better than to push you. Or to run."

"But you were right. I *did* want it." She wanted it still, so strongly and desperately she had to hug her knees to her chest to keep herself from crumbling.

"Yza…to force someone's hand, even if they want it deep down, is forcing them nonetheless. You weren't ready." A long, silent look passed between them that ended when Faty sighed. "You still aren't."

She was unable to deny it. Brites's words sounded in her head, urged her to take the leap, to say what was in her heart. But it was one thing to realize her love for Faty wasn't wrong, or that they weren't the only ones; another entirely to accept it for herself and ask for it in return. "I'm sorry."

"Don't." Faty turned to her, took Yzabel's cheek in her hand. "I was selfish, demanding that you love me as I love you. I was selfish when I tossed aside your friendship as being less-than when it's not." Tears shimmered in her green eyes. "That's what I realized when I was trapped here, listening to you every day. I know you love me. I know we both want something else, but if friendship is all you can give me, then it's all I'll take, because I'd rather be your friend than be nothing to you at all."

It was everything Yzabel could ask for, offered without her voicing anything. Her body was already moving when her mind caught up, and she was already hugging Faty again, who silently allowed her to nestle into her. The curve of her neck was the perfect cradle to Yzabel's face, her arms the perfect home. Yzabel's chest seemed to be expanding, her rib cage too small, too tight for all the feelings spiraling inside her. "I missed you. So much."

"I missed you, too," Faty said. "I even missed your bear-wolf-thing."

Yzabel giggled, remembering that time passed differently here and Lucas was probably sitting in her chambers, waiting for them to pop out of the stone. "Then you'll stay with me?"

"For as long as you'll have me."

The scent of almonds and magic took root in her nose. Yzabel inhaled it deeply, nodding against Faty's warm neck. "Thank you."

Not the words she *wanted* to say—but they were the only ones she had. "You *do* realize you'll have to kiss me if we're both to get out?"

"I do." She lifted her head to meet Fatyan's gaze. "We should make it one worth remembering."

Pressure tingled on Yzabel's lips in the wake of Faty's fingers. "Every kiss shared with you is worth remembering."

Her heart burst with tender warmth, the truth resounding in her memories, where the memory of every kiss with Faty had been imprinted. She smiled as she leaned forward, noses brushing, and against Fatyan's mouth, she whispered, "Freedom from the stone or not, whether I can show it or not, I promise that my heart will always hold love for you."

The heat of Fatyan's strained breath, of words murmured back, of a kiss, gentle and unhurried. The stone's tether snapped, and as the current of magic swept the ground from under them, Yzabel pulled Fatyan closer, desperate to taste more, to feel more, for this kiss to never end and for reality to never come. Their lips remained locked as they emerged, and although Yzabel never wanted to let go, she stepped away.

They were in her rooms in Estremoz, with Lucas jumping at Yzabel, whining with relief. Outside, the first rays of sunlight painted the dark horizon with orange hues. A cold wind trailed inside from the still-open window, the wet marks of the storm scattered along the floor and curtains. Yzabel headed toward it, meaning to shut it, but her hand stopped cold on the frame when she looked toward the town. Over in the less-fortunate part of town, smoke rose from a house close to the wall, a sight that froze the breath on her lungs.

"Matias said he was going to set Brites's old house on fire and have it framed as divine punishment. That he would use that to kill me." The words left her slowly, like a confession. "Why burn it empty, though?"

"That goat-face, shit-eater of a Benzedor." Fatyan's footsteps as she approached the sill were like her voice, rushed and angry. "So that's how he's going to play this."

Yzabel blinked and frowned. "What do you mean?"

"That house wasn't empty." Fatyan scratched at the wooden window frame, marked each conclusion with a tap. "You might've foiled a detail in his scheme, but he can still go ahead with the rest. He doesn't need your body to frame Brites, not if he's desperate enough and can stand the pain of an amputation or four. If push comes to shove, he can always use a pig's to make up the torso that's missing."

His limbs grew back, echoed Brites in Yzabel's head.

"If Brites's house burns while there are either pig or human bones inside, Dom Domingos and Court will tie her to this fire like they tried to in Terra da Moura," Yzabel completed. She could picture his grand arguments and gestures while he made his case before Court. "They'll claim it was dark magic gone awry, and I won't have a choice but to give myself up to save her."

"Or you'll make a mistake while clearing Brites's name. Yusef—Matias, as he calls himself now—won't have to kill you if the Portuguese do it themselves." Fatyan's gaze hardened with resolution. "This won't end until we're dead, or he is."

Arguing against that was impossible. Yzabel had heard the spite in his voice, seen vengeance burn in his gaze, felt cruelty in his actions. His prolonged life stemmed from anger so deep, it seemed to have tainted everything in his life. Still, it wasn't a knife through his heart or poison in his cup that they needed. "The only way for him to die is for you to forgive him. Until then, there's nothing we can do."

"I can't just forgive him like *that*." Fatyan snapped her fingers. "And it has to be genuine, meaning I have to look at the man who stole my life, who used me not once, but *twice*, bound himself to me without my consent, and let that sight overcome me with enough pity and selflessness, I *voice* the emotion. You couldn't forgive your sahar when you thought it evil—how can I do the same to someone who truly is?"

"You said you'd given up on hating him and your father.

Surely it can't be hard to—"

"Giving up on hate isn't the same as forgiveness," Fatyan cut Yzabel off with a hiss. "And even if I could forgive Yusef for putting me in the stone, I can't so easily forgive him for trying to kill you. Or for doing everything in his power to make your life miserable."

"Then work on it, like I had to work on my gift," Yzabel argued softly. "Meanwhile, we have to put you somewhere. I doubt you want to spend the day stuck in my rooms—"

"I'm not leaving you alone. Not with Yusef around and out to kill you." Fatyan looked at her from over her proud nose. "I'll pose as a castle maid today and wait until night to behead him. We can ask the convent to hide his infant self, and I'll pass as him until we have time to think of something better."

In Yzabel's chest, something tightened and softened all at once. "You hate taking a man's form."

"Even more so when it's the form of a man you hate. But I will do it if it keeps you safe." Faty's hands settled on Yzabel's shoulders, and her voice steadied. "And Yza, *think*. He can't harm you or spread lies about Brites if he's a baby. My sahar lets me sense danger. He can't ambush you if I'm around, and neither will he be able to recognize me." She brushed Yzabel's cheek. "Trust me. I can do this."

"What if you're wrong?" Yzabel took Faty's hand from her face and held it, the irrational fear that she'd be alone again if she let go. "What if Yusef finds you and puts you inside another stone and I can't find you again? Or someone else notices you're not a castle maid?"

"I'll get out of it and change into someone else. And if Yusef is the one to do it, you can be certain I'll be ripping his head from his neck before he can curse me again. Whoever's there can see him turn into an infant and label him as a demon child." Fatyan shrugged. "Works out well, too."

The thought of plotting someone's demise sat on Yzabel's stomach like acid, but try as she might, she couldn't think of a better alternative. And Fatyan was right about Yusef being unable to do harm if he was reduced to a crying infant.

At long last, Yzabel allowed herself a nod. "You need a uniform," she said while fishing out an older cloak from the closet. "It will be downstairs, in the laundry room." She held onto the wool when Fatyan made to take it. "The other servants will be up by now."

"And have the bear-wolf ready in case Yusef comes in and tries anything." Fatyan tied the cloak around her neck and tugged on the cowl. "Don't leave until I'm back."

Yzabel nodded, hand on Lucas's head. "Don't let them catch you."

"Yza, please." Faty rolled her eyes, changing their color to brown halfway into the motion. Her face rounded, her nose shortened, her brows arched, and when she next spoke, her voice was higher pitched. "You're talking to someone who pried secrets from prelates and slipped evidence into their boots. I'll be fine."

She *had* done those things, had she not? And so secretly that no one, not even Yzabel, had noticed until the results had been shoved in front of her face. Now she could only nod and watch as Fatyan slipped silently out the door and into the castle. The aftermath was different. She had a name for the sweet clenching in her womb, for her shortness of breath, for the way her tongue ran over tingling lips to relive that teasing taste of cinnamon. Before, she'd been starving. Now, she starved still. She would always be starving.

In freeing Fatyan, she'd traded one hunger for another.

CHAPTER TWENTY-SEVEN

Dire Consequences

Not half a chime later, Yzabel finished changing into her regular clothes and the hinges on the door to Yzabel's room screeched. Dread whispered between her shoulder blades, and every hair on her neck stood on end as she jumped from the bed, clicking her tongue so Lucas would know to stay alert. Yusef stepped inside the room, and although her thoughts were running, her body wouldn't move while her dog crouched in front of her, teeth bared, growl rumbling.

Buy time. She had to buy time before Faty arrived, and to appear brave, she crossed her arms over her chest. "Come to finish your job?"

He smirked, scoffed, and said, "Good. We're not going to pretend last night didn't happen."

"It's hard to feign levity when someone tries to kill you," Yzabel hissed, hand on the back of Lucas's neck. "Why would you be here, if not to do what you couldn't yesterday?"

"The king has sent me to fetch you." Yusef's large, calloused hand held open the door, while his other beckoned at her in the smuggest gesture she'd ever beheld. "He thought you'd like to hear the case Dom Domingos is making against that old shrew."

Yzabel's breath hitched, but she made herself stay put and calm. The house hadn't even stopped smoking, and they were already set on using that event for their nefarious purposes. "And you can what, stab me behind my back as soon as I approach you?" She shook her head. "I'm not going anywhere near you."

The look he gave her was of pure arrogance, his short, low laugh even more so. "Why would I kill you when the Portuguese will do that of their own volition?"

Yzabel retreated until the back of her knees hit the bed. "What have you done?"

"What fun would it be to tell you?" He gestured for her to leave again. "Call off the hound, Princess. And keep your sahar to yourself."

Her eyes narrowed and her lips pressed together as she debated her options. Yusef could very well be lying about Denis sending him to get her and be leading her into a trap instead. Her gift had been exposed, and there was a chance he'd told her betrothed. There was a chance he hadn't, too, as Denis had dismissed the stories about Enchanted Mouras outright. It made sense the king would dismiss this one as well, if the idea were presented without proof.

If she went, Matias might push her into a dark corner and kill her. But if he were telling the truth about Dom Domingos making a case against Brites, Yzabel could not stay behind and let him poison the room without resistance.

"Walk in front of me," she said reluctantly. "I'll follow."

Mercifully, Matias did not argue. With him in the lead, they left the royal chambers and crossed the cloister's archways, then came into a Great Hall fallen into dissent.

Tables with assorted breads, cheeses, meats, and wine had already been set up by the servants, and after making sure Matias was several feet away, Yzabel stood on her tiptoes to look at the circle of prelates talking to her betrothed, with the Chancellor-Mor at their center.

"How else do you explain the bread, Your Majesty?" Dom Domingos asked, dabbing the sweat on his forehead with a kerchief. "Many of the people said they found it at their door the morning before. The churches have also reported the same, as has the hospice, only with them, it's much more. At least a dozen loaves."

Hugging her mantle closer, Yzabel looked at a smug Matias over her shoulder and drifted to her seat beside Denis. Goose bumps rose on every inch of her skin, and ugly suspicion quaked in her insides as she sat. She made a nonchalant show of filling her waiting glass with water and taking a drink while her gaze flitted along the crowd, hoping to find Faty in her disguise. Which she realized was silly—Fatyan and Yusef could feel each other's nearness, always had. The only reason Fatyan would be in the same room as him would be to ambush him, and she would not be doing that in front of an entire Court.

"It is the very behavior of a witch! It's their fado to follow the Devil across the streets at night, and to keep her soul, she must pass through seven churches and seven fountains before the sun rises. Because Estremoz does not have such a number of either, she leaves the bread to appease the Devil's hunger, inviting him to feast on those families. And in addition to *that* her own son saw her the night this started, only to be chased off by crows! And last night, when he went to the house that is rightfully *his*"— Dom Domingos pointed to his right, to where Matias stood, jaw set, eyes somber, without stopping his tirade—"Guarda

Real Matias found a woman there, with blood on her hands and a body at her feet, using dark forces to make bread out of human flesh. Dark forces she used against him before he could confront her, giving her time to flee."

Yzabel clutched the arms of her chair, knuckles white, nails shredding against the wood. She had to put a stop to this, to come up with an argument that would both cast doubt on Matias's testimony and keep Brites safe.

Gathering her privilege and nerve, weapons she despised but had to use nonetheless, Yzabel turned to Dom Domingos with a haughty tilt to her chin. "Brites joined the convent as soon as we arrived at Estremoz. Did you ask the sisters for their testimony?"

The Chancellor-Mor halted, his surprise at being questioned by the princess evident in his rapidly blinking eyes. "Well, yes—and they swore on the Bible she'd been there all night. But nuns protect each other, Your Highness."

"And Matias has admitted to me that he has a vendetta against his mother," Yzabel said, a current of anger lifting her voice and directing her gaze to the culprit. Yusef beheld her like a rabbit caught in an ever-tightening trap, one of his raised eyebrows daring her to keep going. "It's his word against an entire convent's, and yet it's *him* you choose to believe."

"You did say you hadn't seen the woman's face clearly," Denis finally intervened, pinching the bridge of his nose with a groan. "Couldn't it have been someone else?"

Dom Domingos grunted. "Please, Your Majesty. Matias's loyalty has been proven twice over. The same can't be said for Brites, or her friends at the convent, who enable her witchery."

And there it was. Jaw hard, Yzabel kept her eyes firmly on Dom Domingos, regretting that she'd ever considered him an ally. Regretting that she'd let him poison her own mind, as he wanted to do with everyone else's.

"Why must you blame a witch? Wouldn't it make more sense if it were someone distributing their household's surplus of food? A benefactor who wishes to remain anonymous, so they do it during the night, when avoidance is easier?"

A slow nod. "Could be, Your Highness. But every person who has the means to do it swears it's not them. We asked the baker, too, but they say they haven't leftover bread to give. Food doesn't just appear out of nowhere."

She frowned at his condescension. "So someone is feeding the poor, and you have no idea who it is. I fail to see the issue here."

"If it's not her and her dark magic, then how?" He swept his arm in a grand, theatrical gesture, addressing the room. "Then where else could the bread be coming from? The baker says no one is buying more. I assume your kitchen hasn't increased their bread production, either. However it's being made, it's through no conventional means."

"You are very firm on this witch idea," Yzabel commented dryly.

"Because she *is* one." Dom Domingos turned to Denis without pausing. "I was the bishop overseeing this region before His Majesty asked me to become his Chancellor-Mor. Her fame was already of note back then, as someone that people—especially girls—went to in times of need."

"Using herbs is not witchery, prelate, and neither is a house catching fire," Yzabel spoke as flatly as she was able—not much, since Dom Domingos's words incensed her to the point she decided to goad him. "Unless you want to call me a witch as well? I do make plenty of salves for the hospice, after all."

"Forgive me, Princess, but you can't know—"

She cut him off with harshness. "Dona Brites was under my employ for years, and she was nothing but respectful. Yet you choose to put your faith in a man who'd speak against his own mother and who isn't even sure it was her that he saw."

"Snakes such as her know when to play meek, and when to strike. You dismissed her for a reason, did you not?" He directed his question toward Denis, Yzabel's input clearly undesired.

Her hands curled on the arms of her chair. They wanted to ignore her? She spoke louder, "This is nonsense."

"It is," Denis agreed, severe eyes on the prelates, but before Yzabel could sigh with relief, he added, "But we can't overlook the fact that someone is sneaking through town at night and giving everyone bread, or that Matias saw a woman set fire to a house that's his by right." Denis stood, voice booming across the hall. "To put Dom Domingos's suspicions to rest, we'll ask the convent to surrender Brites to us tonight, and I will assign more patrols to the city at night in case the culprit is someone else. If the bread keeps showing while she's under our care, we'll know she's innocent, and reassess our options."

Yzabel's breath stiffened in her nose, and her bones became stone. On the other side of the room, Matias stared at her still, the corner of his lips turned up as if to say, "Your move." Righteous anger and determination blossomed in her chest, and she turned it all into scowling back at him.

Much as the idea of letting them lock Brites up again repulsed her, it was the simplest way to clear her name. But more guards at night meant more danger; more danger meant she'd have to be more careful. It was stopping that was out of the question. It was God's will she carried in her heart when she gave away food, His will that let her turn flowers into bread. He would protect her from their misguided accusations, see her safely past the guards in the night, and help her clear Brites's name.

"It's all we ask, Your Majesty," the Chancellor-Mor said.

After they were gone, Yzabel slid Denis a look, then leaned over to whisper, "You can't keep throwing Brites to the dungeons every time Dom Domingos tells you to."

"Yet you and I both know she *is* a witch of the Caraju." Denis returned her side glare, suspicion unwavering. "If she's innocent, you have nothing to worry about."

Yzabel kept her teeth pressed together as she leaned back on her chair. "It's disappointment I'm feeling, because you had a chance to put them in their place and didn't."

"What would you have had me do? Someone *is* giving away all that food, and at least this way, we'll know for sure if it's Brites."

"Even if it were her! The bread is an act of kindness, and kindness isn't witchcraft, Denis." Yzabel crossed her arms over her chest, frustrated at the little sway she had in this matter. As the saint who left loaves of bread for the poor, she was one person, with that same reach. The saint only had enough influence to be in one place, at one time. But as Portugal's future queen, Yzabel's reach was that of a country. And she'd given enough to Denis to be able to make another demand now. One she could use to both help the country, and clear Brites's name.

"If you're so concerned about it, perhaps it's time to reconsider my proposal to have a charity day every Sunday."

Denis grabbed the boar leg on his plate and took his teeth to the tender flesh around it. "Back to this, are we?"

Yzabel regarded the food displayed around the long

tables with a critical eye. "How much of this lunch is going to waste?"

"That isn't your concern."

"It is. So many people are starving while waiting for the next harvest, and we waste. So. Much."

"I thought you were over meaningless charity."

That offended her worse than any witch rumor. "Charity is not meaningless, and I will never cease thinking of ways to help those who need it. I will inherit your responsibilities when we marry; that means I'll inherit your people, too. I will be damned if I stop my endeavors when it gets hard."

Denis massaged the thin bridge of his nose. "Our responsibility is that we rule fairly. Nothing else."

"By the Lord, can you not hear the privilege in your tone?" The anger boiled her insides, screaming the one way to extinguish it. Her lack of control drew the uneasy stares of nearby servants and lords.

Denis's face turned stern, as hard as granite. "Calm down."

"I will calm down when you listen to what I have to propose with an open mind."

Shaking his head, Denis took a drink from his wine goblet, bringing it down hard on the table when he finished. His jaw trembled, and Yzabel feared she'd provoked his temper—but he breathed out and looked at her from the corner of his eye. "Mention allocating money and this conversation is over."

"There are no dinheiros involved." When her fury didn't subside on its own, Yzabel swallowed it. She gestured about the table again. "Look. Look at how much is going to waste every day from this table alone."

"It's not all going to—"

"Yes, some of it goes to the hounds. But so do the servants' leftovers. And the guards'. The hounds eat well enough. The people, however, do not. I don't propose we give them money to eat. You're against that, and I understand your reasons. But Denis…if it's food we're going to throw out, why not give it to those who don't have any? We'll alleviate their burdens without spending anything. Same thing about clothes we don't use. If we get everyone of means, every prelate to participate, don't you think there's much to gain? Just once a week, Denis, on the Lord's day of rest, we do what He bade us to. We help our neighbors."

A scowl settled on Denis's face, but it was thoughtful rather than angry. "There's some logic to what you're saying," he conceded. "It's true we enjoy a surplus of resources. But you forget something—the Portuguese are a proud people. Do you believe they would accept leftovers? Wouldn't they think we're patronizing them?"

"Look at the other boar shank you didn't touch. Look at the meat on it. Why would anyone turn that away? Why would they object to their king sharing from his table?" Her tone turned placating. "This would lessen the impact of the mysterious bread. If your subjects can rely on you once a week, they might no longer need the so-called witch."

Brown eyes stayed on her, unwavering and unreadable. "Fine."

She shouldn't be so grateful, but she was. On an impulse and much to his wide-eyed surprise, she kissed his cheek and the red beard he insisted on growing. "Thank you. I'll coordinate with the churches and the castle's governess."

It was small, but it was progress. And more importantly, it was progress she could use not just to help Brites, but the entire city.

. . .

After breaking fast together shortly after Court adjourned, Denis took Yusef and the rest of the Guarda Real to the barracks so they could organize the new patrols going out at night, as well as the several to be posted around the convent. Yzabel left the Great Hall to search for Faty, worried she hadn't seen her since the morning, fearing she'd been caught. That concern wasn't very long lived, for as soon as she ventured into one of the cold stone corridors, a hand pulled her into an alcove.

It took only a touch for her to recognize to whom it belonged. Faty, safe in her disguise. "You scared me," Yzabel blurted out, hand on her chest. "Did you run into any trouble?"

"No. Did you?" Faty asked back in her masked voice.

"Yusef came to get me after you left. Did you hear what they said? What Denis is going to do?"

A quick nod. "Listen, Yza. I'm going to find out more about these night patrols." Fatyan kept her tone a hushed whisper. "You need to go someplace where you won't be alone. The more eyes around you, the better." A reassuring touch to Yzabel's upper arm. "I'll come get you once I know enough."

Thus, Yzabel retired to the sewing room with Lucas, and found it already overflowing with gossip and embroidery. She barely had time to pick up her kit from the corner when talk of the bread started, and she wasn't even in her seat when it turned derogatory.

"I've told my maids not to eat it," Lady Violeta said without looking up from her cross-stitch of a hunting scene. "I'll not have servants who eat the Devil's food!"

Yzabel stabbed downward with her needle. This discussion followed her wherever she went, spreading like a sickness. "Perhaps if you paid them more, they wouldn't have need to eat *the Devil's food*," she said.

"My princess! Surely someone devout as you must realize there's devilish sorcery involved!"

She kept her face blank, but anger seeped along the edges of her tone. "I didn't take the Devil to be charitable."

"It's how he gets you," Lady Graciete said, jumping to Violeta's aid. "With promises of salvation that are nothing but a sentence to eternal doom."

Blood spread, a red flower on the aida cloth, and Yzabel realized she'd pierced her finger. She sucked on it, letting the metallic taste spread on her tongue.

Lips pressed together, Yzabel kept quiet while she waited for Faty to come back, thoughts raging a nebulous cloud over her head. She couldn't stop her nightly escapades because of fear, or because others thought it foul play. The gifts she had waiting for her on doorsteps told her enough about the situation. It was the powerful who were afraid, and with their hold on the land weakened, they resorted to baseless accusations. A sign her efforts were paying off.

How could she stop now?

When Faty reappeared in her castle maid disguise a couple of hours later, Yzabel was about ready to burst. As she stood, she dragged her grumpy chair across the Arraiolos rug underneath her. "Excuse me. I have other business to attend to."

Yzabel left the murmurs of "Our princess and her tender sensibilities" behind. Fatyan followed her as she stormed all the way back to her chambers and waited until they were inside with the door locked to shed the fake skin and say, "You can't go out tonight."

"If I don't, they *will* see it as proof that it was Brites." Yzabel slumped on the bed, Lucas climbing at her side. "All I can do is make sure the bread keeps showing. If not during the night, then during the day."

"And get caught yourself?" Fatyan asked with a raised brow. "I heard Yusef asking Denis to join the Guarda Noturna, and he was so insistent on it—because he *has* to catch the witch himself—Denis agreed. He won't be here at night anymore." She tilted her chin toward Lucas. "That is a good wolf-bear-thing you have, but it can't stop Yusef for long. Neither can you."

Yzabel shook her head. "I must. If not at night, then during the day, somehow. Denis is letting me arrange a weekly charity day with the church, so I could—"

"Amazing. He's *letting* you be charitable once a week," Faty interrupted with the dryness of sand. "At least your relationship has improved to the point he's not locking you in your rooms."

"He's not as bad as he first appeared." Yzabel sat up and Lucas took the chance to place his head on her lap for continued attention. "He asked for my help in running the country. I'm glad to oblige."

"And yet, you're still afraid to tell him about the sahar," Fatyan pointed out in a cold whisper. "He won't be in the dark about it for long if you don't change your plan. Forget being caught by the patrols, or Yusef telling him—what would've happened if he'd come to you in the night and you weren't here?"

Yzabel lowered her eyes, embarrassment heating her face. "I, um…went to him first. The second night he retired before I had to."

Footsteps shuffled on the stone floor. Then, too

innocently, "Did it hurt?"

The question scratched at her heart, and Yzabel remembered the moments shared with her betrothed and their disastrous finish.

Fatyan's sigh broke the silence in the room. "I'm sorry. That was mean of me," she said, moving to add more wood to the fire the servants had lit in the hearth while Yzabel had been away. "I shouldn't have —"

"I couldn't go through with it," she blurted at the same time. Fatyan halted. Yzabel's confession didn't, spilling out of her lips in frantic, broken syllables. "He-he has hair all over. On his shoulders, his back, his front — no matter where I put my lips, I'd catch a mouthful. His beard scraped, his f-fingers were rough, and I told myself to lie still, let him do whatever it was he needed to do. His tongue was down my throat, and I kept squirming, so I closed my eyes." Tears had begun to fall, hitting her skirts in wet plops. "Then all I could think about was you, and how unnatural it was to want you. I hated myself for it, was so ashamed of it, that he stopped.

"I betrayed my engagement in Terra da Moura, and I did it again in my head when I was with the man I'll be married to. That's when I realized I was different. Something I never would have known had I not met you, had you not…" Yzabel refilled her lungs with a deep inhalation. "There wasn't a day I didn't miss you, a day I didn't regret how I reacted, a day I didn't wish for you, a day where I didn't remember all the things I felt with you, and how everything else pales in comparison."

Quietude descended. Yzabel lifted her aching eyes to Faty, who stood with her parted lips shivering, thick black hair gleaming gold in the vagrant daylight. Looking at her, being with her, brought that quivering feeling back to her stomach and farther below, that grip squeezing around her heart, the memories of kisses and touches that she wanted to relieve so desperately.

"Was he angry?" Fatyan asked at last, concern deep in her voice. "When you couldn't, you know…"

A shake of the head. "No. He said we wouldn't have to do it if I didn't want to. That he can always legitimize his bastards if we have no children." Heat spread across her cheeks. "He was very understanding, considering."

"Huh." Fatyan blinked rapidly, but the genuine surprise was quickly replaced by a scowl. "And you still didn't tell him that you can make food out of flowers?"

"You saw how he was in Terra da Moura when Brites used the Caraju." Yzabel shook her head and gave a small shrug. "Why wouldn't he act the same way toward me?"

"You won't know unless you tell him." Fatyan's footsteps pounded, ever closer as she crossed the room. "This is one large frog for me to swallow, but…I might have slightly misjudged your husband-to-be." She knelt before the bed and took Yzabel's free hand. "But let's put that aside for now. It's Yusef who's the real danger, and he thinks he has you trapped." A mischievous smile curved her full lips. "Let's find a way to trap *him*."

Yzabel worried her lip as she considered it, and for the next couple of hours, she and Faty went back and forth on how to end Yusef's threat once and for all while keeping Yzabel safe and the suspicion off Brites. The details Yzabel obsessed over were nothing but pebbles in Faty's thinking, easily overcome or brushed aside, and when Yzabel would stick to proven tradition, Faty sought alternatives for improvement. They balanced each other nicely, virtues complementing each other's faults.

Faty made her work better, in a different, yet similar

to the way Yzabel made Denis's work better.

Alone and her way, it wouldn't be long until Yzabel either broke from exhaustion or was caught. But with Faty's help, and her perspective, Yzabel felt like she could not only feed one city, but the entire nation as well.

If the convent helped. If Yusef didn't see through their trap. If Denis was the person she thought he was. And at the end, one reckless leap of faith.

CHAPTER TWENTY-EIGHT

The Last Gamble

After the six o'clock mass in the Church of São Francisco, Yzabel stayed behind to talk to Padre Augusto about her plans for São Martinho in a couple of weeks. The castle would be opening its doors for the commoners to share agua-pé and roasted chestnuts with them; the churches would be providing bread and ingredients for soups to be given to anyone who asked. She was trying to make it a weekly custom and hoped Estremoz would prove a successful experiment, and then she could see it implemented across the country.

She parted from the Padre with a kiss on the cheek, then went to the convent next door while Grand Prior António—whom Denis had assigned to her when he shuffled Yusef in with the added night patrols—followed close behind. The empty vestibule greeted her with ominous silence. Behind the bars in the middle of the door, no sister waited with her knitting. Frowning, Yzabel tugged on the bell's cord, ringing it thrice, tapping her foot while she waited for someone to come, then pacing around the room when no one did.

She rung the bell again—some long moments later, a younger nun who introduced herself as Fabiana emerged on the other side of the bars. "I'm sorry, Your Highness," she said as she rushed to unlock the door. "It's been a most trying day. The prelates and the king demanded we give them Sister Brites; they said her induction had been illegal, and that by harboring a witch among us, we risked not only eternal damnation, but condemnation of these very walls."

"I know." Yzabel noted the sister's red-rimmed eyes, her blotchy complexion. "That's why I came. To help clear Brites's name."

The other woman sniffed. "Sister Zaida will be glad to hear it. She hasn't stopped crying."

Zaida. That was Brites's Enchanted Moura. "Can you take me to her?"

"Yes, of course." Sister Fabiana wiped her eyes with her sleeve. "Follow me."

The nun took her to the same room where Brites had taken Yzabel the night before. A circle of sisters gathered close to the fire, all clad in different forms of grief.

"Sisters," Fabiana called. "The princess is here."

A dozen sets of puffy eyes stared at her. A hawk-nosed sister with sharp cheeks patted the shoulder of the one sitting next to her. "See, Zaida? She came. Like Brites said she would."

"Princess Yzabel." Zaida lifted her head, her features lined only with sorrow, not age. The moment their eyes met, an entire conversation passed between them, unspoken. Enchanted Mouras didn't grow older than the age they were cursed at, and Yzabel would never look older than her seventeen years. *This*, a convent, was what waited her in the future. And before that, she'd have to find a way to hide her preternaturally young appearance. Matters to worry about later—she had some years to figure out how to deal with agelessness, and only today to help Brites.

That was why Yzabel had come, thus she rushed

forward and took the nun's hands in hers. "I'm so sorry. I never meant for this to find its way to Brites."

"She said you'd say that." Zaida's rosebud lips curved into a smile—she had a doll's round features, skin of lovely bronze, eyes brown specked with gold. "We said she didn't have to go with them. That we'd make Dom Domingos get an order from the Pope, which is the same as saying he can go put himself behind the setting sun." She squeezed Yzabel's palms. "But she said she had to buy you time for you to do what you had to do. That you'd save her."

A sister sighed. "All this over bread being given away."

"And now they'll hang poor Brites for it," another lamented. "They said taking her to the dungeons was a preventive measure, but we know how these things end when you're like us. Domingos despised many of us before we joined. He holds those grudges still, and twisting the Court's opinion is playtime for someone as short-sighted as him."

"It'll be one night, then another, then another, and another," Zaida added. "And with Yusef back to remembering himself, Brites will rot in that dungeon until they find you."

"I know. That's why I came," Yzabel said, and rose, steeling herself with a breath before telling the room, "I'm the one giving away the bread."

The sisters exchanged looks, none of which bore any surprise, followed by shrugs. "We know," Zaida said. "About your gift, too."

Short-lived confusion blinked in Yzabel's eyes. "Everyone here knows you're an Enchanted Moura, don't they?"

"Not just me. Many of us in this convent have been blessed by the Holy Spirit," Zaida explained, a hint of humor sneaking past her grief, and nodded to the two nuns at her sides. "Sister Maria can make sugar from salt, make exotic spices out of dust. Sister Edúlia can keep the rats from the stores with nothing but a sweep of her broom. I can change water into any beverage I desire. Small miracles, at the edge of our fingertips, that we practice away from prying eyes and behind locked doors."

Yzabel's marvel flitted between Edúlia and Maria, awe wide in her eyes. "You two as well? How many of us are there?"

"Five in this room. Twelve in this convent—thirteen, if you count Brites," Sister Zaida said. "And so many more, spread around the world."

"But Your Highness"—Sister Maria took Yzabel's left hand, where the gift burned the strongest—"when we find each other, we help each other. It's the only way people like us can survive."

Yzabel could scarcely believe it. "Why didn't Brites tell me you were all here?"

Sister Zaida drew an arm around Yzabel's shoulders. "She was waiting for you to come around on the blessings of the Holy Spirit. Then those things happened in Terra da Moura, and she couldn't."

"That's why people like us often end up in places like this," Edúlia softly said. "We have little choice, when so many outside these walls misunderstand our gifts."

She looked down at her hands, at the magical light twinkling in her breast. Her great-aunt's story played in her thoughts, of the miracle Erzsébet performed when caught doing the very same thing Yzabel did—feeding bread to the poor and needy. Yzabel had drawn the parallel before, when she'd believed her gift to be a curse, thinking it was a fate she had to run from. Now, she realized it was a fate she had to run to. Maybe that was yet another reason the Lord had entrusted Yzabel with her power. Should a queen put her mind to it, she could convince an entire country to pay equal devotion to all aspects of the Holy Trinity. Another responsibility for her to shoulder, and one she was willing to.

"That's why I want to give them a miracle," she said. "With the whole town watching, I want to show them a miracle of roses."

"You mean to be caught," Zaida gasped. "Yzabel…"

It was the one way to lift every bit of suspicion from Brites, the one way to save at least one of them from a terrible fate.

"And miracles are dangerous things, Princess. Open to interpretation." Sister Maria's lips pursed into a bloodless line.

"Maria is right." Zaida's grave eyes looked straight into Yzabel's. "If it goes the other way and they think it a demonic occurrence, they won't simply kill you. They'll trepanate you first, so they can say they tried to exorcise you when your country demands an answer."

A shiver racked her body at the mention of such a practice. Barbaric, to say the least, and a last-ditch effort to rid a mind of demonic influences. Even if she survived it, she wouldn't be the same after. No one was.

"I'll take the risk," she declared, and launched into an explanation. The sisters listened intently, periodically interrupting her to ask questions. In the end, they accepted Yzabel's request without struggle, but much worry.

"Meet us at São Francisco after morning mass. We'll take care of everything else," Sister Zaida was saying as she and the others accompanied Yzabel out. "Do you have a preference for flowers?"

"Estevas are very useful. Pansies, too." Yzabel halted briefly. "But anything you can get, I'll be able to use."

"We'll join you, all of us," Sister Edúlia added. "And we'll ask some of the padres in the church. Augusto and José will definitely come, at least."

"Padres Augusto and José are like us, too?"

"The Lord's magic is everywhere," Zaida said, kissing Yzabel's cheek goodbye. "Especially in His most loyal followers."

That evening, Yzabel sat at the table's head in the Great Hall, ears scintillating with the music of lutes and verses of song. Some of the nobles danced to the troubadour's tunes, and from time to time, Yzabel would find Fatyan in her castle maid's disguise to see the person behind that mask of flesh and bone. It could be the agua-pá getting to her head, but all she could think about was that night in Terra da Moura, and the overwhelming feelings that had arisen. And she knew Faty wanted the same as she did, saw it in her lingering gaze, felt it in her lingering touches.

This time, however, Faty wouldn't take the lead. It was up to Yzabel, and Yzabel had other duties to place before her selfish desires. Though she'd already accepted that there was nothing wrong with craving Faty, her first duty was to her betrothed, and she couldn't be with Faty in that way without seeing to her promises first. Yzabel turned to Denis, intent on asking his plans for the night, but he was as aloof as she was, staring somewhere to the left—she followed it with a squint, to the dancing floor, to

Aldonza. Although she was too far for Yzabel to discern her expression, the pang in her chest she got from seeing Denis's face was enough.

Yzabel wasn't the only one in love with someone she wasn't promised to.

Gently, she lay her hand on Denis's arm, and said, "She loves you, you know."

He regarded her with quizzical lines on his forehead, eyebrows low. "You know about that?"

"For some time." With a parting smile, Yzabel kissed him on the cheek. "Go see her. You deserve that happiness."

Yet as she spun to leave, he grabbed her hand, and looked up at her with hesitant eyes. "Yzabel, I have to ask you something, and I know it might be hard to answer truthfully, but…"

Her heart thumped painfully, and for a moment, she was afraid the red on his cheeks was of rage. But he seemed to have trouble looking at her and kept stumbling over his words.

"Do you, um… How to put this? Are you, um… In Terra da Moura, when you, you know, had that psychotic breakdown…" After several failed attempts, he closed his eyes, inhaled deeply, and blurted out, "Was it because you were in love with Fatyan?"

The blunt question hit her like a punch to the gut. Her jaw dropped. Her eyes widened. Her breath matched her pulse, fast and shallow.

That was all the answer Denis needed. His fingers stiffened, and she readied herself for whichever violence, whichever disgust he would throw at her. Yet he did the worst possible thing of all: rose from his chair and wrapped her in an awkward hug. "It's fine. It's fine," he said, hiding her face against his shoulders, patting her on the back.

Anyone who looked would see the scene exactly for how it was, a king comforting his future wife.

"How are you not angry?" she asked, trembling. "How did you know?"

"I've been in and out of brothels since I was thirteen and seen everything that goes along with it. Including women who were like that. And you were…different with that girl. I had my suspicions then, but it wasn't until you came to me that night that I was sure." He pushed her away just slightly. "I'm no hypocrite, Yzabel. If being with a woman makes you happy, you can. At least this way I'll know to have reason to worry if you show up pregnant and it wasn't me, because you won't be able to surprise me with dangerous infidelities."

Yzabel would've laughed if she weren't so shocked, and if acid guilt weren't churning in her belly. It had taken so much heartache for Yzabel to accept that part of herself, and Denis did it without a blink. Why not tell him of the part she hid from him still?

But she couldn't, not until tomorrow. He couldn't know what they planned to do or appear partial when the time came to judge her. He had to be as unaware of everything as the people she would rely on.

She dove into his chest and hugged him as hard as she could. "I'm sorry. I should've told you."

"I understand why you'd keep this a secret." He held her back, one hand brushing the back of her hair. "And we can't go back down south now, but if you want to send for Fatyan, you can. Or we can return after we're married and tell her yourself." He cupped her cheek when they parted. "You deserve that happiness, too."

"Thank you," she said, and meant it with all she was.

Tonight, Denis would be with someone who loved him.

And all Yzabel had to do was tell Faty she loved her, and maybe, she could have the same.

As soon as she left, Fatyan followed her under the castle maid's guise. Out of the hall, past the cloister, and into the corridor, the silence between them thickening Yzabel's tongue, reverberating in every step, lurking behind every door.

When they reached the solar, Yzabel still didn't know what to say. Her cheeks had grown impossibly hot, her lips dry. Nervous fingers fell on the lever; she inhaled when the door clicked, stepped past the threshold with slurring feet, and it was with anxiety that she nodded for Fatyan to follow. She did, a soft question in her brown eyes.

Yzabel turned the key, leaned against the door as she looked up at Fatyan's false features. "Please change back."

Magic swelled, and like clay being re-molded, Faty became herself, with her stunning eyes and luscious lips. "You know, we can still break Brites out of the dungeons and make a run for it," she said. "If you're worried about tomorrow, we can—"

"I'm not worried." Yzabel stepped closer, traced Faty's high cheekbone with her thumb, the line of a jaw, and felt Faty's entire body quieten. "I'll live with you or die with you." Heart pulsing in her throat, Yzabel brushed the bow of Faty's mouth, felt a hot breath parting it under her fingers. "We'll be together either way."

Tears welled along her eyelashes "What are you—"

"I'm ready now," Yzabel said, and let her fingers fall along the curve of Faty's neck. "If you still want to."

Faty's shoulders slumped, her nostrils flared, her eyes widened. Her teeth bit into her lower lip as her chest expanded and deflated once. Twice. "Yes," she said, one word fraught with pain and helplessness.

Yzabel kissed it away, tasting their mingled tears, tasting sadness because it took desperation for this to happen, tasting happiness because it *was* happening. A shift, and she held Fatyan closer, embracing her warmth, her love, and although Yzabel didn't care to compare them, it was inevitable. This was so different from what happened when Denis kissed her, so much better, filling her with desire and the need for *more*.

They pulled apart, panting breaths mingling. Yzabel wiped the tears on Faty's cheeks while ignoring the ones coating her own, and said, "I love you," before kissing Fatyan again. "I wish I hadn't been so stupid. I wish I hadn't believed this was wrong. And I wish it hadn't taken your absence for me to realize it, or that I had to stare death in the face to admit it."

"Death does have a way of putting things in perspective," Fatyan whispered, her arms falling around Yzabel's waist, her hands resting on the small of her back. "Maybe tomorrow I'll thank Yusef for making this mess and helping you along."

Yusef. A lot of tomorrow hinged on him acting the way they expected, and, ultimately, for Faty to break the ties that bound her to him. "Do you think you'll be able to forgive him?"

Fatyan tensed, a small wrinkle appearing between her brow, then disappearing with a shake of her head. "It will be fine. We know how to deal with him if I can't. Now." She pulled Yzabel against her. "No more talk of Yusef."

Even if Yzabel wanted to, she couldn't. Faty's lips were on hers again, building heat inside her, burning away any thoughts, any feelings that weren't about Faty, who used a gasp to slide her tongue in, brushing it against Yzabel's, supporting her when her knees almost gave. She clutched

Fatyan tighter, lost in feeling, eagerly returning everything, aware of her clumsiness—Fatyan chuckled, angling her head differently, kissing until they were out of breath, kissing more once they regained it.

They came to a stop at the foot of the bed. Over the dress, Faty trailed her fingers over the line of Yzabel's collarbone, drawing a shiver not from cold, but from pleasure.

"Yza?"

"Yes?"

"You can tell me to stop if you want me to."

"I know."

"Then…"

"I don't want you to stop. But…" Yzabel looked away, embarrassed.

Softly, Faty turned Yzabel's face back to face hers. "But what?"

"I know we…umm…did some things already, but…" She inhaled, the pent-up need and anticipation making her shudder. "I'm still unsure how it's supposed to go between us."

Fatyan smiled, the mischief fluttering in Yzabel's stomach. "Do you want me to show you?"

Their night together over a month ago echoed in her ears. This time, she left no room for doubt. "Yes."

Another kiss, and her mantle was on the floor, the dress over her head, the slippers kicked aside. Her hands helped Faty out of the castle maid's outfit, so tight around her ample chest, then the slippers and socks. Yzabel's back hit the covers, and slowly, Faty peeled one sock, then the other, leaving the scars of the cilice exposed.

A rush of warmth spilled from between Yzabel's legs as Faty took her lips to where the cilice had marked her, tongue sliding along the tender flesh.

Then she came up, and they pressed together, nothing but undershirts between them and their kisses. "You can touch me, you know," Faty said with a sinful nibble to Yzabel's neck.

She hadn't realized she'd been waiting for permission until it was given. There was no hair along Fatyan's spine, skin smooth and warm under her palm.

Faty sat up to toss aside the last of her garments, the sight of her mesmerizing. Yzabel was ensorcelled as she followed, baring herself in return, fighting the need to cover her lacking assets in shame, then forgetting all about it. The place where Faty straddled her stomach radiated with heat.

Yzabel closed a hand around one of Faty's breasts, heavy and much too big for her small fingers, and Faty smiled lazily at her, leaning down to brush their lips together.

"How long were you waiting for that?"

The hot flush pulsed on her cheeks. If she were to be honest… "Since I met you."

Faty held Yzabel's hand to her breast as she swung a leg back, leaving them both on their sides, facing each other.

"When you saw my heart…did you see this?" Yzabel asked.

"No," Faty said, gently rolling over so Yzabel was under her again. "But the more I think about it, the more I believe."

"Believe what?"

"That it was my fado to stay in the stone for so long." A kiss on Yzabel's temples. "It was fado that you misunderstood your blessing." Another kiss, this time on her cheek, accompanied by the dance of fingers skimming over her stomach. "Fado that your lady's maid knew where

I was." A third kiss, right in the corner of her mouth. "Fado that you found me."

Faty softly bit at Yzabel's lower lip. "But it wasn't fado that made me fall in love with you."

"No?"

"No." A lick along the seam of Yzabel's mouth. "Fado might've set up the stage, but it was you who conducted the play."

It became hard to think straight, not to fall to comparisons again, but *this*, this was the intimacy she wanted, with the person she loved. It would never be the same with Denis, for he was a man, with a man's touch, a man's needs. The difference between the love she held for Denis, and the love she held for Fatyan had never been as pronounced, as clear.

Her fingers locked on Faty's silken hair, and Yzabel didn't know what was happening inside her—only that it felt better than a great deal of things, pure bliss that kept building with the rhythm of Faty's tongue and fingers. There was another one, now, and she hadn't even noticed— she was calling for mercy, calling for God.

The tide of rapture washed over her, shattering her into hundreds of pieces, and she hadn't even come down from the first wave when another came to drown her.

Faty held her close after, kissing her sweaty brow, her lips—she still tasted of cinnamon, but there was something sweeter on her tongue as well. Yzabel's own taste, she acknowledged with wanton embarrassment.

"I love you," Faty whispered.

"I love you, too," Yzabel whispered back.

And, after Yzabel was done shivering from pleasure, she showed Fatyan how much.

CHAPTER TWENTY-NINE

The Miracle of Roses

The sun dawned to gray mist and cloudy skies, and Yzabel woke to the warmth of Faty's arms around her, one hand brushing her hair. Though she longed to stay in bed all morning, there was a plan to set in motion.

"Last chance to run." Faty's voice came from above, still soft from sleep.

"That would never work." Yzabel nuzzled her neck. "We'd be hunted for the rest of our lives. Matias would still be out there. And Aragon and Portugal would definitely go to war."

"And your deepest wish has always been peace." Fatyan laid a kiss on Yzabel's forehead, then used a finger to tilt her face toward her and lay another on her lips.

Yzabel returned it, checking the contours of Faty's face with her hand. "Thank you for staying."

The smile she received was brighter than the sunrise, more beautiful than the sunset. "Thank you for letting me." She released Yzabel and slipped out of bed. "Let's go. We have work to do."

Yzabel dressed in the clothes of a commoner and placed a spare royal outfit on a leather bag. "I'm ready." Smoothing her skirts, she turned to Fatyan, who had already changed into one of Yzabel's gowns, enraptured as she watched her features morph from one person to another. Fatyan's prominent nose rose and widened, eyes became rounder, her hair curled and browned until she was no longer staring at Faty, but at herself. She would use Yzabel's form to draw Yusef away, and then forgive him.

Or behead him.

Lucas paced around, whining in confusion as he sniffed their hands. Yzabel giggled when he licked hers, then knelt to pet him behind both ears. "Nothing can fool you, huh?" She hugged him and said, "But you'll have to stay here with Faty, all right?"

The dog's wet tongue slid across her cheek. With a final kiss on his snout, she said, "You are the best puppy I could have asked for."

Adjusting the scarf on her head, Yzabel joined Faty by the window she'd used at night. "Are you sure you can handle Yusef by yourself?"

"You handle the Portuguese. I'll take care of him." Fatyan used one arm to draw Yzabel close, and in her ear, she whispered, "Be careful."

Yzabel smiled as she traced Faty's fine cheek. "You too," she said, leaning in for another kiss. Then, cloak over her shoulders, she climbed out onto the lawn and took the cobbled streets to town. This early in the morning, the roads were filled with movement from peasants going to work and servants running errands for their masters. And without her bejeweled crespinettes or fine dresses or an escort, Yzabel mingled seamlessly with them, just another girl going to church for morning mass.

Head low so as not to invite stray eyes to linger, she pressed on, sticking close to groups when she could. Her biggest danger at present was in being recognized and brought back to the castle. Which, with Fatyan currently in Yzabel's form, would lead to immediate catastrophe.

When she reached the São Francisco Church, it was already full of talk about São Martinho and the princess's planned festivities for the entire town. The nuns were there, too, grouped by the sacristy's door, beckoning with smiles for her to approach them.

"We're to proceed with what you told us yesterday, then?" Zaida asked, fingers entwined over her stomach.

"You don't have to come with me," Yzabel assured. "All I need are the flowers. You don't need to risk the possibility of bringing more wrath to the convent."

"*Pff*. Nonsense." Sister Edúlia made a shooing motion. "You're one of us. We'll stand with you."

"And so will we." Padre Augusto emerged from the sacristy's door, black ferraiolo cloak billowing behind him along with several acolytes and priests. "We won't let someone who uses the Holy Spirit for good be labeled a witch."

A melancholic shroud lowered Yzabel's face. So much pain and trouble that could've been avoided had she been honest, had she not hidden what she could do out of fear of judgment. It was fitting that she'd need to let everyone judge her if she was to walk away free.

"I mean this with the utmost respect and humility." She bowed her head. "Thank you. All of you."

Padre Augusto let her into the sacristy, where she changed into her royal outfit, a white cotton overgown and a kirtle as red as the roses that would give today's miracle its name.

Outside the church, Yzabel ripped the scarf from her head, let her curls bounce in the wind as she adjusted the grip on her skirts, now heavy with flowers the nuns had gathered. Before she headed out, she sent one final prayer to the Lord, asking him to trust her, to please let this work.

Please, let the people believe in me. Please, let me save Brites. Please, help Faty forgive Yusef. Please, let Denis forgive me.

Then, with the entire convent behind her, she marched.

The earth squashed under the leather of her shoes, the air cold nails on her throat and lungs. Her movements were clumsy, and she frequently needed to shift her handle on the dress. Still, she did not stop until she reached the first house. On the other side of the brick wall, an infant cried through a mother's lullaby — the Farinhas, Zaida told her, a family of nine who'd lost the patriarch to blood rot.

Yzabel knocked on the door. A young boy opened it, rubbing his snotty nose with the back of his one hand as he said, "Mamã! There's a lady here." He gave her another look from head to toe. "She looks rich."

"Ai, Santa, give me patience," came the mother's tired voice along with a shuffle of feet. "And hurry on feeding the chickens and getting the eggs."

The boy retreated into the home, the widow taking his place with a crying baby in her arms. "You look familiar…" Dona Farinha frowned as she held the child's head to her shoulder, slightly bouncing him up and down.

"I'm the Princess of Aragon, future Queen of Portugal and the Algarves." With a smile, Yzabel produced one loaf, handed it to the slack-jawed woman.

"You…you were the one leaving the bread at night." One of her hands dropped to her side. "You've been feeding us."

"Trying to." The currents of magic traveled the river of her blood, filled her veins with light, and her heart with fulfillment as she turned another flower and gave her a second loaf. "And I'm sorry this is all I can give for now."

A choked intake of breath. The widow set the bread on the table behind her, took four large steps, and embraced Yzabel. Between them, the baby stopped wailing.

"Thank you," Dona Farinha said. "Thank you."

Door by door, Yzabel delivered her bread, the sheer gratefulness of the people fogging her sight with tears of joy. When she ran out, one of the sisters would come forward, dump the contents of a bag into her skirts—flowers that Yzabel turned behind the folds of her clothes.

The crowd behind her swelled with each stop, people come to watch their princess take bread from her skirts, her supply seemingly endless. Terror chewed the inside of Yzabel's stomach, fearing that they would realize she was using her gift every step of the way and not solely in the one time she meant for them to see.

Her worries stayed unfounded as she came to the Church of Santiago, where she climbed the wide steps to the group of homeless sharing the communal fire, gave each of them bread before dumping more into the church's offer basket.

Yzabel went back outside, resumed her trek up the road. A cold weight sunk her stomach, slowing her steps. Voices bent around the road, along with the clicking of horse's hooves on the cobblestones, and a group of men made to file down the street.

Leading them was Denis, in heavy furs over a gold-embroidered surcoat with the Portuguese coat of arms. His eyes speared her with their intensity, lids falling to a squint as he tried to make out her face. Behind him, Dom Domingos and the rest of the king's men looked on, as bewildered as their liege. A flurry of worry tightened around her throat. Her efforts could still take a wrong turn, and she could not count the Chancellor out yet. He might still get what he wanted—Brites dead, and a more malleable girl on the throne.

Yzabel's first instinct was to turn back and run, but she caught herself before following through. She kept walking, shoulders straight, head held high as the men neared, then came to a halt a few feet away from her and her followers.

"Yzabel?" Denis's astonished voice called.

She made herself become steel as he dismounted. Her left hand slipped discreetly into the folds of her skirts, the magic building in her chest, spreading through her arm and into her fingers. Denis came upon her in quick strides. Yzabel funneled more of her gift, felt it spread across the flowers—almost there, almost. They turned to bread and now, she had to make them into roses.

Fingers caught her left forearm and forced it out. The magic retreated into her, glowing in her hand, ready to jump to any target it could find. And the one target currently touching her was Denis, looming over her with a scowl lined with fury, a nose wrinkled in disgust, a mouth drawn in a growl.

Breath shivering and catching, Yzabel desperately tried to hold the magic back. "Let go of me," she said, trying to yank herself free.

The people around them were stunned into silence. Denis's grasp on her arm tightened; the gift inside her burned, begging to be released and defend its master from the threat before her. Pain crashed into her where Denis held her, and where she held herself back.

"What do you carry in your skirts?" he asked.

The question stilled the wind, the world, time itself.

The needle of fear sowed her lips shut with the thread of silence. She knew she must speak, but her tongue swelled and stuck to the roof of her mouth, and the magic, it was too hot, too much, her grip on it slipping and slipping. The vice of Denis's fingers bruised her skin, unrelenting even when she tried to shake herself free.

But Yzabel was no longer the meek girl promised to him. She'd learned to embrace all the things that made her wholly herself, and she believed in the righteousness of her choices. Everything she'd done and everything she was came to a culmination in this moment, and she would not falter, would not doubt, would not relent.

From her lips, one worst burst.

"Roses."

Confusion fluttered in his eyes. "Roses? This close to winter? With that bulk?"

Doors and windows opened, heads sticking out to spy on the commotion. Guards came to surround them, and Yzabel recognized some of the prelates among them, all of them perplexed.

"Yzabel, show me!"

A quick movement and he held her right arm as well. Yzabel yelped in pain, in desolation, for without her fingers to hold the fabric, the skirts fell open, revealing a glimpse of the bread she'd yet to turn.

Above her, the clouds parted, dousing her with sunshine. The force of the gift piled up inside her shivered, coiling tightly around her heart before breaking out of her every pore, swallowing the bread in bright magic.

Dozens of roses, red as blood, fell to the ground with murmurs of petals and stems.

Silence swelled in the streets. A drop of water fell from a roof, hitting the cobblestones. Yzabel's heartbeat thrummed in her ears, but she kept her back straight, her chin defiantly tilted.

"It was you," Denis muttered. "The bread, it was…you."

So much hurt in his wide-open eyes, in the downturn of his lips, the look of a friend whose deep trust had been shredded into pieces. Yzabel's chest cried in return, dejected over breaking Denis's heart.

"A miracle," Padre Augusto shouted from the crowd. "The princess has performed a miracle!"

"It's not a miracle, it's the Devil's sorcery!" Dom Domingos bellowed. "Our princess has been possessed by dark forces and needs to be exorcised immediately!"

Yzabel held Denis's unwavering stare with stony determination of her own. "I was just feeding them," she said. "There never was any witch. There was only me."

His eyes narrowed. "Then how did the roses appear?"

"A miracle," she said. "The Lord's hand, seeking to spare me from your anger."

"She believes herself to be blessed by the Lord!" interjected an outraged Dom Domingos.

Denis held up a hand, silencing the other man. "Why did you lie to me? Again?"

"Because the people were starving and you wouldn't let me give as much as I wanted to."

His small nostrils flared, and he pursed his lips so tightly they disappeared into his scraggy beard. "Release Dona Brites from the dungeons and lock the princess in her stead."

Yzabel didn't protest or try to dissuade him. Escort around her, she marched to the castle with her chin held high, surrounded with whispering on all sides.

Her relationship with Denis might not survive another perceived betrayal on her part, but she was prepared to withstand that backlash. She might lose her future place as Queen of Portugal and the Algarves and the power that came with it—she might even lose her life, and have her death ruled sickness or suicide. She accepted that, too. Anything that happened to her from here on out was God's will and His will alone.

So long as the populace stayed on her side, so long as they knew she'd done this for them, she would die with a full heart and no regrets.

Well, she had one. She didn't want to leave Faty now that she'd found her.

Tears tried to surface. Yzabel disguised them with a cough.

More people came to the streets to see her escorted in shame, confusion thick in their hubbub of voices as she disappeared into the prison. She kept her expression deadpan when the smell of waste punched her in the nose, let her skirts drag along the dirty floor as she was led down the dank corridor.

The jailer opened Brites's cell. "You're free to go."

"Told you this wouldn't last. They—" Brites's words fell away, replaced with a gasp. "Yzabel?"

She embraced Brites before anyone could stop her, and said, "I'm sorry. Zaida will explain," before a rough hand pulled her away and shoved her forward.

Yzabel hit the stone floor with her knees, the impact rattling her to the bone.

When she looked back, the door had already been closed.

With nothing else to do, she lay in the cot and prayed.

. . .

As the hours passed, so did the voices beyond the inner castle walls.

"Free the Holy Princess!" they said, their cries rising to the skies, reaching her in this lonely cell. "Free her!"

Yzabel closed her eyes and basked in the people's passion and determination, unwavering even when the rain returned, when the bells chimed two, three, four o'clock. The sun had set, and they screamed for her liberty still.

From her jailers came no sound, and that alone spoke enough. It was enough for her to assume Faty was safe, and Brites as well.

It was evening when she heard footsteps in the corridor. Clutching at the pangs of hunger in her stomach, Yzabel went to the door, ear to the floor as she tried to spy whoever it was that stood on the other side.

She rolled back when the locks began to turn, frowning as the door opened. "The king will see you now," said Grand Prior António. "You've drawn quite a mob, Your Highness."

Yzabel followed him out. "Are you of their opinion?"

"My opinion doesn't matter." He scratched his thick mustache. "But it's the first time I've seen so many band together for the sake of a future queen consort. That... should tell you enough."

She threw a small smile his way. On their way across the patio between the dungeons and the keep, servants stopped to watch, whispering amongst themselves. The Captain-Mor took her past the great hall, down the stairs to the living quarters, stopping at Denis's rooms.

"Good luck, Your Highness," he said, holding the door open.

With a nod, Yzabel stepped inside her betrothed's solar alight with candles. Elbows propped on the table,

he regarded her with a controlled squint and tight lips.
Neither moved until the lock clicked behind her.

Crossing his arms over his chest, Denis leaned back
on his chair. His left eyelid twitched, as did the corner of
his mouth, rage barely contained. "Is there no end to your
lies, Yzabel?"

She folded her hands behind her back and swallowed
her hammering heart. "I will not apologize for trying to
help the citizens I'll inherit from you."

"I'm not talking about the bread."

His nails dug on the leather arm of the chair. Yzabel
shifted the anxiety in her jittery feet, locked her trembling
fingers together, trying to figure out exactly which of her
many secrets he meant.

By the window behind them, the curtains rustled.
Yzabel didn't look, didn't dare move her gaze from Denis's—

"He's talking about her." An all-too familiar voice said
behind her.

The thumping of Yzabel's heart filled her ears. A shiver
ran through her shoulders and down her spine. Turning her
head seemed to take forever, like she was a statue, stone
grating against stone. There, half coated in candlelight,
with remorse brimming in her eyes and sorrow trembling
in her lips, stood Fatyan—with Yusef behind her, holding
her at sword point.

Fatyan.

CHAPTER THIRTY

Perspective

"Tell me you know nothing about this," Denis said, voice dangerously even. "That you didn't know she was a shape-shifting Enchanted Moura. That it was indeed a miracle back then and not because you have this…sahar."

But Yzabel wasn't looking at him. Yusef and Faty held her attention, Faty saying, "I'm sorry, Yza. I failed," while he pushed her forward, closer but not close enough. "He kept saying terrible things about you. I couldn't—"

"*Yzabel*," her betrothed called, demanding. "If there's any hope to salvage this, you will tell me the truth, and you will do it now."

She inhaled courage, meeting Denis's stare. "Did he tell you who he is?"

His arm blurred, and she gave a small jump when his fist hit the table so strongly the platters clattered. "Don't deflect me."

Yzabel's eyes flickered between the Mouros and Denis, between Faty's hardened jaw, Yusef's smug grin, and her betrothed's scowl. At a small nod from Faty, Yzabel slowly made her way to him and the bread and cheese on the table, left over from dinner. She laid her hand on them, let her magic flow freely, and turned it all into roses and lilies.

"I knew she was an Enchanted Moura, and I do have a gift, and I'm sorry I hid it from you, and I will tell you all you want to know about it later," she said, brisk lips filled with terror and urgency. "I know you don't have much reason to trust me, but if you ever had any esteem for me, you'll believe me when I say the enemy in this room is Yusef—the man you know as Matias."

A small furrow appeared on Denis's brow as he regarded her, then the Mouros, then her again. Yusef scoffed, pulled on Fatyan's hair to further expose her throat, where his sword was pressed. "My king, all she says are lies—"

"I want to hear it," Denis said without looking at him, his undivided focus on Yzabel. His voice wavered, and she realized she'd misread him again. It wasn't anger that coated his words; it was sadness, and betrayal, and confusion. "I want to know why you did what you did. Why you felt like you still needed to hide from me even though I've been nothing but kind and patient with you."

The hideous sound of blade rending flesh spun Yzabel around just in time to see the tip of a sword protruding from Fatyan's ribs, and her body falling to the floor.

Denis stood so abruptly his chair crashed backward, but Yzabel barely registered the noise. It was Brites's reminder of when she cursed Yzabel just as Yusef had Faty that sunk its spectral fingers into her ears, the same sentence repeated over and over in her mind.

I don't know if both of you will die when one does.

Yzabel stepped back, hitting the table as an agonized shriek ripped out of her. Although every inch of her body tugged at her to run to Faty, Yusef was there, snorting at her, blocking her. "Oh, don't be dramatic. You know death doesn't stick to her." His tone was of mocking dismissal as he stepped over Fatyan's body and the blood pooling around it. Red dripped from his sword as he advanced on her. "But it will stick to you."

It happened before she could blink, his speed unnatural, his strength ungodly. Denis shouted. Pain burst through her stomach, and Yzabel looked down, to the hilt of the sword splitting her middle, and all that left her was a gasp.

"Your greatest mistake was in believing Fatyan can forgive," Yusef taunted as he thrust the blade upward with a twist, shredding her insides into pure agony, and even then, no sound left her. "The more she hates me, the more powerful I grow. And now I'll be sure she dies in an explosion of spite. And you"—he turned to Denis—"you are weak, Denis of Portugal. But your country will be weaker with you gone."

Yusef removed the sword and side-stepped Yzabel as she fell to her knees, then to her side. Agony radiated through her, spiking to excruciating when her shoulder hit the floor. By the window, Faty's fingers, still and stiff, *dead*. Behind her, Denis screamed for the guard, feet rushing to the corner where he kept his sword and shield.

"You told them to leave after she was brought," Yusef reminded with a chuckle, the sound of his steps unhurried. "You didn't want anyone else overhearing the conversation, remember?"

Yzabel's mouth filled with blood, and in vain, she coughed. It kept on coming and coming, and soon she couldn't breathe, and she was gasping, flailing—

"Why?" Denis shouted.

"Because you weren't going to. It's the only way to kill the Moura." He gestured toward Fatyan's unmoving body. "And the quickest way to ensure the Christian kingdoms go to war."

Steel clashed against wood, then steel, the sound of

strife growing distant. Her throat spasmed, fighting to kick the blood from her airways.

"It will be mostly amusing to watch the Portuguese try to explain what happened tonight," Yusef's voice trickled into her ears as if behind several doors. "Her brothers will never forgive this country if she dies under your care, and Castela will be happy to aid them in the upcoming war. The Kingdom of Portugal and the Algarves will be erased from the peninsula, and with the forces of Castela and Aragon depleted by the conflict, the Caliphate will take back the land you *reconquered*."

The room dimmed and blurred. A terrified whisper blew into Yzabel's left ear—no, not a whisper. A primal wail that tore the air in half, born of the deepest sorrow and the most furious of wraths. It was Yzabel who was too far gone to hear it.

Fatyan's crying face filled Yzabel's fading sight. "Yza, hang on, please don't go. Yza, please, Yza, Yza, Yza."

She was alive and saying Yzabel's name, over and over like a prayer. While her vision faded in and out, Yzabel mustered enough strength to cup Fatyan's jaw and turned it to Denis.

Her limbs lost their strength. Darkness fell on her like a blanket but did not claim her.

The light did.

At first, Yzabel thought herself in Hell, and the fire sweeping through her insides was that of eternal punishment. Then, her senses returned at once, and she saw no flames and smelled no brimstone.

Broken clay and glass littered the floor, and beyond the upside-down table, the fight raged still. Denis backed into a corner, lifting his cracked shield over his head to deflect a heavy blow from Yusef. Fatyan, meat knife in hand, aimed for the back of the Mouro's neck, him twisting out of the way to take the blow on the shoulder, and the crunch of broken bones when his elbow met her face.

Neither of them noticed the light in Yzabel's chest knitting her back together.

"You should've died when the princess did. How are you still alive?" Yusef slammed the sole of his boot against Faty's stomach without looking back, flawlessly parrying a sword thrust from Denis.

Faty clutched at her head, swaying as she tried to get back to her feet. Her knees hit the ground again, and in doing so, she looked back.

The brief meeting of their eyes came to an end with the crash of Denis's shield as it broke in half. The next blow, he blocked with his sword, yet Yusef proved too strong, too experienced against a young king who preferred women and poetry to bloodlust and battle. He kicked the weapon out of the king's hand.

Behind him, Fatyan changed, adding more muscle to her limbs, growing taller, broader, hands so big they wrapped around the full length of Yusef's arms. "It was *you* who made the mistake, Benzedor Yusef." With him firmly in her grip, she spun them both around. "You forgot that the difference between a blessing and a curse is *perspective*."

Yusef's eyes landed on Yzabel standing before him, teeth gritted as she held the gift in her left hand, the light burning hotter than the summer sun at its pinnacle. He'd sentenced Faty to a stone and tried to use her to live forever. He tried to kill Denis, calling him soft when he was strong, and throw the realms of the Catholic Church into war.

This was for peace. Including his.

Yzabel shoved her fingers deep into his hair, dug her nails into his scalp, and shot the magic straight into his skull. Between seconds, hair withered, skin charred and fell off in ashen flakes that burned off into petals of all colors and shapes, and she didn't let go until the light spread to every vein, every organ, every limb.

A growing flurry of flowers and vines sagged under the mounting weight to fall flat on the carpet. It jerked and spasmed until his chest faced the ceiling. The sound of cracking branches and the slithering leaves haunted the room as what had once been a chest bloated and burst.

At its center, a cradle of moss, and within it, a weeping newborn.

Dizzy and sapped of power, Yzabel fell to her knees, breathing hard, and deeply. Fatyan was immediately at her side, proportions back to normal, and together, they stared at the infant, bellowing with all the strength in his tiny lungs.

"Devils take me," Denis let out, a hand over his heart. "Is that…"

"Yusef. Or, as you knew him, Matias." Fatyan leaned forward to grab the baby, careful to keep her hair away from Yusef's vicious, tiny fists. "He told you I'm an Enchanted Moura, and that much was true. But he neglected to mention that *he* was the one who cursed me, and that he bound himself to my hatred so he could live forever. This will keep on happening until I forgive him."

Denis's widened eyes blinked to Yzabel, still not quite recovered. "I saw him stab you. How…?" He gestured to both of them.

"I'll tell you," Yzabel said, respiration somewhat close

to normal now. She stared at Yusef and touched Faty's thigh. "Can you do it now?"

Faty set Yusef on the mossy cradle and stared intently at him as if waiting for hatred to fill her with its violent needs. Yet it was pity in her voice, when she spoke, pity and weariness. "I've despised you for a long time, Yusef. I hated you for telling my father that Sal and I were something other than friends, I hated you for suggesting I marry Bráfama as her, I hated you for the beatings, and the insults, and the despair you thought you were cursing me to." She splayed her fingers on his chest, and a chubby hand started to slap it away. Unfazed, she closed her eyes, let a breath leave her, and sent the rancor along with it. "You bound yourself to me because you thought I was like you—but you underestimated Yza and how she makes people better." She grabbed Yusef's small hand. Green and dark brown eyes locked, and he quieted.

"For putting me in that stone, for giving Yzabel a chance to find me, for giving us what will turn out to be an eternity, I thank you, Benzedor Yusef." Fatyan smiled. "And I forgive you."

Yusef hiccupped, and the fingers around Faty's fell away, a lifeless hand belonging to a lifeless gaze that withered to dust.

Faty turned to Yzabel, cheeks streaked with tears, and crashed into her waiting arms. "It's over," she cried, wetting her neck.

"No," Yzabel said, looking up at Denis. "It's not."

Denis approached, and his presence loomed over them. His gaze surveyed the destruction, and, breathless and stunned, he asked, "What the thunder just happened?"

• • •

While the people outside cried for the freedom of their future queen, Yzabel told Denis everything. They sat, Yzabel and Faty on one side, him on the other, the table back upright and between them, pitcher and glasses on top.

He never interrupted her as she spoke about the blessing she'd believed a curse, about how she'd starved herself because all the food she touched turned to flowers. How her great aunt Erzsébet had the same gift before her and used it to perform a miracle years ago in Ungarie, how Brites had told her about an Enchanted Moura, and how she'd sought out a legend to put an end to her troubles, only to find out there was no way to drain the magic from her veins. How Faty had helped her see there was no curse, only a blessing from the Holy Spirit, meant to be mastered and wielded.

How Yzabel had sneaked out of the castle twice at night, feeding the people with nothing but flowers, how Matias had tried to kill her and Brites and she'd accidentally killed him instead, only to find out he was an Enchanted Mouro, too, named Yusef. How he made up the story about Brites, forcing her to be caught. How she went back inside the stone to get Fatyan back, she had become magic—and, as it turned out, immortal.

After two long breaths, Denis filled his glass with wine and took a long sip. The brown of his eyes shifted between Yzabel and Faty several times until it settled on the princess. "You women, I swear." A defeated sigh left his shaking head. "Why don't you tell the truth to begin with?"

"Because we're afraid you might kill us for it," Yzabel answered. "All I wanted was to help the Portuguese by using the gifts I've been given."

His fingers shifted on the wineglass's stem. "You resorted to deception and deceit. Made me look the fool in front of my men, my *people*. Had you been honest from day one, Vasco would never have perished. A death on your conscience because you refused to tell me the truth."

"You had just dismissed Brites because she practiced the Caraju, and then locked me in my rooms! And today, a miracle transpired in your presence and your answer was to lock me in a dungeon." The impotence wavered in her voice. "Can you blame me for being afraid of telling you the truth?"

Shame turned his head to the side and heated his sharp cheeks. "I never wanted you to be terrified of me."

"And I never wanted to hide anything from you," Yzabel softly admitted. "We've both made mistakes, but Denis... I still consider you a friend—and we *can* marry as friends. Or, I hope we can." She looked up at him, pleading. "I would keep working with you to make this country better."

He gestured toward the window, to the mob chanting her name beyond the glass and walls. "The people are obviously on your side."

"They can be on yours, too." Yzabel reached across the table to cover his hand with hers. "We can work for them. Together."

He scoffed but didn't slap her away. "You have turned them against me."

"I turned no one against you. They're not asking for you to be ousted, are they?"

"No, but if you suddenly disappear, they will. There might be a war, like Matias, or Yusef, or whatever he's called, wanted." He gave a harsh frown. "Is that not what you wanted? To trap me between two bad decisions?"

"I know being king makes you all-important, but not everything is about you, Denis." Yzabel sighed. "I never sought to put you in a difficult position. I never sought to involve you, which is why I kept it a secret. I did not want you to have to choose between believing your wife performed a miracle and believing her a Devil's servant."

"Those aren't the words of one who regrets their actions."

"I don't. Had I the option, I would've done it again."

His downcast eyes were on their hands as he asked, "Why?"

"Because even though it didn't last long, even though it might have cost me my life…it made their lives easier. And that's what it was about; helping those who couldn't help themselves. I saw a problem. I tried to fix it one way, the *proper* way, and couldn't. As much as I think you can be a miser, Denis, you were right when you said we can't pay for the food that goes in everyone's bellies. It'd bankrupt the kingdom. So I thought around it and worked my hardest to feed them another way."

"And in doing so, you went against the king's orders— the penalty for which is death," Denis finished for her.

"You've changed many laws already; no reason you can't change that one." Yzabel held her betrothed's stare. "No reason to admit you've made a mistake."

Next to her, Fatyan shifted on her seat, finally speaking after holding her silence. "If you must hold someone accountable, hold me."

Yzabel's head whipped toward her. "Faty, no."

But the Moura kept speaking. "I was the one who taught her how to reverse the *curse* she was born with, a curse she'd have hidden her entire life had it not been for me. I was the one who poisoned her mind. I was the one who brought Yusef to your doorstep. Yzabel is innocent, and all she ever wanted was to make the lives of the people a little bit better, without wasting your precious money."

"And when Yzabel doesn't age?" Denis cocked his head, features unamused as he slid his eyes to her. "You've already played your miracle card. You can't do it again."

"I can be her in public," Faty said, unwavering, her features changing to Yzabel's, then wrinkling and sagging before going back to normal.

Elbows on the table, and hands on a steeple, Denis leaned forward. "Why would you do so much for her?"

"Someone else would've watched the commoners starve to protect herself. But she never did." She looked the King straight in the eye. "Yza is the best queen you could ask for. And if you'd rather sentence her to death than forgive her, then I pity you. I pity your country, because they will never have a queen that genuinely cares as much as she does."

"I know that—why do you think this marriage contract wasn't annulled as soon as she told me she was in love with *you*?"

Faty flinched, then turned to Yzabel. "He knows?"

"He asked me last night," she answered.

"And it didn't occur to you to tell me he's all right with it?"

Denis sighed, once again turning to the window. "If you love the people so much, why not tell them the truth? That you can make bread out of flowers?"

"Because then it will be magic, and not everyone sees it for the blessing it is. If you doubt that, all you have to do is look to Dom Domingos." Yzabel sighed. "It's not a miracle if it happens every day. But I will keep on using my gifts as I have, and now that you know, we can use it together, for greater effect. And today, you just tell them the Miracle of Roses made you see you were wrong in your ways."

"And you?" Denis asked Fatyan.

"If you let me stay with Yza, my abilities will be under your command," she replied. "I will be your ear on the walls, your eyes among the people. And I will stay loyal to you so long as you stay loyal to her."

Fingers smoothing his beard, the king's dark eyes glazed, running over countless of possibilities. Yzabel's hand tightened around Faty's, her entire body on edge.

Then, finally, a nod. "We'll try. If you can promise me no more lies."

"I promise," she said, relieved. "No more lies."

Denis regarded her for another long moment, then rose with an offered hand.

Yzabel smiled and took it.

RECIPE FOR AÇORDA ALENTEJANA

2-4 garlic cloves
A bunch of fresh coriander or pennyroyal, roughly chopped
A pan (six and a half cups) of boiling water **
A loaf of bread, preferably stale/hard
Four spoons of olive oil
Four poached eggs

Slice the garlic, then grind it with the coriander and the salt until it's a paste. Scrape it into an empty bowl and add the olive oil. My dad always taught me to say, "One for you, one for me, one for the old woman in Quiriquiqui," while pouring the olive oil into a spoon, and to stop at the end of the sentence—but you can use four tablespoons.

Poach the eggs, then set them aside. Pour the boiling water into the bowl, stirring as you go, and put the eggs in the soup.

On a plate, put some cut-up slices of the stale bread. Cover it with the soup you've made above, and there is your açorda!

** You can also boil a piece of cod in the water and poach the eggs along with it—then use the remaining water in the açorda soup.

ACKNOWLEDGMENTS

They say it takes a village to publish a book—well this one required three villages, spread across three different countries.

First of all, I owe a huge thank you to Jen Bouvier for scouting me out of nowhere when I was almost ready to give up, and for being a friend throughout all this. Jen, you're a star, and every book you touch shines brighter because of you.

Lydia Sharp, who worked their damned hardest with me to make this book the best it could be. Thank you, Lydia, for your endless patience and showing me how to make Yzabel's story sing to its fullest potential. A huge thank you to my agent, Travis Pennington, for sweeping in to save the day several times. Also, to Russ Galen, for the years of mentorship and advice.

Leonor, and actual ray of sunshine in my life, and the rest of the Ferrão family (yes, Manuel, even you with your bad jokes) for sharing their history knowledge and books with me, but also for letting me cat-sit for them when they're away. And for pet-sitting for me when *I'm* away. My cat nephews Matthew and Margot, as well as my great-nephews Scott and Artur, for always making my day a little better. And Mimi and Lucas, who're now two bright stars in the sky, special to the point I named the dog in this book after one of them.

My second family, the Sanistas. Anna Dooland, Adam

"Bunny" Rampling, Amy Parker, Ashton Connolley, Jenn Brown, Lynsey Wood, Nik Nevin, Dmitri and Ksenija Lenselink, Sonja Milicic, Allison "Jordy" Watson, Danica Lundin, Rich Mossop, Lotta Markkula, Toni Green, Artemisia "Arty" Bellamy, Lindsey Glinka, Karen, and Annabelle Gralton. The moment we crossed paths online all those years ago was one of the most fortunate of my life. Thank you for being the best possible friends, and for shining light in every one of my moments of darkness.

To the Walrus Writers, Ron Delaney Jr., Kathleen Palm, Hannah Johnson, Emma Wicker, and Tasha Raulerson, for listening to me moan and cry about this book and the books before and telling me how to make them better.

And to the person who is in both of the above, not just ANY person, but MY person, my sun-and-stars, my Alaskan snowflake, and best fucking friend forever in the whole world: Dana Collins. None of this would be happening if it weren't for you, and never have I wished for instantaneous teleportation to be a thing so I could cross the world in the blink of an eye to hug you whenever.

The Writing the Unreal class at Highlights Foundation: TJ, Steph, Kim, Liz, Laura, Olivia, and Kurt. Unlimited thanks to Laura Ruby, Anne Ursu, and Christine Heppermann for the guidance, and to Highlights itself for not just being a wonderful place staffed with wonderful people, but also for the scholarship that allowed me to go.

My former team at HighSkillz: Edgar, Zé, Fred, Badim, João, Manuel, Marco, and Maria, both for the support, and for being the best place I've ever worked. Members of my academic family who've always supported me: Sofia "Sofy" Teixeira, Renato Vieira, Francisco Guerreiro,

Pedro Mira Lopes, Carlos Margarido, and Pedro "Jola" Nogueira. To my Portuguese and English teachers who've always encouraged me to write: Luís Cabanejo, Anabela Tomé, and Teresa Ramalho. To Harry, my teacher at Cambridge Portugal, who pulled me aside and said, "You should really look into being a writer."

The Twitter writing crowd, and our NaNoWriMo Portuguese group, that are far too many to name, but I'll endeavor: Dakota Shain Byrd, Parmita, Tylia "Norberta's #1 Fan" Gardner, Maria Hossain, Kate Foster, Mariana Serra, Jenny Ferguson, Soraia Imperial, Sara Calvim, Mário de Seabra Coelho (sorry about using your name for a minor villain, Mário), Francisco Martinho, Renata Nunes, and Alexandra Freitas. The whole #TheRoaring20s debut group, who made this unbearable debut year better. The Corte do Norte: Cláudia Silva, Sílvia Ferreira, Rafaela Ferraz, Diana Sousa, and Inês Montenegro. Lyn Miller-Lachmann and Carly Heath for keeping my head up above water while I wrote this book, and providing me with invaluable feedback (and, in Lyn's case, giving me a couch to crash on!) Meredith Tate, for being 100 percent awesomeness, and Mia Segert for her referral, and Cass Newbould and her indomitable spirit and love.

To Miguel, as well as his parents and relatives, for their love and support, and for making Moura feel like home. A special mention goes to Ana, who is like the gamer sister I never had and lets me borrow all the PS4 games she buys.

Mom and Dad, for the continued love and support through this tumultuous journey that was getting a book out. To Grandma Sílvia and Grandpa David, who're still here, and to Nana Nini, and Grandpa Arnaldo, who aren't, but I carry in my heart as if they were.

And I know a bunch of you will laugh at this, but I don't care. I'd be remiss not to mention my cats, Sushi and Jubas, and Norberta, my bearded dragon, for making my life better every day and being the best depression/anxiety shields a girl could ever dream of, but also Tux and Melke, the original cloud kitties who started the cat craze in our home.

A lush, unique fantasy trilogy about a girl tasked with stealing the prince's heart...literally, from New York Times *bestselling author Sara Wolf.*

BRING ME THEIR HEARTS

Zera is a Heartless—the immortal, unaging soldier of a witch. Bound to the witch Nightsinger, Zera longs for freedom from the woods they hide in. With her heart in a jar under Nightsinger's control, she serves the witch unquestioningly.

Until Nightsinger asks Zera for a prince's heart in exchange for her own, with one addendum: if she's discovered infiltrating the court, Nightsinger will destroy Zera's heart rather than see her tortured by the witch-hating nobles.

Crown Prince Lucien d'Malvane hates the royal court as much as it loves him—every tutor too afraid to correct him and every girl jockeying for a place at his darkly handsome side. No one can challenge him—until the arrival of Lady Zera. She's inelegant, smart-mouthed, carefree, and out for his blood. The prince's honor has him quickly aiming for her throat.

So begins a game of cat and mouse between a girl with nothing to lose and a boy who has it all.

A thrilling journey full of magical secrets and swoon-worthy romance, perfect for fans of Stephanie Garber and Mackenzi Lee.

MADELINE J. REYNOLDS

1898, London. Saverio, a magician's apprentice, is tasked with stealing another magician's secret behind his newest illusion. He befriends the man's apprentice, Thomas, with one goal. Get close. Learn the trick. Get out.

Then Sav discovers that Thomas performs *real* magic and is responsible for his master's "illusions." And worse, Sav has unexpectedly fallen for Thomas.

Their forbidden romance sets off a domino effect of dangerous consequences that could destroy their love—and their lives.

Let's be friends!

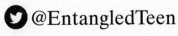 @EntangledTeen

@EntangledTeen

@EntangledTeen

bit.ly/TeenNewsletter

entangled teen

an imprint of Entangled Publishing LLC